HOW *(Not)* TO HAVE
A PERFECT
WEDDING

BEFORE SHE CAN LIVE HAPPILY EVER AFTER...
SHE HAS TO SURVIVE THE BIG DAY

Arliss Ryan

SOURCEBOOKS, INC.®
NAPERVILLE, ILLINOIS

Published by Sourcebooks Landmark, an imprint of Sourcebooks, Inc.
P.O. Box 4410, Naperville, Illinois 60567-4410
(630) 961-3900
Fax: (630) 961-2168
www.sourcebooks.com

Library of Congress Cataloging-in-Publication Data

Ryan, Arliss.
How (not) to have a perfect wedding : before she can live happily ever after—she has to survive the big day / Arliss Ryan.
    p. cm.
 ISBN 978-1-4022-0974-1 (trade pbk.)
 1. Weddings—Fiction. 2. Wedding etiquette—Fiction. I. Title.

PS3568.Y262H69 2007
813'.54—dc22

                                 2007020229

Printed and bound in the United States of America
RRD 10 9 8 7 6 5 4 3 2 1

For Eric

ACKNOWLEDGMENTS

It is my great pleasure to thank the people who helped make this book possible.

My agent, Robert E. Guinsler of Sterling Lord Literistic, Inc., worked energetically to find a publisher and guided me through the process with care and consideration. Hillel Black, executive editor at Sourcebooks, took my manuscript under his experienced wing, and his suggestions and encouragement brought the novel to its final form. My book and I are fortunate to have made the acquaintance of two such gentlemen.

Month after month, my writers' group in St. Augustine, Florida, listened to my novel-in-progress and provided invaluable feedback and friendship. I am deeply indebted to R. J. Feliciano, C. J. Godwin, Jim James, Drew Sappington, Claire M. Sloan, and Marie Vernon for their input and for hearing my tale to the end.

Living with a writer has turned my husband Eric and our children Kira and Dane into astute editors and literary critics. They shine a bright light on everything I write, and I would be lost without their honesty and enthusiasm.

Finally, to the many fine people I worked with at the mansion in Newport, thank you for your fellowship on those memorable nights. And to all those wedding party members and guests who sniffed, "My, what a boring job you have!" as I stood on duty at the end of the hall, I simply smile and say, "You have no idea."

1

WELCOME TO ROSECOURT

Anne

"Good afternoon! Come in! Welcome to Rosecourt! I hope you're all rested and ready for the wonderful evening ahead. Yes, isn't this weather fantastic? You couldn't have picked a more perfect day for a wedding!"

Another bride, another groom, another Saturday in June. Another smile on my face, although, as I was advised when I started at Rosecourt as a hostess some ten years ago, "The smile on your face doesn't have to be sincere, just present." I remember the jolt I felt when the previous event supervisor imparted that wisdom in her most gracious tones, beaming a patently false smile at me in demonstration. I smiled back—already I was learning—but how could she be so two-faced, so cynical?

I was then in my late thirties, and having reached one of those family-career crossroads the advice gurus extol as an opportunity for self-exploration. I was optimistic about trying a new job in a new field. For that matter, I was still optimistic about marriage, and you'd have to be coldhearted indeed not to be entranced by a wedding in such a romantic setting. Though neither as large nor as grand as some of its more famous neighbors, Rosecourt to my mind is still the most beautiful of the Newport mansions, its neoclassical white stone exterior a sugar-icing confection, its airy interior furnished, as far as our tenuous budget will allow, with objets d'art and period antiques that the Lamont family might have owned when the house served as their summer cottage during the Gilded Age. Our landscaped grounds front on fabled Bellevue Avenue, where millionaires' carriages once passed on parade. In the rear, where the outdoor weddings are performed, a lush green lawn unrolls from the columned verandah to a vista of blue Atlantic Ocean. On the south side of the property, through an archway in a privet hedge, the rose garden first planted by Augustus Lamont, an amateur horticulturalist, has just burst into bloom, a profusion of peach and scarlet petals, the air scented by their collective sigh of release . . .

Forgive me—I'm beginning to sound like a glossy brochure—but to maintain the aura of wealth and history, to sell the illusion, is imperative. Like the former Astor and Vanderbilt properties we're nestled between, Rosecourt has been in the tourist trade for several decades now, and the guided tours by day, weddings and corporate parties by night, saved our mansion from condo conversion or worse. *Our* mansion—I do love the place—and now that I'm the event supervisor, I try to revive my optimism for each guest who walks through our doors. But tonight will be especially hard, and I'm secretly dreading the impossible expectations, volatile egos, and obnoxious behaviors a wedding too often brings.

"Allison, let me have one of our hostesses escort you up to the suite, where you and your bridesmaids can dress.

Mead, you and your best man might like to remain at the front of the house to greet the guests as they arrive. The remaining groomsmen can position themselves on the verandah to assist with seating. And here's our little flower girl, Fiona. Doesn't she look sweet!"

Faux smile. Tonight's event isn't a ceremony, it's an extravaganza. New York people, two hundred and fifty guests. Years ago, when the group of investors who bought and restored Rosecourt first opened the mansion to the public, a minimal office staff worked overtime to produce the few evening events. Now, with upwards of a hundred parties and weddings a year, the office handles the bookings, and a separate function staff, which I direct, steps in at night. It spares me from meeting the bride and her family until the rehearsal—the office is usually sick of them by that time—although copious notes and a code scribbled inside each client file cue me in on what to expect.

Allison's file bears the fatal VHM notation—very high maintenance—not surprising when the wedding party alone consists of the bride and groom, seven bridesmaids, seven groomsmen, a junior bridesmaid, ring bearer, and flower girl. Add to that lineup five parents—the bride's mother and father being divorced and the latter remarried to a twenty-two-year-old trophy wife—and you can appreciate the degree of tact that will be required. At the rehearsal, one of the groomsmen was missing due to a delayed flight from Chicago, three of the bridesmaids were distracted by hair/humidity issues while a fourth sulked in an unexplained pout, and two-year-old Fiona whimpered with exhaustion from the travel and excitement as her yuppie parents alternately bullied and coaxed the poor child to perform. Deirdre Hollingsworth, Allison's mother and the mastermind behind this shindig, watched tight-lipped as a snake hoarding its venom when Gordon, her ex-husband, practiced escorting their daughter down the outdoor aisle. Conspicuously absent was Kimmy, the trophy wife, and I confess my staff and I are dying of curiosity to see her.

Yet despite the flusters and tension, Allison remained coolly collected, a sculpted blond of the Hitchcock variety, while Mead, in sunglasses, is laid back and joking. Not quite the pairing you'd expect, but they're in their early thirties, a career couple, and should be mature enough to know their own minds. Another plus: his parents, so far, seem to be the noninterfering kind. Best of all, I can count on the caterer and band the Hollingsworths have chosen. Riverside is one of the premier restaurants in Providence, and Hank, the catering manager, is a pro; likewise the Glen Gold Orchestra. Both have been at Rosecourt before, and their familiarity with the house is a big advantage. To pull off this bash, Deirdre Hollingsworth has also engaged a phalanx of florists, a photographer, a videographer, and a valet parking service.

Now all these people are swarming over the lower floor of Rosecourt, steaming up the kitchen with boiling pots on the cast-iron stoves, plunking crystal and flatware onto the ballroom tables, rolling keyboards and drum sets into place beside the grand piano at the head of the dance floor. They're overwhelming the mantels, the marble table in the foyer, and the grand staircase with lavish floral displays. Toss in the rehearsal dinner, the gowns, the tuxes, the suite of rooms at Newport's poshest hotel and my guess is a price tag in excess of $200,000.

"Yes, Mrs. Hollingsworth, everything's on schedule. As your guests arrive, our front door butler will direct them inside, where our hostesses will help them locate their place cards and ask them to sign the guest book. The box for money cards is on this side table. Guests will then turn right through the music room and head outside for the ceremony. We won't open the ballroom doors until it's time for dinner so everyone can get the full breathtaking effect. Would you like to go upstairs to help Allison dress or would you prefer to see the seating arrangement on the lawn? The seating? Of course. If you'll come this way, please."

I gesture for Mrs. Hollingsworth to accompany me and suck in a battle-ready breath. Deirdre Hollingsworth is one of those nipped-and-tucked, salon-perfected women in their late fifties who aren't afraid to spend money in pursuit of a lifestyle that succeeds in pleasing them only when it succeeds in making their friends overtly jealous. They always have better taste than the interior decorators they've hired, their gourmet kitchens feature a granite-topped island with gleaming, never-used copper pots hung from a ceiling rack, and their walk-in closets—wedged with designer clothes—are large enough for several homeless people to camp in. The opportunity to stage a daughter's wedding provides the ultimate showcase for their talents, yet a risky showcase at that. Image, prestige, and status, not to mention the bitterness provoked by her ex-husband, are all riding on Deirdre's bare, tanned shoulders as she descends the verandah steps and walks up the aisle, inspecting the rows of padded gilt chairs radiating in a semicircle from the altar. She's already dressed in a gown that is nothing short of gorgeous, a strapless, full-skirted, burnished gold-bronze affair, the satiny fabric appliquéd with vibrantly colored beaded peacocks. Her short chic hair has been expertly dark-blond highlighted to match.

"You look stunning!" I'd normally say to the bride's mother, and mean it, but in Deirdre's case I hold back. It would sound too familiar. So I merely stretch the smile on my face as I await her verdict. How can she possibly find fault? The rows of chairs are arranged to the precise width she specified, the lawn, thanks to a relentlessly rainy spring, is as plush as emerald velvet, and the aisle cloth upon which Allison will walk has been laundered to a virginal whiteness. The florists have been laboring since one o'clock to erect an eight-foot-high bower of white dogwood branches to frame the bridal couple as they speak their vows. A catch rises in my throat at the loveliness of it, the serendipity of beautiful weather, the brilliance of blue ocean dancing beneath a few cotton-puff clouds.

Like a seek-and-destroy missile, Deirdre zooms in on target: a single blossom in the bower, slightly bruised by handling, its petal edges browning in the heat. Frowning, she snaps it off. Not our fault. As with the caterer and musicians, we provide a list of recommended florists, photographers, and other wedding suppliers, and leave it to the client to interview and select. Nevertheless, Rosecourt ultimately gets the blame or the credit for everything, including the weather, so every detail must be scrutinized and triple checked.

I divert Deirdre's attention from the bruised dogwood to the minister, a handsome silver-haired man they've brought from New York. He's pursing his lips in contemplation of a sailboat on the horizon, and I leave them to confer, the smile dropping from my mouth as soon as I've turned my back.

Inside, I'm ambushed by my staff.

"Anne, the caterer wants to know what time to send out the servers with the champagne welcome."

"Anne, the toiletries baskets for the restrooms—is the bride supplying them or should we get ours?"

"Anne, the photographer's in a snit because the waiters are still setting up in the ballroom, and he says he needs everyone out so he can get an uncluttered shot. We told him he'll have to work around them, but he's being an asshole about it."

"Anne, the bride's father just arrived with his Barbie doll, excuse me, his new wife."

"Okay." I point a finger around the circle, delegating tasks. "Tell the caterer we're expecting the first guests around five thirty and we'll give him a heads-up to send out the champagne. The bride's supplying the toiletries baskets; look in the upstairs office, one of the bridesmaids brought them to the rehearsal last night. Ignore the photographer, he'll get over it. I'll go greet Mr. Hollingsworth. Where's Allison, our bride? Still upstairs in the suite?"

"With a gaggle of bridesmaids."

"Good, keep them there. And someone go tell Glen and the band they're absolutely not to announce a special dance for the parents of the bride and groom or to play 'The Anniversary Waltz' tonight."

"Anne," says Leon, our head butler and my second-in-command, and we all pause at his deep, barrel-chested voice. "I presume you'd like me at the front door?"

"Yes, thank you, Leon."

He nods and departs, and the others dart away on their assignments, my battle-tested troops. Usually, I try to conceal from them a VHM code, not wanting to prejudice them against the wedding party and guests before the evening starts. But two hundred and fifty is the maximum head count for Rosecourt, and they already know it's going to be a long, hard night. They reported at three o'clock for setup, cleaning and vacuuming the entire first floor, ferrying the more valuable antiques upstairs to safety, and arranging the rented ceremony chairs on the back lawn. Then they manually hauled another two hundred and fifty chairs and twenty-five six-foot round tables up the narrow basement stairs to the ballroom, Rosecourt's original investors having neglected to install any kind of elevator, let alone a helpful freight elevator, in their historically accurate nineteenth-century house. By the time setup was complete, the staff had fifteen minutes to change from their sweaty work clothes into their uniforms, formal butler's suits with black tailcoats for the men, and for the women, long black skirts, white blouses, and gold vests embroidered with the Rosecourt crest.

Now they'll be on duty for the ceremony at six, the cocktail hour at seven, the formal dinner and reception from eight until midnight. Then they'll re-don their work clothes and break down the party, hauling tables and chairs back to the basement, repositioning antiques, mopping floors and vacuuming the debris left by the mob of eating, drinking, dancing guests. If they're efficient, they'll have the last stain out of the carpet by two in the morning, an eleven-hour day spent mostly on their feet. And for many of them, it's a second or third job. If I could share one trade secret with our unsuspecting guests, it is this: my staff hates you. You are the only thing standing between them and a paycheck.

I step forward to greet the bride's father, Gordon Hollingsworth, suave, early sixties, and Kimmy, the trophy wife. *So this is what men can get away with.* Kimmy—blond, naturally—is cheerleader pretty and wears a bright smile and coral lipstick. On a slender chain around her neck, a diminutive gold cross points down to the suggestive cut of her silky black halter dress. I don't know when black became acceptable for weddings, but on Kimmy this backless gown with its alluring drape is downright hot. Alongside the Hollingsworths are Mead's parents, Joseph and Donna Morelli, stocky and down to earth, easy to lose sight of in a crowd. Looking at them, you wouldn't quite have predicted Mead's tall, dark good looks.

"Dr. and Mrs. Hollingsworth, Mr. and Mrs. Morelli, welcome to Rosecourt! I'm so glad the traffic on Bellevue didn't hold you up. I believe the caterer and florist have finished in the ballroom. Would you like to take a peek? And isn't this weather fantastic? You couldn't have picked a more perfect day for a wedding!"

I guide the quartet to the ballroom and slide the heavy doors open a few feet. Sometimes, I hope, if I prime everyone sufficiently, if I tell them that everything is wonderful, breathtaking, exquisite, they'll buy into the illusion and believe me enough to discount any evidence that may arise to the contrary. Because a perfect wedding is what all clients want, even though, in a saner moment, they would admit it's an impossible feat. In my ten years at Rosecourt I have worked virtually every type of wedding and witnessed every type of disaster, the rings lost en route to the altar, food poisoning and allergic reactions, kitchen fires, flooded toilets in the restrooms, elderly guests suffering heart attacks, even a drunken bride and groom in fisticuffs—all nonfatal to date. So to emerge at the end of a major production like tonight's with only minor grievances ought to be as close to heaven as it gets.

But no, it must be *perfect*, because a wedding that is flawless to the last detail is somehow a promise that life together thereafter will be perfect too, and why shouldn't it be, why couldn't it be, if only you can get the beginning exactly right? Such yearning, when the real mystery is why people continue to marry at all. It's hardly necessary; cohabitation is mainstream and respectable, and given the divorce rate, surely no one can have the blind faith that their union will be the one shining exception, the happily-ever-after into-the-sunset that not even death can part. I should know. I got my own divorce papers this morning.

The Hollingsworths and Morellis have nudged forward for a peek into the ballroom, and I prepare to second their exclamations, the instantaneous gasps. But then I look too, and my eyes can't seem to retract. It *is* beautiful, it *is* exquisite, a fairy-tale scene of crystal and flowers, a swirl of candles and elegantly set tables reflected in gilded wall mirrors, a snare of brightness and promise that constricts my throat. *What happened? What went wrong?* Mrs. Morelli is speaking—to me, I think—but I can't seem to reply. The wire around my throat cuts through my voice, and the sparkle of the ballroom swims before my gaze in a hurtful white light.

2

You're Kidding Me, Right?

Fredericka

I'VE ALWAYS SAID MY BROTHER Mead is an idiot, and the fact that he's about to commit matrimony in this three-ring circus only underscores that opinion. It's not that Mead is stupid, he has brains enough. They're just so well mothballed that if he ever unpacked them he'd no more recognize them as his than he would a long-outdated suit of clothes. Besides, Mead doesn't require a brain. He has no ambition, no drive, no long-term plan. At thirty-five, he's perfectly happy being heir apparent to Dad's business, and Dad is still far too much the king of his realm to feel any need to be grooming a successor. He'll probably continue running Morelli Development Inc. till he dies, which, given his robust health, could be another twenty years. So all Mead has to do is hang around till Dad expires, then sell the company and retire quite profitably in his early fifties without ever having done a lick of real work. It's a great job being Prince of Wales—no responsibility and unlimited access to the royal bank.

I, on the other hand, can't stifle my brain, so I went to Harvard. From which I graduated, much to Mom's distress, not with a rich husband on my arm but with a *summa cum laude* law degree and a predilection for radical feminism. After getting my feet wet with the ACLU, NOW, and the United Farm Workers, I'm presently a legal affairs counsel at the Women's Justice Organization in Washington, DC. So how is it I've ended up in the bridal suite of an übercapitalist Newport mansion on this hot June day, wearing a strapless red bridesmaid's gown and a spray of baby's breath in my French-twisted hair, while Pammy, the nice bridesmaid, presses onto my fingertips a set of frosted acrylic nails that would make a raptor proud?

"Freddie, guess what? I got engaged! Pretty wild, huh?"

That was how Mead announced the news to me over the phone approximately one year ago.

"Why?" I responded, systematically shuffling the papers on my desk. I have two bad habits, one of which is putting something down and being unable to find it again even when it's right in front of me, and I had just misplaced a brief on a new case.

"What do you mean why?" Mead gave one of those bemused chuckles for which he's known to be so charming. "Because Allison wanted a ring for her birthday, because it seemed like I finally ought to take the plunge, I don't know. Why do you think?"

"Because you're an idiot."

Mead chuckled again. It's never bothered him that his little sister always outshone him academically. One of our grade school teachers, who had Mead first and then me three years later, had asked our parents in all sincerity if I was adopted.

"Well, Mom's thrilled. Allison wants a big wedding in Newport next June, and—don't say no, Freddie—she's going to ask you to be a bridesmaid."

"Sure," I said. *Damn it, where is that brief?* "Why not?"

"Freddie, thanks! That's great. You're a pal. I know it's not your thing, but hey, it'll be a lot of fun. Allison's planning to host a bridesmaids' luncheon for you all to get together on the twenty-seventh of July. Since that's the weekend you're coming for Mom and Dad's anniversary party, can I tell her to count you in?"

"Sure, why not?" I repeated, voicing a mental *aha!* as a corner of the missing brief poked out from a pile. With more thanks and the news that a formal invitation from Allison would be forthcoming, Mead rang off.

Now, let no one make the mistake of thinking I agreed to become a bridesmaid because I was too distracted to pay attention to what my brother had said. Quite the opposite, I heard every word. But I'd learned long ago that the easiest way to deal with family obligations is simply to accept them and waste no further thought or energy on the matter. Since I'd already written off the weekend of my parents' fortieth anniversary party as one of those unavoidable duties, the scheduling of Allison's luncheon offered a convenient way of killing two birds with one stone. Besides, how hard could it be to be a bridesmaid? You buy a dress, you walk down the aisle, you're done.

Yet there is one other reason I accepted, and here's a confession that will both confound my feminist colleagues and astound those right-wing conservatives who have

denounced me as a heartless bitch. The real reason
I accepted is that although I truly do believe marriage is an
antediluvian institution and my brother is an idiot, I'm also
rather fond of him. Mead is a well-meaning idiot and, more
important, a well-meaning brother. Who do you think
stood up for me all those years when the other kids were
calling me nerd and four-eyes and egghead? Who do you
think planted himself between a trembling, skinny eight-
year-old and an onslaught of angry fourth-graders in the
playground when I dropped the baseball and let the other
team score yet again? In those early days, Dad's business
hadn't yet succeeded to the point where he could send me
to an expensive private school for gifted kids. If it weren't
for Mead, I'd probably have ended my life pounded to a
pulp in the public schoolyard where all those noble
mantras about diversity do not include the acceptance of
eggheads. You'll notice Mead is the only person in the
world I allow to call me Freddie, not Mom, not Dad, not
any of my past lovers. Only Mead. Everyone else has to call
me by my full name, Fredericka.

So I willingly agreed to be a bridesmaid, assuming the
wedding came off as projected. Mead had never stayed with
any of his girlfriends for more than two years, and there was
plenty of time for him to disengage from Allison before
next June. Even if he did march to the altar to the strains
of *Lohengrin*'s "Bridal Chorus," he was probably figuring he
could always get a divorce if things went wrong. The big
surprise was that Allison would ask me, since we'd met only
twice and clearly had nothing in common. However, I supposed it was a matter of tradition—isn't the bride more or
less obligated to include the groom's sister in her wedding

party?—and with that settled, I proceeded to put the entire business out of my mind.

I still wasn't thinking about it when I sat down at the restaurant table for the bridesmaids' luncheon three weeks later. My new case at the Women's Justice Organization involved a young Ecuadorian woman named Teresa who worked in an office complex scrubbing toilets and vacuuming floors after the nine-to-fivers went home. On her way outside for a cigarette break, she slipped and fell in the concrete stairwell. For the next two days she limped and then hobbled to work, until a security guard found her on the third night, crying on the floor beside a wastebasket, her knee swollen to twice its normal size. Though the office complex that employed her provided medical insurance, the insurer blandly stated that because the accident occurred on Teresa's break, her own free time, they weren't liable for coverage. Moreover, the accident wasn't reported within forty-eight hours, a clause in the insurance policy of which Teresa, a recent legal immigrant who spoke only broken English, had never been advised.

"I didn't want to make trouble. I thought it was not serious," the translator relayed, as Teresa implored me in Spanish to understand.

Dismissed from an overcrowded ER with cursory medical treatment, struggling to keep working, in chronic pain—the story only got worse, and it had been going on for over two years as her appeals were ignored or denied.

"They told me, 'You must have had water on your shoe from when you mopped the bathroom. That's why you slipped. It was your fault,'" the translator explained.

Bastards!

I already knew I would get them. I was chomping at the bit to begin. As I sat down in the restaurant for the bridesmaids' luncheon I smiled brightly at Allison's introduction of the other women, ordered a lemon sole without opening the menu, and went on mentally channeling my outrage over Teresa's case into a strategy that would level the arrogant power structure that had sought to disempower her.

As for the bridesmaids, their first order of business was to exclaim over Allison's ring. I had to admit it was hard to miss, a perilously sharp and glittering chunk of ice nearly large enough to sink the *Titanic*. As Allison extended her hand to the center of the table to flash it in the light, Pammy, the bridesmaid on my right, helpfully informed me it was a 1.2-carat marquise-cut diamond set in platinum with petite diamond and ruby accents. I nodded agreeably; no doubt Allison had directed Mead on which ring to buy.

I'd already summed up the bridesmaids at a glance: four sleek creatures I automatically dubbed the Beauty Queens, the helpful but merely pretty Pammy, and Susie, Allison's sister. Or rather, poor Susie, because this, I soon discovered, was how everyone, and especially her own family, referred to her. Poor Susie had a big nose, hair like a dirty string mop unraveling down her back, and a beefy face and figure on a tall, large-boned frame. Truly, you'd be hard-pressed to identify blond, pedigreed Allison and the two-years-younger Susie as issuing from the same parents.

I say this as someone who has no physical illusions about herself. At thirty-two I'm practically as skinny and flat-chested as I was in eighth grade, when the other girls got boobs and I didn't. Although I've been told my face is pert—meant as a compliment—the follow-up usually consists of effusive recommendations to play up this promising bone structure by rectifying my straight brunette hair, black wire-rimmed glasses, and aversion to makeup. With regard to my personality, I'm no charmer either, being brusque, tart-tongued, acerbic, articulate, and full of nervous energy which I expend by biting my fingernails to stubs, my second bad habit. So when I describe Susie's physical attributes as I've just done, I'm not being mean. Some have beauty, some brains, some both, some neither. It's a fact, get used to it.

"First, let's consult our organizers to book our future planning sessions," Allison directed, pulling out her calendar.

The other bridesmaids did likewise, while I forked up a mouthful of sole and returned to Teresa's case. For the insurance company to argue that a worker was not covered for injuries sustained during a legally sanctioned break was so ludicrous I could slay them on that one alone.

"What works for me," said Allison, "is the first Saturday of every month. We can do lunch here in the city, one to two o'clock. That means, not counting today, which is my treat, you'll each have two luncheons to host between now and the wedding, and you can pick the restaurant."

The bridesmaids began scribbling in their calendars.

"Um, Allison?"

"Yes, Susie?"

"I can't come for lunch, not once school's in session. I'll be back in Montana, teaching."

"I know, Susie, but you don't have to be here, do you? I'll tell you everything. Next item, dresses."

I thought of interrupting to say I wouldn't be able to make those lunches either—and why would we need monthly planning sessions anyway?—but instantly realized that Allison no more required my attendance than she did Susie's. Maybe she even hoped I'd drop out—who needed seven bridesmaids?—and the silent observation that Susie was seated on my left and the nice but innocuous Pammy on my right was already telling me something. I gave an inward shrug and got back to Teresa. The forty-eight-hour clause for reporting an accident was indeed in the insurance policy handbook, if you could read through an eighty-six-page document of convoluted language to find it. But no one had ever given Teresa a copy, much less a copy in Spanish.

"Now, for your dresses I've chosen cinnabar. I think you'll all agree it has to be Vera Wang."

"What's cinnabar?" Susie again.

"It's mercuric sulfide, symbol HgS," I said without thinking, the brainy girl automatically kicking in. I can't help it. I just know these things.

"It's a reddish color, Susie," Pammy explained. "A vivid red almost with a touch of tangerine orange in it. Not quite scarlet, not quite vermilion. Picture a color about three-quarters of the way from poppy orange to rose red and you'll have it."

"Oh, I see. Thank you, Pammy."

"Sounds good to me," I said, feeling I ought to say something of a rah-rah-team-spirit nature to obliterate the brainy girl remark before I got back to contemplating how I was going to twist the balls off Teresa's oppressors. *You must have had water on your shoe. It was your fault.* Had they no shame?

"Now for flowers—are you ready?—this is really unusual." Allison paused, holding her breath for effect until she had everyone's attention. Even I looked up. What? Were we going to clench a long-stemmed rose between our teeth? Wear Hawaiian leis? Carry potted marijuana? "Renaissance," breathed Allison, and out came a chorus of oohs and aahs, although I noticed one of the Beauty Queens was smiling rather stiffly. I must have been looking confused myself because Pammy leaned toward my ear and whispered, "Lots of ivy."

"Hair up," Allison continued, lifting her own highlighted tresses and turning her profile in demonstration. "I'll book stylists for us in Newport, and we'll get our hair and makeup done the morning of the ceremony. No false eyelashes, please, and Fredericka . . . ?"

"Huh?" I'd begun mentally calculating how much the insurance company was paying its corporate lawyers to stonewall Teresa's claim—probably a fraction of what it would cost for an MRI and outpatient arthroscopic surgery to correct her injury and alleviate her pain—

"Fredericka, you are going to stop that in time for the wedding?"

Allison was sending me a pointed smile, and following her gaze I realized I was gnawing my fingernails again. In the three seconds before I could shift my mind to answer, one of the Beauty Queens interrupted.

"Excuse me. Could we go back a minute to the cinnabar?"

Around me, everyone froze. Pammy halted her water glass halfway to her lips, Susie swallowed a gulp of fried potatoes. The other three Beauty Queens ceased nibbling their salad with low-fat dressing on the side. I sat forward, immediately alert. I wasn't sure what was up, but I haven't been involved in cutthroat union negotiations without sensing at once that tension was prickling.

"Yes, Lauren?" Allison's tone was as sweet as that of the Beauty Queen who had spoken.

"Well, I know cinnabar is very trendy now, but anything in that spectrum . . ." Lauren tossed off a little laugh as if her meaning should be obvious, and to everyone else it apparently was. Pammy bit her lower lip, and the other Beauty Queens deliberately wilted back with an uh-oh-we-have-trouble look on their faces. Even Susie registered alarmed comprehension, before dropping her gaze to her plate as if she were somehow to blame. "I think a little discussion before a final decision is made would be helpful," Lauren concluded through a pressed smile.

"But it's really not a topic for discussion, is it?" Allison smiled back.

"Well, perhaps you've forgotten that it's also going to be June."

"I doubt I would forget the date of my own wedding."

Oh boy. I still hadn't a clue what the problem was, but it was clear we had a situation, and I was instantly fascinated. All my debating instincts, my joy of confrontation, sprang to the fore. Leave it to me and I would have locked down the restaurant, sealed all parties inside, and refused to let anyone out until we had a contract to vote on.

"Maybe," said Pammy in a carefully neutral tone, "Allison could bring a fabric swatch to our next planning session, and we can have a look at it then."

Susie perked up from her plate, and although the issue clearly wasn't resolved to Lauren's satisfaction, she made enough of a concessionary smile to allow the luncheon to proceed. Pammy continued to be extra cheerful to everyone, and Allison resumed command. In the beauty and/or brains equation, I would soon learn, Allison possessed not only the physical prerequisites but a trait that is a highly viable substitute for real intelligence, namely, complete self-confidence. The meal concluded with Allison handing out laminated cards listing our names, addresses, phone numbers, and email addresses so we could stay in touch between meetings, about what I couldn't imagine. As the others hugged, kiss-kissed, and departed, I pulled Pammy aside.

"Pammy," I said, doing my best to adopt a sunshiny girlfriends' tone, though I've never been good at any such thing, "I hope you won't mind my asking, but I've never been a bridesmaid before, so maybe you could fill me in. What's the problem with the cinnabar?"

Pammy looked around to make sure none of the other bridesmaids might overhear, then she pinched a lock of her own toffee brown hair and held it out toward me. "Redhead," she confided. "Lauren's a redhead."

"Ah, so she doesn't want to wear a red dress," I surmised. Give me credit for a little fashion sense.

"Well, she might if it's the right shade of red, but it's also a matter of skin tone."

"It is?"

"Oh yes, because if you're an ivory redhead you can stay pale all summer and look devastating in a red gown, but as a pink-tone, Lauren burns very easily and freckles massively on her shoulders if she's not careful about pacing her tan. That's hard to do anyway because she plays tennis so she's out on the courts a lot. When you factor in the beach you can see it's a real problem. We're all going to have to coordinate our tans as it is, so we harmonize for the ceremony and the photos. If Lauren's the least bit splotchy or peeling and if the cinnabar tends more to orange than to rose, she could wind up looking crimson, and that would spoil everything."

We had walked outside as Pammy spoke, and I continued with her toward her bus stop. Her explanation had been delivered without the least hint of farce or amusement. She appeared to be one of those genuinely good-natured people who never said or thought anything bad about anyone but was perpetually kind, thoughtful, and obedient, a peacemaker and a team player. In other words, a Girl Scout. Oddly, I liked her.

"Might Allison change her opinion and pick another color?" I asked.

"Well, it is the bride's prerogative to choose the color and style of her attendants' dresses, although a considerate bride will try to pick something that suits the majority. Then again, with seven of us, it's going to be hard to make everyone happy." Pammy took my arm to steer me out of traffic. "Of course, there are always the standard pastels— pink, lavender, yellow, sky blue, mint green—but no one wants to be caught dead in those anymore. The jewel tones like amethyst, garnet, sapphire, and emerald were popular a few years ago, but they're also getting overdone. If you're having an autumn wedding, I personally think the fall colors are lovely."

"What colors are those?"

"Oh, you know, copper, bronze, burgundy, sienna, those very warm, rich tones. Or you can go for a more subtle shade like heather, sage or moss green. Once I was in a January wedding where we wore winter white velvet with white faux fur trim. Then come spring you get into the sherbet and fruit colors, like lemon, lime, raspberry, peach, mango, honeydew, tangerine. Last summer's big color was seafoam, but it was tricky. Get the wrong shade and it looks like you're wearing Crest toothpaste."

"Well," I said as we reached the bus stop, "it certainly sounds as if you've done this before.'

"Oh yes, this will be my fourteenth time."

I shook my head, wondering what was wrong with my ears. I couldn't have heard that right.

"You've been a bridesmaid fourteen times?"

"Oh yes, it started right after high school for my best friend. Then there were my sorority sisters in college, my three first cousins, and my friends from work. It's an honor to be asked, although . . . Well, you know what they say, 'Always a bridesmaid . . .'" Pammy laughed, a little sheepishly, then she extended her hand. "It was really nice to meet you, Fredericka. Will you be bringing someone special to the wedding?"

"No, just myself. It was nice to meet you too, Pammy. Or do you prefer Pamela? Pam?"

"No, Pammy's fine. See you soon."

She stepped onto the bus with a wave, and I signaled a taxi and put the bridesmaids' business out of my mind. I wasn't worried any more about Teresa—I knew I could get her the compensation she deserved—and three months later, after the Women's Justice Organization hyped Teresa's story to the media as a cause célèbre, the insurance company capitulated for a gratifying sum. I have no objection to winning my cases by trial in the press. But there was always another Teresa, another new brief on my desk, and my blood pumped in fury at each fresh injustice.

I was working late in my office the night before Thanksgiving, answering emails about the latest case, when an inbox message from Allison caught my eye. We bridesmaids had been receiving regular bulletins from her since our luncheon, the first of which had contained a list of ten perfumes with names like Obsession and Poison, followed by Allison's personal critique of each scent. Apparently, we were not to wear fragrances that "competed" with each other or with Allison's own selection, which was tending toward Diva but was still under debate, the final decision to be communicated in due course. After that, I'd deleted the messages unread. This one, however, was addressed to me alone. It was headlined "Fingernails," and perplexed, I clicked it open.

Dear Fredericka,

As you know, time is running short to my Wedding Day. To help you along with your preparations, I'm attaching a pledge for you to read, acknowledge, and return.

Love, Allison

What? I thought.

The pledge read: "In honor of Allison and Mead, I, Fredericka, promise to stop biting my nails by January 1 and to have grown them out to a minimum of one-eighth-inch long by May 31."

An underline indicated where I was to affix my electronic signature.

Get real, I typed back, and went on to important stuff.

An hour later, Mead phoned.

"Um, Freddie . . . Allison says you insulted her."

"When?"

"A little while ago, by email."

"Oh yeah, she sent me some pledge about not chewing my fingernails. It was a joke, right?"

"Well, no . . ."

"No?"

"See, Freddie, this is kind of important to her, and if you could just . . ."

I listened in dawning disbelief. Allison was serious?

"Mead, no one cares about my fingernails. No one's even going to notice my fingernails."

"Well, Allison thinks they will. She says people always turn to admire each bridesmaid as they walk down the aisle in the processional."

"Fine, I'll hide my hands under my bouquet."

"C'mon, Freddie. Be a sport, be a pal, do it for me?" Mead pulled out his charm, but beneath it I detected the incipient cringing of a soon-to-be pussy-whipped husband.

"No, Mead. I've been biting my fingernails since I was in kindergarten. I like biting my fingernails. I probably couldn't quit biting my fingernails if my life depended on it. Do brides normally boss their bridesmaids around this way?"

"I think so, if it's for their own good . . ."

"What? What do you mean?"

"Uh, nothing, Freddie . . ."

"Spill it, Mead."

"Well, it's nothing, really, just that Allison made Susie sign a pledge to lose thirty pounds by the wedding."

Susie—my brain reeled backward—poor Susie, Allison's fat, homely sister with the big nose and stringy hair. Allison made Susie promise to lose thirty pounds?

"And Susie signed this?" I demanded.

"As far as I know."

"What if she doesn't lose the weight?"

"She's out of the wedding party."

For a minute I was too stunned to speak.

"Mead," I began in a menacing tone.

"Gotta run, Freddie! Talk to you soon!"

The phone went to a dial tone before I could blister a tirade into my brother's ear. What the hell kind of sadistic cultural ritual empowered a self-centered bitch like Allison to dictate that her own sister lose thirty pounds or be banned from the wedding? What kind of perverted body perceptions did women hold that would compel Susie to agree to this shameful blackmail? Why would a sensible girl like Pammy consider it an honor to appear in a rainbow of gastronomically and metallurgically colored gowns as the runner-up in somebody else's pageant, not once but fourteen times? And how the hell could anyone possibly care about the state of my fingernails when women in America and around the world were still being victimized by faceless bureaucrats, as Teresa had been, and far worse, being disenfranchised, abused, raped, and murdered by repressive political systems, if not by their own husbands?

I glared at my mutilated digits and prepared to snatch up the phone and deliver to Allison a furious two-word message: "I quit." But this was more than personal now. I needed to understand how women like Allison and the Beauty Queens could exist in such isolation from women like Teresa, how they could invest time and energy in something as monumentally trivial as the scent of perfume, how they could bully and manipulate each other under the guise of honoring a supposedly unimpeachable tradition such as marriage. If I couldn't comprehend the mechanisms of their desires and fears, how could I expect to enlighten them to the plight of their less-fortunate sisters and secure, if not their activism at least their superficial sympathy and financial contributions? I had to subject myself to their mind-set, observe, listen, and learn . . .

All of which explains why I'm here in the bridal suite of a lavish Newport mansion on a hot June day, begowned and bedecked in cinnabar and baby's breath, watching Allison and the Beauty Queens preen for their grand entrance, while Pammy applies to my fingertips the frosted acrylic press-on nails that would make a raptor proud.

"There, all done!" Pammy exclaims, as the other bridesmaids, sans Susie, cluster around to coo their approval. "Go on, Fredericka. Take a look."

I rise to inspect my disguise in the full-length mirror. Expecting to see a confident spy, I'm startled by the unknown woman who appears.

"Now take off your glasses," Allison commands, holding out her hand for my wire-rimmed spectacles.

I comply, and they burst into exclamations and applause. Then, mission accomplished, they turn back to their mascara and eyelash curlers, leaving me to squint at the stranger in the mirror.

 3

LOSE DA ACCENT

Joey Morelli
Hey, nice joint.

That's what I would have said once upon a time, if I'd ever been invited into a classy place like Rosecourt.

Some ballroom, huh? Whaddaya think they forked out for that crystal chandelier?

I'd have swaggered a bit as I spoke, thumbs cocked in the pockets of my jeans, shoulders twitching forward in my leather jacket like a boxer itching for a fight. But I doubt anyone older and wiser would have been fooled by my scorn. Scorn is almost always a defensive measure, mixed of equal parts jealousy, admiration, and fear, and for Joey Morelli, punk kid from the Bronx, to come out and admit he aspired to a lifestyle like this would be to confess his own nagging sense of inferiority. Turbulent kid, that Joey, but he got straightened out in the end. Today I'm Joseph Morelli of Morelli Development Inc., with a skyscraper office in Manhattan, a five-bedroom executive home in Montclair, New Jersey, a pair of hand-rolled Havanas in my tuxedo pocket, and a son about to be married in one fancy joint.

"Excuse me, are you all right?" says my wife Donna, as Anne, the Rosecourt supervisor, brushes her cheek with one hand and turns away from the sliding ballroom doors where she's let us peek inside.

"It's nothing," says Anne. "I always get a little misty-eyed at weddings."

"Me too." Donna pats her shoulder. "I expect by the time Mead and Allison say 'I do,' I'll be a bucket of tears."

Anne smiles—*Nice-lookin' dame*, I would have said once upon a time—and closes the doors.

"We'll start the ceremony promptly at six, providing we can get the bride and her attendants ready on time," she says, sending a knowing glance up the grand staircase. "Dr. Hollingsworth, I'll need you here in the house no later than five forty-five so you can walk your daughter down the aisle. We'll form the processional in the ballroom, then we'll open the doors to the verandah. I'll signal the musicians to begin, and all heads will turn to see the bridesmaids, ring bearer, and flower girl appear. I promise you, when the bride and her father pause together at the top of the steps with the full impact of Rosecourt behind them, the effect will make chests swell and hearts flutter."

Everyone chuckles, me included. We rehearsed all this yesterday, but with so many people fussing around some confusion still remained, and you can hear the careful way Anne is repeating her instructions now. You have to be a diplomat to manage a show like this, know when to use a light touch, when to peel back that velvet glove just enough to reveal the iron hand. The minister, in particular, offered a few too many windbag opinions, which Anne and Deirdre Hollingsworth firmly declined. Personally, I'm not a fan of these write-it-yourself vows with limp-wrist poetry that Mead and Allison have chosen. It seems to me if you're going to take marriage seriously, you ought to make it a solemn sacrament with organ music swelling and the priest pronouncing and the full weight of the church and a higher authority bearing down on the occasion—helps keep you in line later on. Besides, I happen to like the way the light falls through stained-glass windows. But who am I to talk? I got canned as an altar boy for stealing from the collection plate, and I haven't been to mass in years, though I do sometimes slip into St. Patrick's Cathedral on Fifth Avenue to get my bearings. I like the quiet, there inside the busy city. As I stand before the altar, I wonder what old Father Ignacio, who swore I'd go to hell, would think of me now. Anyway, it's only Donna who's still religious, the kids gave it up long ago, and the Hollingsworths are just lip-service Episcopalians. So what are you gonna do when your kids want to get hitched? Hire a Unitarian.

"Well, I think it's awfully cute that the groom doesn't get to see the bride until they meet at the altar," says Kimmy brightly, her first foray at conversation.

"Actually," says Anne, "there's a less than romantic reason behind that tradition. In the past, when marriages were often arranged by fathers without the couple's consent, many times the young man and woman had never met. So to prevent the groom from bolting from an unattractive bride, it became bad luck for him to see her until the vows were spoken, the veil lifted, and it was too late. In Europe, some brides wore opaque yellow veils, and they couldn't see out any more than the groom could see in. That's why the father had to escort the bride to the altar."

She gestures to Gordon, and we chuckle again. "Just a bit of wedding history trivia," Anne concludes. "If you'll excuse me, I must check in with the caterer."

She heads off, leaving the four of us in the foyer, and now it gets awkward. Donna and I have hardly met Allison's parents before this weekend, though she and Mead did host two dinners, one with Deirdre, one with Gordon, to introduce us. Also, Donna invited Deirdre out for lunch, an episode about which Donna remains tight-lipped. I have to admit I'm curious to see how this ex-wife/new wife scenario is going to play out. Donna says the respectful thing would have been for Kimmy—*da broad*, I would have said once upon a time—to absent herself this weekend entirely. My wife's exact words, in private, were, "Gordon should leave her home and buy her another piece of jewelry instead."

But I didn't see that happening. You think a man is going to pass up a chance to make an appearance with a piece of eye candy like that on his arm? And that slinky black gown Kimmy is wearing . . . *mama mia!* There's barely a string holding the top tied behind her neck, and the way it's cut in front is one hell of a tease, the fabric slipping open each time she moves but without revealing anything. You keep staring, hypnotized, imagining what's in the shadows, hoping for a glimpse when she shifts her arm, a cusp of soft flesh, a peep into heaven. It takes a good minute to realize Kimmy's actually not that busty, but no sooner do you start to lift your eyes than that little gold cross at her throat points them downward again. It makes you think you'd be fucking a virgin, which only drops your eyes further to the seductive "v" between those sleek hips.

"Ahem," says Donna, and I yank my gaze upward.

"Ahem," I repeat, trying to look as if I wasn't looking where I was. Gordon and Kimmy pretend not to notice. It's funny. Your kids meet, fall in love, marry, and suddenly you're stuck with these other people, you're in-laws, and what do you have in common? Left alone together, what are the four of us going to chitchat about while we await the first guests? We've already covered the weather; I suppose I could say something nice about the mansion or the flowers. Then I remember I paid for the flowers—as the groom's father, my only responsibility was to foot the bill for the rehearsal dinner, but I chipped in the florist as an extra wedding present—so to mention them might sound like I was fishing for thanks or compliments. Maybe we could discuss the stock market?

"We're going to Europe in September," says Kimmy, as if trying to jump-start the conversation while we adults falter.

"How nice for you," says Donna, taking up the theme. "What itinerary do you plan to follow?"

"London, Paris, Rome . . ."

Gordon joins in with a reflection on the Borghese Gallery—Donna and I have been there, as a matter of fact—and I let the other three talk. I note that Kimmy had no trouble with the word "itinerary." Maybe she heard it from a travel agent? Donna carries on smoothly, observing that between the *Davids* of Donatello and Bernini, she far prefers the Baroque interpretation. On the drive from New Jersey to Newport, we debated how we should act toward the Hollingsworths this weekend. The smart course, we decided, was to lay low and take our cue from Allison's parents themselves. So far, Gordon has been friendly enough, dropping an occasional word of praise for Deirdre's wedding planning efforts. But Deirdre has kept a frigid distance from her ex and her successor, and, in our company at least, pretends they don't exist. When she has to refer to Gordon, she calls him "the bride's father," although Donna bets that's not what she calls him in her head.

Well, it's always a sad business, a family breakup—*da pits, ya know what I mean?*—but something tells me we're not going to have a close relationship with Allison's family in any case. I'm not saying we dislike the Hollingsworths—though Donna has made herself pretty clear to me about Kimmy—nor they us. But although on the surface there's a parity of income and social status, something just doesn't click. Gordon and Deirdre have class, and I'm not talking about the phony refinement you get by hoisting your pinky when you hold a teacup. I'm talking about birthright, the assurance that you have only to step on the floor pad and the automatic door will swing open for you to enter, whereas I was always butting my head against the glass. For Gordon it was Yale, med school, chief of surgery, hospital president. I dropped out of high school twice before I graduated—Donna's mother sure didn't think much of me as a son-in-law, I can tell you that.

"We gotta get ourselves some class, Joey," Donna would nag me in the one-room apartment her parents let us have for cheap over her father's shoe-repair shop. "We gotta get out of here and move up."

"Yeah, yeah," I'd reply, hoping she'd drop the subject.

We'd married at nineteen because of a pregnancy scare; Father Ignacio threatened eternal damnation if we didn't. Donna was clerking in the dime store, and I was kitchen help at the pizzeria, not a place with many prospects. Our apartment had a moth-eaten sofa bed, hot plate, and drippy shower, and smelled of soaked-in shoe polish. On Saturdays we visited my mother, who raised me and my two younger brothers by working as a seamstress after my father skipped out when I was ten. Mom and Donna had hit it off early on, and they spent hours in the kitchen making pasta and gabbing about food, babies, and the perfidies of men. On Sundays, Donna dragged me to mass and then to her parents' house where, over ham dinner, her mother kept track of my shortcomings while her father chewed in morose silence.

Come Monday, Donna would renew her campaign. "We gotta get some class, Joey. We gotta pull ourselves up."

"Yeah, but how, Donna? How we gonna do that?"

"We're goin' back to school, nighttimes, the both of us."

"School? Aw, Donna, not that."

"Yes *school*, Joey, 'cuz I know you're smarter than you think you are, and education is how people get ahead in the world. And another thing, we're gonna lose the accent."

"What accent?"

"*Da* accent. You know very well what I'm talkin' about. It's gonna be like *My Fair Lady* where the flower girl learns to talk right."

"Aw, Donna, you can't go changin' a guy like that."

"Yes, I can. You listen to me, Joey. We're goin' to school and we're gettin' some class 'cuz I am not spendin' the rest of my life as Donna Dombrowski Morelli from the Bronx."

So here we are, not that it happened overnight. I took business courses, ditched the pizzeria, and got an office job with a construction firm. Donna studied English literature and sociology and observed the manners of the upscale clientele as she sold Italian leather handbags at Bloomingdale's. She put a dictionary on a fruit crate beside the sofa, set the TV channel to PBS, and whenever a word got used that we didn't know, she made me look it up. On weekends she hauled me to art museums and free music recitals. To my surprise, I began to enjoy it. On Monday mornings, if senior management happened by the water cooler, I had more than baseball scores to talk about. Gradually, I advanced to management and then started my own company specializing in retail developments. Along the way we moved from the Bronx to New Jersey, starting with a two-bedroom bungalow in Hackensack. When the kids were born, Donna insisted they have names with class.

"Like what?" I asked.

"Like Mead." She pointed to a page in a baby names book.

"Mead? What kind of name is that?"

"It's Old English. It means 'from the meadow'."

"For a boy? Don't you think it sounds sissy?"

"No, it sounds distinctive. Should we spell it with an *e* on the end or without?"

"Without. Otherwise the kids might call him Meady."

"And if it's a girl, we'll name her Fredericka, which is Old German and means 'peaceful ruler'."

"Okay," I gave in, and as usual Donna was mostly right. The kids never teased Mead about his name. Tall and handsome, he was always the most popular boy in his class. Too bad he didn't get his sister's brains—I have no false hopes about that. But hey, my little Fredericka, who is anything but peaceful, is a Harvard lawyer, which will come in handy someday if the IRS ever catches up with my books. Because, you see, while Donna was mostly right about the benefits of education, I learned by reading between the lines of all those business texts that there are quicker ways to boost yourself to the top. Donna doesn't know, of course, and for Fredericka, always off on somebody else's crusade, her father is her one blind spot. But she'll stick by me, she's got that family loyalty Donna and I instilled in both our kids. I thank my father's absence for teaching me the value of that.

So as I say, we made it—and yet, not quite. *Nice joint.* You can't erase who you are, and I think that's what Gordon and Deirdre and even Kimmy sense about Donna and me, a suspicion that we don't really belong, that we'll never quite reach their level, that there still clings to us a whiff of pasta and Polish ham and shoe polish, a beaten-down but not defeated accent from the Bronx.

And you know, there's one funny thing about my wife. She always wanted class, but now that we've acquired as much of it as we're probably going to get, what does she care about most? Her kids, her house and flower garden, the grandchildren she wants Mead and Allison to have. She doesn't fret about a few extra pounds on her hips, and she still cuts recipes out of the women's magazines and makes the marinara the way my mother taught her. She says she has enough jewelry and what she wants for her birthday is to take a watercolor painting class. She's become a kinder, gentler version of old Mrs. Dombrowski, who never liked me to the end, and in many ways she resembles my mom as well. And though I haven't always been faithful in thought or deed, I never forget that I owe Donna everything I've got. So I understand her—and every other woman's—resentment toward Kimmy. How else should the first wife feel when she's spent the best years of her life making a boy into a man to be proud of, then along comes someone else to claim the prize?

"Oh, here come the first guests!" exclaims Kimmy, and with a measure of relief, we Morellis and Hollingsworths part. Having paid for the rehearsal dinner and the florist, my only remaining duty as father of the groom is to sit back and enjoy the night. Donna says her role as mother of the groom has been clear-cut from the start: wear beige and keep your mouth shut.

"Come on," I say, taking her hand. "We done good, Donna, and now we're gonna live it up. You are da best thing to ever smack me between da eyes, and I'm gonna love ya till da woild stops."

Which is exactly what I did say, once upon a time.

4

SIBERIA

Isabel

AH, HERE WE ARE ALIGHTING AT the front door of Rosecourt for Allison's wedding. Isn't it the perfect evening! Blue skies, balmy air, and what's this? Waiters, offering flutes of champagne on a tray, a sweet red raspberry floating in each glass. What a nice touch! As I said to John as we were dressing at our hotel, you can always count on Deirdre to put on a quality show. Although I was a bit perturbed at the unprofessional greeting we received from the parking attendant at the entrance. Here we'd already endured the horrendous traffic along Bellevue Avenue, what should have been a five-minute drive from the hotel turning into a twenty-minute crawl amidst sightseeing trolleys and bumper-stickered cars full of tourists gawking at the mansions en route. So when we reached Rosecourt it was most inconvenient to find yet another line of cars backed up at the gate.

"What do you suppose is the delay?" I asked John, peering ahead.

"Looks like a parking attendant stopping the cars," John replied, lowering his window. "Did you bring the invitation?"

"No, of course not. It didn't say we had to. If we have to present the invitation when I've left it back in Westport—"

"Good evening, sir. What event are you here for, please?"

"The Hollingsworth-Morelli wedding."

"Thank you. If you'll proceed straight up the drive to the front door, one of our parkers will take care of your car."

"Excuse me." I leaned over John's seat to make myself better seen and heard. 'Do you mean to tell me there's another wedding booked here this evening as well?"

"No, ma'am. We just want to ensure that no tourists are coming in by mistake."

The attendant waved us forward, and not wishing to delay the cars behind us, I let the matter pass. But really, could anyone imagine that John and I resemble tourists? Our attire alone ought to have afforded sufficient evidence to the contrary. And what business do they have putting guests on the spot with a trick question about which event they're attending when there is only one? I said as much to John, and he said it was probably a polite way of screening for gatecrashers. As if we even faintly resemble gatecrashers!

"Relax, Isabel," John replied. "Let's go in and have a drink and see who's here."

Now, sipping champagne, we pass a butler who bows slightly as he holds open the front door. Another nice touch—although I do find it suspicious the man is black. It smacks a little too much of servitude, that whole southern plantation thing, and I wonder at the mind-set of the management to put an African American in a position like that. Wasn't it only a few years ago there was an uproar about those black jockey statues being used as lawn ornaments? Moreover, I'm surprised any person of color would acquiesce to fill such a post. If black men don't want to perpetuate stereotypes, they shouldn't accept inferior jobs. Well, I won't mention it when I spot Deirdre. She's been under enough strain, trying to produce this wedding with no support whatever from Gordon. The things I would like to say to that man—

"Good evening, ma'am, sir. May I help you find your place card?"

"No, thank you." I step past the hostess posted at the marble table in the foyer and begin scanning the neat rows of miniature envelopes propped like little tents on their flaps. A dozen guests are already bunched around the table, trying to collect their cards and sign the guest book. Really, what poor organization to display the place cards here in the foyer, causing a bottleneck as soon as people enter. And the hostess is a mere freckle-faced girl who looks no more than seventeen. You'd think they'd insist on hiring only mature staff at a place like this.

"I'll be happy to help you if you'll tell me your name," she persists.

"No, thank you," I repeat. As if I can't alphabetize to find my own name, although the calligraphy on the envelopes is not the most legible, and I have to pick up several in the *N*s to read ours clearly, *Mr. and Mrs. John Newsome*. Slipping out the card, I can't help but think it's a little pretentious. Nice quality stock, naturally. Deirdre doesn't skimp. But isn't it a bit much to have Allison's and Mead's initials entwined in gold inside a red rose wreath on every single place card? Personally, I think plain embossed ivory speaks volumes in elegance.

"We're at Table 7," I inform John, handing him our card as I search for and open the rest of our friends' envelopes: Andretts, Table 17; Langleys, Table 4; and Morestones, Table 17 also.

"Is there something else I can help you find?" says the obsequious girl, pointedly straightening the cards I've touched.

"Yes, I want to know who else is at our table," I say just as pointedly in return. You can't let these people act as if they run things.

"I'm sorry. Each card is labeled individually. I don't have an overall seating chart."

"Well, someone must have one. The bride's mother certainly prepared one."

"There may be one in the supervisor's file. If you'd care to wait, when she returns, I'll ask her."

The girl turns away, as if it's imperative she assist another guest, when it's perfectly clear she's deliberately putting me off.

"Isabel, over here," John calls. I can see he's found Jack and Cassandra Copmann. What a pleasure! It's been ages. That's the delightful thing about weddings, meeting up with old friends. How thoughtful it would be if Deirdre has seated them at our table.

"No, we're at Table 17 with the Andretts," they say. "Don't you love Newport? We had the most delicious lobster dinner last night! Oh look, here come Dick and DeeDee Falherne."

"Table 7?" I ask them, after hugs and kisses.

"No, Table 4 with the Langleys," they reply.

Everyone begins reminiscing about the last time we were together at a surprise birthday party in Greenwich two years ago for Josie Andretts.

"I still remember dancing with you beside the pool, beneath those Japanese lanterns," says Dick Falherne, sending me a roguish wink.

"Oh, Dick," I say, feigning embarrassment, because everyone knows he's a notorious flirt. But what is going on here? So far John and I aren't seated with any of our regular friends, although there are still plenty to arrive. In April when I saw Deirdre at the salon, she told me the guest list had ballooned to two hundred and eighty.

"Personally, I've drawn the line at first cousins," she confided as the technicians waxed our eyebrows, "but Mead's parents both come from large families. You know how that is."

"Italian?" I asked.

"And Polish on his mother's side," Deirdre answered, emitting an "Ouch!" as the technician ripped the waxing paper off her eyebrows with unnecessary savagery.

"Say no more." I patted her shoulder in sympathy. "Oh dear, it's not going to be a Catholic wedding, is it? Ouch!" I glared at my technician as she demonstrated a similar incompetence. Where do they get these people?

"No, Allison and Mead are scripting nondenominational vows," Deirdre replied. "Well, I'll simply have to cut the list, although I'm frankly counting on the more geographically distant friends and relatives to decline. You don't suppose they'll mistake a courtesy invitation for a real one, do you?"

I sighed. "You never can tell. Some people just don't understand when they're not wanted—ouch!"

Now, looking around Rosecourt, I'd say Deirdre has done an excellent job of keeping out the riffraff. John, the Falhernes, and the Copmanns have segued to comparing golf scores, but I really must settle this matter of our tablemates. I excuse myself to locate Deirdre and follow the stream of guests heading for the verandah past another door-holding butler—white this time, that's better. But even outside it's crowded; guests seem to be arriving in droves. Deirdre must be mingling somewhere. I stop a young man and woman in waiters' outfits who are hauling between them an open ice chest loaded with Pellegrino bottles.

"Where is Mrs. Hollingsworth?" I ask.

"I'm sorry, ma'am, we don't know who she is," says the young woman cheerily, attempting to maneuver past me toward what I see is an outdoor bar. "One of the hostesses might be able to help you."

"You work for Rosecourt and you don't know who the bride's mother is?" I repeat, incredulous.

"No, ma'am. We're not with Rosecourt, we're with the caterer, and we haven't been introduced to the bridal party. Would you excuse us, please?"

She gestures that they'd like to pass by me, and with the growing crowd on the verandah, I'm jostled as it is, so I let them go. Really, though, who do they think is paying their salary tonight? The least they could do is to familiarize themselves with the members of the wedding entourage so if a guest wishes to find someone during the course of the evening, they can direct the guest accordingly.

Well, the good news is, there's a bar out here, and although the champagne was a nice touch, it was only a token drink, the flute barely half full. I approach the white-clothed table where the same two waiters are depositing the chilled Pellegrino beside the rows of liquor bottles.

"I'll have a vodka and tonic," I inform them.

"I'm sorry, ma'am," the young woman replies with another bright smile, "the bar isn't open yet. We do have water, soft drinks, and fruit juices available. May I get you something?"

"What do you mean, the bar isn't open?" I eye the bountiful array on the table, inviting her to acknowledge the evidence. "You have a full setup here."

"Yes, ma'am, and we'll begin serving cocktails right after the ceremony. Meanwhile, we can offer you Evian water, Pellegrino, Coke, Diet Coke, Sprite, ginger ale . . ."

"Never mind." I turn my back on the girl, who once again doesn't appear to be more than twenty with those perky breasts and ponytail. And why doesn't the other waiter or bartender or whoever he is speak up? He happens to be black—I guess it's acceptable for a black man to be a bartender—as well as lithe and rather handsome, and you'd think he'd take charge instead of letting this bossy young female do all the talking. And why on earth would Deirdre not have the bar open as soon as guests arrive? Is she trying to skimp on costs? Good heavens . . . is she going to have a *cash* bar?

"Isabel, darling! What a fabulous dress!"

"Where's John? Did you get here last night?"

"Love that Wedgwood blue color!"

I'm swamped by the Kendalls and the Radcliffes, followed by John arriving on the verandah with still more of our favorite chums.

"Please." I motion for attention after the pleasantries have been exchanged, all of us laughing in a convivial circle. "John and I are dying of suspense. Who else is at our table?"

"Not us."

"No, we're Table 4 with the Langleys."

"Not us, we're Table 13."

"Oh, how nice, we're Table 13, too!"

"Well, who in the world *is* at Table 7?" I demand in mock despair, though privately, I'm thinking this is getting a little ridiculous and extremely puzzling that not one of our best friends—

"Did you say Table 7?" burbles a voice, followed by an unwanted invasion of flesh as a curly-haired woman in a sleeveless orange paisley dress and a large straw hat bundles into our circle. "Pleased to meetcha! I'm Madge Dombrowski, fourth cousin of Mead's mother. Well, actually, it's my husband Arnold who's the fourth cousin of Mead's mother's father, but family is family, as I always say, so let me pump your hand. Isn't this a peachy keen day for a wedding? We've come all the way from Nashville in our Winnebago, and lordy, isn't this Newport a swell place? Let me just catch my husband Arnold . . . *Ar-nooold!* Come over here and bring Stanley with you! Don't you mind our boy Stanley. He'll catch on if you speak real slow. And meanwhile I can do you the favor of answering your call about our fellow citizens at Table 7, because I've been rounding them up and we are in the best company. There's

Mead's great-aunts Iris and Edna, and a single gentleman from Toledo who I know you'll be happy to meet, and of course here's my Arnold and our boy Stanley . . ."

"Would you like me to get you a vodka and tonic, Isabel dear?" John says, and I can see he's already casting eyes at the ponytailed bartender with the perky breasts.

"Make it a double," I say faintly, remembering too late the bar's not yet open.

Around the circle, our friends have begun backing away with smiles designed to disguise their pity while simultaneously putting a safe distance between us. *Wait,* I want to shout at them, *I'm sure there's been some mistake.* Because it's beginning to be only too obvious what Deirdre has done. For no earthly reason I can conceive, she's assigned John and me to the table reserved for the lonely females, the hayseed cousins, the boorish colleagues, and the village idiots. She's banished me to the hinterland known as Siberia, the dumping ground for misfit guests.

"My, my, isn't this going to be the most perfect evening?" burbles Madge, patting a hand to her orange-paisley bosom to still the heaving of her excited chest.

Well, we'll see if I'm going to stand for this!

5

WE HATE YOU

The Rosecourt Staff

ANNE SPOKE THE TRUTH.

The secret is out.

We hate you.

It doesn't matter that when you walk through the front door, we'll greet you effusively as our most honored guest. You are trouble incarnate, the bane of our existence, and we deplore every one of you, starting with the bride. We've met her before, and though she cleverly morphs from one wedding to the next, it takes us mere minutes to size her up.

Presenting—trumpet flourish!—our lineup of most dreaded brides:

The Control Freak strides in and snaps, "Move the guest book to that sideboard. Make those candles ivory, not white. The ballroom tables are too close together. Get a tape measure and reset them three inches. Turn down the air-conditioning, turn up the lights. Fetch the band leader. I'm rearranging the order of the dances." Move it! Hop to it! Her bridesmaids, her groom, her own parents jump.

The Drama Queen arrives breathless and overwhelmed and must be fanned by her attendants as they bear her up to the suite. Every five minutes, one hurries down with a new request. Could we send up some white wine with ice, the bride is overheated. Do we have any aspirin, the bride has a headache. Can we come open the windows, the bride needs a sea breeze. Would the caterer have any strawberry cream cheese and crackers to ease the bride's empty stomach. The Drama Queen will hold up the ceremony for forty-five minutes, the guests twisting in their seats, until she finally appears, near swooning on her father's arm, clutching an embroidered lace hanky, joy illuminating her tear-streaked face.

The Princess Bride flutters and flusters and can't make up her mind. She has no mind to make up. When she breaks a fingernail, the whole world stops. How could this happen to *me*? Her lower lip trembles, her eyes well with tears, a whimper escapes her mouth. She is easily distracted, most often by her own reflection, but responds well to coaxing and sugar-coated promises. "Come outside and see the pretty ocean," we coo with devious intent, and the broken fingernail forgotten, she steps onto the verandah, one step closer to the altar and good riddance. With practice, the Princess Bride will become a Drama Queen when she grows up.

The Olympic Bride runs a decathlon wedding. The activities include a maypole on the front lawn, a photography station in the rose garden where each guest may have a souvenir picture snapped, a harpsichord player in the foyer, a strolling violinist on the verandah, a raw bar, a martini bar, a documentary video of the engaged couple on endless loop in the library, a five-course dinner in the ballroom, a special appearance by a concert pianist, and a separate children's party—with magician—in the morning room to amuse the youngest guests. You need a team of broadcasters to cover all the venues, the myriad events.

Psycho Bride laughs and smiles, then discovers a hair on her plate and goes berserk. Calm restored, she chats and dances as if nothing has transpired, until the sight of her maid of honor flirting with the best man inexplicably drives her insane.

Bridezilla embraces all of the above charming traits, topped with a monster-sized dollop of egomania.

But wait, there's more. In addition to gracing one of the above categories, it goes without saying that our antagonist of the evening will also be a Rich Bride, because to enact your wedding fantasy in our Gilded Age mansion overlooking the ocean in Newport, Rhode Island, your daddy has to have some pretty big bucks.

We hate Rich Brides.

As for the wedding party, where shall we start?

We could do without the flower girl, the angelic tot. Oh, she may look adorable and pink-cheeked now in her frilly white dress, but by evening's end she'll be a tired, cranky, bawling child whom no one's had the sense to take home early and no one wants to leave off their partying to watch.

Ditto the ring bearer, the snot-nosed brat. In no time he'll be belching soda pop and pushing the flower girl down on the lawn, snickering at the slime-green grass stains ruining her dress.

We'd like to gag the bridesmaids, the whole gabbling flock. At least one of them will be envious and subversive. At least one of them will be chronically unhappy because she thinks she weighs too much. At least one of them will misplace her lipstick, shoes, or an earring during the evening and expect us to find what she lost. All of them will talk too much.

In the interests of equality, we're none too fond of the groomsmen. They crack stupid guy jokes and slap shoulders and pat each other on the butt. Although they can come in handy if we need to strong-arm any drunken male guests—that is, if they're not already drunk themselves.

Ah, but look at the proud parents, beaming upon their children's happiness. Surely they deserve our respect? No! We flee from the bride's mother, especially those of the VHM ilk. From the moment they start to plan the simplest ceremony, they become brutal despots. Crack the whip! Take no prisoners! This isn't *fun*, do you hear me? This is serious! We take perverse delight in watching the bride's and groom's mothers go at each other's throats when their opinions conflict. Meanwhile, the two fathers turn into spineless, sniveling whelps. Yes dear, no dear, whatever you want.

Finally, the guests. You have so many opportunities to make us miserable tonight! Depending on how obnoxious, rude, and critical you are, we'll revise our opinion of you up or down the Animosity Scale until we pronounce the final judgment at twelve o'clock. At best, we may grudgingly admit you weren't so bad after all. But it's better to start with the assumption that we hate you, because chances are, we will.

And you hate us.

Oh yes you do. Don't deny it.

You take offense when we impose rules that spoil your fun—no dancing on the tables, no sliding down the banister, no sex in the cloakroom.

You're miffed when we decline to laugh at your bad jokes or to be flattered when you hit on us.

Though you try to pretend we didn't see, you resent us for watching as you rack up an entertaining list of faux pas, spilling food down your front and tipping over your own feet on the dance floor.

And by the way, everything you suspect we're thinking about you, we are.

But one thing about us you do love. Every time you make our job more difficult, you're validating your self-congratulatory observation that this isn't a party for everyone.

Don't worry. It's all right. No doubt it's been that way between masters and servants since time began. In the Gilded Age, when Rosecourt and her sister mansions were the epitome of social climbing, the rule of thumb in our illustrious household was four servants for every aristocrat. The upper crust liked to imagine their loyal staff were devoted to their welfare and grateful for the generous pittance of their wages. What a shock should they discover these same employees not only did not enjoy their menial jobs but didn't like their lordships very much either.

Nowadays we'll credit you with a little more perspicacity. We both know that anyone who works at Rosecourt could not afford to be married here. But that still inclines you to feel superior, while we modern servants don't feel inferior, so the battle lines are drawn. And by the way, our sentiment is shared by everyone else you've hired tonight: the wait staff, the musicians, the parking valets. We compare notes with them throughout the evening, we relay stories of Guests Behaving Badly to our mutual mirth. Nothing you do goes unobserved, and the report circulates to all quarters of the house. Every last one of you has the potential to be our secret laughingstock.

Yet there is one person among you whom we don't dislike: the groom. That's because, except to meet the bride at the altar and say "I do," he's invisible. The wise groom will shelve his personality entirely on his wedding day and recognize that this rigmarole has nothing to do with him. It could be any man up there; a cardboard cutout would suffice. The wise groom will practice saying "I do" often before walking to the altar.

"Honey, do you like Newport for a wedding destination?"

"I do."

"Do you think we should have a champagne welcome for the guests?"

"I do."

"Don't you agree with me that cinnabar is the only possible choice for the bridesmaids' dresses?"

"I do."

When asked more directly by family and friends what form the wedding will take, the wise groom will smile lovingly at his fiancée and reply, "Whatever she wants. This is her special day."

Standing at the altar, he will think to himself, "Relax, this is almost done. Just keep smiling and at the end of the night you will get sex."

In his future married life, the same rules will apply to shopping expeditions, attending the opera or ballet, and visits to his in-laws.

And, correction, there is one person at the wedding we are predisposed to like enormously: the bride's father, the moneybags who is the source of our paychecks—we love our paychecks!—and who has the potential to make us ecstatic by capping off our evening with a big fat tip.

So don't say you weren't warned, don't plead ignorance, don't act as if we're your personal slaves tonight. Though we're at your beck and call, we are far from powerless and have ways of taking our revenge.

Beware.

We hate you!

 6

THE BEAUTY QUEENS

Lauren, Carolyn, Jessica, Nicole

OOH, LOOK AT US! Aren't we just perfect? And we love this gilded ballroom with its mirrored walls—we've already added it to our list of places to hold our own wedding someday. Being Allison's bridesmaids has given us lots of insights and ideas on that subject, and we'll be forever grateful to her for that alone. Now the big moment is almost upon us. Look at the rows of guests outside, craning in their seats! In a few minutes we'll step onto the verandah and pause between the stone lions flanking the stairs. Then with every eye upon us, we'll descend the half flight to the lawn and glide up the aisle. But first, we'd better check our appearance one last time.

"Carolyn, one of your hairpins is sticking out!"

"Oh no, where?"

"Don't move! We'll try to fix it."

"Does anyone have a comb?"

"Where's the hairspray?"

"Upstairs in the suite."

"Someone needs to run and get it for us!"

"Could you hurry to the suite and get our hairspray?"

we implore the butler. "It's a purse-sized lavender metallic mister—"

"Excuse me! Could I have everyone's attention, please!" Anne, the supervisor, plants herself between us and Carolyn. "Leon cannot go upstairs to fetch hairspray. He has to stay right here to help you ladies over the door-sill in your gowns and high heels. Then he has to fluff Allison's train as she and her father start down the aisle so it will be picture-perfect for the photographer. Carolyn's hair looks fine. You've fixed it beautifully. Please get back in line with your groomsmen because we're already twenty minutes behind schedule. Now where is the ring bearer? Nicholas . . . Where is the pillow I gave you to carry?"

Jessica gives Carolyn's hairpin a last delicate tap, and we exhale. There, it's all right. Because despite what this supervisor thinks, it's far more important to make the right impression than to be late by twenty or thirty or forty minutes. People will wait for us. They always do. After the effort we've put in for Allison's special day, we're certainly not going to be rushed now. We awoke bright and early at ten a.m., stretched luxuriously, slipped on our Versace halter tops and capris, and gathered at the hotel café for our preordered breakfast of hazelnut coffee, fresh fruit, and croissants. Well, all of us but one. Pammy reported that Mead's sister, Fredericka, would be delayed.

"She was talking to our chambermaid about her health care benefits. It seems the hotel management switched them to a cheaper policy that doesn't include prenatal or maternity care, so Fredericka is organizing a grievance meeting for them with some union representatives." Pammy stopped, as if a little surprised at the words coming out of her mouth. Then, remembering our priorities, she added, "She said she'd be back in time to get her hair done as you want, Allison, and I'm sure she means it."

The rest of us rolled our eyes. Honestly, if you want prenatal and maternity benefits, get a job that offers them or get your husband's company to cover it or better yet, don't get pregnant if you can't afford it. Stick to a vibrator, like we do. It's much more convenient. Secretly, though, we were just as happy not to have Fredericka join us. Don't you think she has to be a serious lesbian or something to go around befriending women on all these legal causes and wearing those unattractive glasses when there are so many flattering shades of contact lenses available?

Meanwhile, we had tons to accomplish.

"First, a head-to-toe spa treatment," Allison announced. "Cucumber facial, herbal body wrap, and a luxurious aroma-therapy massage. On me, of course." She waited for our *oohs* and *aahs* to subside. "Now, do we all have our tans coordinated?" Giggling, we held out our bare arms to compare the delicate golden hues we'd achieved by diligent timing and judicious spacing of our visits to the tanning salon. Even Lauren, despite her tennis and her obsession with her pinkish skin tone, had managed to finesse a sexy tawniness. Nevertheless, she displayed her arm rather stiffly. She had a big fight with her latest boyfriend three weeks ago, and he disinvited himself from the wedding and still hasn't called to apologize. Also, she's still miffed about the cinnabar. Sometimes we wish she'd grow up and get over herself.

The one arm that didn't stand up to inspection was Susie's, which was plump and white except for the short, spiky, dark hairs that poked up from the flesh like miniature porcupine quills. Honestly, don't you think she could do something about that? Hasn't she ever heard of bleaching or depilatories?

"Susie . . .?" Allison said.

"I tried, Allison, really, but it's hard to get a tan in Montana in the spring. We had snowstorms right into May."

"I'm sure you did, Susie. Here's my suggestion: right after breakfast, while we're at the spa, why don't you go out to the deck chairs by the hotel pool and get a little sun? You can catch up with us later."

"Yes, Allison."

The rest of us smiled encouragement, but honestly. Susie didn't lose the thirty pounds Allison asked her to either. She'd barely shed fifteen, and her ideal weight loss would be closer to sixty. If she smoked a few cigarettes to curb her appetite, like we do, she could have been practically svelte by now. Allison was more than fair about it, and the rest of us made personal sacrifices too. Lauren's wearing the cinnabar, Jessica exercised night and day to take another inch off her hips, Carolyn never said a word against doing her hair up, and Nicole abstained from chocolate all last month to avert the slightest hint of a breakout.

Which reminds us, did you see Fredericka's fingernails? Not only did she not grow them out as Allison requested, they were nibbled to pathetic rinds. Fredericka claimed she'd tried—not very hard, we suspect—and she told Allison not to get huffy, she'd slap on artificial ones. Apparently, she has no inkling that even artificial nails can vary greatly in color, shape, size, and quality, and it's not as simple as walking into a drugstore and pulling something cheap off a rack. Pammy came to the rescue—what would we do without Pammy?—

and found something in one of the hotel boutiques before the rest of us got up. Anyway, with Susie and Fredericka out of the way, we proceeded from breakfast to the spa. While the technicians started on our body wrap and facial, we began a discussion of current events.

"Guess who's sleeping with her gynecologist?"

"No! I thought he was gay."

"You're confusing him with that art dealer we met at Allison's gallery."

"Speaking of hunks, has anyone booked a private lesson with that new tennis pro yet?"

Our eyes slid slyly toward Lauren, who affected a cool profile in response. *Getting a little slutty lately, aren't we, Lauren?* Bouncing from one bed to another so soon after a breakup. We've heard from more than one tennis player why you're suddenly so devoted to improving your ground strokes. Paulo, the new pro, is a Brazilian charmer, with seductive brown eyes, a tangle of hair, and a bronzed torso that glistens with sweat at the open V-neck of his white polo shirt. *Is he any good, Lauren? No? You're not the least bit interested in him? Then you won't mind sharing if any of us take a fancy to him?*

"Help yourselves," Lauren replied with chilly indifference, as the spa technicians undid our body wraps and rinsed us off. We don't mind being nude in front of other women. On the contrary, we enjoy them pretending not to stare at us. We're quite enviable, especially Jessica, now that she's dieted off that extra inch. No one who works at a hotel spa in a two-tone pink uniform is ever going to look like us.

"Next, hair and makeup," Allison directed.

Of course, we'd each brought our own cosmetics case

and color chart so we could instruct the stylists on our personal palette. For our hair, sometimes it's hard to decide which is more fun, wearing it up or down, but Allison decreed up for her wedding so we all got some variation on the classic French twist. The beauty of a French twist is that it can make even bad hair look good, which for Susie, when she returned from suntanning, would be an absolute must. Could you imagine her appearance otherwise, that ratty dishwater mop straggling down her bare back? A French twist can also disguise limp hair, which would be vital for Fredericka, who still hadn't shown up. Honestly, how could she be so selfish as to go off organizing health care for some chambermaid when Allison had spent over a year meticulously planning this perfect wedding?

The one person who might justifiably take exception to the French twist was Carolyn, who is a natural blond, unlike platinum Nicole and Allison herself, who was blond as a little girl but then her hair darkened, so now she's frosted. And not only is Carolyn a natural blond, but she has tons of hair, ripples of it, a cascade, a mane, a *crescendo* of silky, wavy locks. It streams down her back nearly to her waist, so marvelous it's almost alive, floating like the shimmering strands of some filamented sea creature. It's princess hair, the kind you see in fairy-tale books, and you know no one in real life could have tresses like that. Well, Carolyn does. It turns both women's and men's heads—we admit we're all a little jealous of it—and hairdressers invariably treat it as a sacred trust.

Carolyn herself is in love with her hair. She can't seem to leave it alone, can't keep her hands off it. We've seen her, within the space of an hour, pin it up, tumble it down, braid it, clip it into a ponytail, and swirl it into a topknot. When she brushes it, she croons and sighs, stroking it between her fingers. By the way, Carolyn's pubic patch is equally blond and glorious, and although we've never caught her at it, we suspect she's equally fond of devoting personal attention to that. In short, Carolyn has never been in love with a man as much as she is with her hair, yet she didn't object to wearing it up tonight where she can't touch it for a whole evening. That tells you how seriously we bridesmaids take our responsibilities, and why it's hard for us to be tolerant of others who do not.

As the stylists completed their ministrations, we wrapped up our current events discussion with our favorite subject: who we're having sex with. Allison's with Mead, of course, and Carolyn's preferences have been noted. Jessica has been dating a stockbroker for three months but didn't bring him to the wedding because she wanted to scope out who else might be here. Lauren fucks everybody and any-body because of her low self-esteem—her breasts, you see, aren't quite as nice as the rest of ours—but although we've concluded she's hopped the net with that tennis pro, she stubbornly refuses to own up and share the titillating details. That left Nicole to dish.

"Come on, Nicole," we demanded.

"Well . . .," she teased out the word with a coy look, "there is something I've been saving up to tell you. I may have found someone I can finally be serious about."

"Who? Who?" we demanded, and she revealed a name.

"You're kidding! I dated him four years ago," said Allison, and we squealed. As long as two of us don't want the same man at the same time, we're fine with serial boyfriends. Allison beckoned us in closer. "Try this on him and he'll be the proverbial putty in your hands," she confided, demonstrating.

"How do you do that without gagging?" Jessica giggled.

"Trust me, it's all in the angle," Allison replied, and she should know. Allison has personally studied porno movies to perfect her methods, and anyone can see how happy she keeps Mead.

We were nearly hysterical with laughter by that time, until we noticed poor Pammy blushing furiously. Oh dear. She's so undemanding it's easy to forget she's there until we need her. She's one of those moderately pretty girls for whom makeovers don't produce much impact, and since everyone already compliments her personality, there's very little we can do to improve her. Some women would find that a blessing, but we don't. If you already like yourself the way you are, isn't that like settling for less?

"Okay, I'm here. What do you want to do with my hair?" said Fredericka, walking into the spa and interrupting our conversation without preamble. Honestly, how thoughtless could she get? Here we were prepared, in spite of her attitude, to coach her and be role models so she could see how perfect it is to be one of us. But if she doesn't care . . .

"Sit here," said one of the stylists, conveying with a polite chill what we think of someone with such scant regard for friendship. "I'm afraid we won't have time to do anything as elegant as we've done for the other bridesmaids."

"Whatever, just tuck it up," Fredericka said, hopping into the chair. Her fingernails still weren't done either.

Then Susie hurtled in, breathless, and our jaws

dropped. Oh my God, oh my God, oh my God—

"I'm sorry," she whimpered. "I fell asleep in the lounge chair."

She was the color of a giant boiled lobster.

"Susie, what have you done?"

"Oh my God, Susie, you're scarlet!"

"Your face is swollen!"

"You look like you're on fire!"

"Look at the strap marks on your shoulders!"

"How long were you out there?"

"Didn't you set a timer?"

"Didn't you use sunscreen?"

"I'm sorry, I'm sorry!"

"Oh, Susie," said Pammy. "It must hurt. Come with me and we'll find something to take out the sting."

"You may need a doctor," said Fredericka, jumping out of the stylist's chair and joining Pammy.

They led Susie away, and what could we do but stare at each other in shock? After we planned this so carefully, after Jessica dieted and Nicole sacrificed chocolate, after Carolyn imprisoned her locks without a whimper and Lauren went to exacting lengths to get a tawny glow—to think that Susie spoiled it all by carelessly getting sunburned.

Slowly, we turned our gaze to Allison, seeing what she must be imagining: her perfect bridal procession ruined by her fat, homely sister trundling down the aisle among the rest of us, like a roasted-alive pig in a Vera Wang gown . . .

Allison closed her eyes and drew several long breaths.

"Oh, Allison, we're so sorry!"

"We'll dust her in powder to tone down the redness."

"We'll fill in the strap marks with artificial tanner."

"No." Allison opened her eyes, speaking with absolute authority and calm. "Susie is far too sick to be standing outside in the hot sun for a wedding. I wouldn't dream of letting her risk her health to do it. She needs a doctor's attention, then total rest and recuperation in her bed here at the hotel."

"But then you'll have an extra groomsman in the processional."

"He can escort Madeline, the junior bridesmaid."

We stopped, picturing it. Instead of Madeline making a solo entrance, we'd have her on the arm of an obliging groomsman, then us with our escorts, followed by the ring bearer, the flower girl, and finally a radiant Allison and her proud father. And no Susie . . .

We nearly broke into applause. Brilliant. Allison is brilliant, that's why we admire her, why she's our inspiration, our heroine, our undisputed leader. Who else could be so resourceful and decisive? Here we had a near disaster, and with a simple flip of the lineup, Allison had saved the day.

"I'll tell Mead and the groomsmen," said Jessica, as we galvanized for action.

"I'll alert your mother," said Carolyn.

"I'll tell Pammy so she can persuade Susie to stay in bed," Lauren promised.

"I'll get Fredericka back here. She still doesn't have her hair and nails done," Nicole chipped in.

"Thank you." Allison hugged us in turn, then we all hugged each other.

Now a whole year of preparation has come to fruition, and we're lined up in the Rosecourt ballroom, ready to make our grand entrance. Straighten spine lift head, deep breath. Anne raises her finger for our attention, then cues the musicians on the verandah to begin. This is it! Our audience awaits, and we won't let them down. Isn't it wonderful how things always turn out so perfectly for us, beautiful us . . . ooh!

7

A PORTRAIT OF THE ARTIST

Allison

To avoid an ordinary life, you must surround yourself with beauty, and I have certainly accomplished that tonight. The weather is idyllic, the reconfigured processional—minus Susie—will be as photogenic as I'd always dreamed it would be, and I love the way my gown feels, the sensuous brush of ivory silk against my skin. Every one of the seed pearls nestling on the bodice is hand sewn, and they glisten like tiny teardrops to accent my figure in subtle luminescence. Most important, I know the vision I'll create a few minutes from now will exceed the highest expectations and set a standard of artistry to be admired and emulated by everyone present. I have spared absolutely no thought and no expense to make this the most significant occasion of my life. Oh, I know what people say—it's the marriage, not the wedding, that's important, and I agree. But what's wrong with having both? Why would anyone settle for a commonplace ceremony in a poky little church when they can have a sumptuous celebration like mine?

"Let's do it," says Anne, directing Madeline and Steve, the first groomsman, to step onto the verandah. For my processional I've chosen "Hornpipe" from Handel's *Water Music*, and it couldn't be more right, the music stately and regal but not overbearing. I can't see outside yet, but I picture our guests nodding in approval as my first couple appears.

"Well, sweetheart, this is it," says Daddy, patting my hand as he stands handsome and stalwart beside me in his tux. I give his palm a return squeeze. Last night at the rehearsal dinner, he jokingly admonished Mead about "taking care of my little girl." Anyone can see he's relishing his role as father of the bride.

I'm about to be married!

What will my new life be like?

For a start, Mead and I will have our own apartment in Manhattan. We've found the ideal place on the Upper West Side in a building that fronts the park. People seem to think it's quaint that we didn't move in together as soon as we became engaged, but it simply wasn't convenient. Mead was living near his parents in New Jersey, and I was sharing an apartment with Jessica and Nicole in the city and needed to commute to Connecticut every weekend to plan the wedding with Mom. Once we've returned from our honeymoon in Italy, we'll move in and begin decorating, converting one of the three bedrooms to an office. Mead doesn't really need one, since his work day starts and ends at his father's company. I, on the other hand, have built up a prominent clientele since joining the Naomi Wyatt Gallery as a sales associate four years ago, and as Naomi says, you don't earn commissions by hanging a "Closed" sign on the door at six o'clock. It was good of her to phone best wishes from the auction in London this weekend. Thanks to her mentoring, I plan to open my own gallery soon.

"Okay," says Anne, "Madeline and Steve are down the steps. Fredericka and Blaine, move into position. Remember to keep yourselves evenly spaced."

I'm not surprised that I'm the first of my crowd to get married. Of course, none of us wanted to relinquish our independence too early, while we were building our careers, traveling, getting the most out of life. But once I hit thirty, it became necessary to implement a serious timeline. My agenda was straightforward: engaged and married by thirty-two, continued advancement as a professional couple, pregnancy and first child by thirty-seven. That will still leave time for a second child before forty if I decide to pursue that option. But I notice that many women choose to stop after one baby, and I may too. After all, one is enough to give you the experience of pregnancy and parenthood, and with one child you can be sure to provide plenty of undivided attention when the nanny is off-duty in the evening. However, the first step was to get married, and since I'd recently begun dating Mead, he deserved consideration. What happened next was unexpected—my heart acted before my head, and we fell in love.

"Pammy and Patrick." Anne sends the next couple out the door, and the rest of us take a step forward. I can see over my bridesmaids' heads now, to the guests seated on the lawn. I can make out Mead's figure at the altar, though I can't read his face from this far away.

Love—there's nothing in the world like it, is there? You're going along, perfectly happy, painting your life to suit yourself, when suddenly the brushstrokes take over and the composition is transformed. You still recognize the basic elements, but in startling new colors and configurations.

It's as if you took a still life by Cézanne and handed it over to Picasso. It's giddy, dangerous, and exciting, thrilling to discover a fresh vision in a timeworn genre. It rearranges everything—the perspective, the lighting, the relationship of each object to another. I've been in love before, of course—who hasn't? Yet no matter what your past experience, you embrace the new picture as if it's a masterpiece. The real question is: how do you feel after staring at this canvas for weeks, months, years? To fall in love is so vivid and easy; to marry, to live with someone day after day, can be like watching paint dry. So in these last few minutes, I can't help but ask: is Mead the right man?

There's some commotion over Lauren's shoe, but for an instant I lose contact with everyone around me. *Is Mead the right man?* To be honest, I'm not sure, but how can anyone be? No one my age contemplates marriage without simultaneously conceding the dismal rate of divorce. Even when a couple has survived the early ups and downs, there are no guarantees. Look at my own parents and their clichéd ending—all the more reason not to make the same mistake my mother did, giving up her career in real estate to take care of Daddy, Susie, and me. When a woman does that in the midst of her prime earning years, it makes her look as if she's not serious. She loses contacts, momentum, and what does Mom have to show for it now? Nothing—I can see her sitting there alone in the left front row. Daddy has the hospital and Kimmy. I have the gallery, my goals, and Mead. Even Susie has a career, albeit a dreary one, teaching in Montana. But Mom opted for a false sense of security, and she's left with an empty house and alimony. No one respects a woman who has to ask for alimony.

"See, all fixed," says Anne, displaying a pebble from Lauren's shoe. "You and Dave just watch your step over the doorsill. Nicholas, I asked you to stay in line."

Daddy leaves my side temporarily to steer Nicholas back into place, and I peer ahead again to Mead. I still can't make out his expression. Does he have any qualms? Is he thinking the same thoughts as I am? Actually, I believe we'll be quite content together for a while. Falling in love aside, Mead was the only one of the men I knew when I formed my timeline at thirty who was ready to get married. The others still wanted to play the field, and why shouldn't they, as long as they're getting all the sex they want, commitment free? But Mead took up with enthusiasm the idea that we should get married and throughout our engagement has never expressed any doubts.

Sometimes I wonder if he's taking it all too much for granted, assuming we'll coast along with no incompatibilities. Because I can foresee one probable area of disagreement, namely that he's not fulfilling his potential with his father's company. Commercial real estate development simply isn't his forte. I would like to see Mead as a VP in advertising or broadcasting, particularly in a sports division. One of my clients is a VP at NBC, and I've mentioned Mead's capabilities. Naturally, he'll have to work his way up just as I've done, starting with a college internship at the Museum of Modern Art where a friend of Daddy's was on the board. But unlike me, Mead has never had to struggle, and I think the experience will invigorate him. Since we keep our bank accounts separate, I'm willing to be patient. Of course, it goes without saying that I also have my own trust fund and an ironclad prenuptial agreement.

"Carolyn and Rob," says Anne, and Carolyn turns to blow me a good-luck kiss as she steps from the ballroom. Jessica and Nicole move up in line, tittering.

"Pretty girls," says Daddy, patting my hand.

I nod, my emotions suddenly welling. Jessica and Nicole especially are my two dearest friends, and we've had such a great time sharing the apartment these last three years. We'd take off for skiing weekends in Vermont or shopping in Montreal, and it doesn't hurt that Jessica, as a buyer for Saks, has an absolute knack for spotting a trend even before it hits the runway. And it was Nicole, a paralegal, who got her boss to negotiate such a fantastic deal on our apartment. It would have been hard to choose between them as my maid of honor, so in a sense I'm grateful I had to ask Susie. Poor Susie. She means well, and she has a good heart.

But don't I also have a good heart? When Mead and I got engaged, I never once said Susie couldn't be a bridesmaid. I bit my tongue and welcomed her, even when the others cringed. I knew Daddy would be proud of me and he was, and maybe it's because I did the right thing that fate intervened and Susie couldn't be in the processional after all. I doubt anyone will notice she's missing, and if she's feeling up to it, she can come to the reception later. The formal photos will have been shot by then, and the photographer can take a few of me and Susie for the family.

"Jessica and Todd," says Anne.

"I'm on!" Jessica gasps, holding her bouquet to her nose for a bracing inhale before she steps out the door.

"You look divine!" I call after her.

"You all look lovely," says Anne, smiling at the rest of us. "It's going perfectly. See how the crowd's eyes follow each pair of attendants up the aisle, then swing back to the verandah to see the next couple poised at the stairs?"

"You know," says Daddy, "I never thought to ask before, but why is it the bride's family sits on the left and the groom's on the right? Is there some particular reason?"

Anne chuckles. "That's another bit of wedding trivia. In the old days, if there weren't enough marriageable young women within a community, the groom would have to capture a bride from a neighboring village. He'd take his strongest friend to help him—that's the origin of the best man—and once he captured the bride, he placed her to his left in order to have his right hand, his sword hand, free to fight off her relatives if they tried to rescue her. I doubt any grooms carry a sword up the aisle today, except perhaps for a military wedding, but the left-right tradition remains. Okay, last couple. Nicole and Brad, out you go."

Nicole reaches back to clasp my hand, then she glides toward the stairs. If I'd known she was dating one of my old boyfriends, I would have insisted she invite him, though I don't think he'll pan out as she intends. Neither she nor Jessica have great taste in men, unfortunately, which is why Mead and I went to such lengths to pair his groomsmen with my bridesmaids on the basis of both appearance and personality. It would be a nice legacy of my wedding if one of my friends met her future husband here.

The *Water Music* lilts on the breeze. Now it's only Nicholas and Fiona ahead of me. Naturally, the ring bearer doesn't carry the real wedding rings, merely a pair of symbolic gold bands tied by a ribbon in the center of the white satin and lace pillow. Fiona's basket does contain real rose petals, dewy fresh and soft as pink velvet, and after the butler leads her down the stairs, she'll sprinkle them as she walks up the aisle. Mom was against having any children in the wedding party, adamant that if they didn't follow instructions precisely it would ruin everything. But I was willing to chance it, picturing how precious the moment could be.

You see, my mother doesn't quite share my concept of beauty. Her idea of beauty is fixed and hard. She needs things to be perfect to show everyone else she can do it, and the result feels set in concrete. Whereas my vision can accommodate risk and spontaneity. Yet it does start by surrounding yourself with beautiful objects and possessions, by pleasing your own senses of sight, taste, touch, sound, and smell. It *should* matter to you whether the clink of your wineglasses is Baccarat or Swarovski, whether the painting in your living room is a Rothko or a small Monet. That's why I'll have to invest constant time and energy in Mead's and my new lifestyle, hiring and supervising painters, decorators, and a cleaning service, shopping to find the furnishings that express our unique individuality. We'll need to eat at the right restaurants, keep the right company. And if I'm to be part of this ideal picture, I have to wear only designer clothes, devote attention to my hair and makeup, work out at the health club, and drink eight eight-ounce glasses of sparkling water daily. I can't be caught in a sweat suit having a bad hair day.

Let me repeat: to avoid an ordinary life, you must surround yourself with beauty, and that means creating a whole embracing atmosphere that disdains whatever is demeaning and ugly and demands only what is high-minded and lovely. It's the difference between peeping enviously into an art gallery in passing and walking in and vowing never to leave.

"Nicholas," says Anne, and I see her cross her fingers behind her back as she sends him out the door.

I cross mine, too, though privately I told both Nicholas and his parents that if he misbehaves during the ceremony, I've designated Steve, a former football player, to remove him. I am, above all, a realist, and I know when to cut my losses and move forward.

In the end, what *is* beauty? Keats wrote that beauty is truth, truth is beauty, but did Keats write the truth? Did he pen unvarnished newspaper accounts of starving children in the smoggy London slums, of syphilis-ridden prostitutes plying their trade, of ragged families evicted from their dwellings? No, he wrote poetry because he aspired to create not truth, but lasting beauty. And with the exception of natural wonders such as the Grand Canyon, beauty is rarely accidental. Whether it's a Tiffany egg, the Taj Mahal, a Japanese garden, or Beethoven's Ninth, beauty is conceived, designed, structured, landscaped, engineered, orchestrated. It is manipulated, in a thousand different ways, to achieve a vision that ravishes the heart and mind. How many corrections, changes, amends did Keats make to his ode before it came right? How many painstaking brushstrokes did da Vinci lavish on the *Mona Lisa* to create what is arguably the most beautiful painting in history? And when he finally had to declare it finished, it was put inside a border, framed as a testament to its artificiality. Truth is what *is*, beauty is what we would like things to be. Beauty is inherently *dis*honest. So don't blame me for striving to make my wedding a work of art that every guest can cherish and remember with joy.

"Fiona," says Anne, and Daddy and I watch as the butler, solemn and proper, conveys her down the stairs. Fiona is nearly at the altar when the coos of the crowd inspire her to skip and toss her petals high into the air like a fairy child. I did say there was room for spontaneity.

"Allison, it's you."

Anne indicates the way forward with a gentle upturn of her palm, and Daddy leads me onto the verandah. We reach our spot between the stone lions at the top of the stairs and pause while the audience's eyes leave Fiona and their heads swivel to find me. Then for just one minute, time stops. The sparkling white façade of Rosecourt rises behind us. Overhead, puffs of cotton clouds look on like mischievous cherubs in the cerulean sky. The butler stands erect at a discreet distance, ready to lift my train as we descend the steps and fluff it out to spread perfectly as I begin my walk down the aisle. All faces are turned my way, shining with delight, my bridesmaids quivering in anticipation, the groomsmen in a handsome row, the minister smiling above his open book. And Mead, my husband-to-be, awaits me at the altar with a grin on his face.

"This is it," Daddy says, patting my hand for what must be the tenth time, and my heart nearly buckles when I see tears wetting his eyes.

I nod, take a deep breath, and banishing every negative thought, I bask in the moment.

"I'm ready," I reply.

8

LAND OF DREAMS

Anne

"DEAR FAMILY AND FRIENDS, as we gather on this beautiful afternoon to celebrate the wedding of Allison and Mead, I can't help but be inspired by the glorious setting before us . . ."

And they're off, the ceremony's begun, and for a few minutes I can catch my breath and regroup. Inside the house, my staff will already have dropped onto the grand staircase, snatching a precious quarter hour off their feet, while Leon keeps watch for late arrivals at the front door. Any sound from that direction will cue the others to spring erect, smooth their uniforms, and smilingly greet the tardy guests. It is a rule at Rosecourt that no butler or hostess, no matter how tired, no matter how long the event, shall ever sit down, lean against a wall or doorframe, or slouch at their post. At least, it's a rule that no one shall ever catch them at it, and if I were smart, I'd go sit down now, too.

In my ten years at Rosecourt, and contrary to an oft-depicted scene in the movies and on TV, no bride or groom has ever bolted once the ceremony was underway. Although on one occasion we did lose a bride prior to the processional.

While I penned the rest of the agitated wedding party in the ballroom, my staff scurried high and low in a frantic search. Finally a hostess found her locked in the bathroom in the suite. "I'm not coming out until my hair is absolutely perfect," she sobbed. An hour and several Valiums later, her hair lacquered to helmet hardness, her face swollen like a blowfish, she floated down the aisle. Allison apparently has no doubts, about her hair or her vows, so I could safely slip away and ease off my shoes. But this evening I can't seem to break free, and as I watch from the verandah, the minister's words carry to me on the sea breeze.

"Here we are on a sweeping emerald lawn overlooking the boundless Atlantic Ocean, calm and peaceful under an azure sky. Here and there, we glimpse the white sail of a gallant yacht reaching for the far horizon, and it occurs to me that Allison and Mead are about to embark on a voyage, a voyage of great adventure and personal discovery . . ."

So it's to be the voyage of discovery metaphor tonight. Well, there's nothing wrong with that, and it will carry nicely in the minister's resonant voice. Usually for an out-of-state client like Allison, we tactfully recommend to the bride in search of a perfect wedding that the dear, doddering parish priest be left at home. They inevitably get lost in Newport's bumper-to-bumper tourist traffic, forget to bring some necessary text or document, muddle through the ceremony in a voice far too frail to be heard beyond the first row, and then fall asleep over their coffee while waiting for the wedding cake to be cut. Sometimes a bride responds laughingly to our concerns, "Oh, but I couldn't possibly be married by anyone but Father Flanagan. We'll provide a driver for him, and we're used to not hearing a word he says in church." Then we know it will be all right. But I'm willing to bet that when our office staff delicately raised the issue with Deirdre and Allison, they immediately exchanged a calculating look, and without a word passing between them, poor old Father Flanagan was dumped. I wonder how many potential candidates they auditioned before informing this gentleman he got the part?

I have to say, they made a good choice. Tall and patrician, he'll look well cast in the photographs. He enjoys hearing himself speak, he prides himself on his eloquence, and he imagines no one performing a wedding ceremony at Rosecourt has ever before lit upon such a fortuitous theme as the voyage of discovery. Besides, it *will* sound new and poetic to the assembled guests, most of whom are already exhaling a breath—thank heaven this isn't going to be a long, boring, religious speech!—and will therefore be receptive to a pleasant daydream of sailboats and summer sunshine and balmy ocean breeze.

In fact, I'd say the voyage of discovery is our most popular wedding metaphor here at Rosecourt, followed closely by the obvious comparisons of marriage to our fabled rose garden itself—a paradise when lovingly planted and tended, yet not free from the thorns of life. Other recurrent images include two travelers embarking on a winding path, two dancers performing a pas de deux, the tree and/or circle of life, and the lighthouse/faithful beacon in the dark. Standing here on the verandah, observing ceremonies Protestant, Catholic, Jewish, Hindu, Buddhist, Muslim, inter- and nondenominational, I believe I've heard them all. I wish I could summon a unique image to describe my own marriage and its failure, but everything I come up with rings hollow, clichéd, and trite.

"What is the first thing Allison and Mead will require for their voyage? They will need a sturdy boat, a seaworthy vessel that can stand up to the rigors of wind and wave and conflicting currents, a protective hull in which to ride out tempests and storms. That vessel is their love for each other, a conviction that they are meant to sail the course of life together . . ."

Oh, please. We believed that, Greg and I. We believed with startling confidence that we would stay together to the end of our given time. We met our very first week of college at a rally protesting the university's involvement with firms doing business in South Africa. My sign read "End Apartheid," Greg's demanded "Free Mandela," and we accidentally thwacked each other as we got turned in the crowd. Our eyes met, the world stopped—yes, it really was like that. Anyway, we decided to leave the rally to the seasoned protesters and headed to a nearby coffee shop. At midnight, we were still talking in the TV lounge of my dorm, two virgins just past their eighteenth birthdays, rapt with our own intelligence and our untarnished dreams. If we'd stayed together, like some of the older couples here tonight, our fiftieth anniversary announcement in the newspaper would have trilled that we were college sweethearts. But there's no joy in that hopelessly naïve image if your marriage doesn't last; even if it was true once, the words have the sharp, rueful taste of vinegar after you divorce.

One of the most romantic moments between us happened only a few months after we began dating. It was a Saturday afternoon in early December, and with the magic of the first snowfall evoking a Currier and Ives scene, we'd strolled off-campus to the downtown stores to do our Christmas shopping. We held hands, flushed with the excitement of the excursion, flirting with domesticity. Our conversation was alternately bantering and serious.

"What can I get for my brother?" I lamented. "He's such a jock. All he ever thinks about is baseball, football, hockey."

"Get him an athletic supporter."

"Greg!"

"And some cologne that smells like a baseball glove. If he walks into a party wearing nothing but the cup and the cologne, no woman will be able to resist him."

Greg grinned and flicked a snowflake from my nose—he had a great smile, a flash of white teeth that could jump-start my heart—and I tsked at him in pretended disapproval as I towed him along. As we passed the jewelry store window, a cameo brooch in a gold filigree setting caught my eye. It would be perfect for the high-necked blouses my mother liked to wear, but the tag, as on all the other items in the window, was tucked facedown and out of sight.

I was chewing my lip and guessing at the price when Greg nudged me to look his way. A little farther along the street, an elderly couple had halted before a toy store. They were dressed almost alike: plaid—although not identical plaid—wool jackets, corduroy pants—his olive, hers tan—tucked into rubber galoshes, fuzzy red earmuffs over their gray hair, her scarf yellow, his blue. They looked the way a couple will when they've donned their outfits at random, then halfway out the door they'll poke a laughing finger at each other as they realize they've unwittingly become twins. Their faces had aged in unison also, softly withered like the vellum pages in an ancient manuscript. They stood holding hands before the store window, absorbed in a discussion of which puzzle or doll would best suit each grandchild.

"That's going to be us someday," Greg said, as simply as if he'd looked into a crystal ball and made sure of it. We were barely eighteen as we stood there amidst the Christmas lights and the falling snow, and he was sure even then.

From a distance the minister's voice intrudes.

"Of course, Allison and Mead will need to provision their boat wisely, stocking it with patience, commitment, and mutual respect. Most of all, they'll require dreams and goals, for dreams are the wind that fills your sails . . ."

A sigh ripples through the audience. They're eating this up, I'll grant him that. It occurs to me that the few wedding traditions I've mentioned to the families tonight smack of violence—forced marriages necessitating bridal veils, the groom raiding the countryside to kidnap a wife. There are happier traditions, of course. The diamond as the engagement stone of choice originated with Maximilian I, who in 1477 presented a diamond ring to Mary of Burgundy as a token of his love. The "ring finger" itself came from the Greeks, who believed the third finger was connected to the heart by the "vein of love." From Roman times comes the expression "to tie the knot," though in convoluted form. According to the wedding trivia book in our office, the Roman bride wore a heavily knotted girdle that the groom had the "duty" of untying. Whether true or not, these nuggets are invariably received with delight by the wedding party, and I've found them helpful in easing pre-ceremony jitters and bridging awkward pauses between in-laws.

Allison's minister has segued to the inevitable admonitions about steering clear of rocky shoals and weathering matrimonial storms. I try not to remember what Greg and I said at our wedding ceremony a month after our college graduation. A far cry from Allison's gala, it was performed by a hippie minister in the arboretum on a Friday evening in July before about sixty of our family and friends. I wore an Indian print dress, white sandals, and a wreath of pink carnations in my hair. Greg wore an aquamarine jacket with black lapels and a psychedelic bow tie. We each had one attendant, my sister and his brother, and a friend played ballads on his twelve-string guitar. We wrote the ceremony ourselves, featuring quotes from Rod McKuen and Kahlil Gibran. If I heard it today, I'd probably be embarrassed, but everyone our age thought it was beautiful and liberated. The minister cost twenty-five dollars, and my mother insisted on a sit-down chicken dinner afterward at the VFW hall. The weather, I remember, was blissful.

"Don't you wish we could get married again?" Greg's mother had sighed to his father as our families gathered to send us off for our honeymoon. "We had the stuffiest old priest in a gloomy stone church."

"All to please your parents," Greg's father grumbled in reply.

"Don't ever go to bed angry, that's my advice," avowed my cantankerous grandfather. "Quarrel if you must, but be sure you've cleared the air before your head hits the pillow."

My grandmother beckoned the minister aside and asked if he had any marijuana.

"You and Greg are going to have a wonderful life together," said my mother, pressing me to her, and the earnest inflection in her voice proclaimed that you had only to believe your wishes to make them come true. Then, in a shower of rice, we left for a week of backpacking on the Appalachian Trail.

If people could live forever, could a marriage last forever as well? We believed it, Greg and I. Throughout college, we had proven supremely compatible. Friends were astounded that we could count the number of our serious disagreements on one hand. Thrashing about in relationship throes, they begged us for advice, and we sat awake long nights, dispensing sage counsel to forlorn couples while the Moody Blues's "Nights in White Satin" played on the stereo and a candle dripped multicolored wax down an empty wine bottle on the coffee table.

With marriage, it only got better. We took turns supporting each other through graduate school until Greg earned his master's degree in architecture and I completed mine in special ed. When Greg landed a position at Coburn Design Collaborative, a prominent architectural firm in Providence, we began saving for our first house. I was hired to teach elementary school students with an alphabet soup of emotional, behavioral, and learning disabilities, and I loved it.

How predictable and conformist! Looking back, it's easy to scoff at our shiny new lives. Yet Greg and I were happy, while all around us other couples were not. We watched colleagues bicker and squabble, indulge in vengeful affairs, freeze each other out. We heard through the grapevine of college classmates whose marriages hadn't made it to their fifth anniversary and listened to our parents cluck over long-married neighbors divorcing after thirty-five years. It seemed incomprehensible. What had they done wrong? What were we doing right? We'd lock bodies in the dark, knots in our stomachs at the mere idea of separating, pledging never to let anyone or anything come between us. We weren't smug enough to believe we had the only answer, yet we were blind enough to believe we deserved our good luck. If you always keep sight of your love for each other, if you treat the other person with honesty and respect, you'll withstand the assaults that any relationship encounters over a lifetime and grow stronger together, right?

"There's a poem," I told Greg one night as we lay in each other's arms, watching the moon rise through our bedroom window, "by Matthew Arnold. It's called 'Dover Beach.' Do you know it?"

"Nope." He twirled a strand of my hair, using it to brush my cheeks like a feather.

"'Ah, love, let us be true to one another!'" I quoted, then faltered. I didn't really know the poem either, a leftover from some English class, though my mind held an opening image of two lovers standing before a moonlit sea. But the closing stanzas I remember, more or less, to this day.

> Ah, love, let us be true
> To one another! for the world, which seems
> To lie before us like a land of dreams,
> So various, so beautiful, so new,
> Hath really neither joy, nor love, nor light, . . .
> And we are here as on a darkling plain
> Swept with confused alarms of struggle and flight,
> Where ignorant armies clash by night.

Those lines said everything; they stopped my heart. And that, silly me, is how I pictured the two of us, eternal lovers on a glimmering shore, proof against the terrors whirling around them though the rest of the world has gone mad. But Greg didn't chuckle when I told him. There in the dark, in our bed, he drew me closer and held me to him, tight, tight, tight. And I knew we'd always be together. Our vigilance would protect us.

"Anne, there's a friggin' bird in the foyer!"

"Anne, a car got rear-ended at the front gate!"

"Anne, two couples arrived late, and we told them they couldn't interrupt the processional to find seats. We led them down the side slope from the verandah and sneaked them into the back row, but they're pissed about it and want to lodge a complaint."

"Oh, fuck them," I say, and my staff startles and gapes. They knew my divorce was pending but not that today was the day. "There's an old butterfly net somewhere in the cellar. See if you can chase the bird out with that. As long as the accident doesn't involve any guests, let the parking attendants and the police settle it. I'll speak to the miffed couples if they come to me, but chances are they'll forget it once the bar opens and they've drowned the insult in a few drinks. And remember . . ." I tilt my head at a jaunty angle and widen a smile across my mouth.

"The smile on your face doesn't have to be sincere, just present!" they chorus, laughing, and speed away. Leon lingers, raising a curious eyebrow at me. He's a minister at his church, and though I know he'd understand, I'm ashamed to have used the profanity.

"I'm sorry. I'm just a little stressed . . ."

"It's all right," he says. "Let me know what I can do to help."

I nod my thanks, and he departs. I cast a last glance at Allison and Mead standing at the altar. From a distance, they look happy, and I wish them well. Beyond the minister's back, flitting toward the horizon, the sailboat has diminished to an insouciant dot on the vast blue sea.

9

What Joy?

Deirdre

"... Of course, Allison and Mead will need to provision their boat wisely, stocking it with patience, commitment, and mutual respect. Most of all they'll require dreams and goals, for dreams are the wind that fills your sails . . ."

Oh, shut up! What the hell do you know?

That's what I want to jump up and shout at the minister. What the hell do you know about love and marriage and betrayal? Who are you to moralize and pontificate about other people's lives? And what is this improvisational crap about boats and bliss? No one wants to hear your poetry. You're just a stuffed shirt we hired for the occasion to make it legal. I don't go to church, Gordon and I never went to church, and the only reason we had the girls baptized was to satisfy his prick of a father. Stick to the script! Or if you must extemporize, I'll tell you what you should be saying, that marriage is a shit hole, a fraud, the biggest sucker game on earth—

I clamp my fingers to my lips before the words can burst out. Oh, I must stop this, I must stop ranting, even if it's only inside my head. Control yourself, Deirdre, don't make a scene, it's not the minister's fault. There's nothing he can do to undo what's happened. Get hold of yourself, no matter how unbearable it is to sit watching your daughter be married while your ex-husband and his baby doll sit two rows back, innocent as lambs, when he's nothing but a rutting old ram and she's a smug little slut—

Stop it!

Tears spring to my eyes, as if I've been slapped. Do you have any idea how unfair this is, how unjust? This was supposed to be the prime of my life, the time of my rewards. All those years I spent raising the girls, supporting Gordon's career, entertaining his colleagues and friends. I can show you a resume full of hospital fundraisers and service on nonprofit boards, most of which I chaired. What am I supposed to do now? Go back to selling real estate? Open some quaint shop? Anything I do will be a comedown. No one's going to hire a fifty-nine-year-old woman who's spent the majority of her adult life out of the workforce. This past year, I at least had Allison's wedding to plan.

"Deirdre, how are you doing? What are you up to these days?" people would ask.

"Oh, you wouldn't believe how busy I am!" I would respond. "Allison and Mead got engaged, did you know? They want the wedding in Newport, so we've booked Rosecourt, one of the mansions. There are a thousand details on my to-do list."

"How wonderful, how marvelous," they'd say. "It's sure to be splendid! You have such a talent for organizing these events!"

But once the wedding is over, what account will I give of myself? Aside from the charity boards, what else is left?

And where do I go now to meet people, to meet new men? Do I sign up for ballroom dancing classes, go back to college, join the Sierra Club with the other recent divorcees? Please—my life is supposed to be beyond that. I have too much to lose by letting it appear I've fallen to that level, that I'm obsolete. Do you have any idea how hard it is not to look rejected?

Picture the dilemma over my own daughter's wedding. Gordon is there flaunting Kimmy. I'm on my own. How do we arrange the seating for the ceremony? In a happy family, the bride's parents occupy the front row on the left. In cases of divorce, modern etiquette gives the bride's mother the front row and the maternal grandparents may join her so she doesn't have to sit alone. Both my parents are dead. As an alternative, I could invite my brother and sister-in-law and their two teenage boys to sit beside me. But that would give the second row to Gordon and Kimmy, and can you conceive how it would feel to have the two of them directly behind me, staring over the back of my head? In the end, I took the first row, put my brother's group in the second, and Gordon and Kimmy in the third. Gordon didn't object, and there's some comfort in having my brother's family as a shield between us. I thought, too, that sitting erect and dignified by myself in my glamorous gown would send a powerful message to everyone present, simultaneously rebuking Gordon for deserting me and announcing my confidence in going it alone. But now I wonder, do I just look pathetic? I glance at my beaded evening bag, resting on the empty chair beside me. I'm spending my daughter's wedding sitting next to a purse.

The minister babbles on about anchors and a compass, and I reset my shoulders, aligning them to project self-assurance. Hopefully, it will be better after the ceremony when the crowd mingles over cocktails on the verandah. But that's also the time we've allotted to go around and greet our guests, and Gordon won't be shy about it, not with Kimmy to introduce. How am I supposed to avoid bumping into them? I vetoed a reception line because of the awkwardness. And who am I going to dance with all evening? If Mead has any manners, he'll squire me for one or two numbers, my brother will step in, Mead's father, maybe some of my friends' husbands. Otherwise, I'll have to pretend I'm too busy to dance, looking after our guests, making sure they're enjoying themselves. I thought of calling the one or two single men I know, but it smacked of desperation—see, I have someone too!—and a casual escort doesn't belong beside the bride's mother on such an occasion. Besides, how many unattached men my age are there? There are too many Kimmys running around for a handsome, wealthy, straight man to go long without a wife or mistress.

I have murder fantasies about them.

In one, I buy a gun, walk into Gordon and Kimmy's new Greenwich house, and blast them while they're screwing in bed. In another scenario, I ram them with my car, feel the satisfying thump of their bodies rolling like rotten logs beneath the wheels of my Mercedes. Remember that woman who ran over her cheating doctor husband not once, but again and again? She has my complete admiration. You go, girl. And what about tonight? Could I bribe the caterer to poison their dinners with mad cow disease, E. coli, salmonella? I'd be willing to have this whole wedding ruined, written up in the society columns as the disaster of the season, if they expired with their faces in their surf-and-turf. And wouldn't it be delicious if Kimmy somehow stumbled over the cliff where Rosecourt's lawn meets the sea? I can feel my hands on her back, the gentlest push . . . too bad there's a high fence. You read constantly about women assaulted by their boyfriends and ex-husbands, victims of domestic abuse, and no one blames them anymore for wasting the bastards. Don't you think I'm a victim of abuse? Don't you know that's how I feel? I don't have any appalling bruises to prove it, no black eye swollen shut, no broken teeth or a fractured collarbone. But isn't that the trademark of a skilled abuser, making sure to hurt her where it won't show?

I've stopped paying attention to the minister now, and I don't care. My favorite fantasy is Death by Viagra because you know, of course, that Gordon's on it. He's just a little too peppy, too pleased with himself for a man of sixty-three. Ha-ha, I can get it up whenever I want. His dick is probably twitching in his pants right now as he sits two rows back, his thigh pressed against Kimmy's, a benevolent father expression for Allison on his face. Isn't that the last thing we need in this country, more sex, more horny men on the loose? Where do you suppose they got that name anyway? Viagra—*vital, virile, vibrant, vibrate* combined with *Niagara,* foaming water plunging over a cliff, towering spumes of white spray. You can't tell me that name is an accident.

And it could be fatal, I've researched it. If the man has undetected heart problems, if he increases his dosage, if he is otherwise ill, weak, debilitated, and on alcohol, drugs, or potent prescription medications . . . All right, it's a long shot, but bear with me and picture it, a panting Gordon pumping himself into nymphomaniac Kimmy until they both explode. "Prominent Doctor Fucks Himself and Trophy Wife to Death" the headline would blare. A lovely case of poetic justice. But it's not really murder, is it? And perhaps to murder them is what I want, no matter the cost. It could be so easy! Just walk into Wal-Mart, fill out some paperwork, plunk down your money, and in due course you, too, can become the proud owner of a petite pearl-handled avenger. Or how about a kitchen knife, screwdriver, letter opener? It all depends on how much blood you'd like to see spilled.

"How long have you been seeing her? Is she the reason you're leaving?" I cried in disbelief when the truth came out. Friends had been dropping hints. I'd brushed them off. Then Isabel Newsome insisted we meet for lunch at an Indian restaurant in Greenwich Village. What could she be thinking? I'd never liked curry and was irritated when, fifteen minutes late, she still hadn't shown up. But Gordon and Kimmy did, and shrunk into my corner booth, I learned three things about my rival: she was younger than I could have imagined, she thought it was cute to rub noses with Gordon across the table, and she adored tandoori chicken with raita and saffron rice.

I say "my rival," but I never had a chance.

The minister's voice intrudes, more nautical metaphors about celestial navigation and the ship staying true to its course. I would have done that. If Gordon had confined himself to a short fling with Kimmy, I would have forgiven him, though some of my friends insisted that would be too lenient. "The only response to a cheating husband is to divorce him at the first infidelity and sue him for everything he's got," they declared. Easy to say for those who weren't, as far as they knew, in my shoes. Yet I could see the reason in it. If you forgive him after the first affair, what about the second and the third? I didn't ask Gordon to go on the Viagra. It wasn't fun watching him develop a swelled head to match his newly swelled cock. He practically strutted. He practically crowed.

Meanwhile, I had to watch my own reflection diminish in the mirror. It happened almost overnight. Oh, there'd been a few gray hairs, but I'd been highlighting since my twenties so no major change was required there. Tennis and the spa three times a week kept me fit, and discreet plastic surgery had given my facial contour a smooth lift. When I started to miss a few periods, I assured my gynecologist that menopause was not going to break my stride. I expected to sail through it and come out on the other side still looking fabulous, still being Deirdre, with the added benefit of no more bothersome periods.

Then one evening as Gordon and I were dressing for a party, I bent over to adjust the strap on my high heel, and when I straightened, I saw the skin above my breasts had wrinkled like a dried apricot. I smoothed and stretched it with my fingers, but even when I stood perfectly erect, there was a faint uniform puckering, a flaccid texture where once all was taut. I worked in some moisturizer, which helped, and switched to a different necklace that covered more of my décolletage. But the next day there it was again, and within weeks the skin on the back of my hands was crinkling, and despite my latest liposuction, my butt had started to dimple like bread dough that has risen once and then fallen flat.

"Put me on estrogen," I ordered my gynecologist, but he refused.

"Deirdre, you must have heard about the dangerous connection between hormone replacement therapy and cancer, about the study they stopped after thousands of women had served as guinea pigs," he said. "And you have a family history of breast cancer, both your mother and your aunt."

"Do you think I care?" I shouted at him. "Why can Gordon bounce around taking Viagra while I have to shrivel into something ugly and dried out?"

I switched doctors, but they were all too ethical. So I went for more plastic surgery, and I can confidently say you will see no crepe-paper skin anywhere on my body tonight. But it made no difference. Gordon had decided to leave me anyway. How much longer can I keep fighting this losing battle with my body when it's no longer enough to look good for your age? No, now you must look *ageless*.

Perhaps the final insult is that my own daughter didn't stand up for me.

"How do you want to handle having your father at the wedding?" I asked Allison, as our preparations got underway.

She was supposed to say, "That bastard? He deserted and humiliated you, and I refuse to have him at my wedding. I never want to see him again!"

Instead, she looked at me as if I'd asked a perfectly dumb question. "Well, he's going to walk me down the aisle, of

course," she replied, and went on about the registration of
her china and silverware patterns. She simply expected me
to be accommodating, and isn't that what you read in the
advice columns and books nowadays? Don't make the children take sides. Don't blame or belittle your spouse in front
of them. Strive to keep the divorce amicable for their sake.
Reassure them that even if Daddy doesn't love Mommy
anymore, he still loves you very much. But Allison isn't a
child, she's an adult woman, and she ought to understand
my pain. No, as always, she gets what she wants, and I'm not
even allowed this one small satisfaction of having my
daughter on my side. I wonder how she's going to feel someday when she discovers Mead cheating on her.

Meanwhile, Gordon pays for it all with a smile, and I'm
reduced to taking petty revenge where I can. He gave me a
budget of two hundred thousand dollars for the wedding,
and whenever Allison wanted something extravagant, I'd
feign concern and say she'd have to get her father's permission. I hoped to at least create some friction between them,
but Gordon invariably acceded without a protest. So
I upped the ante, spending money without asking and
sending him the bills with no explanation of why we needed etched hurricane lamps for the candles instead of plain
glass or imported pâté de foie gras when domestic would
suffice. And still Gordon paid. In the end, this wedding
cost damn near a quarter of a million dollars—I've pro-
duced a quarter-million-dollar event to perfection, but will
I get any credit for that on my resume when I try to look
for a job?

What am I going to do? How will I live? I got the house
with its mortgage, a modest financial settlement, my car, and

alimony for three years. Three years, then I'm expected to be self-supporting. Maybe I can claim to be some kind of society consultant, a wedding or party planner, for example. I could say that so many people called me after Allison's wedding, begging for advice on their own children's nuptials, that I found myself with a career before I knew it. I wonder what this woman Anne makes?

"And so, as Allison and Mead hoist their sails for this momentous voyage, let us summon up for them a tide of heartfelt joy . . ."

In the right front row, Mead's parents are holding hands, and from the whole assemblage there seems to waft a glad wish echoing the minister's plea. Do you know what it's like to be cast aside after thirty-three years of marriage? Do you know how it feels to watch your former husband with his arm around the waist of a woman half your age? Do you know how important it is to keep your chin up and the smile on your face as you watch your daughter walk down the aisle on the arm of the man who betrayed you? And after he handed Allison to Mead at the altar, Gordon turned and smiled at me as if everything in the world was fine.

What joy? Tell me, what joy?

10

It's Good to Be Gordon

Dr. Gordon Hollingsworth

I WANTED TO SLEEP with a beautiful woman. It's as simple as that. For a man of my age beauty means, first and foremost, youth.

Dewy skin, supple limbs, an elasticity of flesh.

Thighs that quiver, breasts that spring to the touch.

A stomach as sleek and taut as stretched silk.

I stroke Kimmy's hand, docile in mine, marveling at its creamy color, its unblemished tenderness. Who doesn't love the springtime, when all the world is soft as a first kiss? Yet this hunger for youth is something neither sex can begin to understand when you're in your twenties, as Deirdre and I were when we met. If we'd been asked then to list the qualities that attracted us to each other, we'd certainly have checked off physical appearance, along with intelligence, kindness, mutual goals, and all the other noble, prosaic traits one is supposed to value in a spouse. But it would never have occurred to either of us to mention youth. At that age, youth isn't a quality, it's a given, and like every blithe young creature since time began, we took it for granted. *Get old? Who, us?* Not until your hair grays and your cheeks threaten to jowl do you look upon your body with disbelief and growing distaste and come to identify youth as an attribute in itself.

"Don't you love the poetry?" Kimmy whispers, twining her fingers in mine, and for a minute I pay closer heed to the ceremony. I admit my mind started to wander when the minister went on his extended sailing metaphor, and it's not coming to anchor—if you'll forgive the pun—on the faintly familiar lines Allison is reciting to Mead now. *If thou must love me, let it be for naught, except for love's sake only . . .* Shakespeare? Allison will have chosen the selection and has her lines memorized, naturally. Mead, when his turn comes, stumbles a bit over the response. He also looks a trifle worse for wear, though he's grinning bravely. Must have been some bachelor party last night.

"*Sonnets from the Portuguese*," I whisper to Kimmy during the brief pause that follows the recitations, pleased the source of the quotation has come back to me. There is no substitute for a classical education and cultivation of the intellect.

Kimmy scrunches her forehead in puzzlement, but she'll wisely save her question about why a Portuguese poet is writing in English. I'll be the first to tell you Kimmy isn't bright, but neither is she the dumb blond Deirdre would like to cast in the role. She was a hospital secretary, a job that requires an average amount of intelligence, and she performed it adequately. She doesn't work now, of course. Mostly she shops, seriously and with good taste. Deirdre got the Westport house and furniture in the divorce, so I bought a new place in Greenwich for Kimmy and myself, and there are lots of rooms to decorate and fill. Kimmy is also under the illusion that as wife of the hospital president she has a position to uphold, and her good qualities include serving without ego on a few inconsequential committees and waiting patiently without complaining those nights I'm working late.

The truth is, I don't really need a wife at this stage in my career. The ladder climbing is over; I'll retire in a few years. I've proven myself as an administrator, deftly handling the latest round of hospital mergers; barring any major scandals or malpractice lawsuits, I'll leave with my reputation admirably intact and my portrait joining the distinguished line on the lobby wall I could have divorced Deirdre without repercussions and simply slept around, and as long as I was circumspect, no one would have cared. But I had no desire to be promiscuous. Marriage suits me fine, and besides, keeping a body like Kimmy in the shadows would be like parking a Ferrari in the garage and never bringing it out for your friends to drool over.

I glance two rows ahead to where my ex-wife sits, hostility radiating from her ramrod spine. So far this weekend we haven't exchanged a word. She was already stage-managing when I arrived at Rosecourt yesterday for the rehearsal, and she kept her distance at the dinner afterward. For civility's sake, I would like to speak with her.

Deirdre, you've done an outstanding job organizing every aspect of this wedding and you've given Allison and Mead memories they'll cherish forever. I appreciate that we were able to work around our differences to include not only Kimmy but many of our mutual friends to share this special occasion. You look wonderful, and I wish you well.

Not a word would be insincere, but neither are the statements entirely truthful. We never discussed the issue of including Kimmy. I simply made it implicit that she would be here. She is my wife, and I will not have her shunted to a corner. I would have proudly brought her to the rehearsal; it was Kimmy who suggested she skip the prenuptial activities.

"That's for you and your family, Gordon," she said. "You have to practice walking Allison down the aisle. I can keep myself occupied. I saw lots of cute shops on the way to the hotel, and I can stroll along the waterfront and go exploring. I've never been to Newport before!"

How can you not find her lovable? And as it turns out, in missing the rehearsal, Kimmy was on hand at the hotel to smooth over a potential crisis when the fiancée of one of Mead's groomsmen arrived three hours late and angry after a pileup on I-95. But Kimmy asked me not to mention that to anyone, so she'll get no credit there.

The other sentence of my intended speech that would stick in Deirdre's craw is, *You look wonderful.*

If I look wonderful, why did you leave me?

A justified retort. Those of our old friends who have remained loyal to Deirdre would argue she is still a beautiful woman, and I don't deny she's both attractive and glamorous for fifty-nine. But consider Deirdre's own reaction to growing older. She spent the last few years of our marriage running from one plastic surgeon to another, like a frantic Dutch boy trying to plug each newly sprung leak in the dike. Creams and liposuction, Botox and collagen, moisturizers and mud packs and teabags on her eyes. I came home one night and could have sworn it was some blue goo-faced, shrink-wrapped alien from a primal lagoon giving herself a bikini wax there in our bathroom.

At times like that I feel sorry for women. Of course it's a double standard. Yet how can they so brazenly crave youth and then blame men for lusting after it? About the only area of her body Deirdre didn't attempt to surgically rejuvenate was her hands—I guess they don't do hand-lifts—but she made up for it by slathering them with lotion and wearing gloves to bed. To little avail. Blue veins crawling over tendons made prominent by the loss of flesh, wrinkles of skin pouching around her knuckles like sagging elephant hide. Her hands give her away. They whisper her dirty little secret. I'm old, I'm fading, oh, the injustice!

If it's any consolation to Deirdre, she's in good company. I gave a quick glance around when Kimmy and I arrived tonight, and it's fair to say that every other woman here of Deirdre's generation has a plastic surgeon's number in her private address book. Ironically, this is the same generation that forty years ago was trumpeting women's lib and female empowerment and glorifying older women who refused to disguise their crow's-feet and graying hair. Now that they're the graying ones they've reversed the credo, and pursuing every means to thwart the signs of age is what's liberated and empowering. At the same time, they don't hesitate to freeze Kimmy with a glacial stare. More hypocrisy. What right have they to disdain Kimmy for possessing naturally what they're so desirous of artificially achieving?

Well, let them stew. Doesn't my Allison make a pretty bride? Last night at the rehearsal dinner, I took Mead aside to offer a few ritual admonishments about taking care of my little girl. Mead took it in the right spirit, two men joking about how to keep a woman happy and commiserating that we really don't have a clue. I must say, I like the boy.

And with Allison, no mind reading will be necessary. Allison has always known exactly what will make her happy and never hesitated to demand it. Deirdre protested I was spoiling her, but I approve the simplicity of her method. Why not be spoiled? It doesn't preclude the fact that Allison works very hard to meet both her own and others' expectations of her—as I have done all my life.

"You will go to Yale and specialize in neurosurgery," said my father, reminting for me his own career.

"You will marry a woman who can support your aspirations and provide me with darling grandchildren," said my mother. Ditto.

"You will ascend to the top of your chosen field," said my professors, chests swelling vicariously.

"You will provide us with a home, cars, and possessions that will be the envy of our social class," said Deirdre, my wife.

Don't get me wrong. I wanted what others wanted for me. I put my nose to the grindstone and did everything right, including adding an MBA to my medical degree. I benefited many people in the process, my family and the thousands of patients and employees who have passed through the hospital during my tenure.

But now is the time of my rewards, and the reward I claim is Kimmy. Deirdre, despite her moans, will survive. There wasn't much love or mutual interest left in our marriage even before I met Kimmy, though I confess my eyes had been roaming for some time. I believe it was Isabel Newsome, by the way, who sicced Deirdre on me and Kimmy at that Indian restaurant in Greenwich Village, though Deirdre didn't confront me until that night.

I'm grateful to Isabel; I was looking for a tactful way to break it to Deirdre that I was leaving, and Isabel saved me the time. I could give her the name of a Japanese restaurant she ought to check out in return, but her husband John is the hospital's lead attorney, and I don't want to lose him.

"How could you? She's half . . . she's a third your age!" Deirdre spluttered and ranted. "She's a child! Why, why, why?"

I shrugged. Not long ago in the hospital cafeteria I overhead a senior nurse counseling a weeping young one on her boyfriend woes. "Honey," the veteran said, shaking her head as she delivered the familiar adage, "it's just as easy to fall in love with a rich man as a poor one." The simple corollary is that for a man it's just as easy—no, make that far *easier*—to fall in love with a young woman as an old one. You can partly blame our youth-obsessed culture. Nubile sex is thrust at us daily on magazine covers, in advertisements, on TV. You'd have to be dead to be impervious to the blandishments.

You can also rightly accuse men of taking up with younger women to stave off facing their own mortality. Being with Kimmy does make me feel and act younger, and in so doing, it may indeed add years to my life and vice versa. Or let's just go with the biological imperative, that it's inefficient for a male of any species to waste sperm on a female who is no longer fertile, and the physical signs of aging are nature's way of alerting a male that a female is beyond her reproductive years. We're *supposed* to be turned off and even repulsed by withered breasts and coarse white pubic hair. So it's no wonder women go to extreme lengths to conceal their age and project the image they're still fruitful, since in nature the protection of an alpha male may be crucial to a female and her offspring's survival. Sure, you can take the high road and argue for loyalty, affection, and commitment, but my money's on good old Darwin.

"Now, may I have the rings to be blessed?" says the minister, and the expectant hush of the audience recalls my thoughts to the ceremony. Kimmy clasps my hand and sits forward in her seat, shining eyes riveted on Allison and Mead.

"Oh, Gordon, this is so exciting!" she whispers. In deference to Allison's upcoming nuptials, Kimmy had agreed to a private, justice of the peace service for ourselves in January. "Everyone knows it's the marriage itself and not the ceremony that's important," she told me. It's a pleasure to see her taking such delight in today's festivities, enjoying them without a single envious thought. The European trip I've booked for us in September will be our honeymoon, and whether it's a hot-air balloon ride over the French countryside or a shopping spree in Rome, there'll be no expense spared to fulfill her heart's desires.

Poor women, poor men. In the end, it really is all about sex, isn't it? Or perhaps it's a holy trinity: sex-money-power. Either way, I'm in the catbird seat. Look around and this is *my* money you see flowing tonight, in every bow by a butler, in every glass of champagne poured. I can buy my daughter her dream wedding, buy off my ex-wife, and buy into a lifestyle a man half my age would envy, thanks to my golden checkbook and a little help from Viagra.

Which, by the way, I'm not sure I even need anymore. My failure to perform with Deirdre during the last few years of our marriage was due as much to her disinclination as to any physical shortcoming on my part. Whereas with Kimmy, I have only to slip my hand between her legs and she goes wet, tongue her nipples and her breasts flush. Her body is luscious and compliant, and when I pleasure her, she squirms and orgasms with a scent of overripe strawberries. I love just walking into our bedroom and seeing the silhouette curve of her body as she lies naked under the sheet. And although I don't kid myself that at my age I'm still an Adonis, I have always been a very skillful lover. I glance sideways now, letting my gaze wander deep into her cleavage where no other male's eyes dare overtly roam. Ah, there it is, a sweet bud of nipple, all mine.

Maybe I can't buy off death, but I can have a damn good time until I get there.

 11

In No Particular Order, the Groomsmen

Steve

SAVED, I AM SAVED! I can't believe my luck! Thank you, powers that be, whoever and wherever you are! Give me a minute and I may even pay attention to this minister. Here I was supposed to accompany Allison's sister Susie down the aisle, and she went and got herself so sunburned she's missed the ceremony. Yes, I am home free!

Look, it's not just that Susie is butt ugly. I'd have slapped on a smile and done it for Mead. In fact, I volunteered for the dolorous duty after my fiancée Lynne made it clear how she felt about me being paired with any of Allison's other bridesmaids.

"Carolyn? He's matched you with that airhead?" Lynne sputtered. "If you think I'm going to sit quietly by while you escort that . . . that Rapunzel—"

"Okay, okay, calm down," I said. "It's just for one evening. I'll ask Mead to put me with Lauren."

"Lauren? That snotty slut? If you think—"

"Okay, okay."

The real issue is that Lynne is pissed as hell that Allison didn't invite her to be a bridesmaid. I didn't dare say this out loud, but why should she? Lynne and Allison barely know each other; it's Mead and I who are longtime pals. And I don't think Lynne being my fiancée changes the protocol, although, being a guy, what the hell do I know?

Anyway, I stepped up to the plate and requested Susie, which mollified Lynne and earned me the undying gratitude of the other groomsmen. I was prepared to go the full nine yards and be as gallant an escort as Susie ever had. But when I tried talking with her at the rehearsal dinner last night, it was a complete flop. The girl has no personality, no confidence, no spark. I pride myself on being a good conversationalist—I'm a sales manager for a line of fitness equipment, and wining and dining our dealers is my forte—yet with Susie, it was impossible to establish any flow. She hasn't seen the latest movies, she doesn't follow sports, and when I tried to generate some conversation about her teaching job in Montana the best she could do was elaborate on her recipe for papier-mâché. Even her voice lacks animation. There's no inflection, no sense of excitement. I'm sorry, she's a dud.

Now, instead of Susie, I'm escorting Madeline, the junior bridesmaid, which makes me look like a hero in everyone's eyes. I saw the beaming smiles and heard the chuckles as we walked together up the aisle. It's also going to earn me a lot of future husband points with Lynne, and a man can never have too many of those.

As for Madeline, what a great little girl! She's smart and kind and pretty, and when Allison announced the change in our lineup, Madeline said to me, "This is very sad for Susie and for Allison not to have her sister with her, isn't it? If Susie's still too sick to come to the reception later, can we save her a piece of wedding cake?" It makes me think how neat it would be for Lynne and me to have a daughter like that someday, which really surprises me because not long ago the mere idea of ever becoming a father would have made me laugh out loud. But when a guy like Mead is willing to take the plunge, it makes you reconsider your own priorities. If he and Allison can do it, maybe I will let Lynne talk me into setting a date.

Could I be growing up?

Nah, not yet!

Brad

Whoa, that was some bachelor party last night! Am I the only one still having trouble standing up? What's my bridesmaid's name again? Nicole? And she's a paralegal, right? Or is she the buyer for Saks? Aw, man, I should have written this on my cuff . . .

Dave

Whoa, this Lauren is hot! Redhead—I like that. Didn't Mead say she's a tennis player? Hmm, maybe I could tip one of these butlers to slip out and get me the latest Wimbledon scores . . .

Rob

Whoa, this Carolyn is hot! Wonder if she's as blond below as she is up top?

Todd

Whoa, look at that speedboat zooming on the water! Whoa, those waves are making my head swim! Whoa, that was some bachelor party last night! Am I the only one still having trouble standing up?

Blaine

You can't not like Mead, especially when he's saved your life. It happened over twenty years ago when my parents sent me off to a camp for the summer, and Mead and I were assigned to the same bunkhouse. Mead was a camp regular. I was the bookish boy in glasses—still am, for that matter; my PhD is in medieval literature. When I climbed onto my bunk clasping my paperback Chaucer, Mead hopped right up beside me.

"Hey," he said, giving my arm a friendly thwack, "my sister reads that stuff!"

Mead was good at every sport, lousy at arts and crafts, a fearless explorer on the trail hikes, and the leader of secret nighttime expeditions to scare the girls at their camp across the lake. Within a week of the first raid, the girls were loving it, squealing "Mead! Mead!" and pretending through their giggles to be outraged and offended when he pushed me through their bunkhouse window as they were undressing for bed. I was always red-faced as the shrieking girls pummeled me with their pillows, feathers swirling in the air. Mead and the other boys whooped like Indians, dragging me out just in time to avoid being caught by the counselors in their nightgowns and face cream. Afterward, I'd be agitated with myself. Why did I let Mead drag me into these escapades? They were juvenile and undignified, and I was going to be a great scholar, the discoverer of priceless long-lost texts, a literary archaeologist.

I have to laugh at that now. What an uptight little egghead I was! Yet I couldn't quite say no to Mead when he was rounding up a crew for some adventure, nor could anyone else. Mead would sneak you ice cream from the cafeteria if you missed lunch, smuggle *Playboy* magazines into the cabin after lights out. He'd give you his allowance without a second thought, although by the same token, if you loaned him money, it would never occur to him to pay it back. Even today he has no concept of fiscal responsibility, and I'd guess that's why his father shunts him off with public relations assignments for his company that don't really amount to much. But when Mead was around, we always had a ton more fun, and when he was missing, even being on the winning team seemed to fall flat. He lives his life the way we all sometimes wish we could, without a care for rules or consequences, a completely feel-good existence, an endless Saturday night keg party at a frat house.

The day Mead saved my life was near the end of a sweltering August. In spite of the heat, I'd somehow caught a nasty summer cold and was tossing with a fever in my bunk while the other kids swam to the floating raft in the lake. I could hear their shouts and splashing through my open window and was miserable at being left out. It was a matter of pride for pubescent boys to fearlessly cover the hundred-yard distance in greeny-brown water that was over our heads. You never let on how your heart clutched as you struck out, arms and legs churning through thick, fluid space, the imagined suck of sea monsters at your ankles, strength draining from your body—then the heave of exhaled breath as your hand grabbed the ladder and you hauled yourself onto the raft, dripping both water and relief. Having recently mastered this feat, I wanted to be out there with my friends, and rising with unsteady determination, I wiggled into my bathing trunks and weaved to the shore.

Swimming relay races were in progress, and unnoticed by the counselors in the hubbub, I slipped into the lake. At first it felt so cool on my fever, I thought, "I'm cured!" and I set out with false hope. A dozen strokes later, the stomach cramp hit. A strangled cry left my throat, and the next minute I was glubbing murky water and losing consciousness. I sank, down, down, as if weighted with cement. Then something slammed into my chest like a huge fish, and I was pushed up and above the surface, doubled over the shoulder of a body wet and slick. It rammed me to the shore, the skin of my back abrading on coarse sand and rocks. When I opened my eyes to the pressure of hands pumping my goose-pimpled chest, I saw Mead's looming white face and heard his terrified pant, "Please God, please God, please God, please." As I rolled over to vomit, I remember thinking it was funny that Mead was the last person you'd have expected to pay attention in lifesaving class.

After that summer, my parents divorced, and in the custody war that followed I never got back to camp. It wasn't until our junior year in college, at neighboring campuses, that Mead and I met up again. When we did, it was as if we'd never been apart as far as he was concerned. From then on I was invited to his frat house and fixed up with any number of sorority girls. Football games, rock concerts, and spring break in Fort Lauderdale were all preceded by a phone call from Mead *halloo*-ing me to come along with whatever crowd he was assembling. I didn't always accept. I knew at heart that Mead and I didn't have enough in common either in our personalities or our goals to develop a truly deep friendship. But we kept each other in balance. I reminded Mead there could be a serious side to life; he was my cue to lighten up.

Most of all, neither one of us could forget he'd saved my life, invoking an inescapable bond. So even after we left college and went our separate ways—Mead to work for his father, me to the hallowed halls of academia—we kept in touch. Mead asked me to be a groomsman in the same phone call he announced his engagement, and I said yes at once. It was a given I would be there; I suppose one day whoever of us dies first will be the other's pallbearer.

"By the way," Mead had said at the end of his phone call, "you'll be escorting my sister, Fredericka. Is that all right?"

"Sure, I'll be happy to," I replied nonchalantly. But here comes the real truth: though Fredericka and I had never met, though neither Mead nor anyone else in the world knew it, I'd been half in love with his sister since that summer at camp.

It started with his comment that she read Chaucer. A girl who liked Chaucer? The very words thrilled my ears. The preteen girls I knew read movie magazines and paperback romances. They collected stuffed animals and sighed over rock stars. Intrigued, I listened for Mead to drop other tidbits about his sister, and I wasn't disappointed.

"Mom's having a fit because Freddie contradicted the priest in catechism class," he hooted, waving a letter from home. "Freddie said the very fact that the first commandment says 'Thou shalt have no other *gods* before me' proves that God himself acknowledges the existence of other deities."

From another letter, I learned that Fredericka had circulated a petition demanding that drivers slow down on residential streets after a neighbor boy's dog was killed. Though at age twelve my experience with girls was nil, I felt strangely turned on by this intellectual rabble-rouser. But being among boys, I was reluctant to reveal my interest.

"How old is your sister?" was the most I dared ask.

"She just turned ten," Mead replied. "You know, you remind me a lot of her."

I took it as a rarefied compliment.

Then summer camp ended, Mead and I lost touch, and Fredericka faded to an unattainable daydream in the complexities of growing up. After Mead and I were reunited in college, I got up the courage to ask about her. I wasn't exactly carrying a torch, just curious.

"Here, I'll show you her picture," said Mead, pulling out his wallet. Fredericka attended some private high school for brainy kids, and Mead's mother had sent him a copy of her senior class photo. Usually those pictures make you both laugh and cringe when you open your yearbook a decade later, the girls all striving to appear glamorous and sophisticated, the boys hip and cool. But there was something far different in Fredericka's expression, an intensity, an impatience, a flicker, as if the next instant she might jump away from the fixed image and leave only a blur. *Take my picture, quick, and let me out of here,* she seemed to say. *I have to move on to the next step, I have to get to the real world, I have to do things that matter.*

"She's going to Harvard," said Mead with undisguised pride. "Someday I'll introduce you to her."

"I'd like that," I said, straining for a last glimpse as he flipped his wallet closed. It hadn't even dawned on me whether or not I found Fredericka attractive. I just had to meet that girl.

But again, I didn't. When Mead made an offer to introduce someone, it could mean next week or sometime in the next twenty years. Twice he invited me home for a weekend and Fredericka wasn't there. She was on a scholarship in London or an internship in Washington, DC. I sat at the Morellis' dinner table, discussing *Sir Gawain and the Green Knight* with Mead's parents, and foolishly wishing she'd appear. I dated other girls meanwhile. I'm actually pretty good-looking for a bookish type, and at college and grad school it wasn't difficult to meet smart young women who shared my passion for literature. Yet in my mind lingered Fredericka's photograph, that intelligence, that drive and desire. I wanted to tell her, *Take your time, don't hurry, don't burn yourself up while you're setting the world on fire.*

And perhaps I knew there was no rush for me to meet her. Sooner or later, with or without Mead's direct agency, I was destined to come face to face with Fredericka.

And now I have. Look at her, standing among those vapid bridesmaids, so alive she practically crackles. Everything about her is quick, her laugh, her eyes, the expressions that fly across her face; you can almost see her mind darting from one idea to another. Is she thinking of me at all? Last night's delay at O'Hare caused me to miss the rehearsal and the bachelor party. I've no regrets about the latter, if the hangovers I saw this morning were any barometer of the night's activities. But it also deprived me of precious time to meet Fredericka, and today I was told she'd be sequestered with the other bridesmaids at the hotel spa. Only later did I learn that she'd deserted them on a private agenda. Apparently they got her strait-laced into that gown in time, but those little white flowers they stuck in her hair are already falling askew. I love that! Not only is she bright and passionate and creative, she is downright sexy.

What do I say? What do I talk to her about during dinner? Does she still read Chaucer? Instead of a long head table for the entire wedding party, I understand Mead and Allison have their own table for two. They've grouped the rest of their attendants at a table nearby, except for Fredericka and me, who will be sitting with her parents. I hope they remember me from college—and favorably. *Um, excuse me, Mr. and Mrs. Morelli, I know it's rather sudden, but may I have the hand of your daughter Fredericka in marriage?* I won't say that, of course, but I will have to work fast. At midnight this affair will be over; Fredericka's booked on a seven a.m. flight to DC.

Most of the other groomsmen are already plotting how they can score with their respective bridesmaids, but that's not my goal. Please, please, just let Fredericka like me enough to let me call her and see her again. Please, don't let me lose her.

Midnight—less than six hours and the clock is ticking.

Ω

Patrick
Whoa, that Blaine is hot!

12

Wait a Minute . . .

Mead

OUCH, THE SUN ON THAT SEA IS BRIGHT! Sticks my eyes like pinpoints. If only I could slip on my shades. Don't suppose Allison would let me. Man, I must have been totally wasted last night. This morning my skull was gonging like a steel drum someone was banging from the inside out. It's still echoing. Great party! Good work, guys! We really did the town. We must have hit half a dozen bars before we ended up at that strip club. Whoo-hoo! Great stripper! At least, I think there was a stripper . . .

"Now let us reflect on the symbolism of these wedding rings . . ."

Yeah, yeah, right. I know I should be taking this official stuff seriously, but at least I got through my part of the poetry recital okay. Why we need poetry to get married is beyond me. Still, I suppose we have to say something to make it legal, and I'd rather reel off a few verses here at Rosecourt than get sucked into a church. Mom is disappointed about that, I know. She heads to mass every Sunday, faithful as can be. But Dad doesn't give a damn, and after two years of terrorizing her catechism priest,

Freddie at age twelve declared herself an atheist. I don't think you should go that far. As long as religion makes people happy, where's the harm? You want to believe in some guy in a long robe and white beard, be my guest. Me, I put my faith in the Yankees, a cold six-pack, and a sixty-inch plasma screen. Come to think of it, I wonder how the game finished last night. Last I recall we were up two runs in the seventh when we checked in at that sports bar . . .

"From the beginning of time, the ring has symbolized many kinds of human relationships. Kings and queens wore them to signify their imperial authority. Friends exchanged them as pledges to come to one another's aid . . ."

Damn, why can't I remember about that stripper? Did she pop out of a fake cake or what? The whole episode's pretty bleary, and when we got back to the hotel, the guys had a case of beer waiting in my room. Whoo-hoo! Good thing there's some superstition about the groom not seeing the bride on the day of the wedding until he meets her at the altar because I didn't even crawl out of bed until noon. My posse had to drag me into a cold shower to get my eyelids open. Thanks, guys! Good work! That's what friends are for. Now if I stand straight and look intelligent, Allison will never know. Yes dear, no dear, whatever you say. Just keep the little woman happy, that's my motto. Besides, if Allison wants an all-out wedding in Newport with seven brides-maids, a ten-piece band, and a hundred-fifty-dollar-a-plate dinner, it's no skin off my nose. Her old man must be even more loaded than I thought to pay for this. He'd have to be, at his age, to snag that Barbie doll for a wife. Say, Gordon, how'd you like to introduce me to my new twenty-two-year-old mother-in-law . . .

Ouch—banging skull! Okay, that was a bad thought, and I'll get it out of my head this minute. But you have to admit Kimmy is an eyeful. and this is the first time I've met her. A month after we started dating, Allison hauled me to Connecticut to pass inspection by her parents. A few weeks later, Gordon took us to lunch at an Indian place he'd discovered in Greenwich Village—said he had someone he wanted to impress and he needed our opinion on the cuisine. We gave it a thumbs-up, figuring it was some hospital industry bigwig he meant to entertain. Not until much later did we learn it was Kimmy. *Hey, Gordon, hope our recommendation helped you get into her tandoori!* After Gordon and Kimmy's quickie wedding in January, Allison had what she described as a "very pleasant luncheon" with them at that same Indian restaurant.

"We're going to get along fine," she said. "Oh, and Daddy has no problem at all about the caviar I want for our reception."

Anyway, it's not Kimmy but Deirdre I have to salute as mother-in-law. Now there is one scary woman. Mean, bitter, angry. She looks at every man as if she'd like to castrate him with a dull spoon. Since our engagement, she's been a regular wedding Nazi, like Martha Stewart and Hitler rolled into one. If she's that uptight all the time, no wonder Gordon dumped her. The guys say a woman always turns into her mother sooner or later, which does not bode well for Allison and me, but then I look at Mom and Freddie, who are poles apart. Wait a minute . . . did I have sex with that stripper?

"Yet these simple bands of gold—or in Allison and Mead's case, platinum—have achieved their highest significance as symbols of the marriage relationship, and wearing them bears witness to your marital fidelity . . ."

Naw, that can't be right. No sex, no stripper. Forget it. Concentrate on the ceremony and once it's over we can get to the important stuff, namely one big blowout party. You know, ever since we got engaged, Allison's been nagging me to fix up my compadres with her bridesmaids on a more permanent basis. Apparently, once we became a happy couple, it became our responsibility to play matchmaker for our single friends so they can be as happy as we are. Well, Freddie doesn't want to be fixed up—Mom worried for years she was a lesbian and then wished she *was* a lesbian when she started bringing revolutionaries home for dinner—but Freddie and Blaine can always talk books for an evening. Poor Susie is now out of the running, thank God. I'm sorry, but that girl is so ugly, she'd have to sneak up on a water fountain to get a drink. It was hard enough recruiting one of my amigos to march down the aisle as her escort until Steve volunteered.

Otherwise, though, I think I've done pretty well. Dave's got Lauren, the redhead, a long, cool drink, although a little too icy, if you ask me. Rob already seems hot for Carolyn, and Todd, who's a clotheshorse, has Jessica, who's a buyer for Saks. Brad's with Nicole, and if they don't hit if off in the sack she can at least give him some free legal advice about his car import business. Finally, I matched Patrick with Pammy. He's always been kind of shy, needs to get out more, and she seems to be the nurturing type, nice personality. *Good work, Mead, have a pat on the back. Thank you, I will.* Actually, I think it's better when men and women meet the old-fashioned way, at a party or in a bar. There's no pressure, you can buy her a drink, take a little time. You can pretty much tell within fifteen minutes whether it's worth a second round. Damn, I could swear I had sex with somebody last night. Do the guys know about this? Wait a minute ... I'm having a flashback ...

"Mead, please take the ring you've chosen for Allison and repeat after me ..."

Boobs! I had a pair of boobs in my hands last night!

"Ha-ha, that's all right, Mead. It's natural for the groom to be a bit excited. Don't worry, the ring's right here in the grass. Now repeat after me ..."

Boobs! They weren't huge boobs either, not like you'd expect on a stripper. They were medium-sized, soft, delicious, with tantalizing nipples. Was there a strip club? Was there a stripper? I remember a lot of bars, Yankees ahead by two in the seventh, then we ended up at the hotel, case of beer, woke up about noon, head bonging. Couldn't have been Allison, she was with her girls. But if someone else was in my room, Allison must not know or we wouldn't be standing here now ...

"Ready, Mead? With this ring, I, Mead, wed thee Allison ..."

"With this ring, I, Mead, wed thee Allison ..."

Shit! I think I had sex with some other woman the night before my wedding! Who was it? How could my posse let that happen? Does anyone else know?

"I pledge to share my life openly with you and to speak the truth to you in love ..."

"I pledge to share my life openly with you ..."

Oh my God, I am in so much trouble.

"I promise to honor and tenderly care for you . . ."

Shit, was it that cocktail waitress in the hotel? We stopped in the bar there before going to the rehearsal, and I remember her teasing us that she got off her shift at one a.m. Did we hit the bar again when we rolled in last night? *Think, Mead, think! Try to remember her boobs!*

". . . to cherish and encourage your fulfillment as an individual . . ."

Stand straight! Repeat the words. Try to look intelligent. Don't let Allison know!

". . . and to stand by your side through all the changes of our lives . . ."

A stripper? The cocktail waitress? Someone else in the hotel? One of our own wedding guests? *I was drunk, I swear it, Allison, I barely made it to my room . . .*

". . . till death do us part."

". . . till death do us part."

But then I remember the door opening . . .

"You may place the ring on Allison's finger."

Wait a minute . . . did I just get myself married to Allison till death do us part? Shit!

WHAT KIMMY IS THINKING AS THE CEREMONY WINDS TO A CLOSE

Kimmy
WHOA, THAT MEAD IS HOT!

MEANWHILE, BACK AT THE HOTEL

Susie

HEY, DID YOU HEAR THE ONE about the girl who was so stupid she fell asleep in the sun and burnt herself to a crisp on the day she was supposed to be the maid of honor at her sister's wedding?

No, what happened?

I just told you. She fell asleep and got sunburned and missed the wedding.

But what's the punch line?

There isn't one. That's the whole story.

That's not funny.

No, it isn't, is it?

But that's my life, a bad joke with no punch line and no laughs. I imagine it's how those stand-up comedians feel when they're on stage in some basement club with a fuzzy spotlight overhead and a dozen people in the audience and forty-five minutes to fill. Half the audience is already bored, and the other half is trying to help you along with forced chuckles and encouraging smiles because they're too kind-hearted to want to see anyone fail. So you dredge up one more wisecrack—*hey, did you hear the one about . . .?*—but you know it's a lost cause. You can hear the words leaving your mouth with the deflated *flup-flup-flup* of a flat tire. Even the air around you feels dead, but you're doomed to keep trying, standing there clutching the mike, trickles of sweat wetting your armpits, your body language giving off involuntary apologies as desperation claws into your voice.

Help me, I'm dying up here!

Over at Rosecourt, I expect Allison is married now and walking back down the aisle on Mead's arm, looking radiant. No, wait, that's not the right word. Radiant, I would tell my second graders, means illuminated, alight, as if the sun is inside you shining out. Radiant is how I would look if I ever got married, glowing with wonder and joy to believe there really was someone special for me. But Allison has always expected to be married. She's never doubted that finding a husband would be as easy as plucking fruit off a tree. How Allison looks is how she always looks, confident, and that, I would tell my second graders, means certain, secure, self-assured. Confident is how you appear when you know the sun is always shining on you.

I ease my nightgown off one shoulder, wincing as the pink nylon slips over my seared skin. One glance dashes any hope that the burn might have faded. See, I didn't put on sunscreen right away because I thought if I did, I wouldn't get any tan at all, whereas if I got a little tan first, then I could apply the sunscreen to protect it. But between flying in yesterday and the rehearsal party and jet lag, I fell asleep at the wrong time. Maybe I should go to Rosecourt anyway. I don't feel too bad, really. If I hurry and dress, knot up my hair, I could be there for the cocktail hour to help greet the guests. But if I get sick while I'm standing there, if I get the chills or throw up . . . I look so awful, my face as shiny red as a birthday balloon.

Well, you'd cry too if your skin was burned and swollen and you're supposed to be at your sister's wedding but you can't because you screwed it up, because you're nothing but a big, fat, stupid screwup . . .

I tell myself I'm not a worthless person. I got through college. I teach second grade in Butte, Montana. My two-bedroom apartment has yellow daisy wallpaper, and for Valentine's Day my students made me lace-trimmed hearts that I pinned on the bulletin board. On Tuesday nights, I go bowling with my friends from the school, and nobody cares how many gutter balls we roll as long as we have a good time. I make hand-painted ceramic pots that I sell at an annual craft fair. But when I come back home to visit, it's as if everything about me is second-rate. No one here would want to trade their life for mine.

The irony is, I wasn't supposed to be in Montana at all. See, about three years ago I read an article in the newspaper about how farmers in the northern plains states were having trouble finding wives. It's a hard life on a farm, the article said. Even with those huge tractors and combines and other modern equipment, it's a seven-day-a-week job. The winters are long and harsh; in summer the mosquitoes and black flies are so big you can swat them with a baseball bat. It's lonely—not as isolated as in the pioneer days before cars and telephones and computers, of course—but on a thousand-acre farm it can still be a fifteen-minute drive to visit next door and an hour or more to a decent-sized city.

And there's not much of a view. "You look out the window and all you see, day after day, is wheat," one woman said. Lots of young people had given up farming altogether, which I guess is no surprise.

The main point of the story, however, was that so many women were leaving for city jobs, for occupations that hadn't been open to them thirty or forty years ago, that the young men who stayed were going to extra lengths to promote the rural lifestyle and attract wives. In one town, they'd organized monthly Ladies' Night dances, and there were dating websites and even weekend getaways for city girls who wanted to experience farm life. It was pretty creative, I thought, though it didn't strike me as a personal option at the time.

Six months later at our school Christmas party, I was eating pfefferneuse and drinking rosé wine from a paper cup. I was teaching third grade in New Haven, and Luis, the custodian, and I had decorated the teachers' lounge in the basement for the holiday. Red and green crepe paper festooned the overhead pipes, and in one corner we had a real tree hung with ornaments, a popcorn string, and silver tinsel. I'd strung the popcorn myself over the course of three nights, sitting in front of the TV with my needle and thread and a huge bowl of microwaved kernels. When the party ended, I planned to drape it outside in the bushes for the birds, even though the popcorn was already stale.

Our bash had begun at three o'clock, right after class let out for the holiday; soon after we exchanged our secret Santa gifts at three thirty people began to leave. They had Christmas shopping to finish, pies and cookies to bake, their own trees to decorate. The principal, Mr. Slapinski, stayed a little longer, shaking hands and expressing his thanks for how calm everyone had remained during the knife incident in the cafeteria earlier that week. Several of my colleagues had already belted back more than one cup of wine, and with Mr. Slapinski's departure, more bottles were opened. Luis, grinning, brought out a flask and topped up the Cokes, to everyone's applause. I couldn't really approve, but Luis had been a big help in organizing the party, so I went ahead and had another cup of wine myself. By five o'clock the dingy gray of a winter afternoon had turned to darkness, and I was ready to leave, not that I had anything special planned. But the handful of teachers remaining had sunk into the usual litany of complaints about poor salaries, no respect from parents and kids, and the spineless school committee.

"Well, it's Christmas vacation and we don't have to think about it for two whole weeks," I said, hoping to brighten the mood.

"Oh yeah, Christmas," said one, "two weeks of listening to my mother-in-law's nagging."

"Two weeks of my kids whining that Santa didn't bring the right presents," said another.

"Two weeks of trying to figure out how I'm going to pay the credit card bills in January," groaned a third.

"Oh, but it's Christmas," said Luis, offering round his flask. He began dancing and singing "Feliz Navidad" to jolly them along, his hands clicking imaginary castanets, his pot belly stretching the buttons of his frayed brown coveralls. His antics helped a little, and I sent him a grateful look as we all drank more wine and spiked Cokes. I was feeling sleepy, but as hostess I couldn't leave until everyone else did. A dull rain began beating a monotone against the basement windows, rectangles of double-paned glass set just above ground level, and I watched the drops splatter and trickle in the darkness outside. Then words caught my ear—someone had relapsed into gripes—and I felt myself sinking, as if a hole were slowly opening beneath my feet and I couldn't climb out.

"I'd quit in a minute if I could," one teacher groused, and another proposed immigrating to Australia. My mind slipped in and out of the conversation with the wine. Luis seemed to know how I was feeling. He began those tactful maneuvers a host employs to let guests know they've overstayed their welcome, collecting paper cups and packaging cookies for people to take home. Gradually, they got the message. We saw the last teacher out at six thirty, the rain now pelting the panes like a barrage from a nail gun.

"We'll have one more drink," Luis told me, "and maybe it will let up some."

We had two more drinks—I'm not sure when I lost count—but I remember it was while we were untangling the popcorn chain from the tree that we bumped into each other, front to front, Luis half a head shorter than me, my chest poking his shoulders, his thick salt-and-pepper hair tickling my nose. I'd like to think he was as drunk as I was, that he didn't plan it or take advantage of me. What I know is that I woke up at midnight on the torn blue leatherette couch in the crepe-papered teachers' lounge, naked except for the stale popcorn string draped around my middle, a naked, hairy Luis snoring on top of me. He had a fleck of popcorn in his mustache, and as I squirmed out from beneath him, he squeezed my breast, and murmured lovingly through whiskey breath, "Susie, mamacita, mama gorda, Susita."

When my head stopped aching the next morning, I sat at my kitchen table searching the Internet for anything, anything at all, about lonely farmers seeking wives in a place as far away as I could get. What I got was a list of websites selling videos of women having sex with barnyard animals, gyrating preview clips included, that made my fingertips recoil from the keyboard. Finally, taking a different tack, I landed on a job posting site for teachers, and, long story short, by mid-January I was in Butte. It wasn't that I feared further advances from Luis, who hurried away guiltily when our paths crossed at school after the holiday. Nor had I been a virgin; there are fat, homely boys at college who want to have sex too, you know. It was that sense of sinking, of being dragged down, down, down into the earth while the last glimpse of sky above me paled and shrank out of sight.

Later, I learned it was mostly in North and South Dakota that the lovelorn farmers dwelt. Western Montana, where I landed, is mountainous, and Butte, with its huge ore deposits, was once called the "richest hill on earth." Thanks to open-pit mining, it's now the nation's largest Superfund site. But in its own way, Montana served its purpose. I like my job, my students, my colleagues, and the people overall are friendly and more accepting. Since no one's interested in coming to visit me in Butte—as they might if I'd moved to Hawaii or Florida—I can write home glowing accounts of my new life with the knowledge they'll never be disproved. Yet when I come home, no one envies me. It's a life that's good enough for Susie, but not for anyone else.

Well, maybe I should splash some cool water on my face. Maybe I should call someone at the reception to see how it's going, although Allison said absolutely no one in the wedding party was to carry a cell phone tonight. If they know what's good for them, no one will. Fredericka might be the one exception—she doesn't seem intimidated by Allison at all, and I do have her number from the list Allison prepared after the first bridesmaids' luncheon—but I don't know her well enough. Mom and Daddy probably have their cell phones, but they'll have them tucked away and switched off. Everyone of importance to them is right there in person, and they've put too much into this evening to allow any intrusion from the outside world.

Why hasn't anyone called *me*?

Susie, it's Daddy. How are you, sweetheart? I didn't hear about your sunburn until we got to Rosecourt, and I've been worried about you all through the ceremony.

Susie, it's Mom. Are you feeling any better? I feel so torn, I should be there taking care of you. Darling, there are plenty of doctors among the guests, and I'm going to send one of them to the hotel to check on you.

Susie, I'm married! How I wish you'd been here to be my maid of honor! Everyone missed you and is asking for you. Please, Susie, hop in a cab and hurry over.

Fat chance.

Most mornings I wake up, hoping things might be different. Is it possible that overnight, in my sleep, my life could have changed? I'm not asking for anything drastic. I don't expect to step out of bed and suddenly look like a model or discover I've been zapped with a talent I never had before. Just a small transformation, like maybe I'll be five pounds thinner, or my hair won't be so greasy, or the ring of the phone will be that handsome firefighter who spoke at our school assembly instead of my landlord reporting he's finally found the right bolt to fix my leaky toilet. I try to get out of bed with some optimism in my heart, but then I look in the mirror and sigh. They say God doesn't make mistakes, so what was he trying to prove with me? That he's bored with his job and just doesn't care anymore?

The funny part is—maybe my story does have a punch line—that I'm supposed to teach self-esteem to my second graders every day at school. *Act like a winner and you'll be a winner!* declares the red-lettered banner in our entrance hall. Okay, so I try to reach deeper, to mine my inner sunshine, and it helps, a little. But there are always moments like now, when I'm sitting alone, when I've screwed up again, that the truth worms into my soul. I am a lump on the face of the earth, and even if I do find a farmer or a teacher or any man to marry, he's going to be a lump, too.

Well, I bet everyone's having cocktails now at the reception. I bet they're mingling on the verandah, while the waiters offer silver trays of asparagus tips in puff pastry, and grilled scallops en brochette, and all the other delicious appetizers Allison ordered. I bet they're laughing and joking and exclaiming to each other, *You look divine! I love your gown! How fabulous to see you!* While I'm sitting alone in a hotel room in my XXL nightgown with an ice pack and a bottle of acetaminophen, looking like one huge, puffed-up blister. If you were me, you'd cry too . . .

Wait! There's the phone! Oh, what's the point? It's either the front desk with some courtesy call or a wrong number. But maybe, maybe . . .

"Hello?"

"Susie, it's Pammy. I'm on a pay phone by the restrooms. How are you feeling? Is your sunburn any better?"

"Pammy, I'm so glad you called! Yes, I think it is getting better. How was the ceremony? Is Allison happy?"

"Oh yes, it went beautifully. The minister made a lovely speech about Allison and Mead sailing toward new horizons, and Fiona was so cute tossing her rose petals along the aisle. Listen, Susie, I have to go for photographs, but I was thinking, if you're up to it, you could still come to Rosecourt. It's not the same without you."

"It's not?"

"Of course not! I—we all—miss you and wish you were here. You mustn't stress yourself. If you're feeling at all achy or nauseous, it's better to stay and rest at the hotel. But we do miss you, Susie, and I'm sure it would make Allison's special day complete if you could share it with her."

"Oh Pammy, I want to be there, too!"

"I know you do. Take your time and don't worry about your hair or makeup or wearing your bridesmaid's dress if it's uncomfortable. Just come and join us."

"I will! I'm on my way! Oh, thank you, Pammy!"

I fumble the receiver into the cradle, my eyes a blur. Tears of joy this time—how could I have been so gloomy and morose? No one likes a sad sack. Act like a winner and you'll be a winner! I'll bet I can even get into my bridesmaid's gown. I jump up from the bed and pull it from the closet, unzip the garment bag and hold the dress before me in the full-length mirror. *Yes, you can do it, Susie.* I wriggle my nightgown over my head, tear through my suitcase to find clean underpants and the strapless bra Allison said

I should wear. Then I shimmy and jiggle into my dress, contort my arm behind my back to pull up the zipper. On the vanity in the bathroom is my small zip bag of makeup, hairpins, and perfume. The scent stings when I dab it on my neck, but who cares?

"Hold on, Allison! I'm coming!" I yell, as I grab my purse and dash to the door.

They miss me, it's not the same without me. They like me, they really, really do!

15

BELLY UP TO THE BAR

Tracy and David

"OKAY, DAVID, THAT'S IT, ceremony's over. Bride and groom steppin' down the aisle, groom looks like some judge just handed him a life sentence—too funny! Guests rising, chitchat, eyes shifting our way. Oh yeah, you know what you want. We got ice, soda, fruit juice, mixers, and enough beer, wine, and hard liquor to float an ocean liner halfway to Bermuda. Brace yourself, David, my friend, your introduction to the glamorous world of bartending is about to begin."

Jack Daniel's and a double vodka and tonic . . . Give me three beers . . . A beer, make that a lite beer, a screwdriver, and a rum and Coke . . . Two Chardonnays . . . Vodka martini— hee-hee—shaken, not stirred . . . I'll have a frozen strawberry margarita. Wait a minute, is that a mix you're using? Don't you have fresh strawberries? Well, can you go see if the caterer has some? Oh, all right, if that's the best you can do . . .

"And we're . . . clear! Still standing, David?"

"Yes, barely, Tracy. Do they always come in a rush like that right after the ceremony?"

"Count on it. You'd think they'd been parched in the desert for weeks, wouldn't you?"

"At least nobody asked for anything unusual."

"Except for the bridesmaid with the frozen strawberry margarita. Duh, no, I'm not hiding fresh strawberries under the table, your highness. Duh, no, I'm not going to leave the bar and trot to the kitchen for fruit and a blender. First lesson, David: if we don't have it, we don't have it. Suggest the closest alternative but don't let anyone coax or bully you into a wild goose chase for ingredients, especially when people are piling up in front of you. Heads up . . ."

A rum and Coke . . . Orange juice, please, no ice . . . A beer and a Shiraz . . . Could I have a white wine? Do you have a Riesling?

"And we're . . . clear! Still with me, David? You'll find you usually get a surge right after the ceremony, then it's steady but manageable throughout the cocktail hour. We'll get a second wave after dinner when people get up from their chairs. So you teach at a private school in Providence, huh?"

"Yes, it's my first year. I hope to switch to public school though."

"More money?"

"Yes, I have some hefty student loans to repay. But it's also more of a challenge."

"Ah, an idealist."

"Well, you can blame it on my grandmother. She raised me on Sidney Poitier movies, and her favorite was *To Sir, With Love.*"

"A classic. Oops, look sharp, David, more customers. Hello, ladies, what can we do for you?"

"Hello, I'm Iris, and this is my sister, Edna. We're the groom's great-aunts, and we'd like to get a little pickled, please. Wouldn't we, Edna?"

"Eh?"

"Pickled, I said we'd like to get a little pickled, wouldn't we, Edna?"

"Eh?"

"Edna's hearing aid is acting up. You'll have to forgive her."

"No problem, ladies. I'm Tracy, this is my friend, David, and you just tell us what's your pleasure."

"Well, we'd like to get a buzz on, I believe that's the word, but we don't do this very often, so I'm not sure. Edna being pretty deaf, I'll order for her."

"Eh?"

"I said, I'll order for you, dear. Now could you young people recommend something not too strong that will give us a tickle? They usually don't let us out of the nursing home, you know."

"Oh, escapees, huh? Well, you've come to the right bar. How 'bout I start you off easy with some white wine spritzers until we see if you can handle your liquor. We don't want you tearin' up the place like a couple of roustabouts."

"Roustabouts, oh my, isn't that the word for us, Edna? Yes, we'll take two of those spritzers. Now don't spill on yourself, dear. Cousin Madge says we're going to be sitting at Table 7 with some very sophisticated friends of Allison's mother and a nice single gentleman from Toledo, so we want to make a good impression. Thank you very much, young lady, and you too, young man. Tally ho!"

"Tracy, do you think you should have given them any alcohol? They must be near ninety."

"Don't worry. I made the spritzers good and weak, and if they come back for seconds, the drinks will just keep getting weaker. No, I'll tell you who we have to watch out for. Remember the couple who came up first, the Jack Daniel's and the double vodka and tonic? That's a serious drinker with an unhappy wife. Remember she tried to order from us before the ceremony and got all hissy that the bar wasn't open? Plus, he was scoping out my tits."

"Would you like me to intervene if he returns?"

"Oh, David, you are the last of the true gentlemen, aren't you? No, I can take care of him, and besides, tits equals tips, so let him stare. As for our other customers . . . the Scotch and mixed drinks like gin and tonics are too early to tell. Some people like to start off with a belt, then they tone it down and sip wine during dinner. But the classy wine drinkers can fool you. If they keep it up, they'll be under the table. Ditto the beer boys, they tend to like to party. Whereas the Camparis and piña coladas we won't have to worry about, they're sissies. And anybody who's loud and cracking stupid jokes or doing a bad James Bond impersonation even before they start drinking is guaranteed to get pissed. They're already under the delusion they're the life of the party, and they think alcohol is only going to make them wittier. If I had a dime for every time I've heard 'shaken, not stirred,' I'd be one rich girl."

"You sure know a lot about the psychology of this, Tracy."

"Actually, I have a degree in psychology."

"You do? Then why are you tending bar?"

"Because it gets me where I want to go, free wheelin', out to see the world. I came up to Newport on a yacht from Miami and I'll hop another back down to the Caribbean come fall. Meanwhile, you stick with me, David, my friend, and I'll teach you stuff they never taught you in bartending school. Now keep your eye on who's getting refills . . ."

A rum and Coke, please . . . Jack Daniel's . . . A cranberry juice and a lite beer . . .

"See, David? You notice our Jack Daniel's came back without the double vodka tonic? That means he's temporarily slipped his leash. I heard from the Rosecourt staff that it's VHM tonight, very high maintenance. Most rich people are. But don't let that stop you from becoming one of them. I'm going to have my own beach café in the islands someday.

"What about your psychology degree? Don't you want to make use of that?"

"I do, every day. I'm a real people watcher. But I didn't go to college to earn a degree to pursue a career. I'm not that disciplined. I just wanted to study interesting stuff and come out after four years with an education. Revolutionary concept, huh? Well, well, look who's back, and with a couple of empty glasses in their hands. Did you ladies enjoy your wine spritzers?"

"Yes, very much, didn't we, Edna?"

"Eh?"

"I said, we enjoyed our drinks, but we have to pace ourselves because they'll be serving wine with dinner, and if the mood takes us, we may get up and dance. May we leave our glasses here?"

"You sure can, and David and I thank you for being so considerate to return them. If I peek in the ballroom window later, I expect to see you two cuttin' the rug."

"I used to do the Lindy Hop, you know. I had quite nice legs as a girl."

"Then you go for it, ladies! You too, Edna. Kick up your heels."

"Eh?"

"I said, kick up your heels! Never mind, off you go . . . Uh-oh, here comes Miss Frozen Strawberry Margarita. She looks like a frozen strawberry margarita with that red dress and red hair, although she's going to melt pretty fast if she keeps belting back the tequila. Go on, charm her, David."

"Good evening, miss. What can I—"

"Whiskey sour."

"Certainly . . . here you are. I hope you enjoy—"

"Whoa, nice try, David, but did you see that glassy look in her eyes as she turned her back on you? That first drink's already starting to hit her, and now she's bouncing from one yuppie cocktail to another. How much you want to bet she hasn't eaten anything since breakfast? Women like that have a calorie counter in their heads set just a notch above starvation level. The problem is, once she gets nicely tipsy, she'll want to keep feeling good, and there's no way nibbling a few hors d'oeuvres is going to make up for her intake of alcohol. Ten bucks says she'll be back."

"Is that psychology again, Tracy?"

"No, my friend, it's stereotyping, and let me tell you something, it works. Because contrary to what the do-gooders spout, we are all stereotypes, you and me included. I'm Tracy, the perky bartender with the heart of gold, and you're cast in the role of the noble Sidney Poitier by your sainted grandmother who scrubbed floors on her knees to raise you."

"Now wait a minute . . ."

"C'mon, David. I'm not saying that to be offensive. Did she or didn't she do some kind of domestic labor to raise you?"

"Well, yes . . ."

"And there's no shame in it. It's what a lot of black women her age had to do."

"But you can't make snap judgments like that about people, Tracy. You don't know. My grandmother could have been a doctor or a lawyer."

"But if she were, you wouldn't be working a summer job to pay back student loans, would you? Mix a little Freud with a dollop of Sherlock Holmes and it's not hard to peg people. Why do you think they have police profilers? Because criminals fit stereotypes. Why do you think advertisers pay big bucks for demographic info? Because it tells them precisely what brand of toothpaste you'll buy based on your age, sex, and income level. And if you break the mold, you're only creating a new mold for other people to fall into."

"That's not true! Is it?"

"Sure, it's like the women's movement was supposed to destroy the stereotype of the passive, cookie-baking housewife, and instead its major accomplishment was to create a new stereotype of the supermom who's expected to do it all."

"You talk too much."

"Just watch me put my silver tongue to work. Because now that the first rush is over, we can slow the pace, exchange some friendly banter with our customers and subconsciously twist their arm to leave a generous tip in our glass. The truly happy people won't linger; you have to hit them quick and right on target to score. But as the night wears on, the lonely, the lovelorn, and the loquacious are going to start looking for a sympathetic ear. It's our duty to validate their experiences with words of solace and understanding, as if we haven't heard it a thousand times before. Then we let out a glimmer of our own wistful dreams—your struggle to earn a PhD, my quest to become a restaurateur—"

"Wait a minute, who said I want to earn a PhD?"

"Don't you?"

"Well, yes."

"Then do your part. Be Sidney Poitier and leave it to me to let it slip about your sainted grandmother."

"You're a hustler, Tracy, a shameless hustler."

"With a heart of gold and a push-up bra. Besides, I raise this lowly job to new levels. I make it an art. I see every guest coming toward me as a potential tip, and that in itself puts a welcoming smile on my face. If I get the payoff, I come out ahead, and if I don't, the guest still gets my heartfelt service."

"Well, when you put it like that . . ."

"That's the spirit, David! But one thing I'm serious about. We've got to watch the drinkers, starting with Jack Daniel's and Strawberry Margarita. I'll bet you my tiki bar they're in trouble before the night is over."

16

SIBERIA

John

"EXCUSE ME, MISS? I'm sorry to bother you, but I wonder if you could double-check our seating arrangement. My wife feels there may have been a mistake."

I reach inside my jacket and hand over Isabel's and my place card to the Rosecourt hostess in the foyer, smiling as anonymously as possible. It's not as crowded inside as when we arrived—the majority of the guests are on the verandah imbibing cocktails—but handfuls of people are passing to and from the restrooms, and others are wandering through the open rooms on the mansion's first floor. I hold my Jack Daniel's casually at waist height, itching for a sip. God, I wish Isabel wouldn't make me do these things. What the hell does it matter where we sit? It's one night, one lousy night. All I want to do is get drunk.

"Certainly, sir." The hostess reads the front of the place card aloud. "Mr. and Mrs. John Newsome." She flips it open. "Table 7." She looks up, smiles, and gestures toward a pair of large, gilt-trimmed doors. "That will be on the left side of the ballroom, sir, in the far corner. We expect to invite people in for dinner at about a quarter to eight."

She offers to return the card, but I pretend I don't see it, mentally grit my teeth, and press on.

"Yes, I know it says Table 7, but my wife feels that may be a mistake. Is there an overall seating chart you could check?"

"Let me ask our supervisor."

She excuses herself with a polite nod and steps away from the marble table where the guest book and a dozen or so unclaimed place cards remain. God, this is embarrassing. The hostess is the same freckle-faced girl who was handing out the cards when we arrived, and I'm sure she remembers Isabel pawing over them and has made the connection. Though I'll have to give her credit—you can't tell it from the expression on her face. Damn, all I want to do is get drunk and sit down to a juicy steak dinner on old Gordon's tab.

"Good evening, sir. I'm Anne, the supervisor. You had a question about your seat?"

"Yes, well," I clear my throat to make my case, "our card says we're at Table 7, but my wife feels that could be a mistake. Is there any way you could double-check?"

"Of course. Let me get my file." She crosses to a side table, takes a folder from the drawer, and compares our place card to a list. "Yes, here it is. Mr. and Mrs. John Newsome, Table 7. That's correct."

"Is there, um, any way we can change that?"

My brain squirms at the words leaving my mouth. God, will you listen to me? Would anyone believe I'm a highly competent corporate lawyer? Why am I doing this? All I want is to get drunk, chomp into an expensive steak dinner, and fuck that perky bartender with the cute tits.

"I'm sorry, sir. The bride's mother prepared the seating chart, and the tables are full."

"Well, is it possible some of the guests aren't coming?"

My eyes slide to the unclaimed place cards still on the marble table. God, I hate myself! I'm actually thinking about swiping one in the hope it contains a different number just to placate Isabel. The Rosecourt supervisor and her assistant exchange the merest glances and smiles. They've seen this before, so help me. I am pathetic.

"Some of the guests went straight around to the lawn to be seated for the ceremony rather than coming through the house," says the supervisor, her smile as bright as it is unyielding. "I'm sure they'll be in afterward to pick up their cards." She pauses. "You know, sir, once the dinner has been served, most people don't stay at their assigned table. If you'd like to get up after the meal to dance or socialize with friends around the ballroom, there'll be plenty of opportunities."

She tips her head slightly, inviting me to take this scrap back to Isabel and save face. I should grab it and run. Isabel will already be pissed that I'm not back yet with another drink for her. God, please, all I want to do is get drunk, eat steak, and fuck that cute bartender or a waitress or any woman who isn't cold as a corpse on a slab in the morgue.

"Naturally, if there's a serious problem with your seat," the supervisor continues, "I'll be happy to bring it to the attention of Mrs. Hollingsworth."

She ends on a querying note, but she's got me and she knows it. Even Isabel wouldn't dare complain to Deirdre.

"No, no, that won't be necessary. Thank you for your assistance." I can feel my tail curving between my legs, the smile turning cheesy on my face.

"You're welcome. Please excuse me. I have to locate the bridesmaids for photos."

With a quick nod, she departs, and I edge away from the freckle-faced hostess. God, I'd divorce Isabel in a minute if it weren't for the fact that she'd clean me out. My best tack is to keep her supplied with vodka and tonics and shoehorn her over to one of the other tables at the first opportunity. But who says I have to go back yet? She's not looking over my shoulder now . . .

I glance around the foyer—no one we know is in sight—and treat myself to a surreptitious belt of Jack Daniel's. *Ahhh.* Maybe I'll stroll around the first floor here, admire the architectural details and the portraits on the walls. It's better than circulating on the verandah, pretending to be sociable, like a pack of dogs sniffing and nuzzling each other's balls. Hell, who are any of these people to me? I've never met the groom or his family before tonight. Though we used to see Allison as a teenager when Gordon and Deirdre invited us for dinner, it's been more than a decade since she left home for college. Nor have we seen Gordon socially since the divorce—he's persona non grata in Isabel's eyes—though he and I have kept up the buddy-buddy thing through the hospital. Gordon himself made no qualms about turning over their old friendships to Deirdre, as if we were an unspoken part of the settlement, as if we didn't matter. The majority of people he's invited to the wedding appear to be doctors and hospital administrators, and I'm hardly eager to rehash the same old complaints about malpractice lawsuits. Which leaves about a half dozen couples for Isabel and me to hook up with, the very people we're apparently not seated with at the leper colony table. What Isabel said or did to Deirdre to provoke this banishment is anybody's guess, and I frankly don't care. Hell, I would have been happy to send the newlyweds a generous check and buy my way out of this whole overblown affair.

I take another slug from my glass. *Ahhh, that's the stuff.* Well, now it's just me and my pal Jack Daniel's, two lonely, mellow dudes looking for the meaning of life in a bottle and a pretty woman with a tender heart and a sympathetic ear. And what's this I spy near the far end of the hall? Why, it's another Rosecourt hostess, not the freckle-faced kid but a shapely brunette, standing by herself at the back stairs. Don't you think she looks a little lonely, too? I take my time ambling toward her, stopping to shake hands and blather a few words with some Indian doctor whose name I can't remember, touching an appreciative finger to an elaborately carved wood cabinet against one wall.

"Well, *hello.*" My expression registers surprise to see her there. "Don't tell me they make you stand here alone the entire night at the end of the hall?"

"Not at all, sir. Is there something I can help you find?"

"Is there something I should be looking for?"

She smiles, obviously impressed by my quick repartee. "Most guests who come this far are looking for the restrooms. The gentlemen's is right around this corner." Her palm tilts in demonstration, her breasts shifting ever so slightly beneath her Rosecourt vest. There's no disguising that pair of beauties.

"What's behind that door?" I lift my drink to indicate a plain, painted panel a few yards beyond her at the dead end of the hall.

"The kitchen. The catering staff is working in there."

"So you're standing guard to keep meandering guests out." I chuckle, playing the interested tourist. I peg her in her mid-thirties, just the right age to find me sophisticated and debonair. "Why is this staircase roped off?" I tap the banister. "What's upstairs?"

"It leads to the old servants' quarters."

"Any old servants up there, ha-ha? Seriously, if these walls could talk, I bet they'd tell some fascinating tales." I swirl the amber liquid in my glass. *We're on a roll here, Jack. Don't rush her.* "Take that portrait in the foyer, the old gent with the mutton-chop whiskers. Who was he, pray tell?"

"That would be Augustus Lamont, who built Rosecourt. If you're interested in history, sir, there's a write-up about the house in the glass display case in the library." Her hand and her big brown eyes swing toward an open door halfway up the hall. "It's very informative."

"As are you." I pause to let her savor the compliment. "So where did old Augustus get his money?"

"He inherited a banking fortune, sir."

"Ah, a banking fortune—tough life, huh? Then he spent the money on this cottage, which is pretty impressive, I must say." I nod around, though this end of the mansion is fairly utilitarian save for the carved wood cabinet against the wall. "One of the original antiques, I presume?"

"Eighteenth-century Italian, in walnut with exotic wood marquetry. You know, sir, if you're still in town tomorrow, Rosecourt will be open at ten a.m. for guided tours. The butler at the front door can give you a brochure."

She sweeps her smile and her hand toward the front of the house, but a look of consternation is my reply.

"Don't tell me you have to work this wedding late tonight and get up early tomorrow to give tours? Why, that's unconscionable! Let me get you something to drink, a little wine, some sparkling water." I extend my glass as proof of my ability to procure an equally refreshing beverage for her, but the hostess takes a step backward.

"No, thank you." Still smiling, she skirts around me. "Sir, if you'll excuse me, I have to go replenish the supplies in the ladies' room."

"Okay, ha-ha, see you later."

She disappears through yet another hallway door, leaving me standing by the back stairs. Damn, I'm not that drunk yet not to recognize a brush-off when a woman hits me over the head with it. I take a sustaining draught from my glass. *Too bad, Jack, my friend.* She was a looker, but no score there. Probably the wrong time of the month—that's why she's on her high horse. Well, the night is young, and so am I. Time to ramble back to the bar for a refill. Of course, if I venture outside, I'll have to look sharp to avoid Isabel.

But wait, what's this? I turn as the kitchen door opens behind me with a gust of noise and hot air, and a waitress emerges. Why, she's just a little bitty thing, Hispanic, barely five feet tall, and here she's carrying on the palm of one upraised hand a heavy silver tray decorated with hors d'oeuvres. Her curly hair bounces like a doll's, and her skimpy black skirt hugs her hips as they swivel to balance the off-kilter load.

"Well, *hello*. Looks like you have some delicious egg rolls there. Let me be the first to lighten your tray . . . You sure I can't carry that for you? No? Ha-ha . . . Well, let me just walk you along the hall and make sure no one bumps your elbow . . ."

Ah, Jack, you smooth devil. You debonair dude, you.

17

OH, BROTHER!

Fredericka

UGH! HOW THE HELL are you supposed to change a tampon in a cramped toilet stall while wearing a full-skirted bridesmaid's dress and artificial fingernails?

Picture it: High heels planted on the tile floor, I'm squatting like a quarterback in a football huddle, attempting to wrestle yards of billowing fabric above my knees without dipping the hem into the toilet bowl. Foreseeing this would take some maneuvering, I've already extracted the new wrapped tampon from my purse, which is slung on the hook on the stall door. Ideally, I'd have set the tampon atop the toilet tissue holder where it would be right at hand, but in keeping with Rosecourt's Victorian decor, the pink-painted ladies' room is all frou-frou and frills. To balance the tampon on the curving gold bars of the toilet paper holder is to risk it rolling off into the neighboring stall or out into plain view on the floor. Then you're faced with the prospect of a strange hand popping up at you from below, accompanied by a cheery voice inquiring, "Excuse me, did you lose this?" To obviate this embarrassment, I've sucked every last drop of saliva from my mouth and gingerly pinioned the wrapped tampon between my incisors. So far, so good.

"Fredericka? Is that you in there, dear? It's Aunt Iris. Are you all right?"

"I'h fine, Aun' Iris."

"Edna and I saw your red dress swishing below the door."

"I'h fine, Aun' Iris."

"Are you sure? You sound funny, and Edna and I heard you grunting. Well, Edna didn't because her hearing aid is acting up, but I did. Do you need some assistance, dear?"

"No, Aun' Iris. Is jus' a lil'—ugh!—cramp in here."

"All right. We're going to powder our noses."

Great, already this stupid dress is announcing to everyone, hey, there's a bridesmaid peeing in the third stall, and I can't exactly tell Aunt Iris the reason I sound funny is because I'm talking with a tampon in my mouth. I'll admit this is one time that old goat Freud was right: I *would* prefer a penis. Vaginas are nothing but trouble. I probably should have gone upstairs to the suite to do this—the bathroom there is certainly more spacious and private—but as I reached the grand staircase so did a trio of the Beauty Queens bound for another re-makeup session, and I figured the downstairs restroom would be quicker. Now, hunkered on my high heels, the gown bunched under my elbows, I need to get my hands inside the elastic band of my underpants without ripping off these acrylic nails.

Ugh! Despite the air-conditioning, this is June, and there are only four stalls to accommodate over a hundred female guests streaming in from the verandah to relieve their bladders of cocktails. The temperature in the restroom is fast approaching tropical. Sweat prickles in my

armpits and beads on my forehead, and I suck up moi
Will someone please remind me why I'm doing th
Mead, right, and to figure out why women not on
cumb to but take pleasure in this whole maddening ritual.
I wriggle down the panties, transfer the bunched skirt to
my left forearm. and probe with my free hand between my
legs for the string of the resident tampon. Of course, the
string is not hanging down nice and dry but has happily
nestled itself into the damper, more convoluted parts of my
anatomy. I poke and pry with the acrylic fingernails—it
feels like I'm being molested by Popsicle sticks. Come on,
come on. The paper wrapping of the new tampon is getting
damp between my teeth.

"Fredericka? You're grunting again."

"I'h okay, Aun' Iris. Ugh!"

"We're standing right outside your door if you need us."

"I'h fine, Aun' Iris. I goh it."

"Well, if you're sure, dear. Did I tell you Edna and I had
a very nice drink? It's called a white wine spritzer."

"Goof for you, Aun' Iris. Tay Aun' Ehna and go haf
anoher."

I shift balance on my teetering heels and gently tug the
string, praying the tampon doesn't swing out too fast and
continue up in an arc to hit the underside of my dress. Oh
well, at least the color is cinnabar. With my right elbow
I nudge up the hinged lid of the unassuming metal box
attached to the side wall and deposit the used item into the
paper bag liner. Halfway there! By now the temperature in
the stall is like a sauna and my underarms are dripping, but
at least I can get the new tampon out of my mouth and spit
out the bits of paper stuck to my tongue. Still holding the

full skirt in my left forearm, I pass my right hand with the tampon under the dress, blindly strip off the wrapping, squat deeper, work myself open with the artificial finger-nails—ugh!—locate the aperture—ugh!—and insert the tampon tube—

"Fredericka?"

"Aunt Iris, are you still there?"

"Yes, dear. Well, you sound better, and we know it's really none of our business, but are you alone in there?"

"What do you mean, Aunt Iris? Of course, I'm alone."

"That's good. We thought you might be having sex in there."

"Aunt Iris!"

Ahh, at last! The new tampon in place, I toss the card-board tube into the metal box, reach for toilet paper to dry myself, hoist up my underpants, and gratefully release the voluminous red skirt. Reclaiming my purse from the hook, I unlatch the stall door and step out, only to confront my reflection in the bathroom mirror: bosom—what little I have of it—heaving, face glistening with sweat, cinnabar dress crushed and disheveled, baby's breath hanging askew in my hair. Aunts Iris and Edna and a half dozen other women peer around me into the stall.

"There was *no one* with me." I hold the door wide for their inspection, and the other women, giggling, return to their gossip and primping at the mirror.

"I'm glad to see it," says Aunt Iris. "It just wouldn't be very discreet, and you've always been such a smart girl. What's that, Edna? Oh, you'll have to excuse us, Fredericka. Edna says she wants a screwdriver. What do you need a tool for, dear?"

They totter out the door, and I make my way to the sink, wash my hands, and finally escape into the hallway and cooler air.

"Oh, Fredericka, there you are!" Pammy hurries towards me, then stops. "Are you all right?"

"I'm fine, Pammy. It was just a little hot in there."

"Well, you can use the suite upstairs anytime you want, you know."

"Yes, thanks, but I saw some of the other bridesmaids headed that way, and I thought this would be quicker."

"Oh, is that where they are? I'm helping the photographer round up the bridal party. Allison wants more pictures. I'll fetch them."

"No, wait, I'll go, Pammy." I catch her back. "I suspect I should, you know, apply a little more deodorant." I confide the last half under my breath, lifting my sticky underarms in demonstration.

Pammy nods conspiratorially at the shared confidence. "Okay, I'll find the ring bearer and flower girl."

She darts back down the hall on her mission. I follow as far as the grand staircase, where a Rosecourt hostess waits to unhook the velvet cord and rehook it after me as I mount the stairs. Do they have a union here? Do they have health care benefits? Sometimes the lowest-paid jobs come with the most expensive-looking uniforms and if—

Low, urgent voices coming from the suite halt me just outside the half-open door.

"No! I don't believe it!"

". . . yes, last night . . ."

". . . no, it was after that, later . . ."

". . . and to think we trusted . . ."

I shake my head. More gossip, what else is new? But can somebody tell me this: why is it women always crowd into a lavatory to dish the dirt? Is it some leftover "we're safe from the boys" instinct from grade school? Here they have an entire mansion full of nooks and alcoves in which to conduct their backstabbing, yet downstairs the tattlers pack into the pink restroom, and upstairs, with a three-room suite of sitting room, bedroom, and bathroom at their disposal, I can tell from the faintness and direction of the bridesmaids' voices that they're huddled in the latter. Time to barge in and break it up—

"If Allison finds out, she'll kill him!"

I catch myself with one foot in the door. There's only one male Allison's likely to kill. Mead, my brother. Oh no, what's he done? I strain my ears, not daring to step in farther and reveal myself.

". . . took advantage . . ."

". . . never should have let him go to that bachelor party . . ."

". . . for heaven's sake, nobody tell!"

A rustle and footsteps approach, and I jump backward, trying to look naïve as the three Beauty Queens appear at the door.

"Um, uh, you're wanted for photographs," I say, as they eye me distastefully from my rumpled dress to the dangling baby's breath in my hair. "I'll freshen up and join you. Won't be a minute!"

I edge past them into the suite, and tsking among themselves they continue downstairs. In the bathroom I attempt to piece together in my mind the tidbits I've overheard while simultaneously repairing my hair. The piecing is easier. Mead did something last night during or after his bachelor party, probably under the influence of alcohol, that Allison would be justified in murdering him for. Hmm, let me think. Do you suppose sex was involved? Mead, how could you? And how could his groomsmen, his best friends, stoop to that juvenile trick of hiring a stripper? Because that's surely the scenario . . . unless they picked up an equally drunk party of bar-hopping women in downtown Newport and an all-out orgy ensued? I shake my head. I can't imagine they'd go that far. But the offense must have exceeded mere flirting, because little as I know her, Allison doesn't strike me as the type to exact capital punishment for a harmless wink or two. Well, whatever Mead's indiscretion, he's safe as long as she doesn't find out.

I stab a last bobby pin into my sagging French twist, squint at my reflection, then grab the hairspray and let go a blast. *Gack!* Why do women use this stuff? It's like spraying cancer on your skull. I let out a second *gack!*—but this time it's not the hairspray. Instead, my mind jolts to a vision of the Beauty Queens descending the stairs and their final whispered words: *For heaven's sake, nobody tell!* Are you kidding me? That's like expecting a sieve to hold water. I hoist my skirt, dash from the suite, and barrel down the grand staircase as fast as I can go. The Rosecourt hostess at the bottom sees me coming and deftly unhooks the cord.

"Careful—" she begins, but it's too late, the momentum has me, and I pitch down the last few steps and flail into open air, only to find myself caught, my nose inches from the carpet, in a pair of outstretched arms.

"Gotcha," says a steady voice, rising from his knees and bringing me upright, although he too looks a little shaken from his reflex action of swooping and scooping me away from an impact with the floor. It's Blaine, my escort for the evening, though between the ceremony and the photography we've barely had time to introduce ourselves.

"Thanks," I say, a trifle breathless, both to him and to the worried hostess, who's hovering to make sure I'm not injured. "I must have caught my shoe on my hem."

"No doubt," Blaine replies. "You looked to be in quite a hurry."

His comment recalls me to my mission—and reminds me that as one of the groomsmen he probably aided and abetted Mead's crime. I raise a terse finger.

"Listen, about last night . . ."

"I know." He takes a deep breath. "Fredericka, I'm sorry to have missed the rehearsal, but my plane was delayed in Chicago, and I didn't get in until midnight. I've been wanting to meet you for a long time, ever since you were ten and I was twelve."

He waits expectantly.

"Huh?" I say.

"Mead used to read me the letters your mother sent him, about you stirring up the catechism class and circulating a petition about the neighbor boy's dog."

"Huh?"

"The one that got run over by a speeding car. It was years ago, when Mead and I were kids at summer camp. He saved my life when I nearly drowned, then we met again in college."

I hold up my hand, and he halts while I fish in my purse for my glasses. Allison had forbidden me to wear them until the photography session was over, but I'm tired of squinting. I hook the wire frames around my ears and finally give Blaine my full attention. What I see is a surprisingly good-looking man with alert blue eyes behind rimless glasses, fair features, and the lean build of a runner. His expression is anxious, as if he's hoping we'll soon find a mutual wavelength, and indeed, my memory is clearing. It was quite a family event when Mead returned from camp wearing a gleaming lifesaving medal.

"Blaine," I say. "I'm sorry. Mead neglected to fill me in on most of the details about his wedding." I don't add that I didn't bother to ask him, either; sometimes I'm not a very good sister. But I do mean to help my brother out of a tight spot now. I cast a glance left and right, beckoning Blaine out of earshot of the Rosecourt hostess and a clump of noisy guests who've planted themselves in the foyer. "So you didn't make it to the bachelor party. Did you happen to talk to any of the other guys about it?"

"A little. I hear it was pretty wild."

"Could you be more specific?"

"Not really, only that they blazed a trail through the Newport bars. Is anything wrong?"

His look turns serious, and I bite my lip, unsure how much to confide. Allison will keep Mead on her arm most of the night, making it difficult to speak to him privately. But if I can find out who knows what about last night's escapade, I may be able to defuse any rumors before they spread far.

"Oh, Fredericka, please come. Allison wants more photos!" Pammy hurries in, waving from across the foyer, and I signal in reply.

"Right this minute!" I call, then I turn and clasp Blaine's hands. "Listen, I need you."

"I'm flattered."

"No, no, I need you to help me with something important that I can't exactly divulge. Can you canvas the other
groomsmen, tactfully, and find out whether anything compromising happened last evening?"

"Compromising to Mead?"

"Yes."

"I'll do my best."

"Tactfully."

"I promise."

"Thank you. Mead's life, or at least his happiness, may
depend upon it."

I dash off, Pammy still frantically waving at me to join
her, a final thought snagging my mind.

Blaine has been wanting to meet me since I was ten
and he was twelve?

Huh!

18

PITY THE POOR
PHOTOGRAPHER

Joel

"PLEASE, COULD I HAVE THE BRIDESMAIDS all the brides-maids, please come forward—that includes the junior bridesmaid and also the flower girl—Allison, a step to the left—we want three bridesmaids on either side of Allison with the roses framing the picture—no, no. you don't need to touch up your lipstick again—please, can someone get the flower girl off the rim of the fountain—"

"I'm getting an ulcer, I know it,' I said to Lawrence over our green chili omelets this very morning. "Or maybe it's stomach cancer. Look at my tongue. Do you think it looks coated?"

"Your tongue is fine," Lawrence said, lazily scanning the newspaper.

"You didn't even look. What about my temperature? My forehead feels hot. Does it feel hot to you?"

"Let me check." Lawrence lowered the paper and leaned forward, putting his hand to my forehead and heav-ing a patient sigh. "Your temperature is perfectly normal. Now stick out your tongue, farther, farther . . ." He turned my chin in his hand, peering down my throat, then his mouth clamped on mine in a sloppy French kiss. "Nope," he said as I squirmed loose, "your tongue is fine."

"You don't take anything seriously anymore," I sulked, eyeing his aqua velour bathrobe falling open to his navel.

"That's right, and it feels *so* good. I wish you could get to that point, too. You're so tense, Joel. Ease up. Let's have sex. That will relax you."

"I don't want to have sex," I said, which wasn't true. After twelve years together, there's still nothing I'd rather do than have sex with Lawrence. Except marry him—but we've agreed to hold out on that. We want a real marriage, a real wedding, not some condescending commitment ceremony that stamps us forever as second-class citizens. We want a full Catholic church ceremony—it's Lawrence's faith, not mine, but I'd happily convert for him—yet for all the progress of late, I worry it won't happen in my lifetime. I'm forty-two, I'm losing my hair, and it'll soon be too late for me to be a blushing bride.

"Come on, I'll massage your shoulders," Lawrence said, rising and walking around the kitchen table. His thumbs stroked down my neck and worked into my muscles. "You're in knots, sweetheart. It's this wedding tonight, isn't it?"

I nodded, surrendering my body to his ministrations while I poured out my woes. "It's my big chance, Lawrence. These are society people from New York and who knows what contacts that could bring. But they're so picky! The bride faxed me a list of a hundred and fourteen required photos, a hundred and fourteen! Bride with groom, bride with mother, bride with father, bride with mother and father, bride with maid of honor, bride with all bridesmaids together, bride with junior bridesmaid, bride with flower girl—"

"I know, I know . . ."

"Groom with mother, groom with father, groom with mother and father, groom with best man . . ."

"Shh, shh . . ."

"Bride and groom in front of mansion, bride and groom on grand staircase, bride and groom in front of fountain in rose garden—"

"Your shoulders are tensing again."

I snuffled up a sob. I've always been high-strung, and this wedding had me wrung to tears. It wasn't the list in itself. Any photographer who shoots weddings keeps a mental checklist of essential shots, and any smart photographer will ask the bride to point out special relatives, friends, and guests she wants in the pictures as well. But the list Allison Hollingsworth had faxed me contained every possible permutation of people in every conceivable setting inside and outside Rosecourt. Since no photographs were to be taken during the ceremony—a stipulation with which I personally agree—the depictions of the bride and groom reciting their vows and exchanging rings before the minister would also have to be re-staged afterward. That meant dozens of outdoor portraits to be taken within the hubbub of the cocktail hour, followed by the indoor portraits after dinner. Plus, Allison wanted spontaneous shots of every aspect of the reception, dancing, cake cutting, tossing the bouquet . . .

"And she's putting those horrid disposable cameras on every table!" I cried to Lawrence, in full sob now.

"There, there . . ."

"I *hate* those little cameras!"

"I know . . ."

Lawrence gave up the massage, pulled his chair next to mine, and cradled me in his arms. I abhor those throwaway cameras! They're the worst idea ever! You'd think a photographer would love them, and we might if guests would stick to using them as they're intended, namely to snap pictures of the other guests at their table. It's an ideal way to catch anyone the official photographer has missed. But that's not what happens, there's always one person at each table who, once they get their hands on that insidious implement, assumes it elevates them to the rank of professional photographer.

"And no sooner do I get a complicated shot perfectly posed than they're climbing over my shoulder, yelling 'Smile!' and 'Cheese!' and flashing away, upsetting my light meter and practically knocking me over. It's anarchy, Lawrence, pure anarchy!"

"I know. Shh, sweetheart, you'll do fine."

"There'll never be enough time to take all the shots Allison wants, and you know how I hate to be rushed. And both my assistants are new, and I'm going to have to negotiate my way around a videographer. Tell me again how it feels not to care."

Lawrence nuzzled his cheek against my head, his aftershave emitting its comforting scent of cinnamon. He looks like Pierce Brosnan, and I'm lucky to have him. I worry I'll lose him to someone younger and better looking if my hair keeps falling out.

"Not to care," he said, "is like reaching nirvana . . ."

His voice grew dreamy, and I snuggled against his chest to listen, like a child nestling into a favorite fairy tale. Lawrence is a poet, but of course poetry doesn't pay the bills. So he writes copy for a giftware catalog, those clever blurbs beside the pictures of cobalt glass bunnies and dancing angel wind chimes and hand-painted ballerina figurines made in China. For the first year or two he actually enjoyed learning a new business, for the next three years he settled into a well-paid routine. Then he started to chafe at the repetition, the cheap merchandise, the mindless consumerism he was promoting. Some days he grew so overwrought, I feared he'd hurl his laptop against the wall.

"If I have to write one more cutesy copy block about collectible porcelain boxes, I'll scream!" he shrieked.

"It buys you time to write poetry," I soothed, a consolation we often shared. Virtually all artists, unless they're independently wealthy, have to pimp to support their true passion. It's why I shoot weddings, to feed my stomach, so I can shoot the landscapes that feed my soul. At least it's a better gig than high school yearbooks.

"But I'm dying, Joel. This catalog is sucking the life out of me!" Lawrence moaned, until one day, about six months ago, his epiphany occurred.

"You know what?" he said, looking up at me from his laptop, a sense of amazement dawning on his face. "I don't care any more. I've reached the point where I don't care."

And from then on, he didn't. He hummed when the catalog company sent over a new cast-iron doggy doorstop requiring a write-up. He whistled as he tapped out a copy block rhapsodizing over a sherbet-striped polyester lounger that resembled a baggy clown suit.

"I don't care, I don't care," he'd sing, and when I worriedly pointed out that his copy would suffer and the catalog company would notice, he shook his head. "No, Joel, that's the beauty of it. I can write this crap with my eyes closed, and they still think it's wonderful. I just send my brain on vacation for the duration of the assignment, and when it's done it's like I'm back from another planet, and I can get on with my poetry."

I shook my head, thinking this euphoria couldn't last. It was a bubble that had to burst. But it didn't. And the more Lawrence revealed his transformation to other people at parties or social gatherings, the more people, to my horror, responded in kind.

"Oh yes," enthused a doctor, a banker, two store clerks, three MBAs, a car salesman, and six teachers, "I gave up caring eight months, two years, five years ago. Isn't it great?" And they chattered happily, as if they'd just come out of the closet together.

"But it *has* to affect your performance," I insisted, distraught. I turned to the doctor, pleading. "You're a brain surgeon, for Christ's sake!"

"No, that's the remarkable thing, it doesn't," he replied. "It's like a letting go, a release. You don't question or fight it anymore, you simply do it and stop worrying."

"Besides," two of the teachers interjected, "who's going to fire us? We have tenure."

"Don't worry," Lawrence assured me, "it will happen for you, Joel. You'll stop anguishing about the outcome and realize how insignificant it all is in the grand scheme of the universe. Then all the crap that comes with a job, the office politics and bureaucracy, will melt away too. It's like flipping a switch: brain-off, brain-on. Most jobs require only half a brain anyway. The beauty is, once you let go of the grief, you also lose the bad attitude, and that in itself is enough to make your bosses think you love your work. Look how much happier and more relaxed I've become."

He was right. Since he'd stopped caring, Lawrence no longer suffered headaches or had to drag himself out of the bed in the morning. Instead of two unhappy artists living together, we'd become one unhappy artist and one who took up yoga, made green chili omelets for breakfast, and lapped up sex like a cat in cream. Which only made me worry more. If I *couldn't* stop caring, how long before Lawrence got tired of me and my neuroses and lit out with someone new? I felt like one of those people who can't see the 3-D picture hidden amongst the colored dots while everyone else is turning the pages and exclaiming, "Wow! Look at that! This is so cool!"

"Just breathe deeply and do your best," Lawrence coached as I left for Rosecourt that afternoon. "And remember, I love you, Joel."

I do remember that; his words stay with me, cached in my heart. But meanwhile, if I stop caring and miss a single one of these shots on Allison's list . . .

"Okay, good. Now the next picture Allison wants is herself, Mead, and Fiona beside the fountain, so the brides-maids can go. Thank you for your cooperation."

The bridesmaids flutter off—thank heaven, the three of them on the right were driving me crazy with their whispers and huddles—and one of my assistants plops the flower girl in place. In a way, the list helps. Instead of me being the bad guy who keeps interrupting the fun to make everyone pose, I can point to the list to emphasize this is Allison's agenda we're bound to obey. But that only frees me up to worry how the final photos will appear. The portrait I took of Allison with her parents is sure to be a disaster, her father beaming while her mother looks like she's holding a mouthful of vinegar. It's not my fault they got divorced, but guess who'll get the blame when the print is developed? Isn't it my job to get everyone to smile? And why does the groom look so uncomfortable? I'd swear that's a guilty grin on his face.

I wish it were my wedding I was photographing.

For a minute, I blank out of the present, and a vision appears in my head. Yes, it's my wedding to Lawrence, right here at Rosecourt. It's a sublime June day just like this, and the garden is in full bloom. Lawrence and I wear matching tuxes, each with a single rose in our lapel, and maybe an accent color in our vests, robin's egg blue for him, mauve for me. We'd hold the ceremony on the lawn, maybe eighty of our family and friends, and my brother and Lawrence's sister would be our honor attendants. For a band, I'd choose rock, Lawrence will prefer swing, but we'd agree the dinner has to be a Tex-Mex buffet. We're both mad for tamales, the spicier the better. My mother will kiss and hug everyone and prop that picture of my late father in his golf cart on the seat beside her so he can witness the service. I'd like to think Lawrence's parents would attend, but they haven't spoken to him since he came out the year he won the poetry prize in college, and Lawrence would reject that "hate the sin, love the sinner" compromise, even if they were inclined to make the offer.

"It's not a sin, Joel," he says. "I love you, and I will love you to the day I die."

"Even if my hair falls out and I get an ulcer?"

"You worry too much, sweetheart."

Then the happily-ever-after vision vanishes, and I'm back at Allison's wedding, although the pleasure lingers a moment longer like a sweet mint melting on my tongue. You can do this, hang in there, I tell myself. It often seems to me that people at a wedding this large never really experience it while it's happening. That's why they demand everything be obsessively photographed and videoed, so they can discover their story afterward. The right pictures prove what they want to believe: *See, I was happy, I was radiant, that pimple on my nose didn't show at all.* Of course not, because I erased it in editing, when in reality it was a honker. But I can't fix everything, and maybe if people accepted the wedding photos, pimples and all, they'd accept that marriage isn't perfect either.

"Okay, that's it, we're done with the rose garden shots." I release an immense sigh and signal my assistants to start moving the equipment inside. Now if only we can get to—

"Wait! Wait! I'm here!"

My jaw drops in horror as a lumpy figure in a red gown thunders toward us, bouquet held on high like a triumphant football player crossing the touchdown line. The face is nearly the same color as the dress, and the chest is puffing like a bellows. The creature leaps through the arch in the hedge and lands with a thump before me, its shoulders shuddering. It draws a happy breath and a smile wreathes its face. No, no, please . . .

"I'm here, Allison! Where do you want me for the pictures?"

No, no, please, don't make me start over . . .

"Why, Susie," says Allison serenely, "how nice that you could come after all. Go find Mom and Daddy and we'll get a family portrait. Pammy, could you run and fetch the other bridesmaids?"

No! No! I swear I'm getting an ulcer.

19

SO VARIOUS,
SO BEAUTIFUL, SO NEW

Anne

"ANNE, THE CATERER has an emergency in the kitchen."

"Anne, Mrs. Hollingsworth—the bride's mother, not the bimbo—wants to speak with you."

"Anne, Glen and the band want to know if they're supposed to introduce the bridal party into the ballroom and if so, they need a list."

"Anne, the ring bearer—aka *brattus horribilus*—has been harassing one of the servers, and she says if he bothers her again, she's going to dump a tray of egg rolls and soy sauce on him, accidentally, of course."

"Okay," I fire off answers in more or less reverse order, "no one lays a hand on the brat, unfortunately, but I'll speak to his parents. Tell Glen, yes, he will be introducing the bridal party, the list's in my file. Tell Hank I'll get to the kitchen as soon as possible. Where's Mrs. Hollingsworth?"

Leon shoots a look over my shoulder, and I turn. It's a no-brainer that when everyone's clamoring, the bride's mother takes precedence, and here comes Deirdre Hollingsworth bearing down on me in her gold peacock gown. She doesn't look happy. What now? I drape the faux smile across my face.

"Mrs. Hollingsworth, what can I do for you?"

"I'm concerned we're running late." Deirdre pauses to flash her own smile and a wave at guests entering from the verandah, then drops the pretense as she ushers me into an alcove. The transformation from Jekyll to Hyde is unsettling, but before I can reflect on it, Deirdre snaps her displeasure. "The ceremony didn't end until seven fifteen, it's seven forty-five now, and according to the schedule that's when guests are to be invited into the ballroom for dinner. That's barely a half hour to mingle, and I've hardly begun to greet the people I'm supposed to."

I nod sympathetically. "Yes, I'm afraid that the extra time Allison and her bridesmaids required to get ready has pushed back the entire agenda. Lest Deirdre miss the point, I innocently rub it in. "I understand your other daughter has only just arrived, and now Allison wants to reassemble the bridesmaids for additional photos?"

Deirdre glares, her anger palpable, but I refuse to accept her blame or let her lay it on my staff. It's not our fault your husband left you. It's not our fault your daughter is a self-centered bitch. It's not our fault you feel compelled to put on a flawless show to prove to everyone present, and most important to yourself, that you're still in control.

"This is sheer incompetence!" she snarls. "How dare you people call yourselves professionals when I have to do your job for you. We'll extend the cocktail hour until eight fifteen, and the caterer can make up the time during dinner. If you ruin this wedding, I'll have you fired." She sweeps away, the gold gown hissing behind her.

Oh! I've been rebuked by upset clients before, but that was uncalled for and she gave me no chance to reply. I blink back unexpected tears.

"Bitch," intones Leon's deep voice at my side. "I saw the look on her face when she dragged you in here, and I couldn't help but overhear." His half smile invites me to join him; the deliberate profanity lets me know he took no offense at my language earlier.

"Thanks, Leon. It's just that tonight . . ." I spill my news, and Leon murmurs condolences. He's met Greg and our two girls at Rosecourt Christmas parties and other employee functions; he was shocked and saddened last fall when I revealed that we had separated.

"Are you having second thoughts?" he asks.

"No . . . no . . . I just have to pull myself together."

He hands me a tissue from his pocket, and when I nod that I'm all right, he leaves to get the bridal party list for the band leader. I take a deep breath. Deirdre's response shouldn't have surprised me. Even when it's the clients' fault, they expect us to run faster to cover for them. Well, I have news for her. That's not going to happen. Weddings are timed for a reason—from long experience we know what's involved in getting two hundred and fifty people wined, dined, danced, and out the door at evening's end— and when a narcissistic bride holds up the show for an extra half-hour's primping, you can kiss your schedule good-bye. We're already running as fast as we can. Then I remember there's an emergency in the kitchen.

"We forgot the salad dressing! We've searched every-where!" Hank, the Riverside catering manager, clutches my shoulders as I enter, while Chef Laszlo swings his cleaver and bawls at his staff in Hungarian. Catering is not a business for the faint of heart, and it's rare for Hank to panic. But then it's rare for Riverside to commit such a blunder, they're the crème de la crème, and Hank seems truly stunned. "I'm sure we packed it, I saw it on the counter ready to go, how could it not be here?" he keeps repeating, while his kitchen crew in their white tunics tear apart crates of supplies.

Meanwhile, servers dash in and out for more hors d'oeuvres trays, steam plumes from boiling pots on the cast-iron stoves, and latex-gloved hands fling chopped walnuts over salad plates on an assembly line. Don't be fooled by the commotion. Rosecourt's kitchen dates from the early 1900s, but even then its raison d'être was to feed large crowds on a grand scale. The stoves are black monsters of heat, huge oak tables provide ample work space, and the adjoining pantry boasts a commercial-grade refrigerator and dishwasher concealed behind sliding panels in the antique cabinetry.

"Don't we have anything?" Hank pleads to his staff, as if they can produce the ingredients from thin air. "We must have olive oil, herbs, something we can throw together."

"What type of dressing do you need?" I demand.

"Aged balsamic vinaigrette with a hint of lime. It's Chef Laszlo's secret recipe." Hank flinches as Chef Laszlo slams his cleaver into a cutting board and emits a frustrated roar. Then he turns to me, a wild hope dawning. "Did you have a function last night? Is there anything left over in the refrigerator?"

"No, but we have a supermarket about a mile up Bellevue Avenue. Tell one of your people to get in a car and dash up there to the customer service desk. I'll phone and ask them to have twenty bottles of Newman's Own and a receipt waiting."

I reach the office at a run, stab in the call, and interrupt the woman who answers before she can get out the store name. "Pick whatever brand comes closest to the description 'aged balsamic vinaigrette'," I tell her, "and if you don't have enough of one brand, mix and match the most expensive ones."

"We'll have it ready," she promises in a competent voice that leaves no worry on that score. But even after I deliver the news to the kitchen, Hank looks like a condemned man. An unscrupulous caterer would have no qualms about serving a substitution; some do it routinely to pad their profit margin. You present the expensive truffles the bride specified to the head table, for example, and ordinary mushrooms to the guests, then charge overall for the higher-priced item. Or as the evening wears on, you replace the French champagne with an equally palatable but less costly domestic bubbly. Who's going to suspect? The biggest snobs are often the most easily taken in.

But Hank and Riverside are not of that ilk. This is a genuine mistake, and he stands in his shirtsleeves and bow tie, wringing his hands. If he explains, apologizes, and offers to discount the bill accordingly, will Allison and Deirdre understand? Might they laugh and play along? It's unlikely any of the guests will pause, smack their lips, and ask their fellow diners, "Excuse me, but doesn't this taste to you like bottled dressing?" Except that Deirdre has placed on each table a lavishly worded card detailing the dinner menu . . .

I shoot Hank a sympathetic glance. He looks queasy, his faded crew cut and sallow complexion at odds with the colorful bustle and tantalizing aromas swirling around him. He's been in this business for ages, though for some reason it took me a long time to remember his name. On less hectic nights we might exchange war stories or some conversation about how our kids are doing. But I can't solve his dilemma, and with a whispered, "Good luck!" I leave him to wrestle with his conscience. Sometimes it's better if I don't know everything that's going on.

I step back into the hallway just in time to see Nicholas, our grinning ring bearer, about to trip a server ferrying a tray of empty wine glasses to the kitchen. I yank him by the arm.

"Nicholas, you must be careful!" I feign alarm before he can protest the brutality. "You nearly had a load of dishes land on you. Let's go find your parents." I haul him out of the house, luckily spotting his mother almost immediately, and march him across the grass. "I'm so glad I found you," I say to her before *l'enfant terrible* can utter a word. "Nicholas nearly collided with a waitress carrying a tray of glasses, and he could have been seriously hurt. It's getting very busy in the house, so you will keep him with you now, won't you?"

My smile grits as if I have sand stuck in my teeth. Just for once I'd like to tell the truth: your child is an unmitigated brat who is deliberately trying to hurt people and it is your responsibility to keep him under control. But Nicholas's mother would never believe me. What, her little darling misbehave? Unthinkable! Those waitresses should watch where they're going! *Come here, precious pussycat, are you rumpled? Are you hurt?* She's murmuring almost these exact words as I return to the house. Nicholas himself knows full well I'm on to him, but he also calculates shrewdly that the moment for charging me with child abuse has passed. I've been too quick for him, his mother is the easy target, and precious pussycat will get whatever he wants.

And suddenly I'm angry, angry and irritated out of all proportion to this minor event. Maybe it's the encounter with Deirdre or Hank's distress in the kitchen or an overall reaction to people's meanness and selfishness. What is the matter with Nicholas's mother? She won't keep him by her side for more than five minutes, parents like that never do, and the parents of Fiona, the flower girl, are already proving to be worse. Throughout the cocktail hour, they've left her in the care of Madeline, the junior bridesmaid, or rather Madeline, seeing the child wandering unattended, has taken it upon herself to be Fiona's babysitter. Unpaid, of course. I want to strangle Fiona's parents. They could have afforded to bring their nanny. If they had any perception at all, they'd leave now that the ceremony is over and go have a quiet evening with Fiona asleep in the hotel. Greg and I never, ever abdicated our responsibilities like that. We always put our children first—

The pain that grips me is so savage, it feels like a hand has punched into my rib cage and clamped onto my heart. I gasp and back into a corner, out of sight. So that's it. I'm angry because I was a model mother, I did everything right, yet I'm divorced, while here are these selfish, inconsiderate, smugly married women who are obviously doing everything wrong. They don't even deserve to have children. But was it that very devotion to our two daughters that pried open the first crack between Greg and me? If we had remained childless, might we be together still?

I've never been one to go easy on myself, and I'm in no mood to be merciful now. Yet the mere idea of saddling the girls with a share of the guilt is sacrilege, a betrayal. Greg and I didn't enter parenthood unprepared. We were thirty, we had our feet on the ground, and our first baby was planned, wanted, loved. We'd saved enough for me to take a year's leave of absence from my teaching job to stay home with our bundle of joy; no stranger was going to raise our child. Even when we learned that Miranda had been born deaf, we quickly surmounted our grief and fears with unity and an action plan. Though our budget grew tight, I postponed my return to teaching, devoted my days to Miranda, and became active in deaf education. As a special ed teacher, I had knowledge and contacts I could share with other parents struggling to cope with the blow. Greg worked longer and harder at Coburn Design Collaborative to support us and pitched in with housework on the weekends. Once a month we hired a babysitter so we could have a night out. Miranda's needs must come first, yet Greg and I would not forget ourselves.

Three years later we had a second daughter Rachel, to prove our lives were on course. I remember nights of no sleep, Greg's pride at putting ten dollars a week into the college fund he'd started for each girl, the stuffy head cold we started one November that lasted until May. I remember once-a-year vacations in bargain motels and the way our old station wagon always waited to break down until Daddy was out of town. Yet no matter what squabbles the girls had enacted that day, no matter how exhausted I was when we tumbled into bed, I never closed my eyes without thinking how much I loved my children. When our daughters were six and three, Miranda thriving in a day school for the deaf, Rachel the precocious darling of her preschool, I returned to teaching part time. We had survived what should have been the most difficult and stressful years of our marriage. We had made the transition from a dedicated couple to a dedicated family. People smiled at us when we took Sunday walks in the park. Short of a major illness or accident, nothing could rock our boat.

We're happy! Miranda would sign, and we'd sign back our assent, Rachel's little fingers almost as adept as ours at mimicking her sister's messages. Even the girls understood how bright and beautiful was our little world, how special it was to be us.

I take a breath and glance out from my corner. It's nearly eight o'clock, and I've already absented myself from Allison's wedding too long. Any minute now I should send my staff to start herding people inside for dinner. Yet this short corridor is deserted, and the story I've started plays on in my head. How our lives spun in a whirlwind of jobs, school, and activities: Miranda's art classes, Rachel's science projects, taking the dog to the vet. How Greg, his reputation growing, often worked Saturdays or skipped dinner at home to woo important clients at restaurants instead. *This house is like Grand Central Station!* Miranda would sign, rolling her eyes at the craziness of our schedules as we dashed in and out. Then I lost my part-time teaching job due to a budget cut. I was stunned, but because of the time I'd taken off to raise the girls I didn't have the seniority to reclaim it. When I chanced upon the help wanted ad for Rosecourt, Greg urged me to give it a try.

"It sounds like fun," he said, "and since you'll be working mostly evenings, we can manage with only a little overlap from a babysitter until I get home at night."

"Okay," I said, "but only if it doesn't interfere with the children."

So I took the job, and though it did present more conflicts than anticipated, we smoothed them over and sailed on. If anyone had asked, Greg and I would have responded with only a little hesitation and a longing sigh toward each other that we were still very much in love. Maybe Allison's minister is wrong. Maybe it isn't the obvious perils that most endanger a marriage, the rocky shoals, the violent storms, the treacherous waves rising out of the depths. Maybe it's an accumulation of small stresses, the tiny leaks in the hull, the undetected fractures in the mast or deck. You could cruise along for years, blithely ignorant of your vessel's unseaworthiness, until you look down and discover the soles of your feet are wet. Annoyed, I shake my head. I'm still searching for an apt metaphor to contain my marriage and divorce, and I'm falling into the same clichés as everyone else.

I step from my corner. Most of the guests remain outside, but those who've migrated indoors are drinking and laughing around the marble table in the foyer, admiring the enormous centerpiece, belatedly signing the guest book. Adults: singles, couples, a few older teenagers who know how to behave themselves. Flower girls and ring bearers aside, we don't get many children at Rosecourt weddings. They aren't invited, they aren't welcome, they fuss and make noise. Nor is it only formal venues that discourage the presence of little ones. Open any wedding planning guide and the advice rings loud and clear: *leave small children at home!* How ironic that marriage, a union that at one time was intended first and foremost to produce offspring, today begins with a ritual that all but bans them from the celebration. What if, instead of being held in evening hours and geared to grownup pleasures, a wedding was held as a picnic or at a playground or amusement park? What if, instead of an overpriced surf-and-turf dinner, the entree consisted of hot dogs, popcorn, ice cream, and soda pop? What if, instead of ball gowns and tuxedos, the bridal party wore tee shirts and shorts?

People are approaching, and I clutch at what's left of my dissolving thoughts. No children—would Greg and I have stayed in love, would our love have lasted longer, without Miranda and Rachel? We'd have struggled less financially and emotionally, had more time and energy to indulge ourselves. I've read studies confirming that childless-by-choice couples are the happiest marrieds of all. Or did our daughters keep us together, would we have split sooner as other differences were revealed? I don't know, I don't know. But not to have had my children is unthinkable. *Please, I love them so desperately, don't let anyone ever think I regret having them, don't let them ever be hurt . . .*

"Yes, it is time to bring the guests in for dinner," I announce, snapping back to business as my staff spots me and converges. "Don't take no for an answer. Be firm."

My troops move out on their assignment. In the opposite direction, far down the hall, one of Hank's crew barrels in a side door and charges for the kitchen, a large brown grocery bag clasped to his chest.

"Mrs. Hollingsworth." I catch Deirdre's attention and hurry toward her. "I have a suggestion to get our schedule back on track. We could save valuable time if, instead of the band introducing the entire wedding party to the ballroom, we limit the introduction to the bride and groom."

Deirdre balks, then her eyes narrow as she weighs my inspiration. I stop to weigh it myself. To omit a single note of her elaborately orchestrated evening will go against Deirdre's nature. Yet having already bustled the bridal party this way and that for the last twenty-four hours, even she shows signs of wearying of the ordeal. And although it will deny her the fanfare of being announced to her applauding guests as "the mother of the bride, Mrs. Deirdre Hollingsworth," it will also deny Gordon and Kimmy the privilege of following immediately after her as "the father and stepmother of the bride, Dr. and Mrs. Gordon Hollingsworth." *That's Kimmy now, remember, Deirdre?* I can see by the shift of expression on her face that she does.

"Yes," says Deirdre ruthlessly. "People already got to see the bridesmaids and groomsmen in procession down the aisle. We'll limit the introduction to Allison and Mead."

She sweeps away in the gold gown. It's a small revenge, depriving her selfish daughter of the full court spectacle and her duplicitous ex of the opportunity to flaunt his now-legal sex kitten. If Allison takes umbrage at not being consulted, I'll support Deirdre by saying her mother felt the spotlight should be on her and Mead alone. I head toward the ballroom to inform Glen and the band of the change in plan, and though no one's near enough to see it, for once the smile that fleets across my face is genuine. I've just bought us back twenty minutes of precious time.

20

What Would Jeeves Do?

Leon

OKAY, I AM RILED, and that's not a good state for a butler to be in. A butler should be dignified and unflappable, like Jeeves in P. G. Wodehouse's books. You ever read those stories? Crack me up! I especially like the way Bertie Wooster always describes Jeeves as "gliding" or "shimmering" into a room, as if he were on wheels. Technically, Jeeves was a valet, a "gentleman's gentleman," but when people think of a butler, he's usually the image they have in mind. It's what they expect of us here at Rosecourt, and at the moment I'm finding it a little bit hard to accommodate them.

"Ladies and gentlemen, the ballroom is now open for dinner. If you'll please come inside . . ."

The staff and I circulate among the guests on the verandah and lawn, spreading the word that dinner is served. You'd think two hundred and fifty hungry people would make a beeline for their tables. Trouble is, they're not hungry; as often happens at a wedding like this, the cocktail hour appetizers are a meal in themselves, and the guests are already stuffed on cold shrimp, asparagus puffs, and other fancy hors d'oeuvres. When we invite them in, they ignore us and keep yakking.

"Argh." the staff groans, after our first pass through the crowd. "What is the matter with these people? Are they just plain rude or don't they understand English?"

"Try again," I say, "only this time, we'll invoke a higher authority."

"Ladies and gentlemen, the ballroom is now open for dinner, and Mrs. Deirdre Hollingsworth asks you to come inside . . ."

That should get a few more of them jumping.

But I'm still riled. Though it probably mirrors the general trend in our society, it seems to me that in the seven years I've worked at Rosecourt, the rudeness I've witnessed is getting worse. Guests think nothing of disrespecting the house. I've caught women stealing candlesticks from our mantels because they want a "souvenir," men peeing off the verandah because the restroom is "too far away." And don't get me started about the cigarette butts we have to dig out of the grass at night's end, when there are ash cans liberally spaced around the grounds. Though I can't cast too many stones there; I used to have the habit. Nothing like a reformed sinner to spot another's faults.

But what really perturbs me is the way the guests treat our staff. The men think our hostesses are there to be hit on. Some people have no qualms about denigrating our work. "My, what a boring job you have!" they'll exclaim as they pass one of us on duty at the end of the hall. Of course, they don't dare say it to me—that would be racism—and along with my size, I can deliver a pretty intimidating look.

But take that encounter between Anne and Mrs. Hollingsworth, threatening to have her fired. That won't happen; Anne is pure gold, and the owners of Rosecourt know it. I'll also grant, Mrs. Hollingsworth, that you didn't know—none of us did, really—that Anne has a personal problem tonight. Yet you did your best to make her feel bad just because dinner may be a few minutes late. Does that make you feel good? If so, shame on you.

Listen up, people.

Every single person waiting on you tonight—be it a butler, hostess, parker, or wait staff—every one has a story. They're single mothers, college students studying pre-med, forensic science, and graphic arts, a freelance writer, a school nurse, a police force candidate waiting for a spot to open up, a landscape worker, actors from our local dinner theater, a retired firefighter, a kindergarten teacher on summer break. I'm a thirty-eight-year-old sinner, married with a wife and son, a substance abuse counselor by day and head butler at Rosecourt several nights a week. And I am a minister, though not in the way you think.

You see, in my church everyone is expected to "minister," to look after every other member of our flock. On Sundays we take stock of people's needs, and if there are elderly folk who can't afford to get their roof fixed or kids having trouble in school, volunteers will step up to the plate. We're a small congregation, so there's none of this looking around, waiting to see who else will raise their hand first. *You've* got to do it, or it doesn't get done. We're also expected to study our Bible and live by its teachings. If you have something compelling to say, some lesson to share, you don't need a degree in divinity. You just let the reverend know, and he'll invite you to the pulpit to speak.

"Hallelujah, brothers and sisters, I've got words dancing on my tongue!"

"Amen! You tell us, Brother Leon! You tell us your mind!"

I'm no great evangelist, though sometimes I do get carried away. My boy, he's four, will ask my wife as we drive to church, "Is Daddy going to boom today?"

"I don't know," she says, winking and rummaging in her purse. "Let me see if I have any cotton balls to stuff in our ears."

Here at Rosecourt and the counseling center, I try to keep the minister stuff under my hat; no one likes to be preached at or feel they're being judged. Then when it does come up, they can take it in stride. "It's okay, he's cool," the staff here will inform any new hires. Or they tease, "You better stay on Leon's good side. He's got pull with the Big Guy." Sometimes they'll ask my advice on a private matter. "What would you do, Leon?" I give them an honest answer and make it clear I'm speaking for myself alone. I've also got a repertoire of religious jokes to help ease any doubts. Did you hear about the minister who was running short of paint, so he thinned what he had to cover the outside of the church. When it washed off the next day in a rainstorm, the Lord thundered from on high, "Repaint, and thin no more!" If you can't laugh at yourself, you've no right to laugh at anyone else, and I'm not about to give up all the humor my fellow human beings provide.

And despite my observations on rude guests, I do enjoy my job. So do my wife and son. There's almost always something to take home at the end of a function, leftover desserts for our next meal or a table centerpiece for my wife—she gets the best flowers in town. I have a good life and good friends, which was not always the case. Well, I did have friends, but they were bad ones. They said, "C'mon, no one'll miss it," or "Here, try this stuff, man." It wasn't church or my wife or anyone else that showed me the light; it happened before either of them came along. I just got to looking around at what I was doing, and I thought, *Where's the respect in this, man? I don't see anyone lining up to shake your hand.* Then I started replacing every one of my *bad* friends with a *good* friend, and I strove to become one in return.

Our second pass through the guests is complete, and some people still linger. If Deirdre Hollingsworth's name didn't scare them, it's time to bring out the big guns. I beckon my fellow staffers and give the word. They grin.

"Ladies and gentlemen, the minister is waiting for you in the ballroom to give the blessing . . ."

Uh-oh, you're in trouble now. I hold in a chuckle at the hurried move toward the house. No matter what their beliefs or lack thereof, people aren't quite rude enough yet to keep a reverend twiddling his thumbs. I don't hesitate to play my own minister card, if that's what it takes to get people to do the right thing. I also humbly thank others when they point out to me the continuing errors of my ways. No man's soul is ever completely out of the woods.

"Okay, nice work, we got everyone inside." I wave my arms to draw the staff toward me on the verandah. "Listen, I've been thinking about something that I want you all in on, and I've only got a minute to explain."

They huddle in, waiting. It's funny, I didn't know I was thinking what I'm about to say. It must have been one of those subconscious currents that suddenly pops to the surface as if it had been there all along.

"Anne got her divorce papers this morning," I say, and there's an automatic eruption.

"Oh no, that's awful!"

"How could anyone divorce Anne?"

"That's why she looks so sad when she thinks no one is watching."

"Listen, listen!" I pat the air for silence. "Anne didn't forbid me to tell you, but this is still in strict confidence, understand? You know already it's a VHM crowd, and now Deirdre Hollingsworth has vented on her." I fill them in—more consternation—and I hush them again. "To get through tonight, Anne is going to need a little help from her friends. What can we do to make it easier for her? Any suggestions?"

"We could gag Deirdre Hollingsworth."

"We could get Anne a card. I could make it to the drugstore on our dinner break if someone covers for me."

"We could send her home early while we clean up."

"She'll never leave early. She always stays to the end, that's her job."

Suggestions pile up—I'm not sure myself what the answer is—then the accumulation of ideas takes shape in my mind.

"Okay, I've got it," I say, and they stop talking. "Two things. First, we're all going to give exemplary service tonight. No matter how badly these people behave, we are going to be completely gracious and charming. We're not going to give them a single reason to complain. Even if they insult you outright, I want you to turn the other cheek. Agreed?"

They nod, a few reluctantly. Of course, we should behave like that all the time, but when guests are surly it's hard not to do unto them in the same vein. The actors are particularly clever; when a guest haughtily remarks on the boring nature of our jobs, they'll burst into tears and say, "Oh no, and I just found out I have cancer, too!" Other subtle ways of taking revenge include cheerfully giving the nasty person the wrong directions out of town at evening's end. I confess I did it once myself—I am still a sinner, Lord!—but I'm satisfied from the nods there'll be none of that tonight.

"Second," I point around the circle, "each of us is going to do one nice personal thing for Anne before the evening is over. We've already got some good ideas, a kind word, hold the door, offer to get her a cup of coffee on her break. Not a card, I'm afraid—that would let on we know. Run an errand for her, save her some of the flowers. Just come up with something you can slip in naturally."

There's a strong murmur of assent, and we head into the house. Most of us don't see each other outside Rosecourt; between our other jobs and our families, our paths rarely cross. But I consider them friends, good friends, and together we're going to give Anne all the help she needs. And I feel better too, dignified, unflappable, unriled.

Now, let's just see if I can shimmer into the ballroom . . .

21

SIBERIA

Isabel

"LADIES AND GENTLEMEN, appearing together for the first time as husband and wife, please put your hands together in a warm welcome for Mr. and Mrs. Mead Morelli . . ."

Oh, this is too much! Exiled to Siberia in the far corner of the ballroom, pestered by those horrible butlers and hostesses to come in and take our seats. I told them twice I wasn't ready to go inside, and they practically yelled at me. Please, please, I don't want to sit here with Madge Dombrowski and Mead's dotty great-aunts and whatever other losers Deirdre has assembled to torment me.

"Well, I don't know about you, Isabel," says Madge, flapping her napkin onto her lap, "but I am ready to chow down. Lordy, isn't this ballroom a real whoop-de-doo, and we lucky folks here at Table 7 can see the whole shebang without craning our necks. You know, Isabel, I can't tell you how nice you look in that chiffony blue dress. When I was trying to decide what I should wear for the wedding, I said to my Arnold, 'Arnold, what do you think about me getting a fancy new dress like a lemon meringue color or maybe shell pink?' and he said, 'Madge, what are you gonna do if they serve spaghetti at the wedding and you spill sauce on yourself?' So I could see at once my Arnold was right, and when I looked in the closet and found my tried-and-true orange paisley I just thought, Madge, look no further if you want to be chick! Besides, what could go better with Arnold's checkered brown suit?"

I'm not listening, I'm not listening, I'm not listening. She said "chick" for "chic"! And my dress is not chiffony blue. It's Wedgwood silk organza, size four, and I paid a great deal of money for it!

"Stanley," says Madge, "tell Isabel and John about your field trip to the potato chip factory."

No, no, don't tell me. I don't want to hear about potato chips. This must be John's fault, how could he not get our table switched? I send him to do a simple job, and he comes back half an hour later with no drink for me and excuses about Deirdre's list. Well, you can bet I'm not sitting at this table one minute longer than I have to. I'll fake a fainting scene, tell them I'm too hot here in the corner, anything to escape.

"Oil. They had hot oil. And lots of salt."

I'm not listening! Let John talk to Stanley, who appears to be about sixteen years old and has a face full of acne, glasses, and crooked teeth, and enough learning disabilities to fill a textbook. The father Arnold is a skinny little man with a toothy grin, and I'll bet Madge buries him under that mountain of flesh of hers when they—oh, it's too repulsive even to contemplate! I must get another vodka and tonic or I won't have the strength to survive this.

"Maybe you could sing the potato chip jingle, Stanley," says Madge. "We are a singing family, you know. Wait a minute—Aunt Iris, did Aunt Edna get her hearing aid fixed yet? I wouldn't want her to miss this."

Please, let us all miss this. Let us all go deaf right now. One of the great-aunts begins tapping the other's ear. They wear Sunday church dresses and little flowered hats with netting, and they blink like birds behind their rhinestone eyeglasses.

"I don't think so," says Aunt Iris. "Edna, can you hear us?"

"Eh?"

"Edna, twiddle your hearing aid! No, dear, the other way, up, up Try talking to her again, Madge."

"Oh, don't you worry, Aunt Edna," says Madge, "because *I'll just shout!* I was saying that *our son Stanley* is going to sing the *potato chip jingle!*"

"Actually," says Stanley, "it's more of a yodel."

No! What could I have done to Deirdre to deserve this? It's true I canceled out of her luncheon for the ballet guild last month, but I had a Botox injection, and she wouldn't expect me to miss that. And there was that little incident where I let it slip that DeeDee Falherne had sworn me to secrecy that she'd heard Gordon and Kimmy were at a brunch at the Morestones. This would naturally make Deirdre furious because the Morestones are supposed to be *her* friends and this could only mean they're playing both sides over the divorce. But that's no reason Deirdre should take out their two-facedness on me. I'm innocent! I can only imagine this is some diabolical nastiness on her part, some imagined slight for which she wants revenge. She's exactly the type to take a minor criticism and blow it up. You can't even mention in a friendly way that her crow's-feet need a touchup without her taking offense.

Stanley begins yodeling. "Boil-oil-oil in oil-oil-oil."

Dear God, kill me now! John just sits here with a smile on his face, pretending to listen while his eyes rove over the waitresses. Three of the seats at our table are still empty, although I thought Madge said one of them belonged to a single man from Toledo. Could it be he's a handsome out-of-town relative in the same predicament as I am? I glance hopefully toward the ballroom doors just as a lurking figure in a slime green suit enters. No, no, don't let him come this way!

"Why, lordy, here's just what we need," burbles Madge, "a debonair gentleman to balance our table! Isabel, this is our bachelor gent from Toledo I was telling you about. Isn't he a catch! Why, I imagine there are any number of attractive ladies here tonight who would swoon over him."

Be my guest! Take him away. No, please, no, don't let him sit next to me. Now I really do feel faint. He's not even quite human. Dressed in a seedy suit the color of pond scum, hair plastered across a bald pate, his fingernails overlong and yellowed, he slinks lizardlike into his seat. Bad breath—oh no, he has bad breath.

"Have you drunk the water?" he asks, his beady eyes boring into me.

"I beg your pardon?"

"The water. Don't drink it."

"All right, I won't." I try to turn away, signaling the conversation is at a close, but he leans forward into my space.

"Because it's cloudy. That means they put chemicals in it. Chemicals give you cancer."

"I'm sure Deirdre ordered bottled water," I say a little huffily to put him in his place. It's not my intention to defend Deirdre after the way she's treated me, but the glasses of ice water on our table look perfectly crisp and clear.

"No, it's tap water. I waited at the end of the hall until the kitchen door swung open, and I saw them filling the glasses right from the faucet. You know where it used to be safe to drink the water?"

How did this man get here? To whom is he related? He looks like someone who salivates over child pornography on the Internet.

"Milwaukee." His tongue flicks in and out, wetting his lower lip. "You used to be able to drink the water in Milwaukee."

Help! Somebody save me! I look across the table to Madge, who's shouting something about panty hose at the deaf aunt. John is giving distracted attention to Arnold and Stanley while eyeing the Hispanic waitress laying salads around our table. Maybe this *is* John's fault. Maybe *he* said or did something to offend Deirdre. He probably doesn't even know he's done it, men are so insensitive! Two of the ten chairs at our table are still empty, and now I pray they'll stay that way. Maybe I can beguile a couple of our friends to join us to give the appearance we're not totally out of favor. But every time I catch their eyes across the room, they immediately lower their gaze or turn their head as if they haven't seen me.

"But then they started putting fluoride in the water everywhere, and you know who did that?" says Lizard Man. "The Communists."

"Really?"

"It was a plot."

"Really?"

"A plot by Khrushchev to give us cancer."

Save me! I jam my spike heel into John's shin under the table.

"Ouch! What the—?"

I smile sweetly, menacingly, at him.

"Oh, a refill on your drink, Isabel?"

"Thank you, John."

That'll teach him to ogle the waitress and leave me stuck in this mess. That'll teach him to be so incompetent at switching our table. What on earth could he have done to alienate Deirdre? The transgression must have been monumental, it must have pierced her to the core. Oh my God, do you suppose . . .? No, it can't be, I was only acting in her best interest, and she never said a word to me at the time. Though if she were going to say anything, it should have been thank you, especially after the clever way I staged it, inviting her to lunch at that Indian restaurant where she could see for herself. Why, I'm the one who enabled her to save face when less true-blue friends were whispering behind her back. If she's secretly been holding it against me all this time and waiting to pay me back when she knew it would hurt the worst . . .

The nerve of her! This is the most vindictive thing I've ever heard. Well, I'll be damned if I'll let Deirdre get the better of me. I'll hold up my head and carry this off as if I'm having the most fascinating evening of anyone here. I'll turn this table of misfits into scintillating, stimulating bon vivants. We'll eat, drink, and make merry till the cows come home. With my most dazzling smile I lean confidentially toward Lizard Man, whose tongue is going *flick, flick, flick.*

"Tell me," I purr. "What else do you know of this conspiracy about the water?"

22

THE WAY TO A MAN'S HEART

Donna Dombrowski Morelli

So THIS IS THE FINAL MENU, sitting on its own little easel stand. Let me get my glasses on so I can read this fancy script.

First Course

ANJOU PEAR POACHED IN PORT AND SPICES
SERVED ON A BED OF BABY FIELD GREENS
DRESSED IN AN AGED BALSAMIC VINAIGRETTE
AND GARNISHED WITH CRUMBLED BLEU CHEESE AND
TOASTED WALNUTS

Four lines to describe a fruit salad? And not just any Field Greens, mind you, but *Baby* Field Greens, *Aged* Balsamic Vinaigrette, *Crumbled* Blue Cheese, and *Toasted* Walnuts.

Bite your tongue, Donna. Read on:

Entrée

SLICED FILET OF BEEF TENDERLOIN
NAPPED WITH WORCESTERSHIRE GLAZE AND

GRILLED SWORDFISH PRESENTED WITH
FRESH MANGO SALSA
SWEET AND WHITE POTATOES ANNA
BUNDLES OF FRESH GARDEN ASPARAGUS TIED
WITH A LEEK RIBBON

Does the swordfish know it's being *presented*?

Dessert Buffet
MINIATURE ÉCLAIRS AND CREAM PUFFS
SUMMER BERRIES WITH CHANTILLY CREAM
LEMON MERINGUE TART
HAZELNUT MOUSSE CAKE
PETITS FOURS À LA PARISIENNE
WEDDING CAKE WITH BITTERSWEET CHOCOLATE-DIPPED
STRAWBERRIES

Sigh. I never was meant to be a size four or six or eight.

Beverages & Libations
MONTE VISTA CHARDONNAY PRIVATE RESERVE
(NAPA VALLEY) 2001
CHÂTEAU LEDUC BORDEAUX SUPÉRIEUR (FRANCE) 2000
GOURMET COFFEES, TEAS, AND AFTER-DINNER CORDIALS

Joey shoulders against me. "Good grub," he whispers
in my ear, and the two of us giggle. I squeeze his fingers
under the table, and we hold hands a moment longer, the
warmth between our palms comforting and familiar as a
small, steady fire. Then I replace the menu card on its
stand before the centerpiece and candles. I can't recall

ever seeing the menu displayed at a wedding before—and Joey and I have been to some pretty expensive affairs over the years—but I suppose when you've gone to as much trouble as Deirdre has, you want everyone to know it. I volunteered to help, of course, but after she declined my first few offers, I got the message.

Now it's done, our children are married, and the waiters are scurrying to pour the wine and lay the salads—pardon me, the Baby Field Greens—before us. In the old days at a wedding, you always had a head table for the bride and groom and their attendants, but in those days we never had seven bridesmaids and seven groomsmen either. So instead of an overly long banquet table, Mead and Allison have a pretty candlelit table for two in the place of honor before the fireplace.

The rest of us are at tables of ten, the family and attendants close by, the other guests in a semi-circle around the ballroom dance floor. It's a nice arrangement, less stiff and formal; you can see it puts people at ease. Deirdre allotted us one hundred and twenty-five seats, half the total, which is fair, and an additional twenty "courtesy" invitations, which Joey and I declined. Why would you invite someone if you didn't really want them to attend? Instead, we quickly filled our side with brothers, sisters, aunts, uncles, and cousins to the fourth degree. I wish our parents could have been here, but Joey's mother and my parents have all passed away within the last ten years.

"It's good Aunt Iris and Aunt Edna could be here as the oldest members of the family," says Joey, his thoughts traveling the same path as mine. I no longer question this phenomenon; Mead and Fredericka tease that we're starting to resemble each other as well.

"Yes, although I see Deirdre's banished them to the Siberia table in the far corner, along with Madge and Arnold." I allow myself a small frown.

"That's all right," says Joey. "Cousin Madge has a knack for spreading hospitality wherever she goes, and from the way she's slapping that woman in the blue dress on the back, they'll be old friends before we get to the Sliced Filet of Beef Tenderloin."

"Napped with Worcestershire Glaze," I add. "But who is that rather peculiar-looking man in the green suit?"

"I don't know." Joey shrugs. "Must be a 'courtesy' invite of Deirdre's or Gordon's."

The minister rises and speaks a blessing, then we fork into our salads. It is tasty, though something about the flavoring seems a little off. I wonder what spices they used to poach the pear? Never mind. Fredericka is at our table, and here I must say Mead has shown some startling good sense. He's paired her for the evening with his friend Blaine, whom Joey and I are delighted to see after so many years. I remember when Mead brought him home from college.

"Mom, Pop," he called, clapping his arm around a slender, bespectacled young man, "guess who this is! It's Blaine, the guy I got the lifesaving medal for that summer at camp. He's at the college next to mine. I want him to meet Freddie. Is she here?"

But Fredericka was either away at a debate meet or on a summer internship or pursuing her own college schedule the few times Blaine visited, a pity because, from his conversation at our dinner table, here was a boy who might be her intellectual match. Thoughtful, a careful listener—he never barged in with an opinion, although he didn't hesitate to politely disagree after you'd stated yours. His passion was medieval literature; his fair skin pinked on the cheekbones when he recited a passage from *Sir Gawain and the Green Knight*. Yet he also seemed a trifle lonely, a dreamer, an only child whose parents had divorced. From the quick way he brushed past the topic, you could tell he'd been hurt. Now here he is, lean, blond, his scholarly face offset by a flashing smile—it's amazing what a late growth spurt can do. Most important, still single, and if the intense private conversation he and Fredericka are having is any measure . . . does a mother dare hope? I nudge Joey with my knee under the table, and catching my glance, he signals back with a downward nod to the crossed fingers in his lap.

But as my gaze wanders to Allison and Mead, my heart falls. It pains me to say it, but I don't think this marriage will last. Maybe it's not supposed to—isn't serial matrimony more the rule nowadays?—whereas I'm sorely old-fashioned, indoctrinated in my impressionable years to believe divorce was a mortal sin that could cast you from God's grace forever. Naturally, I'm glad that's over, and there are many modern changes to marriage I approve, like husbands sharing the household chores and fathers taking a more active role in child raising. Lord knows I could have used more help from Joey when our kids were small. But then his own father didn't set a stellar example, did he? And when Joey tried to babysit, he didn't understand that children are children, not miniature adults, and you have to exercise constant vigilance to keep them from harm. I remember when Mead was three and Joey bounced him on his knee as they cheered the Yankees on TV.

"You should buy Mead a little bat and ball so you can play in the park," I said, nursing a squalling Fredericka and needing some peace and quiet. I never dreamed it should be necessary to specify the bat and ball be made of foam— didn't that go without saying? But no, an hour later, they returned from the toy store with a solid wood, albeit junior-sized, bat and a stitched leather ball.

"You can't give him that bat!" I said, wondering if men ever use their brains.

"Why not?" Joey looked surprised.

"Because it's solid wood, and he'll swing it around and whap himself in the head."

"No, he won't."

"Yes, he will."

"Aw, you worry too much, Donna. It's okay. He's not going to swing it nearly that hard. I'll watch him."

"You'll watch him hit himself in the head."

"No, I'll stand right beside him. I'll grab the bat in time."

So I threw up my hands, and they went to the park, and fifteen minutes later what do you think?

"He swung the bat around and hit himself in the head," Joey mumbled sheepishly while Mead wailed in his arms. "There's no blood, Donna. Jeez, how was I to know a kid could do that?"

It was the same with the root beer and chocolate.

"You can't give Mead that much chocolate, Joey. It makes him sick."

"Aw, Donna, it's only a candy bar."

"It's a huge candy bar. And you can't let him wash it down with root beer. He'll get a stomachache."

"No, he won't. He's got an iron stomach, just like his old man."

So I threw up my hands, and Mead gulped the candy and soda, and half an hour later, what do you think?

"It must have been all the wrestling we did after he ate," Joey pleaded, contrite, as we bowed Mead's head over the toilet. "Jeez, Donna, I didn't know a kid could puke this much!"

Gradually, Joey did become a good father, no, a great father, and I pray Mead will get the same chance. It won't be easy, because his and Allison's children, my grandchildren—please, God, let me have some!—will have a round-the-clock nanny. Allison's not going to be bothered with diapers and nursing and spit-up down her back. It reminds me of Deirdre's "courtesy" invitations—why would you invite children into your life if you don't really want them there? And why get married if it's not to love and cherish the other person until death do you part?

I guess what I'm getting at is that Allison has no real interest in making Mead happy. When she buys him a silk shirt or Armani tie, it's not to please him but to satisfy her vision of how he should dress. She expects his attendance at her art gallery functions, but never joins him on the sofa to watch football and share a pizza in return. Far more important, she has never once asked me about Mead when he was growing up, about his favorite meals or his boyhood friends or how our family celebrated birthdays and holidays. You can say I'm feeling left out, and it's partly true, but before I married Joey, I spent hours in his mother's kitchen, learning to cook the tortellini and the ravioli and the eggplant parmigiana just the way he liked it. Mrs. Morelli showed me, too, the brand of socks he preferred, Fruit of the Loom, and how he arranged his underwear drawer, shirts right, white jockey shorts left, and how he kept his boot polish, black and burnt brown, in a zippered case along with a polishing cloth and buffing brush.

"You're a smart girl, Donna," Mrs. Morelli would say to me as we rolled floury dough into breadsticks and a vintage Caruso recording warbled from the radio. "Not as pretty as some, but smart, and you're gonna make something of my Joey. So I'll tell you some other things you should know."

Then she explained how Joey was afraid of spiders when he was little and they still gave him the shivers if one dropped on him unawares. She told me how he refused to cry when his father skipped out because he was going to be the man of the house from then on. She showed me his elementary school report cards filled with A's, and she cursed the boys he'd fallen in with in junior high and their disrespect for school.

"Another thing, when he gets older, Joey's going to get hairy," Mrs Morelli warned as she held out a ladle for me to sample the marinara and we decided to add more oregano. "He can't help it. All Italian men do. Hair on his back, his ears, his nose. Don't let it bother you. Make him shave it. You're going to get plump anyway, all Polish women do, unless you starve yourself, which I don't advise." Mrs. Morelli could go on for hours, interjecting, "Try this, what do you think, too much garlic?" and shoving bits of food at me to taste and pass judgment on.

We were allies, you see, because you didn't marry just a man or a woman then, you married into a family. Now families are so fractured, so far flung, maybe it's outdated of me to think Allison should care what our traditions are. But we cared about making each other happy, Joey and I, and there were lots of little things he'd do, like rubbing my tired feet when I came home from a long day serving customers at the handbag counter at Bloomingdale's. Maybe people don't have time to make each other happy anymore. Maybe they only have time to think about themselves.

Well, as Mrs. Morelli predicted, Joey did get hairy, and I did get plump, and I did make something of her boy. When he opened his own construction company, I was his office manager, keeping the books and answering the phone. When he negotiated his first big deal and moved his office into Manhattan, I quit working to be home with the kids after school. It wasn't long afterward that our income took some big leaps up, and though Joey side-stepped my questions, I'm no fool. I made a pact with God: I'll be in the front pew every Sunday and the children's wing of our local hospital will never lack what our money can buy, if you'll forgive or at least overlook whatever Joey is doing with the accounts. Well, God is a busy man and he probably figures that if you take a little here and give back a little there, it all balances with no need to scrutinize the ledgers. At any rate, we've never been audited.

"That pickled pear on spinach was pretty good," says Joey, dabbing his napkin to his mouth. "What's our next course, mango tango swordfish or something like that?"

"Swordfish with mango salsa."

"Right, it's you and me who are gonna cut up the floor with the tango tonight."

I smile. It's true that one way to a man's heart is through his stomach, but it's not the only route. The real path to Joey's heart was through his mother. And if you glance across our table at Fredericka and Blaine right now, you'll see it's not their stomachs or their eyes or their libidos they want to feast. It's their brains that are falling in love. The way to Mead's heart would be through a good laugh, but Allison isn't interested in knowing that.

I swallow the last bite of my salad and press my tongue to the roof of my mouth. Ah, that's it—the dressing's a little flat. Not that I know better than the fancy chef in the kitchen, but if it were up to me, I'd add a squirt of lime.

 23

A MEETING OF THE MINDS

Blaine

How DO YOU GET A WOMAN to fall in love with you in just one night? Or to be more precise, in a mere six hours, more than two of which have already elapsed? Having her pitch into your arms as she falls headfirst down the grand staircase of a nineteenth-century mansion is a fortuitous start. Having her entrust you with a special mission on behalf of her imperiled brother boosts your chances another notch. But while earning a woman's trust and gratitude may engender kind feelings toward you, it's not the same as love. What would a knight in shining armor do to win a lady's heart?

"Did you find out anything about Mead's activities last night?" Fredericka asks me, her voice low, though the others at our table, her parents and various relatives, are too busy talking to notice.

"Yes and no," I reply. "I talked to three of the grooms-men, casually, as you requested, and got the usual tale of bars and nightclubs and attempts to pick up women."

"Men behaving like boys, in other words."

"I'm afraid so."

"Did they pick up any women?"

"No. They didn't want to ruin their chances with the bridesmaids."

"What about a stripper?"

"They all denied hiring one."

"Naturally."

A server rounds our table, filling wine glasses, and for a minute we shelve our topic lest anyone overhear. I want to ask Fredericka what her favorite childhood stories were. I have a theory, completely unscientific, completely unproven, that the type of books a person loves as a child will be an accurate indicator of their adult personality. For example, a youngster who begs nightly for *Winnie the Pooh* or *The Wind in the Willows* will grow up to have a gentle sense of humor and a soft spot for animals. A boy or girl whose bookshelf is filled with *Treasure Island* or *Little House on the Prairie* may someday fulfill their adventurous streak by climbing Mount Everest or conquering Wall Street. A child who delights in the crueler aspects of the Brothers Grimm will relish dissecting frogs in high school biology and could end up as a mortician or pathologist—or in jail. It's a totally facile theory, I agree, and kids may explore and discard half a dozen genres in search of who their grownup selves might be. Yet I still think that childhood reading yields an invaluable clue.

My own favorite was a 1930s juvenile version of King Arthur that happened to be in my parents' extensive library before they divorced, not a picture book but a worn red volume with a heavily inked black-and-white illustration prefacing each story. I remember the artwork vividly—a handsome young Arthur standing awestruck before the diaphanous Lady of the Lake, Sir Perceval on bended knee before a floating vision of the Holy Grail, Guinevere leaning over the wall of her father's castle to see the knights riding past, a rose in one hand, her long black hair braided and bound. I dreamed of the chivalrous deeds that I, Sir Blaine, would do to right the kingdom's wrongs. Now I reside in a realm of academia where, gathering students around a seminar table, we analyze and explicate *Le Morte D'Arthur, Sir Orfeo,* and *Tristan and Isolt.* But to this day, I wish I knew what became of that worn red book.

"About the stripper," I resume to Fredericka, the server having passed out of earshot, "I think the groomsmen are telling the truth. I phrased the question as if I were sorry to have missed the revelries and implored them to fill me in. Given that sort of invitation, most guys would be anxious to boast."

"True. Smart tactic."

Her eyebrows raise appreciatively, and I acknowledge it with a modest nod.

"However," I continue, "they did consume quite a lot of alcohol, and they were bummed, to use Steve's words, when the bars closed at one a.m. Apparently, Newport's not an all-night town."

"So then they came back to the hotel?"

"Yes, and had several six-packs of beer waiting in Mead's room. After another spell of camaraderie, they claim to have left him stretched out on the bed in a semiconscious state in his underwear, having thoughtfully removed his clothes and shoes to make him more comfortable."

"Then that ought to be the end of the story. But why would the Beauty Queens say . . ."

Fredericka's forehead creases, and she chews her nails, or rather she chews the long plastic daggers affixed to the ends of her fingers. She seems oblivious she's doing it, and I want to rescue her hand from her teeth before it gets gnawed. Or maybe I just want to capture and hold her hand, to feel a tactile pleasure at the contact, as I did when she tumbled into my arms. *Catch her!* was my immediate thought, and within seconds she was righted and on her feet. Yet in the aftermath of that brief intimacy, my senses registered the feel of her body, and what I felt was a girl so light she might, like a bird, have hollow bones.

"Is there any chance," she looks up at me, "that Mead woke up after the guys left, wandered down to the hotel bar, and met someone there?"

I shake my head. "I doubt it. It doesn't sound like he was in any condition to stand upright. Also . . ." This time I do take her hand, partly to stop her gnawing, partly to secure her attention for what I want to say. "Also, Fredericka, I don't think Mead would do that, even if he was so drunk he could barely remember his own name. Mead loves a good time, he loves to party, and maybe that's a prelude to trouble. But I don't believe he would deliberately go out looking for a sexual encounter on the night before his wedding. He's too loyal, he would never hurt someone he loves, and despite the lighthearted image, he takes this marriage seriously. He wouldn't betray Allison."

The clearing look that crosses Fredericka's face makes my hopes rise. Until now, she's been focused on Mead, and

I've been merely a useful source of information. But with my avowal of faith in her brother—and it is genuine—it's as if she's able to see me for the first time. She searches my eyes, and a smile dawns on her lips.

"You're right," she says. "That's true. Mead wouldn't do that. He would never knowingly hurt anyone. I must have misinterpreted what the bridesmaids were saying." She squeezes my hand—I am still holding her hand, by the way. "Thank you, Blaine."

"Blaine," calls Mrs. Morelli from across the table, "if you're going to sit beside Fredericka, it's your responsibility to make sure she remembers to eat." She nods meaningfully and indulgently at our untouched salads.

"Yes, Mrs. Morelli," I laugh. "I'll take care of it."

I nudge Fredericka's fork into her hand, and with a sheepish grin she takes a bite. A woman who doesn't pay much attention to what she eats probably isn't much of a cook either, and since I can barely scramble eggs, I picture our apartment littered with Chinese takeout boxes. That's a pretty fast leap forward, I know, but I like that picture, the two of us castled in a book-lined den, working late into the night, me poring over an obscure Middle English text, Fredericka jousting with some government policy in a write-up for her latest cause. Perhaps it's her very intensity I'm enamored of, her fervor to plunge into the world of politics and harsh realities and fight battles on behalf of the poor and oppressed. Maybe Fredericka is the knight in shining armor with a courage I don't possess. What, then, can I offer her? To be her haven when she retreats, bruised and weary, from the combat? But does she require a haven? Does she need me or anyone else at all?

"It's nice you could get away from DC for the wedding," I venture. "Do you like living there?" Not exactly scintillating conversation, but the only place I can think of to start.

"The traffic's a pain commuting from my apartment in Alexandria, but that's DC and there's not much you can do about it. Some nights I just crash on the couch in my office."

"You work too hard."

"Yes, I probably do."

"And you were famished. Didn't you eat lunch?"

I nod at her empty salad plate, amused that in mere minutes she's wolfed her food, and she winces, embarrassed.

"Yes, no, I don't remember. Sorry, I've been a little distracted all day."

"That's okay." I don't add that at least it's kept her from noticing the inanity of my comments. I feel like a fifteen-year-old on a first date. "What is it that's distracting you?"

"Well, I was trying to help this chambermaid at the hotel, but it's more than that. It's . . . the foreignness of all this." She tips her head at the scene around us. "Have you ever been married?"

The directness of the question startles me, yet it's clear the answer itself doesn't matter. Instead there seems to be some core knowledge she's after, some underlying truth she needs to extract.

"No, I was almost engaged once, but it didn't work out."

"I'm sorry." She hesitates, then asks more softly, "Why not?"

"We weren't meant for each other. It was the wrong time in our careers and our lives. I wish I knew really . . ."

I shrug. It would be nice to have a compact answer to those endings, even when you don't regret the final outcome.

"Then do you really believe," Fredericka persists, "that there is one 'right someone' you're meant to fall in love with?"

Yes, you! I long to reply. But the words aren't quite ready to be heard and what comes out instead is, "With over six billion people on the planet, I'd say the odds are good that for any given individual there's at least one other person who would be an ideal match."

Dumb! But Fredericka muses over the answer nonetheless. She seems to be wavering between some private concern she needs to resolve and a flickering interest in me personally, and I'd like to tip the scales in my favor.

"What about you?" I ask. "Have you never been in love?"

Dumb again! Have you *ever* been in love, is what I intended to say, but in my eagerness to bring the conversation to a more intimate level, I've made it sound like a challenge. Yet once again Fredericka doesn't take it amiss.

"I don't know," she replies. "I've had relationships, but were any of them true love? They didn't last, so I guess not. I'm probably too much in love with my work."

"Which everyone tells me you're brilliant at."

"Hmm." She brushes off the compliment with a frown, and I take it as a warning not to sidetrack her. "But maybe I don't know when to stop. The thing is, I like being on the edge, I don't want the zeal to wear off, and maybe I'm afraid that if I look around and see people leading entirely different lives with entirely different priorities, I might weaken and doubt myself."

"And that's what's happening tonight," I supply, as she glances from table to table, studying the occupants in sequence, reading their lives.

"Yes. I agreed to be a bridesmaid originally because Mead asked me and then because I needed to understand why women—and men, too—put themselves through this . . . this hoopla." She shakes her head, her voice registering equal measures of curiosity and disdain. "Yet look at me . . ." Her hand fans downward, the fake nails trailing from her hairdo to the billowing skirt of her red dress. "The truth is, I'm confused."

"You're supposed to be confused, Fredericka."

"I am? Why?"

Her eyes meet mine. They're blue as the summer sea, and genetics being what they are, it crosses my mind with fleeting pleasure that we'll have blue-eyed children. But that's the last comment Fredericka wants to hear from me now. She's just confessed to being unsure of herself, an emotion I doubt she's ever felt before in her life, and though it may be only coincidence that I'm the one she's chosen as her sounding board, this is no time to blow it.

"Because that's what weddings are for—to make you stop and take stock, to ask yourself if you're really happy or if you're missing out on something vital in life. Look around and I bet a lot of people here are questioning their lives tonight. Is this really the path they're meant to be on? What happened to the dreams they believed could come true? Then they're following it up with some kind of vow, to strengthen their marriage or pursue a long-lost love, to quit their awful job and go paint in Tahiti. You'd think we could do that any time, but maybe we need someone else's example to embolden us. And a wedding does that, it makes us believe we can ride out, sword in hand, to win love and glory; it renews our hearts for the quest. Because what could be braver than two people pledging before the world that they'll be faithful to each other unto death?"

I catch myself short. Fredericka's lips are curving upward.

"You're a romantic," she says.

I blush, she laughs, then we glance aside, glance back, and laugh together. We've finally connected, now neither of us knows what to say next. She moves her hands in a small lifting motion, as if coaxing words to emerge between us. I open my mouth, but nothing comes out.

"Blaine, Fredericka!" Mrs. Morelli tsks at us from across the table. "The two of you will starve to death!"

We follow her pointing finger to the plates before us. Somehow the remnants of our salads have vanished and a tantalizing dinner has appeared. The server must have passed right in front of us and we were too engrossed to notice.

"Okay, Mom, we're eating," says Fredericka, and we pick up our forks in unison. "I have one more question for you, Blaine."

"Yes?"

"When you caught me, literally, at the bottom of the stairs, you said you'd been wanting to meet me since I was ten and you were twelve. Why?"

Maybe as a lawyer Fredericka's used to zinging questions at people and eliciting a straight reply. Maybe she was simply intent on resolving her concerns about Mead and her own role at the wedding before tackling the next item on her mental checklist. Either way, this is not a woman who will remain confused about her purpose for long. While I, caught off guard, utter the stupidest thing I've ever said in my life.

"Because I love you."

Fredericka gapes, but suddenly it feels right. I want to stand up and shout it to the ballroom. *I love you!* Sure, this is crazy, it will never work, she may not like Chinese food, she may not want children or marriage, we live half a continent apart. But it feels right. Since Fredericka has managed to get the first bite of swordfish halfway to her lips when my confession blurts out, there's nothing for me to do but gently guide the fork the rest of the way to her mouth.

"Chew before you swallow," I say, and still stunned, she obeys. When the food is down her throat, and it's safe to assume she won't choke, I try to explain. "I've had a long-distance crush on you since Mead first told me about you at summer camp, since he showed me your picture in college, and I kept hoping someday we'd meet. That's why I leaped at the chance to be in his wedding."

"Does Mead know any of this? Did he plan it?"

"Not in any strict sense. Allison probably gave him a list of her bridesmaids and told him to come up with an equal number of groomsmen. Mead probably gave it all of five minutes' thought."

She takes a moment to ponder this, then nods. Mead is no plotter. If two people he's introduced happen to hit it off, great. If not, better luck next time around. I nudge Fredericka's fork back toward her plate.

"Okay," she says, following my urging. "What do we do now?"

"We eat dinner, we dance, we stroll on the verandah in the moonlight. If by the end of the evening, you wish to continue the acquaintance, then we exchange phone numbers, email addresses, and so forth."

"I don't dance."

"Me either, but think of it as a public service. If we bump around stepping on each other's toes, we'll make everyone else on the dance floor look good."

She crinkles her nose and laughs, a peal like hand bells ringing in a choir loft, and I record the sound in my memory the way I did the feel of her body when she pitched into my arms.

"Fredericka, I have to know . . . what was your favorite book when you were a kid?"

"Machiavelli. I thought his discourse on the corruption of political systems—"

"No, no, I mean earlier, say before you were ten."

"That was before I was ten." She regards me, puzzled, and I carefully rephrase the question.

"Think even earlier, the bedtime stories your mother used to read to you."

"Oh, that would be Robin Hood. Why?"

I smile to myself. Steal from the rich, give to the poor. "Well, I know it's completely unscientific and unprovable, but I have this theory . . ."

We bend our heads together. Across the table, Mrs. Morelli is beaming.

24

A LIFE ON THE RUN

Hank

WE DID IT! WE GOT AWAY with bottled salad dressing. We pulled it off. Thank you, Paul Newman! Now get those entreés out there—run, run, run!

One server hustles out of the kitchen as another bursts in and slings her tray down at the dishwashing station in the pantry. Latex-gloved hands snatch off the salad plates, scrape the leftovers into an industrial-sized garbage bin, and dump the china and flatware into a sink full of suds. On the huge central table by the cast-iron stove, more gloved hands fling meat, fish, potatoes, veggies, and sauces onto an assembly line of dinner plates amid a constant stream of "ouch, ouch, ouch" as the hot food and heated plates burn sensitive fingertips. The incoming server hurries her cleared tray to receive the entreés, speaking breathlessly above the rattle and clatter and instructions flying across the kitchen.

"You're not going to believe what I heard in there," she begins, but already her tray is full, and I snap my fingers at her to remind her to keep moving. During the summer we hire a lot of college kids—they come and go in a blur before I can learn their names—and this one shoots me a disgruntled look as she hoists the tray onto her shoulder and bumps her way past another server and out the door. The pro waiters know better. You can't let up for a minute at an event like this, and whatever juicy tidbit they may overhear among the guests they'll simply pass to another server coming or going until the tantalizing fragments get back to everyone by the end of the evening.

"Okay, okay, keep it moving," I say unnecessarily, since everyone's already working as fast as they can. I'm still rattled over the salad dressing. How could we possibly have forgotten it? Dumb, dumb, dumb! Chef Laszlo is furious about the substitution, scowling and muttering viciously to himself as he yanks the beef tenderloin from the maw of the oven and slashes off a medium-rare slice for inspection. I am, quite frankly, afraid of Chef, who possesses a luxuriant black gypsy mustache and glittering eyes and wields a carving knife with the zest of a depraved swordsman. His mutterings sound like, ". . . idiots who cannot tell the difference . . . I would make a woman happy . . . a fraud of a movie star who thinks he can cook . . ." He stabs the beef with pleasure, his eyes glinting as the bloody juices spurt out. As I value my life, I would never tell Chef to run, run, run.

But I tell myself that every night. It's the nature of the catering business. People ask how it is I work around so much sumptuous food and never gain a pound. It's because I've been sprinting for the last thirty years, starting when I was a busboy at age fourteen. Restaurant work is how I paid my way through college, where I earned a degree in theater management—you want fries with that?—and I kept on in the industry until I had a wife and two kids, and it was too late. And maybe I like running, there's a charge to it, a zap of not just doing a job well but doing it at full velocity. Every night is an adrenalin rush, and you don't get to breathe until it's over. In its own way, putting on a catered dinner for two hundred and fifty people *is* theater management, creating a production of sight, smell, and sound that climaxes with the touch and taste of succulent food melting on the tongue.

"Excuse me." A nervous boy, another of the college kids, approaches. "One of the guests at my table says he's a vegetarian."

"Shit." Just what we need, some moral individual who won't eat meat but waits until you're about to set a hundred-fifty-dollar-a-plate steak and swordfish dinner before him to say so. "Chef, we have a vegetarian."

Chef Laszlo turns from the steaming pots of asparagus on the stove, face glowering. Given his build, you might imagine he'd once been a circus strongman; instead, he studied in Paris at Le Cordon Bleu. "You did not say we would have a vegetarian."

"No, we weren't given advance notice of any special diets. It's either an omelet or the spinach lasagna."

"Why does he think God put animals on the earth?" Chef roars. "To eat them, to eat them!"

"Yes, Chef, but—"

"He gets eggs!"

"Yes, Chef."

Eggs we have on hand; I've learned from past experience always to bring along several dozen. The pan of spinach lasagna is for our dinner, and we could cut a square and heat it in the oven. But Chef has made his decision. I motion to Rhonda, our fast-as-lightning sous chef, and shove a Styrofoam egg package into her hands. She squeezes among the kitchen staff to grab a bowl, whisk, and skillet.

". . . beat the little eggs," mutters Chef, ". . . ah, if I had a woman . . ."

Two more servers hustle in, exchanging gasps and giggles, but I'm too busy supervising the entrees going out the door to hear what they're saying. Rhonda waves a plate under my nose for inspection—a golden-brown omelet accompanied by two bundles of asparagus and the sweet and white potatoes—and I nod a grateful thank you. Since the bundles of asparagus are small, adding an extra one lends an impression of fullness to the makeshift meal, but Rhonda's real inspiration is the dash of mango salsa atop the omelet.

Garnish, garnish, garnish—it's one of the first lessons I learned in the restaurant business. I was helping to plate and serve green salads for a women's luncheon, and to each one was added a small fuchsia and white blossom. Almost like magic, the splash of vivid color and the delicate shape of the bloom transformed the ordinary mixed greens into something exotic. The effect on the customers was also instantaneous. "Oh, isn't that pretty?" "What kind of flower is it?" "It looks like one of those flowers on a Hawaiian lei!" the women exclaimed as we set the plates before them. When one of the servers informed them the blossoms were edible orchids, the news provoked another outpouring of admiration.

"Wow, it's amazing what a difference that little flower makes," I remarked when I returned to the kitchen.

"Yeah," replied the luncheon chef, a thin, laconic woman, as she tossed on another orchid from the bulk plastic bag. "It makes 'em think we care."

Nonetheless, I've seen this small truth reinforced often. If the visual presentation evokes *oohs* and *aahs* as the plates are laid around the table, people are halfway to a rave review of the food before the first bite is even in their mouths. It will then take a truly bad meal to contradict the initial evidence their eyes have given them. Chef hates this, perceiving it to be an insult to his talents, but having had to stoop to bottled dressing, I give thanks that people are so easily taken in by façades.

"How's it going, Hank?" says Anne, stepping in and holding the door for a server exiting with a tray.

"That's it," I nod after the departing figure, "the last tray of dinners, and we're only fifteen minutes behind schedule."

"No one caught the substitution on the dressing?"

"No, we're in the clear. We have a few extra salads. Would your staff like some? Are they taking a dinner break?"

"I'm sending them in two shifts, starting now. They've ordered pizza, and I'm sure the salad will be appreciated."

"We'll fix a bowl. Have them stop in and pick it up."

"Thanks. Do you need any help setting up the dessert buffet?"

"No, I have a crew working on it in the dining room. We'll open the buffet at ten fifteen, along with the cordials, cappuccino, and espresso stations. They sure went to great lengths to make this complicated."

Anne nods her assent. "VHM. Well, the worst is over, and now we can relax a little."

She pats my arm and heads back toward the ballroom, just as a phone in the rear office begins to ring. The machine picks up before I can start after her—let it go. Our own job is nowhere near done; we still have coffee and tea to pour, the cutting and serving of the wedding cake, the constant replenishment of wine and water glasses, and a massive cleanup awaiting us at night's end. Yet for a moment there's a lull, and everyone feels it. The incoming servers sigh as they lower their empty trays, the college kids on the dinner assembly line pull off their latex gloves and examine their burned fingers. The veterans, like me, have long ago acquired "restaurant hands," alternately scorched and frozen so often by handling hot food and plates, cold drinks and bags of ice, that there's little sensation left in them. It's hard, physical work, and every time I send a server out the door, a fully laden tray resting on one shoulder and gripped by both hands, opposing hip jutting out for balance, I feel the effects of the weight and that tortuous posture on their knees, ankles, and spine.

I'm lucky to have advanced to the administrative level of the business before I ended up in chronic pain. Looking at some of the servers, women mostly, who've been at it twenty-odd years, I marvel they're still standing. I also know what many of them will be doing as they carpool home—sharing joints and pain killers, over-the-counter and otherwise, as they console each other about husbands and shiftless lovers, mothers-in-law and rent due, the cost of kids' clothes. It's rare to see a middle-aged man still waiting tables. Either they don't have the stamina or they don't have the need.

"I want you to have something better," I'll whisper to my daughters, as I stroke their hair tonight, although they won't hear. It will be long past midnight when I reach home, and as any six- and eight-year-olds should be, they'll be sound asleep in bed. God knows I'm not a handsome man. I'm short and near-sighted with a thinning crew cut. My face is about as unprepossessing as a face can get. It's why I always wear a snappy bow tie and have since my busboy days, thanks to advice from yet another of the veteran servers I've known over the years. "If the management allows it, always personalize your uniform with a fancy tie or a smiley face button or a flower you can pin to your vest," she coached. "It makes you stand out as an individual, and you'll get bigger tips." In my case, it was the *only* thing that made me stand out, and even today more people remember me as the "guy with the bow tie" than by my name.

So it's with a sense of reverence that I'll sit beside my sleeping girls tonight, stroking their shining hair and knowing how beautiful they are. I wish I could see them more often, but it's a given of catering that you work nights and weekends, and I've already lost precious time, days and weeks of their childhood slipping away while I was supervising the feast at someone else's celebration of life. *Daddy, Daddy, don't go! Stay and play!* I hear their voices piping like chicks in my head, I see myself plucking off their clinging hands. *I'm sorry, sweethearts, but Daddy has to run.*

A knot constricts my throat. Will they hate me when they grow up? Will someone convince them they should? My wife, a part-time nurse, says no. She tells the girls wide-eyed stories of what I'm doing all those nights I'm not home, about the glorious meals in the mansions or at Riverside's own banqueting room, about the beautiful brides in white dresses and the handsome grooms. But it's hard on her, too, raising our daughters practically alone, and there are times we grow frayed trying to remake our lives to fit the schedules neither of us can control.

"Is not so bad," rumbles a deep voice, and Chef Laszlo's meaty hand smacks onto my shoulder. I can't imagine what I've done to give myself away, but somehow he knows. "I tell you happy joke, ha-ha, there is this Hungarian . . ."

He rolls out a story that involves a chicken, a shepherd, and several Hungarian double entendres, of which I understand not a word. Nevertheless, I laugh heartily, a wise move since Chef is punctuating his tale with the point of a skewer. Two servers burst in and deposit trays of dinner plates in the pantry, and the dishwashers scrape uneaten salsa and potatoes into the garbage pail.

"You're not going to believe what we overheard in the ballroom," the two girls exclaim, coming into the kitchen proper, and since we're in a lull I don't hush them this time. Gossip makes the evening go faster, and it's amazing what guests will let slip in front of the staff, as if servants don't have ears. We gather round as Rhonda pulls our lasagna from the oven; we'll eat standing up or with one hip buttressed on the table if we can find room. The news bearers exchange a momentous glance. "The groom slept with another woman last night!"

"What?"

"You're kidding!"

"Does the bride know?"

"No, she's in the dark."

"We heard those snotty bridesmaids talking."

"It was after his bachelor party."

"Who'd he sleep with?"

"Someone right here at the wedding!"

Gasps and exclamations pour forth, as more servers chime in that they, too, have heard the rumor.

"It was one of the blonds. She said—"

"No, I heard it from a Rosecourt hostess."

"No, *we* told *them*."

"Let's go see who he's sneaking glances at."

"Or who he's trying to avoid."

"Everyone, please!" I snap my fingers on high for their attention. If the news is already running rampant between my staff and the Rosecourt people, how long before a guest or a family member overhears one of us talking? "As much fun as this is, let's keep it in the kitchen. We don't even know if it's true, and the last thing we want is to have this wedding blow up because someone in the family finds out . . . finds out . . ."

For some reason, the faces around me have gone white, jaws have dropped, and eyes are darting frantically left, right, and over my shoulder. My stomach hits bottom like a leftover meatball in a pot of cold gravy.

"Finds out what?" says the acid voice of Deirdre Hollingsworth.

I pivot. She's swept in the door behind me, no telling how long she's been there. Worse, right behind Deirdre, piled in the kitchen sink, are twenty empty Paul Newman salad dressing bottles. Shit! We forgot to dump them.

"Finds out what?" repeats Deirdre, drumming her fingers on the sink counter. A mere quarter turn and the bottles will register in her peripheral vision.

"Uh . . . uh . . .," I pull at my bow tie, gulping.

"About the vegetarian!" cries Rhonda, and heads nod fervently to me and to each other to confirm the inspiration.

"Yes, yes, the vegetarian," I practically shout. "We had a last-minute notice one of the guests was meatless, and we had to make a hasty substitution. Delicious, I assure you, but an omelet nonetheless, and if we'd only known . . ." I gabble on, inviting Deirdre forward to inspect the crusted lasagna pan, and while she stares at my obvious insanity, Rhonda and two waiters lunge to plant themselves before the sink.

"Well, I came in to point out that some of the guests have finished their entreés, and I expect each table to be cleared promptly," says Deirdre, recovering her authority. She adds grudgingly, "Although I did receive some compliments on the salads."

At the stove, Chef roars, and Deirdre jumps backward toward the door. "Well, I never!" she begins, but a second glare from Chef drives her out.

"Okay, you heard what she said," I order. "Hop to it! Clear those dinner plates, everyone out there, run, run, run!"

My fingers snap, and the kitchen empties in a rush of wind.

Chef's eyes glitter and narrow. "She is gristle, a nasty gristle," he mutters, sucking his teeth as if to rid them of some repellant morsel. He sends a uniquely Hungarian gesture after the departed Deirdre, then he turns to the remnants in his pots, crooning. "Ah, my little potatoes, my dead asparagus . . . if only I had a juicy woman . . ."

25

Neither Joy, Nor Love, Nor Light

Anne

WHAT IF, STANDING HERE in the ballroom doorway, watching the guests laugh, dance, in conversational din over the tables, I could stop the entire scene? Hit an imaginary pause button—freeze!—the diners caught in mid-mouthful, the dancers in mid-twirl, the sound vanished, gone. Then what if I could advance the scene second by second, frame by frame, examining each picture in sequence. Would it be possible in the course of an evening to find one instant when every last individual in this panoramic tableau was happy at exactly the same time?

I've often thought that if there were such a moment at a wedding, this postprandial half hour would be the most likely window for it to occur. The stress building up to the ceremony is over; the vows have gone off without a hitch. Now the company is gathered in a beautiful ballroom, paneled with gilt mirrors, bedecked with flowers and candlelight, their stomachs sated by a delicious meal. Just enough alcohol has been consumed to induce a convivial mood

without verging into excess. Any minor slights or inconven-
iences up to this point—complaints over the crowded ladies'
room, disappointment that the upstairs floors of Rosecourt
aren't open to guests—will have been forgiven or forgotten as
the party spirit mounts. Scanning the crowd, I can pinpoint
any number of people having an abundantly good time. The
brunette bridesmaid, the skinny, bespectacled girl who seems
so out of place among the others, is waltzing with her groomsman, the two of them stopping, laughing, and restarting as
they repeatedly step on each other's toes. At the Siberia table,
the woman in the blue gown who was so upset about her seat
is leading a sing-along, while one of the great-aunts nods over
her plate, which is about as happy as old people can get.

You might think this congenial atmosphere would only
intensify until the reception ends, but in another half hour
it will already be in decay. The revelers will start feeling
tired and cranky from the long trip to Newport and from
overexposure to the sun while they sat waiting for the
ceremony to begin. They'll be bloated from the dessert bar,
sweaty and overheated from the dance floor, sore from
straining their voices to shout at each other over the
volume of conversation and the band. Too much alcohol
will have been consumed, and the inevitable bad behavior
will emerge. Wagging tongues will divulge malicious gossip;
well-lubricated libidos will go on the prowl. Though our
ballroom has no lampshades to appropriate as headwear,
the hard-core party crowd will invent other ways to be
uproariously funny, as they sour the festivities by becoming
pathetically and embarrassingly drunk.

So now is the time, if there is to be one, when happiness should reach its peak. And tonight I want more than

a superficial vision, something deeper than this appearance of wide-angle joy. Could there be an instant when not only the small grievances but the greater cares and sorrows each guest brought to the party are banished, when every last smile and laugh are genuine and not a brave or haughty cover-up for some secret woe? What about the job that's on the line come Monday? The mammogram that just came back with a worrisome shadow? The awakening suspicion of an affair between a wife and a best friend? The discovery of drugs three days ago in a teenage son's bedroom? What about the simple human malaise of glancing around a room and feeling that everyone else in it has led a more satisfying, more successful, more fulfilled life than yours? Could there ever be one millisecond when every private tragedy was simultaneously absent from the hearts and minds before me, and all two hundred and fifty souls shared in pure synchronized delight?

Not tonight. At the very least, the rancor Deirdre bears Gordon counts against it, and no matter how she tries to suppress it, I suspect it's never out of her mind. I wish, despite her treatment of me, I could say something to commiserate. With my own divorce papers in hand, I'm probably the one person present who most closely knows how she feels. But Deirdre would despise my sympathy, and even without her pain, I'm asking too much in the way of universal happiness. There's always something to eat away at our felicity, some worm in the rose . . .

One of the hostesses interrupts with an offer to bring me coffee on my break, but I inform her I'm not taking one and send her away. Good grief, could I be any more morbid, more self-pitying? *Stop it, Anne. Get a grip.* You could have asked for the night off; one of the administrative staff could have stepped into your place. Why *are* you here? To prove you can do it? To punish yourself? Go ahead then, be my guest.

I force myself to seek out Allison and Mead at their table before the fireplace, the enormous mirror above its mantel reflecting the splendor they survey. They, most of all, should be happy, and Allison does indeed radiate the confidence of a newly crowned queen presiding over her court. But Mead appears distracted. In between replying to whatever comments Allison is making, he keeps glancing to the tables nearest them as if searching for a particular face. Then he comes back to her, grins, nods. Has the "yes dear, no dear" phase already begun? Before my staff left on their dinner break, they gleefully informed me of a rumor among the servers that the groom slept with some other woman last night. It feels too far-fetched, and I cautioned them against getting carried away with their game. Please, I want to see Allison and Mead romantic and intimate, absorbed in and endlessly fascinated by each other the way Greg and I were before the girls were born. I believed we'd recapture that intimacy once our daughters were older and more independent. We'd take the couple we'd been out of storage, polish it to a bright gleam, and put it back on display.

And how old were Miranda and Rachel when they didn't need me anymore, or rather, when their need changed from the sacred to the mundane? Twelve? Thirteen? Before that, their very lives depended on me. I was the one they turned to for every answer, to share every triumph and console every hurt from a scraped knee to a lost toy. After that, their friends were more likely to know what was going on in their lives than their mother, and to attempt to bridge that gap was to be accused of prying. What they needed me for then was to increase their allowance, drive them to soccer practice, sign permission slips for field trips, earn money for their college funds.

"It's the natural order," said Greg one night, shrugging, as we switched off the light and settled into bed. "They're supposed to grow up and become independent. You don't want them still living with us when they're twenty-five, do you?"

"No. But don't you miss the way it was when we were the center of their universe, when they thought we could do no wrong?"

"You'll get it back when we have grandchildren. You can spoil them to your heart's content. Besides, isn't it kind of reassuring to know that if we both died now, say in a car crash, the girls are old enough not to be helpless?"

"That's not a very cheerful thought," I protested, though I knew what he meant. There *was* a measure of relief in believing our daughters had reached an age where our values were firmly instilled and they could think and speak up in the world for themselves.

"Besides," Greg continued, "isn't it nice to be gaining back some time for ourselves?"

"Time for ourselves," I murmured, picturing us at a candlelit table for two.

But even when Miranda and Rachel reached high school, nothing changed for Greg and me. On the contrary, he continued to work long, then even longer hours than when the girls were small. There were those college coffers to fill, and being absent myself three and four nights a week at Rosecourt, I could hardly complain about his schedule. Yet when free time did fall into my lap and I looked around for my husband to spend it with, there was always something else he had to be doing.

"You're going to the office?" I'd ask, as he packed his briefcase on a Saturday morning.

"Only for a few hours."

"But it's a beautiful summer day. I thought we might play tennis or go see that outdoor sculpture exhibit."

"I'll be home by noon."

In the early days, when he was trying to get ahead at Coburn Design Collaborative, of course it was important for Greg to impress clients by doing it faster and better than anyone else. Now he was a partner with more clients than he needed, yet he couldn't resist making promises with no real motive but to make him look good in his own eyes. He'd take phone calls during dinner, and I'd sit in silent disbelief hearing him tell the party on the other end, "Sure, no problem, I'll have the revisions to you first thing tomorrow morning." Then with barely an apology, he'd leave his meal to get cold on the table and go to his computer for the rest of the night.

"Look, Anne," he'd say, if I objected. "When a client's hired your firm to design a forty-million-dollar hotel project, they expect you to be available."

The professional and civic committees on which Greg served also demanded his attention. In the early days we'd leaped at opportunities for him to participate in trade shows and conventions, to attend industry seminars and community events; I don't deny he gained clients and prestige that way. But when he volunteered for still more committees after the need was gone, I began to wonder if he wasn't trapped on a treadmill of his own making, caught up in a relentless cycle he didn't know how to break. When he ended up at a chiropractor's, his neck immobilized in pain from extended stays at the computer, I put my foot down.

"You have to take some time off, get some exercise," I insisted, at the same time optimistically believing that exercise was something we could do together, besides sex.

"You're right," he conceded, "but how would I fit it into my schedule?"

"We could do aerobics or go running in the morning."

Greg shook his head. Not first thing in the morning because he liked to get to work early, get right to his desk. Something important might have happened overnight.

"Okay, what about in the evening, a walk before or after dinner?"

But either the weather didn't cooperate, or he had a meeting, or I had Rosecourt, or the girls required our presence at a school activity, or he was bushed and just wanted to read the newspaper on the couch. On the rare occasions when all four of our schedules dovetailed at home, it was more important to spend it as a family than for Greg and me to go off by ourselves. Then Greg took up lunchtime racquetball with a colleague at the health club three days a week.

"It's convenient, I can network while I'm there, and you can stop nagging me about exercise," he teased, pleased to have resolved the matter so neatly.

"Great."

What else could I say? Instead I searched for other outings that might tempt him, concerts, sporting events, speakers at the library, nature hikes. Occasionally he'd have a free slot and agree. He thoroughly enjoyed a polo match I coaxed him to attend. "We should do this again," he declared, as we picnicked on the grass, watching the horses thunder and pivot in powerful, heart-stopping play. But when the next match drew near, he'd been there, done that, and besides he had deadlines to meet. Increasingly, I found myself alone on Saturday afternoons, watching the clock creep past one o'clock, two o'clock, three.

"I said I'd be home by lunchtime," Greg said, annoyed, when I mentioned it. "We have the rest of the evening, Anne."

"No, we don't. I have a wedding at Rosecourt. I have to leave in an hour."

"Well then, what do you expect?" he replied.

Why didn't I come right out and say it? Why didn't I use plain English? *I'm lonely, I miss you, this isn't what I expected at this stage of our lives. Can't you spare a few hours for me?*

Later, when the trust was broken, Greg accused me of expecting him to be a mind reader, and as in any divorce, he was half right. How was he supposed to know what I wanted if I didn't tell him? But it hurts when your husband finds you less interesting than a meeting with a cement contractor, less compelling than the numbers on a spreadsheet, and I was too proud to beg for his attention, like a needy teenager whining for a date. And how could I argue with the money he was making? If I'd earned a similar income, maybe I'd be at the one at the office day and night.

Maybe this is the normal arc a marriage takes, I told myself, and I should embrace my growing freedom and stop looking to Greg for companionship. It wasn't as though I didn't have friends. Get busy! I went to morning yoga and joined a capital campaign committee at the library that met twice a month. Secretly I hoped Greg would miss me, but he didn't.

"You're going out tonight?" he'd ask at breakfast, hopefulness dawning in his voice. "Well, I guess I might as well work late then." He'd smile, guilt absolved, off the hook. Glad, I sometimes thought, to be rid of me.

The thing is, Greg loves his life and his job. He basks in the camaraderie and recognition of his peers. They matter, they define him, I don't. Even our daughters had become peripheral to his identity. Greg loves being important, and what makes him important is that he works seven days a week, that he's so indispensable he can't turn off his cell phone, that he had to take business on our few vacations, that he had no time for his wife. Sometimes I think the divorce helps prove how important he and his work are—so important it cost him his marriage.

Please, stay with me.

"Are you happy with our marriage?" I asked him instead.

"What are you talking about?" He screwed his face as if I were asking him to sample something distasteful. "I'm perfectly happy with you, Anne."

"But you're *not* with me. When do we ever do anything together?"

"We eat dinner together most evenings. We go out a lot of nights."

"We eat dinner together maybe twice a week. We go out when it's to entertain your clients and you need me to chat with the wives."

"Well, how would it be any better if we went out alone?"

I couldn't answer that. How would it be any better? What would we talk about when we no longer had any dreams in common?

Finally, I did say exactly what I meant.

"Look at me, Greg." I planted myself in the doorway as he was leaving for a Sunday at the office. "Look what you're leaving behind. I'm a smart, pretty, talented, adventurous woman, and if you can't find the time to spend with me, I'll find a man who will."

The words took him aback, but only for a moment.

"Oh, Anne," he replied, half irritated, half amused. "Don't be ridiculous."

He left, no doubt believing I was far too trustworthy and loyal to betray our marriage vows. But as soon as the challenge left my mouth, I began to contemplate it seriously. What intrigued me was not any notion of clandestine romance or tempestuous sex, but thinking I could probably have an affair and Greg wouldn't even notice. I almost had to do it out of curiosity. So I did.

His name was Rob, he was on the library capital campaign committee, and for the next eighteen months we saw each other almost weekly. A regional director for the United Way, Rob was recently divorced, in no mood to remarry, and an affair suited us both fine. We had quite a lot in common, especially a love of music, and Greg was only too happy I'd found someone to attend concerts with in his stead, though for appearances Rob and I continued to invite him along. Once or twice, he startled us by saying yes, he could use an evening out, and he and Rob hit it off admirably.

"Your husband is an idiot," Rob said to me after one of these occasions. "Doesn't he suspect in the least?"

"You and I behave ourselves," I replied. "We act like friends in public."

"What about when you get home late?"

"He's used to my not getting home till one or two from Rosecourt and just goes to sleep without me. When I'm in by eleven thirty, he thinks it's early."

"Doesn't he see how you're glowing?"

"It's dark," I joked, although the point jabbed. A few of our friends had begun to raise their eyebrows. Shouldn't Greg have caught the illicit sparkle in my eyes, heard it in my laugh, when I recounted to him what fun Rob and I had together? Shouldn't my body have felt different to my husband when we made love in our bed? Until then, Rob and I had availed ourselves of his apartment; now I began to invite him to our house.

"Do you want Greg to walk in and find us?" he asked, as we lazed in bed after Sunday afternoon lovemaking.

"I don't know. Do you think that's my subconscious motive?"

"It might be. You're unhappy, but I haven't heard you say you don't love him. Strange as it sounds, I'd almost be glad to be the guy caught in bed with the wife, sheet clutched around my waist, if it would be the wakeup call that saves your marriage. A marriage should be saved if it can. There are times I think I could have worked harder to save mine."

Rob and I broke it off amicably not long afterward. He was over his divorce and ready to start dating. I examined my own conscience for guilt but found none. It had hardly felt like adultery, and it should have. It should have felt like the end of the world. I almost envy Deirdre her fury, her desolation, her shipwrecked heart. At least she *feels.* Whereas Greg's and my great love slipped its mooring and drifted away, and I didn't know how to bring it back, and Greg never seemed to notice or care that it was gone.

What to do? Leave him? Why—what was wrong with life as it was? I had a nice home, a job, activities, friends. Surely many marriages evolve into what is first and foremost a successful partnership, an efficient, platonic structure for two people to reside within. What do you want to do, Anne? Travel? Book yourself on a tour to Greece or Ireland. You can afford it, Greg will say go, you'll have fellow travelers for company. Or you can quit Rosecourt, devote yourself to some cause, crusade for deaf or disabled children. How many times had I envied the seeming freedom of single women? Now it was within my grasp. Yet how little it would have taken for Greg to win me back.

"We're going away for a weekend," I ordered him in late August. "We'll hole up in an inn in the Berkshires, go to Tanglewood, hike in the mountains. We can do some antiquing or horseback riding . . . why not?"

Already his face was showing impatience, his mind calculating an excuse.

"I'm not the music lover you are, Anne. We can go antiquing closer to home for an afternoon if there's something you want."

"Then pick someplace you'd like to go. Make it your choice. I want a weekend away, just us two."

"Why? Miranda leaves for college next week, Rachel's hardly home. We can have privacy at the house whenever we want. Look, why don't you book us a table at Romano's for Friday night and pick up a bottle of champagne for afterward."

"I'm working a corporate party at Rosecourt on Friday."

"Well then, what do you expect, Anne?"

"I expect that once in a while we could do something fun and exciting together, like take a weekend off."

"But you're always working on the weekends."

"I can arrange to have a few days off if you'll tell me when you want to go."

"Look, let's just go to Romano's."

"Greg, we need to start reconnecting, we need to rebuild the relationship we had or there's not going to be anything left between us."

He gave in then, chose the path of least resistance.

"All right, you arrange something and let me know."

What did I expect? That candlelight and wine in a cozy Berkshires inn would bridge the chasm between us? That we'd look into each other's eyes, see the young lovers we'd once been, and experience a new surge of romance? Yet Greg did come away with me to the Berkshires, after I had to cancel once due to a conflict at Rosecourt, and he did enjoy the drive there, though by then it was mid-October and the fall foliage had already peaked. He also showed some interest in the antique shops and attempted over dinner to engage in conversation. When we made love, he concentrated on the act. But by Sunday afternoon, he was itching to get back, urging the accelerator, and it felt to me as if the episode had been forced upon him, as if he were performing a court-ordered community service for our marriage. He dropped me at the house to make a quick stop by his office, and I sat on my suitcase in the hallway, wondering if I should bother to unpack. I watched the hands on the clock move past seven, eight, nine o'clock.

I left a yellow sticky note on the newel post and my key under the mat.

26

TABLE FOR TWO

Allison

THIS IS IT! I'M MARRIED! How does it feel? Great! But also . . . a little anticlimactic. After a year of effort and anticipation . . . poof! Can it be we have less than two hours to go? Oh well, everyone seems to be having fun, and I'm sure the thrill will catch me up again in a minute. Meanwhile, here comes the photographer for more pictures. He's such a nervous Nellie, though so far I don't believe he's missed any of my specified shots. I nudge Mead to lift his wine glass to simulate a toast, and as our glasses clink, I smile for the camera.

I wonder what it would be like to be a virgin on my wedding night?

The photographer moves to another angle, and I roll the thought in my mind, folding it into the other lore Anne told us before the ceremony. Armed grooms. Kidnapped brides. Obviously, there's no such drama in store tonight. No sexual surprises either; Mead and I slept together on our fourth date. If you're attracted to each other and take the necessary precautions, why wait? Sex doesn't have to mean anything, and though I was already falling for Mead, it's certainly no proof of lasting love. It can be just a physical gratification, like biting into a sinfully rich truffle or surrendering to the strokes of an expert masseuse or slipping naked into a full-length silk robe. To be honest, sometimes the truffle is better. I can take my time, choose any flavor, bite in slowly, let the delicious chocolate ooze onto my tongue and cling to the roof of my mouth. I can eat a single one or a whole boxful—not that I would, too many calories—and indulge whenever I want. I don't have to share them with anyone else.

Whereas for sex, you need a partner . . . well, a vibrator works, of course. But a vibrator can't touch you other places, can't pin your mouth with kisses or electrify your skin with roving fingertips. It can't press a muscled chest against your breasts while it pumps into you the heat from below. It can't overcome your whole body, collapse with a moan of ecstasy in your ear. To do sex right, it takes a couple, and for me it takes a man, although I did try it once with a woman just to experiment. Sorry, not the same. I simply wanted to know what it felt like to have a woman make me come and to see if I could make a woman come in return, and I'm pleased to say I did. Mead doesn't know, of course, and I'll never tell. Men have this tiresome fantasy about watching two women together—for all I know, Mead has watched something like that in the past—and the last thing I want is for him to get any ideas about a threesome.

But although Mead is an excellent lover—probably the best of the dozen or so men I've slept with—I can't say I feel the same level of lust for him anymore either, that mad craving that possesses you at the start. Since we've been having sex regularly for nearly two years, figure three nights a week . . . well, the human body has only so many possibilities. We dim the lights, accessorize with candles and music. You do this to me, then I do that to you. It doesn't take long to become familiar, to explore every texture and surface topography. I assume my newness has worn off for him as well. Men may salivate at every attractive female, but we all have the same basic anatomy. Barring severe abnormalities, the same goes for the male organ, though every man likes to believe his is special. By the time our clothes are off, Mead already resembles a Greek fertility statue, erect and springing to the task.

"Aren't you even going to give me a chance to try to arouse you?" I'll laugh.

"Nope," he grins proudly, "here I am, ma'am, at your service."

He's good about the afterplay, too, which is just as vital to me and to most women as foreplay, although neither the men's nor the women's magazines ever cover that. Maybe I should write an article about it, because there's nothing worse than a man who rolls out of bed as soon as he's done—thanks, ma'am, I'll just have a shower and be on my way. No, it's nice to lie there a while in the dark, nuzzling each other, talking of this or that. Was it good for you? Yes, very. Too bad it's no longer chic or healthy to share a cigarette. Sex grows softer, sweeter, with some shared cordial—isn't that a nice word in itself?—to cap the event.

Would it be better if Mead and I were virgins tonight?

The photographer is still fussing around our table, adjusting the centerpiece for his next shot, leaving me plenty of time to think. There'd definitely be an aura of mystery and anticipation, the blushing bride disrobed by the handsome groom who awakens her to the delights of womanhood. Isn't that what all those paperback romance novels are about? Bodice rippers, they're called, and I assume that's why women devour them, because they hold out the promise of something forbidden and exciting. Yet in reality, two virgins in bed is usually a recipe for clumsiness, and in the arranged marriages Anne mentioned, the sentiment may have been sheer dread. Still, if it were a matter of producing an heir for the kingdom, I suppose you dropped your doublet, shed your camisole, pictured someone else's face, and got on with it. The king saved the real sex for his mistresses while the royal bride probably lay there figuring, *What the hell, it sure beats being underneath some smelly farm oaf.*

"Lean in a little closer," the photographer pleads, and we do. But my point is that if Mead and I were virgins, the most important part of our wedding, the consummation, would still lie ahead. There'd be a real threshold for us to cross over, something special and private, a gigantic milestone to pass. Maybe that's why this feels anticlimactic just now. None of the guests are looking at us with envy or titillation. Even the most antiquated relatives take it for granted we're having sex; our wedding merely confirms the status quo. It's almost as if Mead and I are hosting the first, albeit possibly the grandest, of the parties we'll throw throughout our lifetimes, and after the guests are gone we'll leave the dishes in the sink, yawn, and trudge to bed like an old married couple enacting a patented routine. Yet even if we were virgins with a wild passion to fulfill, we'd still reach the same place a year or two down the road.

If we're really meant to be monogamous, why did nature make it so ho-hum?

I glance at the dancing couples and blow out a breath. Well, even if I'm not contemplating my wedding night as romantically as I might, I'll take the modern version of love and sex. I'm going into this with my eyes wide open and sticking to my plan. Married by thirty-two—check; first child by thirty-seven. That gives Mead and me five fabulous years as a free-spirited career couple, and I don't intend to misuse them. I don't feel angst over what I can't control. I don't waste time on lost causes. I'm not here to change the world or make it better but to get the most out of what it is, and in the end I'll be a lot happier than any naïve bride who imagines an eternity of champagne and roses. So let's enjoy this party, then get on with real life. Besides, if not the ripping off of my bodice, I do have one thing to look forward to at the conclusion of the night— ripping open all those check-filled envelopes the guests have so obligingly deposited in our beribboned satin box.

"Big smile, please," begs the photographer.

No problem.

Mead

Hey, you know, this being married stuff isn't so bad once you get used to it. Sure, I have to be faithful to one woman now, but I've done that for the past two years with Allison and it wasn't hard. Okay, there may have been an exception last night, although I'm still not sure I'm guilty of anything. I've been checking around the ballroom, because if there was an indiscretion, it had to be at the hotel after the guys and I rolled in, and that limits the possibilities to women guests who are staying there. It's not a long list, and most are automatically excluded. My mom and female relatives, naturally. Deirdre—that does make me shudder. Allison herself—nope, she was huddled with her bridesmaids, which rules them out as well. Kimmy—whoa, try not to think about that one. There are a handful of twentysomething Morelli and Dombrowski cousins, but again, family members are disqualified. A half dozen of Deirdre's friends are also checked in at our hotel, but I've never met any of them before today and besides, they're her age. So I'm thinking it was some passing chambermaid or cocktail waitress, although maids aren't on duty at one a.m. and I don't recall going through the hotel bar en route to the elevator. Unless the guys sent a stripper or a hooker to my room after they left as a final bachelor present?

The photographer's moved off, and Allison is handling the conversation with a couple of her father's friends who've come to offer their congratulations. I take a judicious swallow of wine. My hangover's pretty much gone, and I'm in no mood to have it boomerang back, but if I don't drink something, Allison might get suspicious. As my head clears, so does more of my memory. I know the guys dumped me on my bed, alone, and if they hired a stripper they'd have teased me about it this morning. That means I either wandered back out or someone came to my door . . . I remember the door opening . . . shit! Who was it? Could it have been one of Deirdre's friends, who got tight and wandered into my room by mistake? The thought's gruesome, but not impossible. Look at that woman in the blue dress belting out a tune at the table in the far corner. People tend to drop their inhibitions when they're out of town, especially under the influence. For that matter, it could have been any drunken hotel guest who mistook my room for their own and stumbled in. But wouldn't my door have been locked? Shit, I'm right back where I started.

What's the one clear thing I remember? Boobs, a pair of boobs in my hands. Okay, go with it, Mead. Try to picture the women here topless and see if you can visualize a match. Be discreet, not obvious, although hell, why shouldn't I be? The way most women dress nowadays, what do they expect? I've seen women jogging in sports bras that barely cover their nipples, teenagers in pants slung so low you can see their butt crack. There's one secretary in Dad's office who must be a 38D and seems to own nothing but shrink-wrap tank tops. I've even seen female executives in pin-striped business suits that show cleavage. Tonight there's enough swelling bosom on display to goggle the legally blind. Then they excoriate us guys because we dare to look. What are we supposed to do? Could we have a little decency here, please? A little sense of responsibility? And I'm sorry, but you can't enter a guy's bedroom past midnight and then claim he took advantage. What else did you come for, to solicit funds for the orphanage?

Boobs, Mead, focus on the boobs! Whose were they? Not an older woman's, you can eliminate them for good. These were twenty to thirty-five years old at most, sweet, pliable, the kind I'd be happy to get my hands on when

I was wide awake. Also, it's coming to me that whoever the lady was, she definitely wasn't drunk and stumbling into my room by mistake. If she were, she'd have passed out, and I'd have found her naked beside me this morning. But if she wasn't drunk, if it was deliberate—my senses sharpen; this is a sobering thought—what was her motive? That's it, find the motive, and you'll cherchez la femme.

And suddenly I have it, the only remaining possibility: some woman who's secretly had the hots for me and seized the chance to satisfy herself before I sheathed my sword and permanently retired from the dating fray.

My brain zooms in and locks, and I nod, fortunately just as Allison happens to be saying something she wants me to agree with. Hey, it's not vanity. I'm good-looking, but why pick me for a one-nighter when she had my whole squad to choose from and none of them about to be hitched? It was me specifically the lady was lying in wait for, at a time she knew I'd be drunk and easy prey, and why else would she do that?

To stop the wedding? No, or she'd have done it already, blabbed to Allison or pulled a dramatic scene at the altar, though Allison scratched from the vows that old-fashioned bit to "speak up or forever hold your peace."

To blackmail me for the rest of my life? I don't have any enemies, male or female, and besides, I wouldn't buy it at any price. I'd tell Allison, and mad as she might be, she'd forgive me. I know it, although I can't explain why.

Our prime suspect, then, is a cunning, amorous lady no older than her mid-thirties with a pair of mouthwatering but not oversized boobs and an irresistible attraction to myself. Now go through the list one more time, and if the bra fits . . .

A bridesmaid? Not Freddie or Susie; not Pammy—she's too nice. But one of the others could have slipped away from Allison during the evening, though the hour seems awfully late. Early on, I did consider dating Carolyn, but I got the feeling she'd rather spend her time looking in a mirror. Lauren's a little shy on the cup size, Jessica's a bit wide-spaced. Hmm, Nicole's boobs are just about right.

What about Steve's fiancée, Lynne? She was pissed at him for being a groomsman when she wasn't a bridesmaid, then she calmed down when I paired him with Susie, then she got re-pissed when he deserted her for our revelries last night. Could it have been Lynne, getting some kind of revenge? The boobs are a close match, but she'd have been lying in ambush for Steve, not me.

And that's it. No one else fits the Victoria's Secret profile, except a couple of Allison's colleagues from the art gallery and they're not at our hotel. It's funny—I'm only now realizing how many of the guests at our wedding are really our parents' friends, not Allison's and mine. I suppose that's fair, they're paying. Well, Gordon is, through the nose. And can any guy keep his eyes off Kimmy? Look at those boobs—they're perfect, round, firm, luscious. Imagine undoing that slinky black dress and having those beauties drop like warm fruit right into your hands . . . Shit! This is no time for a hard-on. *Down, Mead!* Quick, think Susie, think Susie! There, that's thrown ice water on it.

Wait a minute . . . oh my God . . . did I just say Kimmy's boobs are a perfect fit?

SMILE, GOD LOVES YOU

Kimmy

NOBODY EVER TAKES ME SERIOUSLY. Nobody gives me credit for anything. For example, here we sit at our table, Gordon and myself, with a hospital vice president and his wife, and the head of neurology and her husband, and two other important doctors and their spouses, and no one's paying me any attention. Like I can't make intelligent conversation. I bet they don't know that I have an index card file at home with a separate card for every significant personage at the hospital, including the head of every medical and administrative department, which is the branch I worked in before I married Gordon. On each card I write down pertinent information, like the names of their children and where they went on their last vacation. Then before a social event such as this, I study the cards so I can strike up a meaningful conversation.

I'm also learning to play golf, which many medical people seem to participate in. But during the cocktail hour, when Gordon and Dr. Singh were discussing how to shoot

from a sand trap and I mentioned that Gordon bought me
my own set of clubs, Dr. Singh barely smiled and said,
"How nice. I'm sure you will soon be adept at the game,
Mrs. Hollingsworth." He was about to turn back to Gordon
when he thought better of it, and we talked for two minutes, Dr. Singh nodding as I explained the difficulty I was
having getting my hips to swing just right. "You know who
is a very good golfer?" Dr. Singh said, glancing over my
head and cupping my elbow. "Dr. Zorban, right over there.
I'm sure he could give you some helpful advice. Let me
introduce you." Which he did, leaving me with Dr. Zorban
and some urologists as if he'd done me a great favor while
he went back to finish talking with Gordon.

The whole encounter is typical. They can't completely
ignore me, you see, because to slight me would be to slight
Gordon, but they don't want to waste time talking to me
personally. So they pretend to be interested and pay superficial attention, and all the while they're looking for some
way to shunt me out of the conversation. They don't
bother to learn anything about me, because they assume
there isn't anything worth knowing, and they treat me like
a child. Well, I know for a fact that Dr. Singh's own wife,
who is French and is actually his second wife, is only thirty-
five, fifteen years younger than he is, so he's not the one
who should be condescending. Especially not when I also
know he had a past episode of handing out questionable
drug prescriptions, which is part of the reason he's always
eager to impress Gordon. I picked up that information by
keeping my ears open, and I've recorded it on my index
card for Dr. Singh. Anyway, the wives and husbands of the
doctors and administrators don't treat me any better, though

you'd think, as hospital-affiliated spouses, we'd have something in common. But a lot of them knew Deirdre, and they give me the cold shoulder like I'm some kind of home wrecker. Which is not true. Gordon told me himself that Deirdre hadn't understood him for years.

The one person who does seem to accept me, to my total surprise, is Allison. She isn't mad at her father about the divorce at all, and though we haven't talked much yet, she treats me as if I were an individual human being. If she and her friends could just overlook that I'm her stepmother— I mean, I overlook it, I'm not pretending to be a mother to her or Susie, although I am trying to be especially nice to Susie, because with her living way off in Montana, this is my one chance to make a good impression. But Allison and Mead in Manhattan aren't far from Gordon and me in our new house in Greenwich, and she might invite me into her circle of friends. Because when I look at the bridesmaids at their table, I know I could fit right in. I like all the things they do, clothes, shopping, being independent. Maybe I could invite them for lunch in a month or two, and Allison could bring the wedding video and photograph album so we could look at them together. Especially after what I've done for Allison. She doesn't know it, and never will, but last night I single-handedly saved her wedding.

It started when Gordon called me from the rehearsal dinner about nine thirty. "Kimmy, I have a special favor to ask you," he said.

"Sure, I can do it. What is it?" I replied, muting the hotel TV. I pushed away the paper wrap from my takeout sub sandwich and rolled over onto my stomach on the bed. I love talking to Gordon on the telephone.

"One of the groomsmen, Steve, has been getting calls from his girlfriend. She's en route from New York, but she got held up by a major accident that closed I-95. She was supposed to be at the rehearsal dinner, but it may be over by the time she gets to Newport so she's heading to the hotel instead. I hate to ask, but could you go down to the lobby and keep an eye out for her? She's pretty upset, and I thought it might smooth things over a bit if someone was there to greet her."

"Sure, I can do it."

"I thought you might. You really are special, Kimmy. Don't think I don't appreciate how understanding you've been. Not many women would have the grace to behave as you've done."

"I love you, Gordon. I'm just trying to be good to you."

"I know. You are. I love you, too. Do the best you can, and I'll be back soon. Her name is Lynne."

We hung up, and I switched off the TV, slipped on my shoes, and took the elevator to the hotel lobby. When I got there I realized I should have asked Gordon for Lynne's last name as well. Then I could have gone to the desk and asked the clerk to signal me when she checked in. But although I had my purse and cell phone, I didn't want to call him back and interrupt the dinner, especially when I was deliberately skipping the rehearsal to show everyone I was respectful of their family situation and not trying to butt in. Appearing with Gordon at the ceremony and reception would be enough for a start. As it turned out, with such a large wedding party and so many relatives on the groom's side, Mead's parents had booked a whole French restaurant. But even counting sixty guests, that would still be too close quarters for me and Deirdre to be together. I know it sounds crazy, but sometimes I think that woman wants to poison me!

Anyway, I found a comfy armchair by the marble fountain and sat down to wait for Lynne. I really like hotel lobbies, they're so luxurious and grand. The fountain was surrounded by trailing ivy and potted plants, and I always wonder where they get those huge carpets with the hotel crest in them. They're much wider than the carpet rolls in a regular store, so I guess they must be custom made. I picked up a magazine and watched the people coming and going, but I identified Lynne even before I heard her snarl her name at the poor clerk. She stormed in like she'd strike lightning bolts at anyone who dared glance crossways at her, and the clerk hardly got to say, "Good evening, ma'am, welcome to—"

"Just give me the damn key!" she said, yanking the card from his hand and cutting short his offer to call a porter to carry her bags. She stalked toward the elevator.

"Excuse me," I said, catching up to her while she cursed at the elevator for taking too long to descend. "I'm Kimmy Hollingsworth, Allison's father's wife. Allison and Mead asked me to meet you." That wasn't quite true, but it seemed the best way to explain myself.

"Well, that's just fine," she snapped, tossing back her hair, which really wasn't all that long. "But I've been stuck in a goddamn traffic jam for three hours—three hours not moving, stuck in my car. I don't even know how many people got killed."

"I'm sorry." I stepped into the elevator with her as it opened. "Everyone is still at the rehearsal dinner, though, so it won't be too late to join them. You can freshen up, then I'll call the front desk to get you a cab."

"Who says I'm going?" Lynne punched a button, chipped a nail, and cursed again. Her floor was the one below Gordon's and mine, where all the bridesmaids and groomsmen were staying, and she elbowed her bags out and down the hall. I followed, not sure what to say as she slotted in her card key and kicked open the door. "Well, at least the idiot got us a room with a mini bar," she observed, glaring around. She dropped her luggage, opened the fridge, and pulled out an assortment of tiny liquor bottles. "What do you want, gin, vodka, tequila?"

"Gin," I said, thinking it best not to argue. She tossed me a bottle, wrenched the cap off hers, and began yanking out glasses, cans of orange juice, tomato juice, and tonic, ranting all the while.

"He should never have agreed to be in the wedding party in the first place, not if I wasn't going to be a bridesmaid, which Allison didn't ask me to. Which means I have to sit on the sidelines the entire weekend, sit by myself at the ceremony, wait around while he poses for pictures. I'm his fiancée, not that that seems to matter to anyone. Yet I'm supposed to take a backseat, while he's off partying. If he expects me to twiddle my thumbs tonight while they're carousing at some stupid bachelor bash—"

She belted back her drink and began tossing clothes from her suitcase onto the bed, while I picked hangers out of the closet and hung them up for her. Then she went on.

"I phoned him when I first got stopped by the accident and told him I'd be late, and what does he do? Nothing! 'What do you expect me to do about it, Lynne?' he said.

That's his brilliant solution. And I said, 'You could skip the rehearsal and meet me at the hotel. You could give them your regrets about the dinner and be there to meet me.' But no, this is Allison and Mead's once-in-a-lifetime occasion—ha!—and his job is to be there for them. Now I'll look ridiculous waltzing into the restaurant as everyone's leaving. I called him six times from the road, six times, to let him know where I was, and he couldn't be bothered to come back to the hotel to meet me? If he doesn't care enough to be here, I'll be damned if I'm going to sit around waiting for him."

"Would you like to go out to dinner with me?" I asked, though having eaten my sub sandwich, I wasn't really hungry. It just didn't seem wise to let her charge out alone.

"Why aren't you at the rehearsal dinner? Oh yeah, right." Lynne shot me a scornful look and answered her own question in one. "Yeah, sure, we outcasts will go paint the town."

I could have said a lot of things to her then. I could have pulled myself up to my full height of five feet four inches and said, "Excuse me, you have misunderstood the situation. I am not an outcast. I am Gordon Hollingsworth's wife, and if we have decided it would be best for me to refrain from attending this evening's festivities in the interest of family harmony, that is our business. So there, bitch." Except I wouldn't say those last three words, because rudeness is never befitting. But you can see how people treat me, and though it hurts, I put up with it because I'm trying to do what's best for Gordon. While Lynne went to the bathroom, I quickly phoned him and explained the situation.

"You did exactly the right thing," he said. "Can you stick with her until she calms down? We don't want anyone to create a scene that will spoil the weekend for Allison." Then he said again how wonderful I was, which made me feel really proud to know he appreciates me even if no one else does.

So Lynne and I went out, although not to eat because it turned out what she really wanted to do was go bar hopping. She doesn't eat at all, and she smokes to stay thin, which is horrible, and if I could tell young women just one thing it would be this: don't smoke to stay thin. In fact, I would like to start a campaign at the hospital about it because even though they already sponsor quit smoking clinics, a lot of the staff still do, like the orderlies and food service workers. Not in the hospital building, of course, but they'll go outside or across the street. I used to pass them on my lunch break, and it doesn't look right. Maybe that will be my focus once people accept me a little more and after I get the house decorated, because as wife of the hospital president I have to have a focus and mine could be to coordinate an employee no-smoking program.

Anyway, Lynne and I went to bar after bar, and I don't know if you've ever been in Newport on a summer night, but let me tell you it's not hard to do. Go from bar to bar, I mean. They're all along this one-way street called Thames Street, which runs the whole length of the waterfront and is packed with tourist shops and restaurants. The stores stay open late, and there's shouting and partying and music spilling out the nightclub doors. The sidewalks are like rivers of people flowing up and down. One store had these painted mermaid and lighthouse statues in the window, and I thought, *Wouldn't that be cute on the shelf in our guest bathroom?* If I could coax Lynne to go shopping, she might forget about the bars. But all she wanted to do was drink and talk about herself and complain how badly Steve had treated her. Which is not true. By her own account, he tried to call her back several times, but she was so mad she switched off her cell phone to show him she didn't care.

Then she started flirting with the guys in the bars, and it was all I could do to keep her out of trouble. Believe me, it wasn't easy because the guys were hitting on me too. *Hello! Don't you see this gigantic diamond ring and matching wedding band on my left hand?* I had to fend them off both Lynne and myself, and I didn't dare leave her to call Gordon and update him where I was. Besides, he was probably asleep by this time. See, Gordon is sixty-three, which is really old. Some nights he comes home from the hospital after a very hard day, and by the time he's had a drink and dinner, he's dozing off on the couch in front of the TV. I have to wake him up so he can take his Viagra. He wouldn't want anyone to know that, but if you get up every morning at six then you have to be in bed by ten to get eight hours of sleep, don't you? So I figured Gordon would have dozed off at the hotel, and I didn't have to worry about him. But Lynne's fiancé Steve and the other groomsmen would be out bachelor partying with Mead, and all night long I sneaked glances around, afraid we'd run into them. Finally, about one a.m., I persuaded Lynne we should go back to the hotel.

"Yes, let's do that," she sneered. "Let's give the party boys a welcome committee."

She grabbed my arm and jerked me along Thames Street. The hotel lobby was mostly empty when we got

there, maybe a half dozen other people strolling in from
their night on the town, but no one I recognized as a wedding guest. Lynne wanted to wait there and ambush Mead
and the groomsmen.

"Let's go check your room first," I said, nudging her
toward the elevator. "Maybe they're back already."

But they weren't, and Lynne paced by the bed. You'd
have thought she'd be over her temper by now, that it
would have worn off, but she was so angry she didn't even
seem drunk, like the anger had burned off the alcohol.
Then we heard voices in the hallway, stumbling footsteps,
loud laughter. In a flash Lynne was at the door, opening it
just a crack so no one could see us inside. And there they
were, bumbling along like a bunch of football players in a
huddle with Mead in the center. All of them were pretty
sloshed, and they had Mead's arms around their shoulders
to prop him up as they staggered around the corner.

"If he thinks he's going to come in at this hour and find
me waiting, ha!" Lynne snorted, pulling me out the door.
"Come on."

The guys had disappeared into Mead's room, but just
across the corridor was the staircase and one of those snack
bar nooks, a small room of its own with vending machines
for soft drinks and candy bars, and she pushed me inside. I
was really tired by this time and wanted to go home to
Gordon. But if I left Lynne alone, who knew what kind of
commotion she might make, and as it was I couldn't get a
word in edgewise. It was all about her, how she'd be
damned if she'd give her fucking fiancé the satisfaction of
toppling drunk into bed to find her waiting in a black lace
teddy when she'd been stuck in a traffic jam for three

hours, three fucking hours, and she was supposed to twiddle her thumbs while he was partying and she wasn't asked to be a bridesmaid. She'd show him. She'd march right back out and whoop it up in Newport and let him come in and not find her, ha!

And as I stood there in the snack bar nook, I couldn't help but wonder, show him what? How selfish and immature you are? That'll do it. Why was she going to such lengths to spy and stalk and plot revenge over such a trivial incident? Meanwhile, not once all night had she bothered to hold a decent conversation or get to know me. That's what I would have done in her place, try to make the best of it, rise above personal pettiness. I would have talked to her. But she saw me only as a dumb post to rant to, and I endured it for Gordon's sake and to spare Allison and Mead. Thinking some food in her stomach might help, I bought us each a candy bar, and it must have triggered her appetite because she wolfed two Snickers and three bags of potato chips. Then finally, Mead's door opened and his friends tumbled out, moaning about their aching heads and bumbling off to their rooms.

"Okay," I said firmly, "the coast is clear. It's late, and we should go to bed. You can talk to Steve in the morning, but right now what we all need is a good night's sleep."

Lynne nodded reluctantly, and I breathed an inner thank you that we were finally home free. But as we stepped into the hall, her posture changed and her eyes riveted.

"Well, well, look at this," she said, drawing out the words as if something delicious were on her tongue. I followed her gaze. In their drunkenness, the groomsmen had left the door to Mead's room half open.

"Oh no," I began.

"This is Mead's fault!" Lynne swore. "He's always lead-ing the guys off on some adolescent spree, and I'm going to tell him exactly what I think of him."

"No, Lynne—"

I snatched at her arm, but she lurched past me, and I saw by her flushed face and glazed eyes that the alcohol had finally hit. She barged through Mead's door with me after her, and we both stopped short in front of his bed. There he lay, passed out atop the bedspread, wearing nothing but his boxers and a goofy smile. Beer cans littered the floor, and the bedside light was on.

"Shleeping Beauty," Lynne slurred, then she swayed on her feet. "I feel shick."

We didn't make it to the toilet in time. As I flipped on the bathroom light, the mess splattered over the sink, the toilet, and the tiled floor. Lynne slumped to her knees to heave a final stream of alcohol, liquefied chocolate, and clumps of undigested potato chips into the bowl.

"I'm going to my room," she announced and staggered to her feet. Chunks of vomit hung in her hair and wet brown stains marked the knees of her linen pantsuit. Too disgusted to touch her, I watched from the doorway as she swayed down the hall and around the corner. Thank heaven! Now all I had to do was clean up the mess and my good deed was done. As I was passing the bed, Mead stirred, and I froze in alarm. He settled again in a moment, but as I waited to be sure, I couldn't help looking at him.

Do you know why God made you so pretty, Kimmy? Momma asked me before she died. I was twelve, and I shook my head. *Because he wants you to be happy. God doesn't make* girls as pretty as you to be sad and cry. Anytime you're unhappy, God is unhappy, too. That's when he expects you to change your life to make him and yourself happy again. Then she fastened a little gold cross on a chain around my neck, and I wear it always to remind me of God's will.

And it works. For example, I was happy for a while with Duane, my old boyfriend, who was the manager of a bowling alley. He was handsome and good to me, but we didn't seem to be going anywhere in our lives. I got a new job at the hospital, thinking that would help, and it was surely better than handing out red-and-green bowling shoes in sizes five through fourteen. But after a while I still wasn't totally happy, and I thought both God and I would be happier if I replaced Duane with a doctor. You can see how well I did there. But sometimes I think if I could put the two together and have both a smart, successful, rich husband like Gordon and a handsome, sexy, young one like Duane, then God and I would be happiest of all.

That's why I couldn't help but stare at Mead. I bet he could be a magazine model for *Esquire* or *GQ*. He was almost naked, his navy boxer shorts printed with little baseball bats and gloves, his chest nicely muscled, the dark hair above his forehead just long enough to curl a finger into. There was something cute about his navel and the way that little trail of hair led down from it to the elastic band of his shorts. The smile on his face had slipped to a seductive look, as if he were having sex dreams, and I confess my thoughts went a little further than they should have. I leaned forward, and at that very instant, Mead's hands flew up and landed on my breasts.

"M'mmm," he murmured. "M'mmm."

I stopped breathing, heart pounding, too terrified to move. What if he woke up? What if he saw me? What if— I nearly gasped, remembering the door to his room was still open—what if someone walked in? Mead's palms began kneading my breasts through my tank top. I didn't dare shift my body, and a hot flush was spreading from my nipples to my pelvis like a volcano about to go *ka-boom!* I'd only meant to take a closer look at him.

"Ahh," he murmured. "M'mmm."

Then his hands released—thank heaven, his eyes were still closed!—but as I jerked upright, I heard footsteps coming. In a panic, I flew to the bathroom, flipped off the light, and pressed my back against the wall. It was awful in there, so smelly it nearly made me puke, and now I got mad, thinking about the nerve of that Lynne to come back again! I was about to burst out and confront her, when something warned me to stay put. Those footsteps were too steady, too purposeful to be drunk, and I shrank as small as I could make myself in the dark. The door was still open a crack, but I didn't peek around it to see. All I heard was a voice cooing, "Mead, Mead, come on, let's have some fun." Then there was the sound of two bodies moving on the bed and Mead's voice, "M'mmm, m'mmm."

I shut my eyes, clapped my hands over my ears, and prayed to God. After a while I heard Mead shout, laughing, "Go 'way, you guys!" and, uncovering my ears, I heard a tapping on the outer door. For an awful second, I quaked in fear that the groomsmen would storm in and find me, and I huddled even smaller. But they didn't appear, and then the bed movements resumed, sheets squirming, that heated panting, the breathless shuddering, then a long exhalation like a dying breeze. *Whoa,* I thought, *you sure wouldn't have to give Mead Viagra!* But mostly I concentrated on praying that no one would need to use the bathroom.

Then it stopped, and Mead must have passed out again because the other person got out of bed, and I heard the door click closed. I didn't waste any more time. I flipped on the bathroom light and cleaned up the mess with lots of hot water and a washcloth and towel. I left the rinsed linens over the shower curtain rod, hoping Mead would overlook them come morning; otherwise, every trace of Lynne and me was gone. I tiptoed out of the bathroom, past Mead unconscious beneath the sheet, and held myself rigid beside the door until I counted to ten. Then I opened it and peeked out. The hallway was empty, and I darted across to the stairs. It was nearly three a.m., and sure enough there was Gordon asleep in our room, propped on the pillows in his pajamas, like he'd been waiting for me. I took off my clothes and slipped into bed.

In the morning I woke first, and I teased Gordon a little about how I'd found him. Then he took his Viagra and we made love, and afterward he ordered us room service for breakfast. I had a lobster omelet—it was scrumptious!—and I told him Lynne was all calmed down. I asked him not to mention it; she'd probably want to forget. Then we went shopping on Thames Street, and I bought the painted mermaid and the lighthouse for our guest bathroom.

Now here we are at our reception table. Not far away, Lynne and Steve seem reconciled, though they both look like the night they spent. Whoever else entered Mead's room hasn't said anything either, and now that he and Allison are safely married, it's not likely anyone will speak up. So I think we are all off the hook—whew!—and though certain details are coming back to me and I have my suspicions, you can trust me to keep silent. Because, as I say, God wants me to be happy, and I am happy being Mrs. Gordon Hollingsworth.

For now.

28

How Sharper Than a
Serpent's Tooth

Deirdre

LOOK AT HER, THE SLUT. The smug little slut. Sitting there beside my ex-husband, demure as milk and cookies with that tiny gold cross dangling above her breasts. How I hate her. How I'd like to see her poisoned. That was another of my murder fantasies for Gordon and Kimmy, by the way, to poison them, a ridiculously medieval notion but tempting nonetheless. Did you know that oleander leaves are highly toxic to humans? That one or two castor bean seeds will do in the average adult? Dogs can die if they lap antifreeze, not that that helps.

Of course, I'd be a suspect. I'd have the prime motive no matter how they were dispatched. But poison has the advantage of being sinister and mysterious. It promises a writhing, agonizing death, yet leaves no fingerprints. It would accomplish the deed while conferring upon me the reputation of a woman not to be trifled with. No doubt the latter message would be delivered even more effectively by blasting them with a shotgun in full public view. I wonder, after you've blazed away, if a pistol really does smoke in your hands? Or what is it those IRA thugs used to do to each other—kneecapping, I believe it's called? Are the victims left crippled with broken shins dangling useless for the rest of their lives? Would that be barbaric enough for a cheating husband and his tart? Are there any spare Irish I could hire to do it?

My gaze drifts around the ballroom, and a dejected sigh escapes my lips. Almost ten thirty, barely ninety minutes left. And the dessert buffet still isn't open; once again that incompetent caterer is running late. I'm so tired of upbraiding them. Oh, why can't I ignore Gordon, defy myself, and squeeze some enjoyment out of this night? During dinner, our table had a lively conversation, as my two nephews, my brother's sons, regaled us with their college escapades. Now they're dancing with their girlfriends, likewise my brother and his wife, and though I still have Susie and a few friends who've migrated to join us, I feel so alone and lost.

"Deirdre, what a wonderful wedding!"

"Allison is such a lovely bride!"

"Delicious dinner! The swordfish positively melted in our mouths."

"Susie, how nice that you could be here from . . . where is it, Idaho? Oh, Montana."

More friends drop by to chat—I can't seem to make the effort to go around to the tables—and I make enthusiastically false replies. Susie lumbers into the conversation, a dab of food stuck to her upper lip. Her sunburned skin looks absolutely terrible, her eyes are practically swollen shut. What's more, though I've pushed it down twice, her bra is showing again, a white horizon of extra-reinforced material rimming above the back of her dress. This strapless-style gown with its push-up front couldn't be more unflattering for a fat girl. Where the other bridesmaids look glamorous and alluring, Susie's torso resembles a blotchy sausage protruding from an overly tight casing. Thank heaven she wasn't in the processional! It's painful merely to glance at her, and I give my friends credit that they can smile so blithely and engage her in chitchat.

Susie licks a last lump of potatoes from her fork, and still that dab of food clings maddeningly to her mouth. I can't stand it—I grab her chin and my napkin and swipe it off. It was always a problem for Gordon and me, what to do about Susie. She pained both of us from the start. They say all babies are cute, even the ugly ones, but that isn't true. We knew what a pretty baby looked like, we already had Allison, and one sight of Susie's porkish face told us everything we needed to know. Even the beautiful name we'd picked out for her, Susanna, refused to stick—fled from her, really, as if it couldn't bear to be attached to this homely child. I've sometimes thought it might be different if Susie had been the firstborn when the inclination to bond might have been stronger. Then how could we have helped loving our second, a pretty baby, as well? Whereas Allison so instantly and effortlessly captured our hearts, poor Susie never had a chance. It took a weight off all three of us when, in an unusual burst of imagination, Susie sought and secured the teaching job in Montana. As we wished her bon voyage, we felt whole again, our perfect family restored. I realize the irony in my being the one to boast about family unity now.

"Tell us about Montana, Susie," the friends say generously, taking the vacant chairs.

"Well, Montana is called Big Sky Country and for good reason. Our state is over 145,000 square miles, which makes it the fourth largest in the union, after Alaska, Texas, and California. Our main industries are agriculture, cattle ranching, timber, and mining, and our spectacular natural scenery includes forests, lakes, and high granite peaks."

"And how do you like your teaching job? It is teaching you do, isn't it?"

"Oh yes, I teach second-grade elementary school in Butte. We just finished the semester, and my students made me a big farewell card with drawings of ponies and butterflies."

"How nice, Susie."

I curl my lip. You know what would be nice? If Gordon were to come over here and dance with his daughter. Not Allison. His other daughter. How can he be so thoughtless, so blind? There he sits beside Kimmy, engrossed in conversation with the hospital vice president and the other doctors and their spouses, and not once has it occurred to him to ask Susie to dance. Is it because he refuses to come anywhere in my vicinity? Or is he afraid to leave Kimmy at the table, unprotected from predatory males and harpy wives in his absence? More likely, he's worried she won't have an intelligent syllable to utter without him to prompt her. If she were smart, she'd do what I did as Gordon rose in his career: keep an index card file of everyone who could be useful so she can converse as if she holds them in the warmest regard. I'd like to go over and snipe in Gordon's ear, *What kind of father are you to ignore your other daughter?* But I won't lower my pride. He has to make the gesture. If only I could match Susie up with someone! But even after coercing her to lose a little weight, the best Allison and Mead could manage was Steve, who is already engaged and whose fiancée sat with him for dinner, while Susie sits unescorted at my family table. Damn it, that bra is driving me crazy.

"Susie, let's go up to the suite so I can fix your dress properly," I whisper, as the guests, having paid their obligatory compliments, move on.

"Oh," says Susie, twitching and shifting as she tries to look over first one and then the other plump shoulder.

We head for the grand staircase, and where is the Rosecourt hostess who is supposed to be here at all times to direct people to the amenities and to unhook the red velvet cordon across the stairs so we don't have to do it ourselves? They make such a selling point of having these butlers and hostesses constantly at your service, but here are the stairs unattended. I'll have a word about that with the supervisor when we're done. Meanwhile, Susie hikes her skirt in both fists and stumps up like a sailor planting his feet apart on a rolling deck. How can she not understand the simple act of gracefully and elegantly lifting your dress to ascend or descend? A staircase like this begs for a grand entrance, posture erect, one hand resting lightly on the banister, the other sweeping the skirt with such careless charm that it draws every eye to you as you float down.

We reach the suite, and I search through the mounds of clothes, boxes, and bags heaped on the bed and chairs, the discarded wrappings from the gowns. Finally, I find the sewing kit on the floor.

"All right, Susie, I know we brought safety pins," I say. "Let's get this dress fixed before we miss something important."

Susie stands obediently while I unzip the back of her gown, releasing the seared and corseted flesh. It's all I can do to contain a sense of revulsion as I tuck and pin and prod Susie, the bra, and the gown back together. Even then, I'm not successful, the heavy-duty white band still poking insistently above the rim.

"Why don't you take it off, Susie? You can wear this dress braless."

"Oh no, I don't think it would look right. Allison specifically said I should wear the bra."

"Just try it, Susie. Go in the bathroom." I shove her toward it, a little more rudely than necessary. Why does she always make trouble? I should be downstairs, seeing to our guests, not stuck out of sight with a grown daughter who can't manage her own underwear. Voices are approaching, and glancing outside to the landing I see a Rosecourt hostess and one of the waitresses talking as they mount the last few stairs.

"Mom, I need help!"

"All right, I'm coming." I hurry in irritation to the bathroom and begin unhooking Susie's bra, a job that makes my skin creep. Susie has had particularly oily skin since puberty, and I've never felt comfortable hugging or touching her. The voices enter the sitting room and grow louder.

"There, there's the mess. I found it when I came up to collect glasses."

"Oh my God."

"I know. Wouldn't you think that if you'd knocked red wine onto the carpet, you'd at least notify someone so they could try to clean it before the stain set? Rich bitches. Will that foam stuff work?"

"I hope so. It says to scrub it in and blot. Thanks for alerting us. If I can get this out, it will be my good deed for Anne . . . look, it's working! Where else did you see it splattered?"

"Here, and there's another splotch here. Hey, did you hear about the groom? It seems he slept with someone last night, and it wasn't the bride."

"I know! We heard that, too! Who was it?"

"We're not sure yet, but we're zeroing in. We overheard it first at the bridesmaids' table—well, not overheard it, you know how they talk as if we don't exist—and we've been eavesdropping ever since to get the dirt. Get this—it might even be one of them! Don'cha love it?"

"One of the bridesmaids? You're kidding! And the bride doesn't know?"

"Nope, but at the rate those airheads are yapping, she's bound to soon enough. I'll show you the prime suspect when we go downstairs. Let me get these hors d'oeuvre plates."

"I'll help you. This is too much!"

"Yeah, don'cha love it when rich people act so snobby and then act like trash!"

Susie is nearly gasping for lack of breath, but I keep my hand clamped over her mouth until I'm sure the two gossipers are gone. How dare those people make such comments about us! How dare they go spreading outrageous rumors from one end of the house to the other, laughing behind our backs! Susie yelps as I stab the open safety pin into the back of her dress, but I abandon her and run out of the bathroom, only to see the waitress and the hostess disappearing down the stairs. The nerve of them! After all I've done to orchestrate this evening, keeping my chin up, hiding my own pain, how dare anyone undermine my accomplishment? This could be a disaster!

"Mom, what are we going to do?" Susie, gown undone, cow breasts spilling over the bodice, tugs my arm.

"Shut up! Get back in the bathroom and don't say anything to anyone. Let me think."

"But we have to tell Allison! Mead cheated on her on their wedding night!"

"It wasn't their wedding night. It was the night before the wedding." Can't Susie get anything right? "Get yourself dressed. I have to go downstairs."

I run as fast as my gown will allow to the staircase, then catch myself in time to make a smiling, poised descent. No one must know, no one must suspect. How could Mead? What could he have been thinking? But he probably wasn't thinking, was he? Men never do, they just drop their pants. And which bridesmaid? I reach the bottom of the stairs—no hostess there again to unhook the cord—and my eyes rake the crowd. I can spot any number of waitresses, but no waitress and hostess together, and not having paid much attention to them throughout the evening, I can't begin to guess which two I just overheard. Damn it!

Mead and Allison are laughing and eating at their table, the bridesmaids are scattered around the ballroom, while the servers scurry to bring plates of wedding cake to the tables . . . they cut the wedding cake without me? I jerk my eyes to the stand where it was displayed. Only half of the butchered bottom layer remains, and guests laden with plates and coffee cups are emerging from the dining room, where the dessert buffet, cappuccino station, and cordials are set. My own daughter's wedding and they cut the cake without me?

"Mrs. Hollingsworth, may I speak with you?" Anne, the supervisor, confronts me, and in a deft movement, before I can get a word out, she draws me aside. Is she going to tell me the news is already widespread that Mead was screwing around on his prenuptial night? How dare she presume to inform me when she can't control her scandalmongering staff? "I don't want to cause an alarm, but the parents of the flower girl can't seem to find her."

"Who gave the instruction to cut the wedding cake?" I demand.

"I beg your pardon?"

"The wedding cake, who said you could cut it?"

"Allison and Mead cut it, so we could open the dessert buffet." Anne pauses a moment, as if to let me catch up, then continues. "As I said, the flower girl is missing, and I've sent several members of my staff to search the house. She probably hasn't gone far, but if we don't find her, I'd like to have the band make an announcement."

Oh, this is too much! Those stupid parents can't control their child, and now we have to interrupt the reception to blare it to one and all. I told Allison we should not allow children in the wedding party, period, but she overrode me, as usual. She always gets her way. She couldn't even bother to find me before she cut the wedding cake. Maybe I'll be the one to inform her what her horny groom has done. Why not just blow this whole reception to hell and be done with it?

A bridesmaid hurries toward us, what's-her-name, the pretty but somehow mousy girl, the one Allison and her friends are always sending on errands—Pammy, that's it. Could she be the traitorous wretch? No, too innocuous.

"We've looked once around the ballroom, but we can't find her," Pammy reports.

"Bring her parents here to the bottom of the staircase," Anne replies, "and I'll have one of my staff take them up to look, just in case she slipped past us."

Pammy nods, and repeating, "Excuse me, excuse me," she threads back through the crowd.

"We'll have one more look, Mrs. Hollingsworth, then we'll make an announcement." Anne nods curtly to let me know what she thinks of such careless parents and of people who put tiny children in their wedding party. The nerve of her! She didn't even respond to my complaint about the wedding cake.

"Mom, Mom!"

I turn at the cry to see Susie thudding down the stairs like an elephant, her braless breasts lurching perilously in the strapless gown.

"Mom!" she pants, heaving to a stop. "What are we going to tell Allison?"

"Tell me what?"

I whirl. There stands Allison, flanked by two of her bridesmaids, en route to mount the staircase themselves. She waits, cool and collected as always, while Susie freezes behind me on the stairs. For a minute, I hate both my daughters. Allison, who can so easily dismiss me from the wedding I slaved over, bringing to fruition her every infinitesimal whim, and Susie, unbearably stupid and clumsy Susie, who blunders into every situation with her ungainly body and her big mouth, blurting and ruining everything. What have I done to deserve this? For an instant I'm tempted to step out of the space between them and say, "Yes, Susie, go ahead, tell Allison everything," and relish the consequences. But the lifetime habit is too strong, appearances must be preserved at all costs, and before the rebellious thought can enact itself, different words are leaving my mouth.

"Tell you that Fiona is missing," I say calmly to Allison. "I'm sure it's nothing serious, but we better help look. If you two will circle the ballroom, discreetly, please . . ." I flick my hand at the two bridesmaids, ordering them off, a gesture that both affronts and scatters them to do my bidding. Amateurs! They think they own the world, that it's theirs to command, but they haven't anywhere near my experience at snapping my fingers and brooking no resistance. It's almost as if I've nipped them with the flick of a whip, and they startle away, disgruntlement catching up to them as they go. Was it one of them Mead slept with, and she wasn't about to let Allison be alone in the suite with another who might snitch? Or were they spiriting Allison upstairs for the opposite reason, in cahoots to reveal to her the juicy news about one of their clique? Either way, I'll not allow that to happen. If anyone's going to tell Allison it will be me, at an appropriate time and place, and with proof in my hand.

Allison exhales a weary sigh. "I suggested strongly to Fiona's parents that they ought to leave right after dinner. Go help look, Susie. I have to fix my hair." She brushes past her sister, who stands fumbling to rehook the velvet cord after her.

"You heard her," I repeat, as Susie turns to me for instructions what to do next. "Go look."

Susie nods and bumbles off, but before I can plan my own next move, I'm swamped by a sudden wave of friends.

"Deirdre! Lovely wedding!"

"Allison is such a beautiful bride!"

"Isn't the band fantastic! Everyone's having such fun!"

I clasp their hands. "I'm so glad you're enjoying yourselves. Have you had cappuccino? Have you tasted that divine wedding cake?"

I sweep them into the ballroom, my smile bright as the crystal chandelier above. Such a fabulous evening!

Why do I feel so numb?

29

SIBERIA

John

FREE—FREE AT LAST! That's the way to do it, you sly devil.
Pour Isabel a couple of vodka and tonics and you and Jack
Daniel's are single once again. You don't have much time
left to score, though. Hmm, what are your options?

First choice would be that bartender on the verandah,
the one with the perky tits and ponytail. Last time I had a
bouncy little number like that was—ha!—a mere month ago
with that cocktail waitress in Vegas. God, I love out-of-town
conferences! But so far the bartender girl has been all clever
talk and no action, even after I very visibly slipped a ten into
her tips glass. Besides, she's got that black dude standing
guard beside her like he's protecting her honor. Let a man
barely flirt with her and he gets an icy stare that would freeze
his dick off. Drop the moral stance, buddy, I want to tell him.
You think she wouldn't do it, given the right motivation? I
know 'em, believe me, I can pick out a target a mile away.

Second choice would have been the waitress at our
table, that curly-haired little Hispanic girl I struck up a

conversation with near the kitchen door. Didn't hesitate to retort when I teased her about her size. "Why, you're just an itty-bitty thing," I joked. "Sir, I am not a *thing*," she replied. Hey, it was all in good fun. But I nixed her when I got a better look at her ankles. Pretty up top, cute ass in that skimpy black skirt, but if there's anything that turns me off, it's a woman with thick ankles.

So who's going to be the lucky lady tonight? I wouldn't mind that supervisor dame who's in charge here, even if she did nix my request about the place card. She's a little older than my usual fare, but it looks like a pair of long legs under that skirt of hers and I've already observed she's got finely tuned ankles. I'd be willing to give her a second chance. But she's off bounds, probably all the staff are in a classy place like this because they're smart enough to know any fraternization with the guests will cost them their job.

So let's check out the guests, start roamin', pal. Josie Andrett, lookin' good. Ditto Peggy Morestone. But I know where not to go poaching, if I don't want to mess up a genial golf foursome. I have to say I like the look of that redheaded bridesmaid. Perfect nose, perfect teeth, perfect collarbones, and she knows it. She's also got a bit of a defiant air. Hmm, what's her insecurity, her weak point? That she gained two pounds last week for unfathomable reasons? That her doubles partner gets in more first serves than she does? That her friend Allison is married now and she isn't? Or maybe some cad implied she's not as hot in bed as she thinks she is? That's a good insecurity for a woman like her to have, because I'll be only to happy to help her prove otherwise. And if she's got a complex of these little issues gnawing away at her—even better. She'll be ripe for the plucking. Looks like she's heading outside alone, no sign of her groomsman. I'll just follow and—

"John! Great to see you and Isabel here tonight. How have you been?"

Gordon claps me on the back and clasps my hand.

"Gordon, terrific party! How's it feel to be the father of the bride?" And how does it feel to be the old goat rutting with that blond cheesecake of yours? is what I'd really like to ask him. Having bagged his honeypot, Gordon actually treats his marriage as if we're to take it seriously.

"Broke, I can tell you. But whatever makes Allison happy is worth the price."

"Sure, that's what daughters are for, isn't it, to run you into bankruptcy, ha-ha." As if Gordon is broke, ha-ha.

"What table are you and Isabel at, by the way? I didn't see you earlier."

"Over there, in the corner."

"Ouch, what did Isabel do to Deirdre to deserve that?"

"I have no idea."

Gordon chuckles. "Well, she seems to be having fun."

I glance back at the Siberia table and wince at the sight of Isabel barreling out some song with Madge Dombrowski and the dotty aunts.

"Anyway, that's women for you," Gordon resumes affably, having pointed out to me the spectacle my wife is making of herself. "But as I told Kimmy, this is Allison's day. We'll let Deirdre arrange everything, and I'll just sign the checks."

"Hope you didn't get writer's cramp, ha-ha." Got to get the message across, don't you, Gordon. Got to let us all know how magnanimous you are to ante up and how virtuous the honeypot is to go along.

"I'm also sending Allison and Mead to Italy on a two-week honeymoon," he says. "That's my wedding gift."

"Good choice, Italy. I'm sure they'll enjoy it." Right. I've listened to enough of his self-flattery. Time to get back to my agenda. "Speaking of the happy couple, I haven't yet paid my respects to the groom's family. Isn't his sister one of the bridesmaids? Is she that redheaded girl?"

"No, that's Lauren somebody-or-other, a friend of Allison's from the city. Mead's sister is the brunette with glasses—smart Harvard lawyer, I'm told. Ball-buster." Gordon pauses to give me a sly wink. "I'd go for the redhead, if I were you, John."

"Ha-ha, you read my mind, Gordon."

"Ha-ha, watch yourself, John."

Ha-ha, you self-satisfied prick. Why don't you go toss some more money around, stuff it down the cleavage of Kimmy the trophy bride with the doe eyes and pouty lips. She's ten years younger than Allison, for Christ's sake! Well, I don't want a trophy wife. If I can ever ditch Isabel, I'm calling matrimony quits. Give me an endless series of one-night stands, no strings, no promises, that's my ticket. Now if I can find that redhead . . . And by the way, Gordon, you asshole, thanks for the inspiration you've unwittingly provided. I'm about to execute the perfect setup.

I step outside, loosen my bow tie, and inhale a breath of cool air. I like a good band, but between the crowd yakking and the heat wave rising on the dance floor, it's better to be out of the noise and the crush. And there's my lovely redhead, collecting a drink at the bar. She sways to the wicker furniture on the verandah and takes a seat. I swirl my drink. *Ready, Jack?*

"Hello there! I'm John Newsome, a friend of Gordon and Deirdre's from way back. Are you Mead's sister, the lawyer? Oh, I'm sorry. I was told Mead's sister was one of the bridesmaids and a very sharp lawyer, and I thought that must be you. Well, you certainly look like you could take charge of a courtroom, Lauren, and as a highly paid corporate attorney, I should know. Mind if I take this empty chair? I don't want to intrude if you're with someone . . . Oh, your groomsman's a bore and your boyfriend did what? Well, I can't conceive how any man would pass up the chance to be here with you. But tell me, Lauren, have you ever thought about a law career? Because my firm—did I mention I'm a partner?—is always looking to hire, and legal secretary is how a lot of young women get their start. There's a lot of honorable work to be done in the field. Fighting for the downtrodden, defending our civil liberties, environmental protection—think Erin Brockovich. Wait, that's it! That's why I thought you must be a lawyer. You're a dead ringer for Julia Roberts! Say, why don't we take our drinks and stroll down toward the water, away from the noise of the band . . ."

Putty in my hands, Jack. You're the man!

30

WE HATE YOU

The Rosecourt Staff

YOU COULDN'T GO QUIETLY, could you? You couldn't just dance, drink, and merrily close cut the night. And here we've been doing our best to be charming and efficient no matter what, though it didn't stop us from having a little private fun. During our dinner break, we crowded into the old servants' quarters for pizza and to cast our votes.

Classiest Dresser: Deirdre Hollingsworth, hands down. Hey, we may not like you, but that's one helluva gown.

Most Fun: Lady at the Siberia Table in the orange paisley dress. Last time we checked, she had them all whooping "The Beer Barrel Polka." You're our kind of gal.

Most Obnoxious: The redheaded bridesmaid, the lady in the blue dress . . . the jury's still out.

Now we're back on duty, smiling and bowing, scoping out the ballroom as we nominate contenders for our Worst Dancer award. The candidates are legion; the contest will be hard fought. Except now you've gone and spoiled it.

After an evening of minor crimes and misdemeanors, you've pulled a truly boneheaded stunt.

You've lost the kid, damn it. You've misplaced Fiona, the dimpled flower girl. And after we did our diplomatic best to prevent it. When you let her clamber up and down the grand staircase as if it were a piece of playground equipment, we said, "Oh my, do be careful, Fiona. We wouldn't want you to slip and get hurt or tear your pretty dress." You stood right there when we said it, you caught her at the bottom of the stairs as she tumbled down. We'll give you credit for that; some parents don't even bother to pick up the kid when she falls. You caught her, more or less, mostly less because you were more concerned about not spilling the drink in your hand. Then you put her back on the stairs for another go. We repeated our concern.

"Oh dear, Fiona, did you bang your elbow? This really isn't a safe place to play, is it? Maybe you'd better stay off now."

We shepherded her toward you and endured your dirty look. How dare we reprove you? You might have to stop socializing and actually monitor your child. To keep her amused while you gabbed with your friends, you held her so she could pluck the heads off the flowers in the foyer centerpiece and flutter petals over the floor.

"My goodness, Fiona, that's quite a mess you're making, isn't it?" we observed.

You ignored the hint, until she stabbed her thumb on a thorn and wailed. To pacify her, you gave her a glass of Coke and let her toddle down the hall, splashing soda until the whole, sticky glass slipped out of her hands in a sugary brown *sploosh*. You came just in time to scold her for spilling a drop on her dress, while we dove on all fours to blot the bubbling puddle from the carpet. Naturally, you didn't apologize.

Finally, to our relief, you abandoned all pretense of parenting and dumped her on Madeline, the junior bridesmaid, with whom we sympathized.

"Are you babysitting Fiona now, Madeline?"

"I'm trying, but I can't make her stay in one place. She wants to run everywhere."

"Did her parents bring any toys or a book you could entertain her with?"

"I don't know. I'm sorry. I have to go chase her . . ."

We watched her dart after Fiona and disappear. Meanwhile Nicholas, the ring bearer, was showing signs of being the devil's spawn.

"I want to go upstairs."

"Sorry, the upstairs suite is for the bride and her bridesmaids only."

"Allison is my cousin, so I get to go up, so there!"

"No, we're sorry. Only the bride and her attendants are allowed upstairs."

"I'll tell Allison."

"Yes, why don't you do that."

"I'll tell my mother!"

"Please do."

"I'll tell on you!"

Go ahead, you little bastard, go fetch your mother. Not only will we inform her the upstairs is closed to everyone but the bride and bridesmaids—yes, we love it when we can invoke the rules!—it will be the perfect opportunity to politely repeat that children are not allowed to be unattended in the house anytime, anywhere. But Nicholas was too crafty to risk early exposure with a whole evening ahead in which to foment evil. When next seen, he had pulled the poker from behind the fireplace screen and was about to jab the unsuspecting rump of the bride's porky sister.

"Stop it!" we commanded, snatching the implement none too gently from his hand, and of course, his mother appeared.

"What are you doing?" she demanded, cuddling him as he feigned with great drama an injury so devastating he must cradle the limp, innocent hand.

"Your son was about to jab a guest with this poker."

"Well, I can't believe you'd leave a dangerous item like this out where any child can reach it."

"We didn't leave it out. It was stored inside the fireplace, behind a heavy wrought-iron screen, and he leaned over and helped himself."

"Well, I can't believe you couldn't foresee such a situation occurring and take steps to prevent it!"

For his third trick, Nicholas escaped from his mother—not a difficult maneuver—and, sensing vulnerability, began stalking Madeline.

"Nick, leave me alone! I'm supposed to be watching Fiona!"

"Nyah, nyah, got your sash!"

"Nick, let go! Fiona! Fiona, come back here!"

"Nyah, nyah, got your hair!"

"Ouch! Nick, let me go! I'll get in trouble!"

We grabbed him by the wrist—yes, the same injured wrist, poor boy—and we're sorry, Leon, but he deserved it. "If you bother Madeline again, we'll tell Mrs. Hollingsworth," we hissed in the brat's ear.

Ah, Deirdre, the wedding Nazi. Even Nicholas knew enough to shut up and not push his luck there. But since we couldn't bind him and throw him in the dark closet with the mops and the spiders—rats!—we had to let him go. He gave us a sneer and the finger and bolted into the crowd. Children like Nicholas should be boiled. At least our interference gave Madeline a chance to escape in pursuit of Fiona, or so we hoped.

Now Fiona is missing.

Our first sweep of the house turns up empty. Anne asks the band leader to make an announcement.

"Ladies and gentlemen," says Glen Gold into the mike. "We are looking for Fiona, the flower girl. Could you all please take a minute, check around and under your tables, and if you have any idea where she might be, come speak with Anne here."

Heads swivel obediently, tablecloths lift, then shoulders shrug, and the dancing and conversations resume.

"It's just as well we keep the guests in the ballroom for now," says Anne, though her expression is growing worried. "Having a mob of people running through the house will only confuse the situation."

She delegates us to search again, main floor, restrooms, the closets and crannies only we know. Upstairs to scour the suite, downstairs to the basement; it will be a blow to our pride if the child got past us somehow. We flip on lights in dark hallways, bend to peer under tables and chairs, double-check the locked doors. "Fiona!" we call. "Fiona, are you there?" We know whose fault it will be if she's not found quickly, if she's not safe and sound.

But Fiona isn't there. Anne sends Leon and the valet parkers, armed with flashlights, to scan row by row through the cars. On the verandah, neither the bartenders nor the guests catching the fresh air remember seeing her.

"I want one butler to stay at the front door, one at the door to the verandah, one hostess at each staircase," Anne orders, the severity in her voice betraying her fear. "Everyone else take a flashlight and space yourselves in a line to search down the lawn to the ocean."

"The ocean?" gasps Fiona's mother. "No, no!"

"There's a six-foot chain-link fence with a locked gate," Anne replies, firmly. "I'm sure we'll find her."

The reassurance goes unheeded. "My baby, my baby!" Fiona's mother wails, racing out of the house toward the dark lawn. Suddenly, the child she couldn't be bothered to claim all night is hers.

"Go," Anne says in a low voice, partying guests still flowing around us, and we hurry out, no more sarcasm, no smart remarks now. Something has changed. This is our house, we know its every nuance, every stirring of air, and it's whispering to us this is no false alarm anymore. Fiona is missing, lost from under the noses of everyone here. An accident? A gap in the fence? A child snatcher? A small body crushed out of sight under the wheels of a departing car? We fan into the dark, a pristine full moon rising in the sky, its path dappling on the water.

Fiona is missing.

Find her!

31

ALWAYS A BRIDESMAID

Pammy
Please, Fiona. Come out, come out, wherever you are.

I murmur the words in my mind, still hoping it's a game, though I hardly expect Fiona to pop up among the few guests socializing here on the verandah. This area is well lighted, and I swept over it once when we first learned she was missing. On the second sweep I looked more diligently behind the potted trees, and the bartenders checked under the cloth covering their table. Inside, they're scouring the house, yet I have a feeling she's somewhere outdoors. I keep trying to remember where I last saw her, my memory skipping over images of a little girl in a white dress, fleeting glimpses of her appearing and disappearing among the crowd. It seems impossible she could be lost with so many people around, but that's how it happens, isn't it? *I thought she was with you. No, she wanted to sit with you, remember? Wasn't Madeline supposed to be watching her?* The reality of it still hasn't rippled through the guests, most of whom are dancing, drinking, visiting the dining room for desserts and liqueurs. *No, we haven't seen her. Do you want us to help look? Don't worry, you'll find her.* Now a half dozen Rosecourt staffers are moving across the lawn, flashlights in hand.

Where else should I try? Floodlights on the mansion's eaves illuminate the areas nearest the house, but beyond their reach a soft darkness stretches, and beyond that, if you can hear it above the music from the ballroom, comes the regular *shush* of waves rolling in from the sea. A full silver moon floats high in the sky. My eyes pick up a movement midway down the lawn, a couple emerging from the darkness, strolling back from the water's edge. Fredericka and Blaine. The last time I saw them they were dancing, then they vanished, and I wondered where they'd gone. Funny, from the little I've gotten to know Fredericka, I wouldn't have thought she'd be interested in anything as old-fashioned and unliberated as a boyfriend. Yet here she and Blaine come, not arm in arm or even shyly hand in hand, but talking as intently as if they're the only two people on the planet, which maybe right now they are. Funny, too, that the groomsman Allison and Mead picked for me turns out to be gay. Thankfully, Patrick unwittingly disabused me of any foolish hopes before I could act on them. When we sat down for dinner he leaned close to my ear, and as my heart fluttered in anticipation of some intimate overture, he said, "Pammy, you're such a nice girl I know I can trust you. Would you happen to know whether Blaine is free?"

"Pammy! Pammy, I have to talk to you!" Susie lumbers toward me, panting, skirt hitched in both hands.

"What is it, Susie? Have you seen Fiona?"

"No, it's something different. It's about Allison."

"Then it'll have to wait, Susie. I have to search for Fiona."

"I know, Pammy, but this is urgent."

"All right, quick then, what is it?" I don't mean to sound impatient, but I can see over Susie's right shoulder that Fredericka and Blaine, having stopped to talk to one of the searchers, are now hurrying up the stairs toward us, while over Susie's left shoulder, Carolyn, Jessica, and Nicole are also veering through the guests in our direction. What do they want now? Susie clutches me by both shoulders.

"Oh, it's awful, Pammy!" she cries, and as she grabs a deep breath to continue, Fredericka and Blaine, and Carolyn, Jessica, and Nicole all arrive simultaneously behind her. Everyone's mouth opens at once.

"Mead slept with one of the bridesmaids last night!" Susie blurts.

"What's this about Fiona being lost?" Fredericka demands.

"We can't find Lauren anywhere!" gasp Carolyn, Jessica, and Nicole.

There's a pause, as if the eye of a hurricane is passing over us, then the storm explodes in full fury.

"*What* did you say about my brother?"

"Oh no, no one else was supposed to hear!"

"You know Lauren can't be trusted."

"She's always been a boyfriend stealer."

"Please, Fredericka, I take it back! I didn't mean it! Don't shake me!"

"She's jealous because her own boyfriend broke up with her."

"And she never did like the cinnabar."

"Listen, you airheads, my brother would *not* sleep with anybody the night before his wedding."

"I'm sorry! I only meant to get your advice, Pammy. Mom's going to kill me!"

"Allison will be heartbroken!"

"How could Mead do this to her?"

"Listen, my brother may be an idiot but—"

"Men, they're all alike!"

"Heartless!"

"Cruel!"

"And they never get the right present for your birthday."

"Blaine, let me go! Listen, you bimbos, if my brother slept with anybody, it was a drunken one-night stand with a stripper and certainly not with the likes of you."

"I'm sorry, I'm sorry! Please, don't tell anybody that I told!"

"*Stop it!*" I shriek, hands clapping over my ears. "*Stop it!*"

"Yes, do stop it," repeats a calm voice behind me, and there stand Allison and Mead, arm in arm. Our jaws drop. We freeze. There's no way they didn't overhear us.

"Allison, we're so sorry," I say, racking my brain for some way to smooth things over, though I don't even know what the full story is. Susie looks aghast, Fredericka is pinioned in Blaine's restraining arms, and Carolyn, Jessica, and Nicole are preparing to rush forward and embrace Allison in sympathetic hugs.

With one uplifted eyebrow, Allison cuts us all short.

"You should be sorry," she says, reprovingly, "spreading a silly rumor like that when there's absolutely no truth in it. I can't imagine how you could get a story so completely wrong." She shakes her head as if we're children. "Of course my husband slept with someone last night. He slept with me. Do you think I was going to spend the night before my wedding alone?"

Her lips curve in a coy smile toward Mead, and there's a dawning moment as we take in the news.

"Ha! I knew there was an explanation," says Fredericka, disentangling herself from Blaine.

Carolyn, Jessica, and Nicole clasp their hands to their breasts, gushing sighs of relief. "Oh, Allison, Mead, we're so sorry! Lauren's been drinking strawberry margaritas and whiskey sours and making the most stupid insinuations, and you know how petty she can be. We never really believed it for a minute, honest!"

Mead blinks like a man who has suddenly and miraculously been exonerated from a crime.

"It's all right, I forgive everyone," says Allison indulgently. "Now where is Lauren? I came out here to fetch you because I'm going to toss the bouquet from the grand staircase."

"The bouquet! Oh, the bouquet!"

They clap, squealing, and Fredericka rolls her eyes.

"C'mon, Freddie," Mead nudges her, winking. "Be a sport. Do it for me?"

"But," Susie begins, still not caught up with the rest of us, "the waitress in the suite told the hostess who was cleaning up the wine that another waitress said that she heard one of the bridesmaids say that—" She stops, sinking in the quicksand of her own confusion.

Allison smiles serenely. "Poor Susie, you never get it right. It's very simple. Mead and the boys came back drunk last night, and they dumped him in his room. They made such a racket, they woke me up, and I went into the hallway to quiet them. Then Steve's girlfriend Lynne showed up very much the worse for wear, and I had to help her dig through her purse to find her key. By the time I got her into her room, I thought I'd better check on my fiancé as well." Allison sends another blushing look her husband's way. "Well, you can guess what happened."

Carolyn, Jessica, and Nicole giggle, and Susie nods happily at the explanation. Fredericka snorts a "whatever" and mutters an apology to Blaine, though she's clearly not pleased at being roped into the tossing of the bouquet. I suppose with so much to-ing and fro-ing in the hallway last night, it's not surprising a rumor started that Mead had a woman in his room. And as always, I'm the last to know. I'd seen the other bridesmaids whispering to their dates at our table, but I was busy counseling Patrick, who was working up the courage to come out of the closet to his friends.

"Come on inside then," Allison says, motioning. "Everyone's waiting."

I take a few steps with the other bridesmaids, then fall back and watch them go. What's the use? I've caught the bouquet four times before. At the last wedding, the bride walked over and thrust the flowers directly into my hands. Yet it's not as though, at thirty-one, all my chances are gone; it's just that the men I meet always seem to want an Allison or a Jessica or a Carolyn—or a Blaine. Well, one thing is for sure: I'm not going to be a bridesmaid anymore. Why do they even ask me, except to run their errands, resolve their tiffs, zip up their dresses, and find that last-minute lipstick. It's the same at work, I cover for everyone else while they take the credit, the thanks, and the pay raise. When do I get the raise or the guy, damn it? I won't do this anymore! I'm going to be bold and aggressive and take what I want. I'm going to be ruthless and selfish . . .

Down on the lawn, a line of figures waving flashlights emerges from the darkness, and I jerk back to my senses. Fiona is missing, we're supposed to be searching for Fiona! How could I have been so self-centered to forget her? Concentrate! When did I last see her? Where? Walking down the aisle scattering petals, during the photography session in the rose garden, once or twice in the ballroom, the guests chuckling as she hopped and bopped to the music in that unselfconscious way small children do. A little white dress flitting spritelike through the crowd. The searchers gather at the foot of the stairs, indicating their failure by quick shakes of their heads. I let my eyes roam over the grounds, along the fencing and hedges that separate Rosecourt from the mansions on either side, and suddenly that little white dress is in my mind, running over the dark grass, through an archway in the privet hedge, not flitting now but lying quiet, floating face down . . . oh my God, oh my God, I remember Fiona climbing onto the rim of the fountain in the rose garden while the photographer tried to take our pictures!

A wordless cry leaves my throat, and I dash down the verandah stairs, heads turning in puzzlement after me. Skirt in hands, I run for the arched opening that leads to the rose garden. Water bubbles gaily from the fountain's spout and spills down the tiers, and there in the round basin the moonlight falls on a tiny form, a billow of cloud-white in the cool dark pool.

"Fiona!"

She's too far away for me to reach from the rim, and kicking off my high heels I scramble over the edge, my gown dunking into the knee-high water, my feet slipping on the smooth marble bottom. I hitch my skirt and splash toward her, scoop and clasp her to my chest, then gasp as I straighten and the cold wet bundle flops against my bare skin.

"Fiona! Fiona!" I scream to the night. I try to wade back, cradling her head as it bobbles lifelessly on my shoulder, but my skirt, fallen from my hands, is weighted with water, and the dress clings and twists itself around my legs. "Help me!" I scream, as half a dozen people burst through the hedge, and lunging forward, I almost throw Fiona into their outstretched arms.

"Get a doctor!" someone shrieks.

"Get her mother!" cries another.

"Get out of the way! I am a doctor!" a third voice commands.

A Rosecourt butler leans to help me out of the fountain, but my legs shake, and as more arms reach to grab me I lose my balance and plop down.

"I've got you," says the butler, his forearm slipping firmly under mine.

"I'm fine, take care of Fiona," I insist, waving the others back and rising unsteadily. As I slide over the fountain's rim, I see a small knot of figures bent on the ground, a frill of white dress, pumping arms. Then the white frill rolls over, and there's a choking, spluttering sound. Fiona wails, and tears of relief spill from my eyes. It's the best sound I've ever heard.

"You saved her!" a woman says, clutching my hand, as more voices babble around us.

"Let me help you inside," says the butler, and I nod.

The wet bodice of my dress chills my breasts, the soaked skirt drags on the ground. Someone drapes a shawl over my shoulders, while others cluck for me to get dry, keep warm. Fiona's cries subside as she's carried toward her parents, who arrive to smother her with tears and kisses. *Our darling, our baby, how dare they leave that fountain unguarded?* I look up at the mansion, music, light, and laughter pouring from the open doors, and I shiver and draw the shawl closer. Inside, on the grand staircase, Allison is probably tossing her bouquet right about now. I picture the flowers turning over and over, arcing through the air in slow motion, landing in some excited girl's hands.

32

POWER

Fredericka

REMEMBER WHEN I THOUGHT all a bridesmaid had to do was buy a dress and walk down the aisle? I was wrong.

First and foremost, being a bridesmaid requires you to be embroiled in a soap opera that would make *Days of Our Lives* seem dull. From the simmering mutiny over the cinnabar at the first bridesmaids' luncheon to the calamity of my gnawed fingernails to the crisis of Susie's sunburn, there was enough melodrama before the ceremony started to fuel a miniseries. Now it seems half the night has been devoted to sleuthing and scheming and gossiping about who Mead slept with the night before his wedding when it was—*ta-da!*—Allison. Nor am I too proud of myself for having shaken poor Susie and nearly punched out the Beauty Queens there on the verandah, but I was right, wasn't I? They were slandering my brother, and though it did originally enter my mind that he might have had a close encounter of the naked kind with a stripper, the charge that he'd fornicated with one of the bridesmaids was so ludicrous

I couldn't restrain myself. At least in that department, all's well that ends well.

Another obligation of being a bridesmaid is to smilingly participate in a number of arcane rituals. Take the bouquet toss, which, despite Mead's coaxing, I was still trying to avoid. As Allison hustled us in from the verandah, Mead told me Allison had nixed the idea of him removing her garter and tossing it to the unmarried guys because it was tacky. And a bunch of unmarried women scrambling and fighting over a nosegay in the hope it will bring them a groom isn't? Now I find myself deposited in the front row before the grand staircase among the other female contenders, a considerable subset in a crowd of two fifty. To my surprise, Aunts Iris and Edna are among them.

"What are you doing here?" I ask, frowning at their frailty, as Allison continues up the staircase to take her position.

"Edna wants to catch the bouquet," says Aunt Iris.

"Eh?"

"*I said, you want to catch the bouquet, don't you, Edna?*" shouts Aunt Iris.

"Eh?"

"She wants to catch a man," Aunt Iris reaffirms, nodding, "and I wouldn't mind one either."

I note their eyes look a little glassy. "You'll have better luck back here," I say, hauling them toward the perimeter where the photographer and videographer are balancing on chairs to capture the action.

"Please, please, I must get this shot. It's on Allison's list," the photographer begs as the guests shove around him, their arms sticking into the air to blindly aim their disposable cameras. I catch Blaine's eye, signaling for help, but before he can reach us, the flowers sail over Allison's head, there's a squealing surge forward, and in the mini melee that ensues, a huge lunging red form breaches like a whale and Susie heaves out of the waves to snag the bouquet before sounding again. I grab a great-aunt by each arm to steady them as the photographer topples with a cry. For a minute he disappears entirely in a mass of flailing bodies. Then I spot him slowly rising, rubbing his head, his camera still clutched in one hand.

"I don't care," he says, giving me a dazed, wondering look as I steer Iris and Edna past him. A beatific smile breaks across his face, lighting his whole expression. "I don't care!"

"Are you all right?" Blaine asks at my side.

"Yes, but I think these party girls should go back to their table." I beckon Cousin Madge and turn over to her the lovelorn octogenarians.

Then everyone stops as we hear sirens approaching.

I confess I'd forgotten about Fiona. Since the band was playing and guests were dancing when Allison brought us in for the bouquet toss, I'd assumed her disappearance was nothing serious. Now the band leader is announcing that the flower girl has been found, she's fine, not to worry, her parents are taking her to the hospital as a precaution, all of which seems to be blatantly contradicted by the appearance of Pammy, damp and bedraggled, being led in on a butler's arm.

"Pammy, what happened?" I rush to her, people converging around us, and with a quick promise to take her up to the suite, I relieve the butler of his charge.

"She saved Fiona's life!" several voices proclaim, and as the guests part to let us through to the staircase, the story pours out. As we pass, I see Susie, huffing and panting, jealously guarding her flowers from the Beauty Queens, who are still eyeing it with the certainty it should have been theirs. Allison pauses long enough to praise Pammy's valiant plunge into the fountain, embracing her at arm's length to prevent the soaked dress from making contact with her wedding gown.

"I'm fine. It was good luck, that's all. I just happened to be in the right place at the right time," Pammy insists to everyone, although I can feel her shivering. In the suite, I peel off her wet gown and grab towels from the bathroom as Anne hurries in.

"They've taken Fiona in the rescue wagon. How are you feeling? Do you need to go to the hospital?" she asks, quickly assessing Pammy's condition.

"No, it's only the dress," Pammy replies. "I'm fine."

"What about bumps or bruises? Did you hit your head or twist your ankle when you fell?"

"No, I'm fine. What about Fiona?"

"She seems completely all right. Thank heaven we had a house full of doctors! I can ask one of them to come up here to see you, or we can drive you to the hospital if you'd like to go."

"No, really, I'm okay. That's enough towels, thanks, Fredericka."

Pammy manages a weak laugh at the yards of terrycloth I've swathed her in, and Anne releases a pent-up breath, finally accepting Pammy's reply.

"I'm sorry. I didn't mean to pressure you. It's been a little tense."

"Does this sort of thing happen often?" I ask, locating Pammy's street clothes and helping her dress, while Anne turns her efforts to hanging up the ruined bridesmaid's gown.

"Flowers girls falling into the fountain, you mean? No, that's a first, although we have had drunken adults go dancing in it before."

"You're joking!"

"I wish I were." Anne carries the soggy garment to the bathroom. "And I've had to call 911 for heart attacks, and allergic shock, and guests tripping over their own feet on the dance floor and falling down and breaking their arms. At least no one's died . . ." She stops in the doorway and covers her mouth with her fingertips, one arm pressed against her waist, her wry tone suddenly gone. "I'm sorry. Tonight could have been really serious."

"Here, come here, sit down." Pammy and I both jump to help her, but Anne shakes herself erect.

"No thanks. I have to get back downstairs and make sure everything's under control." She squeezes Pammy's hands. "If you change your mind, if you feel at all unwell, let me know immediately and we'll take you to the hospital."

"I'm fine," Pammy repeats.

"I'll stay with her," I add.

"Well," Pammy drops onto the bed as Anne leaves, "this has been an exciting evening, hasn't it? Was it Susie I saw who caught the bouquet?"

"Yes indeed." I sit down beside her.

"Nicole won't like that. She expected it to be her turn."

"Tough luck. In a heroic leap, Susie snatched the flying florals and won the dubious distinction of being next to march to the altar."

We both laugh, and I think maybe a tradition isn't so silly if it can do that, give two very different women a reason to laugh together.

"I saw you coming out of the shadows with Blaine," Pammy teases, a bit shyly. "What were you two up to in the moonlight?"

"We were discussing the effects of political instability on the creation of a national literature."

"Political instability? National literature? Fredericka, moonlight's for romantic glances and stolen kisses and sweet nonsense whispered in the ear. However did you get elsewhere?"

"Well, Blaine was elucidating his thesis on Chaucer and that led to the War of the Roses and Elizabeth Tudor and—"

Pammy interrupts with a shake of her head. "All I know is that if I had a guy as good-looking as Blaine alone in the dark . . ."

"Did you want to get Blaine alone in the dark?" I stop short, trying to read her. "Listen, I've only just met him and if you're interested—"

"Oh, goodness no, I didn't mean that."

She dissuades me with a smile, but even I, heartless feminist bitch that I am, can sense the loneliness she's trying to conceal.

"Look, Pammy, I'm far from an expert on matchmaking, but it seems to me that any guy would be lucky to find a woman like you. You're kind and helpful and caring. You're a terrific friend who's done everything humanly possible to give Mead and Allison a perfect wedding, from keeping the rest of us idiots in line to saving Fiona's life.

And you did, Pammy, you saved that little girl's life, not by accident or good luck, but by being the kind of conscientious person you are. It just so happens that I know some single, attractive, old-fashioned men in Washington—they're called Republicans, and most of them I've faced across a courtroom, it's true—but if you'd care to come visit me sometime, I'd be happy to introduce you. And if I ever were to get married—which I'm not, but if I were—you'd be the first and probably the only person I'd ask to be my bridesmaid."

"I'd be honored."

We hug each other, and damn if my eyes aren't wetting like a silly girl's. "Okay, now let's go downstairs and party."

"No, you go, Fredericka, I—" Pammy gestures at her cotton skirt and blouse and shakes her head.

"Then you wear my dress," I say, reaching behind my back for the zipper.

"Oh no, I couldn't."

"Don't be silly. We're near the same size, I've been dying for an excuse to get out of it, and besides, it doesn't go with my fingernails." I hold up my hands and waggle my fingers. Somehow during the course of the evening, probably when I was preparing to punch out the Beauty Queens, I've succeeded in breaking, chipping, and ripping off half the acrylic claws. I undress and zip Pammy into my gown. "Now go," I say, shooing her toward the door.

"I'll tell Blaine you're coming," she teases. "I bet he's still waiting for you at the foot of the stairs."

She laughs and disappears, and I rummage among the garments dumped on the bed for the slacks and top I wore to Rosecourt. What a mess! Hangers and garment bags and tissue littering the floor. Enough cosmetics in the bathroom to open a beauty parlor. A lipstick kiss on the mirror—was that the Beauty Queens' idea of being playful or was one of them actually falling in love with her own reflection and trying out a smooch? Yuck! I finish dressing and survey the wreckage around me. *Did you learn anything from this experience in Bridesmaidsland, Fredericka?* I ask myself. *Did you figure out what's going on here?*

Yes.

Women, even in a vaunted egalitarian society such as ours, still lack access to the highest reaches of power, and a wedding is the one—and possibly only—time in a woman's life when she is not only allowed but *expected* to exercise complete control.

Why did we have to wear cinnabar?

Because it's the bride's prerogative to specify the color and style of her attendants' dresses.

Why did Susie starve herself trying to lose thirty pounds, and why was I decked out in artificial fingernails?

Because Allison commanded it be so.

Why did Gordon Hollingsworth get to parade Kimmy under his ex-wife's nose?

Because Allison said he could, she had no problem with it, she invited Kimmy to be here.

Why did Deirdre endure it?

Because the bride's right to happiness supersedes that of everyone else, including her mother.

Why did my parents butt out of the wedding plans and relinquish all say, even regarding events like the rehearsal dinner, which they paid for?

Because Allison intimated they should be invisible.

Why was a child as young as Fiona included in the festivities, a risky decision even without the complication of an alluring fountain to fall into?

Because Allison's vision of the perfect wedding mandated a little blond flower girl.

Why did Allison get to toss the bouquet but Mead did not toss the garter?

Because it's up to the bride what's tradition and what's tacky.

Why did we have to haul ourselves all the way to Newport for this when the majority of the guests live within the New York City commuting area and there are countless charming wedding venues to be had within an hour's drive of the city?

Because it's what Allison wanted, this is her special day, and from the moment she announced her engagement, there has been a year of fevered activity to fulfill her every desire. We have to do this for her now, obey her now, because never again in her life will we grant her this level of power.

C'mon, it's true. Even if you're the female president of a corporation directing thousands of employees—and we all know that's rare—you still have to answer constantly to someone, your board of directors, your stockholders, the competitors nipping at your heels. Whereas a bride-to-be has the ultimate authority to decide every detail of her wedding, from the inscription on the cocktail napkins to the candles on the dining tables. If she's flexible and considerate, sure, she'll accept suggestions, sure, she'll involve the groom. But if it's something she really wants, no one, especially not the husband-to-be, will contradict her. The only constraint is the budget, yet even on very limited funds, it's still the bride's choice whether she wants her guests to eat lasagna or chicken cacciatore. And if, as for Allison, money is no object, the bride can simply sit back and let the royal decrees flow.

I don't blame her. Go ahead, Allison! Speak up, wield your power! Get a good feel for it, then learn to apply it to something that really matters. Because—and this should tell you a lot—you'll notice the men don't *care*. They don't aspire to this kind of attention. They don't live in a "queen for a day" world. They let us have the flimflam because they understand how insignificant it is, and if we're smart, we'll learn from their example. So while producing a wedding, with the help of your bridesmaid/interns, may be a good management training exercise, don't let it stop there. Get out and do something in the world. Women have fought too long and too hard for the power we've gained to blow it on fairy tales.

I leave the suite and cross the landing to the stairs. There at the bottom stands Blaine, chatting with my parents as all three wait for me to reappear. I halt a minute, watching. You can tell my parents like Blaine, though Mom's hopes of seeing me toss a bouquet someday are bound to be disappointed. I meant what I told Pammy; I'll probably never marry. This is not one of those turnaround stories where, after being drafted as a reluctant bridesmaid and experiencing the joys of a wedding firsthand, the hard-driving career woman realizes what she's lost by sacrificing her chance to have a husband and family and falls head over heels for some guy after all. But I'm not adverse to having Blaine as a lover, though it won't be easy. I'm in

DC, he's in Chicago, and he better like Chinese takeout because I live on it. Nevertheless, there are sparks, and we could be very good together. In which case, he may as well see me as I am right now, in my rumpled slacks and top instead of under the false pretenses of a bridesmaid's gown.

"Everything okay?" he asks, eyeing me oddly as I descend.

"Yes, sorry to keep you waiting," I reply.

"We wanted to make sure you and Pammy were all right," says Mom, "but now that we can leave you in good hands . . ." She tips her head from me to Blaine, winks at Dad, links her arm through his, and leads him away. Not very subtle, Mom.

"Listen," I tell Blaine, "I've just had a revelation about the nature of power, and I want to try it out on you."

"You mean about political instability and national literature? As I recall we'd gotten to Oliver Cromwell and the disruption of the English Civil War . . ." He sends me another curious look.

"Something wrong?" I inquire.

"No, it's only . . . do you know you still have those silly white flowers stuck in your hair?"

I put my hand to the back of my head and feel the baby's breath dangling from my sagging French twist. I pull out a few bobby pins, shake my head, and down it falls.

Blaine's face clears. "Ahh," he says, "that's better. Now let's go back to the moonlight, shall we?"

I slip my arm through his and step over the baby's breath on the floor.

33

HAPPILY EVER AFTER?

Allison

WELL, MY WEDDING IS ALMOST OVER, and I must say I'm pretty satisfied with the way everything has proceeded. Given the extent of the dessert buffet, we probably could have done without the extra plate of truffles on each table. Also, we might have been wise to hire two videographers to ensure adequate footage was taken from every angle. I have been very specific that I want a professional-quality video, scored and edited to create a seamless final product, and that means any awkward scenes—bad dancing, braying laughter, et cetera—must be deleted. Speaking of which—

"Allison, I have to tell you those desserts were simply scrumptious! Me and Arnold and Stanley had a plateful of those mini chocolate éclairs, and my goodness, they melted in our mouths! And that band—why, I could dance all night long! You and Mead make such a lucky couple. Me and Arnold wish you as much happiness as we've always had."

"Thank you, Madge, and thank you for coming such a long way to be with us."

"Aw, shucks, thank you for inviting us. I better get back to our table and check on Iris and Edna before those old gals get into any more mischief."

We exchange kisses, and Madge Dombrowski trundles off. It's no trouble to be gracious to someone who lives in Tennessee who you'll probably never see again.

"Want to dance the next one?" Mead asks, inviting me to rise from our table for two.

"I'd love to."

He twirls me into his arms, and I nestle against his shoulder for a slow number. If anyone were to ask for my recommendations about Rosecourt, I would indeed praise the setting but caution that the air-conditioning is slow to catch up with the demands of two hundred and fifty people dancing on a hot June night. I spot Pammy waltzing with Patrick—how nice to see they've hit it off!—and naturally, I'm deeply appreciative of her rescue of Fiona. I blame Fiona's parents entirely for the near debacle. How do they think I would have felt if my wedding had been ruined by a child drowning? One last item: I am disappointed that Mead's father is passing out cigars to his friends on the verandah. It's true I never specifically banned cigars, but I didn't think I'd have to. Doesn't everyone realize how vulgar they are? However, at this late hour, I'm not going to complain. I remind myself that Mead's parents live in New Jersey and we'll probably be too busy to see them much either.

"May I cut in and dance with my beautiful daughter?"

"Daddy!"

Mead chuckles, bows, and gallantly steps aside, and my father takes me into his arms. We've always been close,

Daddy and I, and you can tell how proud he is of me tonight. As I am of him. Tall, debonair, silver-haired, successful—I've always thought my father is the ideal man. It's inevitable that Kimmy, or any woman for that matter, would go after him.

"Is everything perfect?" he asks me. "Is my darling girl happy?"

"Supremely, thanks to you."

"I hope your honeymoon is every bit as splendid."

"My honeymoon . . . I've hardly had time to think of it!"

"Why should you? That's what travel consultants are for. What time do you and Mead leave for the airport tomorrow?"

"At noon. Oh, Daddy, two weeks in Italy! I can't wait to visit the Uffizi again!"

"My pleasure." Daddy grins, then sighs over my shoulder to where Mead is coaching Susie through the steps of a waltz. "I'd do the same for your sister if it's ever her turn. Maybe it will happen now that she's caught the bouquet."

"You know that's only a silly superstition." I second his sigh. "Poor Susie, I hope she doesn't take it too seriously."

"I know. Poor Susie."

The song ends, and Mead comes to reclaim me.

"I'll have my wife back now, if you please, sir," he jokes, and it's Daddy's turn to bow and cede his place.

"She's all yours. By the way, if you kids haven't had a chance to sneak out and see the moon over the ocean, you really should. It's beautiful. Kimmy and I were out there earlier."

He leaves, and Mead checks his watch. "I think we have time before the last dance."

"Let's go," I reply.

We stroll through the ballroom, stopped by this or that friend or relative for a hug, a kiss, a photo, a compliment. It's wonderful to see how many people we've made happy tonight.

"Lauren is still missing," Nicole informs me, descending the grand staircase as Mead and I pass. Jessica and Carolyn behind her nod worried agreement.

"Well, if she chooses to absent herself from the festivities, that's her loss, isn't it?" I smile, though for an instant my voice bears a frosty edge. I let it thaw to a friendly scold. "And why aren't you all with your dates, after the trouble my husband took to match you up with such attractive, eligible men?"

"Oh, we are, we were on our way, we had to fix Carolyn's hair, we're going right back to the ballroom," they chorus, as Carolyn earnestly pats the back of her head in explanation. Really, I've had about enough of them. They've been true friends, all three, doing everything I asked without quibble or pause. But I feel that after tonight I'll have left them behind somehow. I can picture us meeting for the occasional reunion lunch, but I'm not sure they'll fit in with the new dinner party crowd I expect Mead and I will cultivate. Also, I find I take distinct pleasure in saying "my husband."

"I did do a good job of matching them up, didn't I?" says Mead as we proceed to the verandah.

"Yes, you did very well . . ." I halt a moment at the sight of a couple sitting in a pair of wicker chairs. The woman is gesturing emphatically to her companion, a groomsman, who counters with a vigorous headshake as if challenging her opinion. Fredericka and Blaine. Good grief, what happened to her dress? What on earth is she wearing? And after I tried so hard to include her and make her feel welcome. Fortunately, she lives in DC, and we won't have to see her often, either.

"There, look at the moon, my little wife, my sexy spouse, my better half," says Mead, clumsily trying out the new vocabulary. Standing behind me, he slips his arms around my waist and nuzzles my neck. Mead can be so endearing. I imagine at this moment he's truly happy and maybe a little prideful of his new possession, me, as I am of him. A little awestruck as well, yet confident of the step he's taken. He rocks me gently in his arms, humming as we gaze at the moon. He doesn't have a clue what really happened last night, the night before our wedding, and I'm never going to tell him.

I wasn't asleep, as I claimed, when the boys came in from their stag party. I was waiting up for them. The rehearsal dinner had ended shortly after ten, and my bridesmaids and I went back to my hotel room where our dresses were stored. I handed them out and gave the girls their bridesmaids' gift, gold filigree bracelets they could wear to the ceremony. Then we kissed goodnight, and I sent them to their rooms for a long sleep so they'd look their best today. But I stayed up, thinking and waiting. I thought about silly things, like wondering whether the French bread we'd had at the restaurant was baked on the premises or delivered from a local bakery. I thought about switching my brand of moisturizer to include a higher degree of UVP sunscreen. I watched the news on the television—another car bomb in the Middle East, a toddler in Florida who shot himself in the head with the loaded gun his father left on the kitchen table, a politician caught in a bribery scandal—then I flipped it off. I can't help it if people never learn.

Finally, I thought about serious issues, because it seemed I ought to on this momentous night. I searched my soul. Did I really want to marry Mead? Did I love him? Yes. Some people agonize endlessly over every decision, from the life-changing to the trivial, and the net result is that nothing gets done. I don't agonize, I'm a doer, and if a decision I've made doesn't work out, I make another decision and move on. You might contend that if I agonized more I'd take fewer wrong turns on my life path, have fewer regrets, but the fact is I've made the right choice ninety percent of the time. So rather than spend last night second-guessing whether I really loved or wanted to marry Mead, the more important question was how I would shape my course from there on. And for that reason, I needed to see what the story was when Mead and his buddies finally rolled in.

I never said no bachelor party, no stripper. I won't treat my husband like a child. It would have been hard for his attendants to arrange in any case, since everyone was coming from out of town. But if they had booked a private club and a girl popping from a cake, I wouldn't have minded. It's harmless entertainment—a naked gyrating woman—no different from the regular fare in movies and on TV. Yet men still can't seem to get enough of staring—they really are feeble-minded, aren't they?—and given that knowledge, the only sensible question for a woman is where to draw the line. And I was concerned about the drinking. Mead's not an alcoholic; I'd never marry him if he was.

He'll have a cocktail or two when he's partying, pizza and beer with football, and we both enjoy a good wine. When he's out with his friends, it's usually Mead who keeps tabs on who's imbibed how much and gets them into cabs for a safe ride home. It's not the kind of behavior you might expect at first glance, but there's usually more to Mead than meets the eye. He loves to lead his friends in a good time but never at the expense of anyone getting hurt, and this is one of the qualities I truly do love about my husband.

Yet the bachelor party was *his* night, his last fling, and just this once I suspected he'd overdo it. He had, and so had the groomsmen. I peeked around my door and watched them pitch down the hall to Mead's room, wincing at the noise they made and praying they wouldn't wake anyone. Fortunately, most of our floor and the one above were booked for wedding guests, who presumably would be understanding. I left my door cracked an inch, returned to the bed, and sat reading. After a while, a more subdued commotion sounded outside as the groomsmen piled out of Mead's room and dispersed to their own. When the last footstep faded away, I sneaked a look. Finally! The hall was clear; I could go check on Mead. Then to my surprise the door opposite his opened, and out jumped Steve's fiancée, Lynne, with Kimmy close behind.

What on earth—?

The groomsmen had left Mead's door ajar, and Lynne charged in. Kimmy grabbed, missed, and with a horrified gasp, ran after her. One look was all it took to assess the situation. I've met Lynne only twice, but that was enough to tell me she's poison. There was no way I was going to invite her to be a bridesmaid; if she broke off their engagement because of it, Steve should consider himself lucky. From the way she lurched into Mead's room, it was clear she too had been drinking, and I was about to pursue her, but refrained. The last thing I wanted was a scene with Lynne in Mead's room, and a scene there surely would have been. But Kimmy might have more success. Daddy had told me at the rehearsal dinner how he'd phoned and asked her to waylay Lynne, and it was clear Kimmy had stuck to her quarry.

I held my breath, and a minute later Lynne emerged, looking ghastly. She veered into the walls and bounced off them as she headed my way, then stumbled around the corner. I don't know why I embellished the next part, telling my bridesmaids on the verandah that I went to help Lynne find her key. It was just one of those little flourishes you add to a story that pops out in the telling. The truth is, I couldn't have gone to help Lynne if I wanted to, because at that moment another door clicked open. Oh no, now someone else was awake. I closed my eyes and with a heavy sigh went to sit on the bed, expecting my phone to ring any minute with complaints from the manager. If everyone would just stay quiet . . .

Lauren.

That's who I saw when, after a long silence, I returned and peeked into the hallway.

Lauren, wearing a pale silver negligee and the faintest smirk of a smile. She glided up the hall sinuous as a cat, having just closed the door to Mead's room.

Why didn't I confront her? What good would it have done? We'd all known she was still fuming and reckless over the breakup with her boyfriend. I think she'd secretly hoped to announce her own engagement this weekend, though everyone but Lauren could see she was rushing the guy. He bolted like a scared rabbit, and she bolted right back, into the bed of the tennis pro and every available man she could find. In hindsight, I probably should have deleted her from the lineup when she first grumbled about the cinnabar, but we've all grown so accustomed to Lauren's pettiness that I waved it off as nothing. But I couldn't have predicted this turn her jealousy would take, and you can't fire a bridesmaid on suspicion only three weeks before the wedding. Lauren was the one who should have bowed out if she couldn't rise above her personal hurt to celebrate my happy occasion.

And Mead?

Slowly, I walked to his room. Kimmy was nowhere in sight; she'd probably ducked out right after Lynne. "Go 'way, you guys!" Mead called when I rapped, apparently thinking the groomsmen had returned. He stumbled to admit me, and I had to support him back to bed, where he passed out again. I sat beside his snoring form and debated. That he'd succumbed to Lauren saddened me, although he was obviously too far gone to remember the deed. You might say it wasn't a fair test because Mead was inebriated and vulnerable, and it wasn't indeed. But life is always going to put temptation in your path, and if you're a handsome, charming man like my husband, temptation translates to a lot of women willing to throw themselves your way. Even if he weren't handicapped by alcohol, there might be indiscretions in the course of our marriage. The real question was, knowing this, how was *I* going to behave?

If I were starry-eyed about love and romance, I could have pitched a fit there and then, called off the wedding, and some might say I'd done right. It's also true I seek perfection of myself and of anyone else who expects to be part of my life. But I'm *not* some naïve virgin in an antiquated tale. I'm a realist, a pragmatist, and far too intelligent to let human failings stand in my way. If we want to stay together, I'm going to have to forgive Mead a lot of things throughout many long years of marriage, minor sins like not putting down the toilet seat, major disappointments if he doesn't live up to my vision of the professional success I hope he will be. Could it be that the most perfect thing about a marriage is forgiveness? Will there be times I'll need him to forgive me?

I lay down beside him on the bed.

"Come on, Mead," I whispered, "you can do it," and though he groaned, I aroused him and we joined and he came inside me. "Allison," he murmured, slipping off to sleep, and I said, "That's right, it's me." Then I slid out of bed, wrapped my robe close, and stepped into the hall, closing Mead's door tight. Let's see what Lauren would say the next morning, though I doubted she'd say anything. She's a coward. She might hint and insinuate, but she's not brave enough to stand up and reveal her own sordid behavior to declare she knows a reason why this wedding should not go forward. I'd stripped that trite old line from the script anyway. In the end, whatever nonsense she might utter, I had my answer ready, and Mead and I could both pass a polygraph test on it.

Of course Mead slept with someone last night—me.

The moon hangs above the water like a bright, silver-gilt bauble, an out-of-reach toy. My wedding is almost over. My husband is by my side.

"I love you," he says, nuzzling my neck.

"I love you, too," I reply.

"We should go in for the last dance."

"Yes, people are expecting us." I pause. My heart closes around the last of the hurt and seals it there. "Mead, do you think we'll live happily ever after?"

"Of course, my little wife, my beautiful bride, my lady fair."

It's not what I would answer if he asked me the same question. Will we live happily ever after? "I don't know," I would say, "but we'll try."

Yet I like his answer better, and I kiss him for it. Then I take my husband's hand and lead him back inside.

34

SIBERIA

Isabel

CAN'T . . . KEEP . . . MY EYES . . . open. Think . . . I might . . . pass out. Better . . . get . . . some air.

"'Scuse me, Madge . . . 'Scuse me, everybody . . . Be back soon . . . *Oof!* Dizzy up here, isn't it? Be back soon."

There, that's better. Standing up is better. Funny thing about the ballroom, how it's going 'round like that, like I'm inside a virtual tour, *whooeee!* Well, a great evening we're having, yes sirree, never felt so shintillatling . . . scintillatly . . . oh what the hell, you know what I mean. Great gal, that Madge. Iris and Edna, too. Great old coots! And Lizard Man . . . old flicky tongue . . . don't drink the water. He's right about that. Drink alcohol instead!

Should probably find John who's been gone a long, *looong* time. Can hardly remember when he left. Oh, *Johnnn!* Where are you? Must be around here somewhere. Nope, don't see him. Anybody want to boogie with me on the dance floor? Yeah, let's boogie, let's all boogie together. *Shake-shake-shake, shake-shake-shake, shake your booty.* Oh yeah, and mine still shakes with the best of them! You go, girl! Oops, know what? I never said hello to my old friends. Lots of 'em here tonight and I never said hello. Must rectifry . . . rectify that error.

"DeeDee! Dick! Peggy! Cassandra! Great wedding! Lovely blide . . . bride . . . love the bride! John? Nope, nope, seem to have lost him . . . Leaving? No way! Got a whole table of wild party animals over there in the corner . . . fashinating company . . . new best friends. Good seein' you . . . must toddle . . . kiss-kiss."

Whoa! Virtual tour still going inside my head . . . hard to walk in high heels . . . maybe better take them off . . . Whoops! Whoops! . . . Who's that got my arm?

"Ha-ha, good catch, Gordon . . . lost my balance for a minute there . . . Oh, it is you, Gordon, and this is Kimmy, is it? . . . Nice to meet you, trophy bride! Is that silicone popping out of your dress? . . . Aw, whaddaya mean, Gordon, shush, hold my tongue . . . Seems to me that's all anybody's done since you left Deirdre, hold their tongue and be syllabized, cibilized, behave. Well, you can stuff it, mister! I say what I think . . . will not keep my voice down . . . jab you in the chest anytime I please. Who cares well the hell . . . 'scuse me, where the hell, John went. Say what I think, and we all think you're shit, Gordon, I shpeak for every woman here, and li'l Miss Kimmy is a cunning li'l . . . a cunninglingual . . . gold-digger. Aw, don't go away mad, Gordon . . . Okay, be that way!"

Hey, I just discovered something . . . It feels good to say what you think . . . ought to do it more often. Speaking of whish, I'll just go find Deirdre, tell her what I think 'bout being exiled to Siberia . . . just walk straight and find her . . . "Deirdre! Oh wait, you're not Deirdre . . . How come your face is so blurry? Deirdre, oh *Deirdreee*, where are you? No thanks, folks, don't need help back to my table. You just keep on dancin'... And there she is! Deirdre! It's you! Great wedding, lovely blide, did you hear how I told off Gordon for you? Yup, I did, you can thank me later. Listen, Deirdre, old friend, so what if I missed your ballet meeting, was that shufficient reason to sexile me to Siberia?... What am I talkin' about? Your ballet meeting... I had a Botox appointment... Don't tell me you haven't had a few yourself, you wrinkled old nag, ha-ha, just kidding... No, I don't need to sit down... I walk the walk, I talk the talk!... Told that old goat Gordon off for you and this is the thanks I get, exile to Table 7, Siberia, Lizard Man up my skirt... Ought to thank me for putting you on to him in the first place, you snotty bitch—"

"Isabel, Isabel, are you listening to me? What are you talking about? I did *not* seat you at Table 7. You're at Table 17 with the Andretts and the Morestones, remember?"

What?

"I did *not* seat you at Table 7, Isabel, though I thought it was awfully generous of you and John to drop over there and make those poor people feel welcome. I know I should have gone around myself, but then everyone started coming to me. Now stop babbling, Isabel, and let's step away to the corner before you make any more of a scene."

What? We weren't supposed to be at Table 7 after all? But our place card—

"Honestly, Isabel, we're going to have to address this little drinking problem of yours. You see, your place card says... but, but... Oh no, that stupid secretary from the temp agency must have made a mistake and typed Table 7 on the master list for the calligrapher. Isabel, I am so sorry! But then who . . .? Oh my God, oh my God! Mr. and Mrs. John *Newsome,* Mr. and Mrs. Enoch *Newton.* That means the Newtons, the married first cousins from Maine, have been sitting all night with my best friends! I have to fix this immediately!"

A mistake? It was all a mistake? We're still friends? Deirdre didn't mean to exile me? Oh, that's so sweet! Going to weep into this napkin . . . Forget what I said about your winkles . . . wrinkles . . . Deirdre? Where'd you go? Never mind, I'll find you again and when I do I'll apologize profoozy, profrusely . . . We're friends! Now, must go tell John we're saved from Siberia, must be at the bar getting me another drink. Whoo, good to get out of that hot ballroom . . . walk outside.

" 'Scuse me, 'scuse me, bartender . . . What's your name?"

"David, ma'am."

"David . . . David . . . Have you seen my husband?"

"As a matter of fact, ma'am, I have."

"Oh, that's good. That's very good. Wait a minute . . . How do you know who's my husband?"

"Jack Daniel's, ma'am, and I believe you're the double vodka and tonic?"

"You got that right! I'll have another one."

"I'm sorry, ma'am. The bar is closed, and we're packing up."

"Closed? Aw! The inside bar, too?"

"Yes, I'm sorry, ma'am. The bars close half an hour before the wedding ends. I can pour you a soda or fruit juice, Coke, Diet Coke, Sprite?"

"Aw . . . say, David, you're black, aren't you?"

"Last time I checked, ma'am."

"Ha-ha, good sense of humor. You know that Martin Luther King speech . . . I have a dream?"

"I believe I do."

"Always gets me, right here . . . right here . . . Shuffle the little children to come unto me. And that's what the world needs now, David, love, sweet love. Not a problem on this planet we couldn't solve with more shlove, brothers under the skin . . . Take you and your friend here . . . what's her name?"

"My name is Tracy, ma'am, and I can speak for myself."

"Tracy, I know what you and David are thinking . . . I see you eschanging glanshes. You're thinking what does this woman have to say to me that's so important, and I'll tell you, Tracy, it's love. You and David, white and black, side by side . . . always gets me, right here . . . do unto others . . ."

"You know, ma'am, David and I make it a point during the evening to try to get to know our customers, don't we, David?"

"Yes we do, Tracy."

"We like to keep an eye on them, though you can understand it's hard in a crowd this size. But I must say you and your husband really stand out."

"We do? Oh, that's so sweet."

"Yes, you're extremely memorable, and that's why we're able to do you the favor of telling you exactly where he is."

"Who?"

"Your husband. The Jack Daniel's. You were looking for him?"

"Oh, right."

"Would you like the pleasure of telling her, David, or shall I?"

"Let me, Tracy, please. Ma'am, I believe you'll find your husband down on the lawn, on the south side of the property. Look along the hedge, past the archway to the rose garden, that's right. Do you see the landscaped area around those tall trees? Yes, he was out here on the verandah for a while, then he headed that way. Tracy and I will watch to be sure you're going in the proper direction."

"That's so kind . . . I'll just take it from here . . . I walk the talk, I talk the walk . . ."

"You do that, ma'am. Have a nice evening."

See, what did I tell you? Ebony and ivory, just be polite to everybody. Down the steps . . . good lions, good kitty cats . . . Nice cool grass on my bare feet, ahhh. Wait a minute, bare feet . . . What'd I do with my shoes? Had them in the ballroom . . . or did I take them off there? Oh well, they're around somewhere . . . Nice summer night, nice full moon . . . past the rose garden, shame the wedding has to end . . . but I'll be back! Wait for me, Lizard Man! Nice leafy trees, nice bridesmaid with her dress around her hips, ha-ha, getting fucked by some old goat against a tree . . .

"John!"

 35

FINAL FANTASY

Deirdre

IT'S HALF PAST MIDNIGHT, and we stand at the double doors
in the foyer, bidding the last of our guests goodnight. *Thank
you for coming, drive safely, farewell.* On the way, they've
passed the marble table where two of the hostesses are handing out the party favors. So long Allison and I searched to
find a unique memento. How about an engraved bookmark?
Lovebirds sachets? Personalized votive candles? In the end
we decided a simple tradition was best: Jordan almonds.
The hard, sugar-coated nuts are said to represent the bitter
and the sweet of marriage—more irony for tonight. Usually
they're presented in mini gift boxes or gauzy drawstring bags,
but we found a source that offered organza flowers with a
colored almond wrapped in each petal. They cost five dollars
apiece, so for a reasonable twelve hundred fifty we were able
to satisfy the tradition and add a clever twist, as the *oohs* and
aahs I'm now hearing confirm.

Joseph and Donna Morelli encourage me to pump yet
another cousin's hand. When I say "we" stand at the door of

the foyer, I mean I stand on one side of the wide archway with Mead's parents, Gordon and Kimmy stand opposite, and the guests funnel between us. I didn't quite foresee this is how it would be at the end; most of the guests who left earlier sought us out individually in the ballroom to say goodnight. The rest have taken so long to dawdle this way that Allison, Mead, and their attendants have deserted, the bridesmaids to collect their belongings upstairs, the groomsmen to fetch the limo driver and send the parking valets for our cars. Now I'm left beside Mead's parents, as if I were an orphan they've been kind enough to adopt. For the guests, it's a sudden dilemma; given the flow toward the exit, it will be hard to say good-bye to both Gordon and me. Do they stop first at one side of the archway, then cut across the traffic to shake hands or blow a kiss to the other party? If so, who takes priority? The hospital people go straight for Gordon, of course; they know where their interest lies. The numerous Morelli and Dombrowski relatives head naturally to Mead's parents, thanking me heartily for such a special occasion, no doubt pitying me privately.

But the friends, the longtime friends, whom will they choose? I see their glance flick left to right, the vacillation on their faces, the furtive looks as they approach the gauntlet. When the Newsomes' turn came, Isabel grabbed John's elbow to yank him away from Gordon and marched him resolutely toward me. They were both drunk as skunks—the bartenders had confiscated their keys and called a cab—and John had apparently done something to earn an emerging black eye. But I'm grateful to Isabel for her loyalty. I long to see it from our other friends, the Morestones, the Andretts, the Falhernes, the Langleys. We golfed with them in Westport, sailed together on Long Island Sound, played bridge every first Tuesday.

Now they have to take sides, and though the women may want to align themselves with me, they can't risk snubbing Gordon either. Dick Falherne is his accountant, and DeeDee makes a calculated move, pushing Dick toward Gordon while she throws open her arms to me. She repeats yet again what a lovely bride Allison was, all to give Dick time for a quick handshake with Gordon before he cuts over to join us. Peggy and Ralph Morestone come directly to me, and my hopes rise, then they make a deliberate effort to push through to Gordon and Kimmy as well. Peggy owns an antiques store, and Kimmy has a big new house to furnish. The Andretts and Langleys bunch themselves together to chorus their thanks, as if there's safety in numbers and the less they say to either of us, the more diplomatic they'll seem. The truth is, Gordon and I make them uncomfortable. If it can happen to us, it can happen to them, right?

Well, of course I don't approve of Gordon's behavior, they're telling themselves, *but I couldn't exactly cause a scene at his daughter's wedding, could I?*

Why not? Why not? What is so sacred about maintaining civility that we can't speak up even when an injustice has been committed? Why must we deny our emotions for the sham of public neutrality? I would like to see just one man, in dignified tones, tell Gordon that what he did was wrong. But you can bet hell will freeze over first. They all want what he wants, and what they want is piteously little. They burn with ambition to reach the top, then risk it all for a blow job in the Oval Office. So there stands Gordon, as blasé and confident as ever, shaking hands, laughing, sending the women off with a kiss and the men with a genial pat on the shoulder. He's made his point, he has the money, the power, the prestige, and no one but poor, foolish Isabel would have the nerve to contradict him. How can I blame them? How can I excoriate everyone else for their cowardice when I've swallowed my pride and played this charade to the hilt?

And Kimmy, what does she make of us all? She hasn't said one word to me this evening; she's barely looked my way. She simply stands like a decoration on Gordon's arm and lets him do the talking. Does she feel the least bit guilty? Or is she just biding her time, get this over with and then she'll have Gordon to herself? Does she love him? Does she love him more than I did? What about his age? Does she fantasize when Gordon's making love to her that it's really some buff young lifeguard? Could we go out to lunch, Kimmy, and discuss this, and you can tell me where I went wrong?

"... beautiful wedding, Deirdre ..."

"... marvelous job you did ..."

"... everything was perfect ..."

"... Allison looked radiant!"

"Thank you, thank you," my voice cracks like a broken flute, "so good of you to come ..."

And now I admit what I've known all along: after tonight I will probably never see Gordon again, never lay eyes on a man with whom I spent thirty-three years. When would we meet? I've given up the hospital committees, feeling unwelcome, a rejected female in the king of beast's domain. Gordon has left the local boards he served on in

Westport when he moved to Greenwich with Kimmy. There's nowhere for our paths to cross unless I go out of my way to contrive an encounter. I did that, I confess, several times after he abandoned me. I knew his schedule at the hospital well enough that if there happened to be some overlooked file I had to return I could intersect his path. If I played enough golf at the country club, our tee times were bound to overlap. I golfed with a vengeance, though I've never been good at it. Gordon knew these meetings were no accident and patiently tolerated them, part of the price he had to pay until my feelings for him were resolved. Yet isn't it telling that no sooner has he replaced me with her than he tries to make her into me? Now she's the one playing golf, serving on the hospital commit-tees, as if I was never anything more to him than a role to be cast.

Now I'll be alone. Who will I talk to? I don't have a pet. I don't even have my own name. Deirdre Hollingsworth has become an empty identity, and who would remember a young woman named Deirdre Decker? In another family, Gordon, the girls, and I might come together for the chris-tening of a first grandchild, but Allison and Mead aren't likely to subscribe to that ritual. The idea of Susie getting married is laughable.

There's a lull in the stream of departing guests, and glancing toward the ballroom, I see the breakdown has begun. The waiters are clattering plates, glasses, and silver-ware into plastic tubs. They swipe away the floral center-pieces and snap off the tablecloths, like magicians whisking away a concealing veil. The musicians are packing up their instruments, amps, and speakers; the music disappears into battered black cases, a guitar emits a last discordant *twang!* The Rosecourt staff has changed out of their uniforms and into tee shirts and jeans. They swarm in carrying buckets, mops, and brooms, calling to each other, "You take the dining room, we'll get the verandah!" It's like watching a beautiful castle being dismantled before your eyes. I wish they'd close the doors.

Here is my final fantasy:

The last guests depart. Mead's parents hug me and head outside. Allison descends from the suite with her bridesmaids and their luggage, and they bundle into various limousines, along with Mead and the groomsmen, who've been joshing each other as they wait under the stars. Gordon hands his keys to a valet parker and motions Kimmy to wait on the doorstep while he and I bid goodnight to the Rosecourt supervisor. Then she leaves, and Gordon and I stand alone in the foyer.

"You did a great job, Deirdre. I mean that."

I shrug, not needing his compliments. Of course I did a great job. Anyone can see that.

"I remember how many times you organized benefits or functions on behalf of the hospital. You've always had a real talent for it."

Another shrug. Why is he drawing this out? I start to move away, feel his hand on my arm.

"Deirdre? Can we get together? Can we talk?"

"About what?"

"About us."

It's bad dialogue, a sappy movie, and believe me, I've tried to rewrite it a dozen times. It's the crucial scene of the story, the straying husband acknowledging his mistake and returning to his wife, and I want it to sound poignant and piercingly fresh.

"I've realized Kimmy could never be the woman you are. She and I have nothing in common. I'm an old fool, and she's a child. But you and I are soul mates, Deirdre, and we were meant to be together for the rest of our lives."

Damn it, I don't care if it's clichéd, I don't care how he says it, I just want to hear those words. Maybe I don't even want him back. Sometimes when I plot this scene in my head, I spurn him just to spite myself. Then I go on to a new life of triumph and happiness for him to hear about secondhand while he stews in regret. Either way, I'd at least have a choice. Because you gave me no choice before, did you, Gordon? You simply robbed me like a thief in the night. You stripped me of my marriage, my confidence, my identity, all without a backward look.

"Well, you did a great job, Deirdre, as always."

I startle out of my reverie.

It's Gordon's real voice I'm hearing, not the wished-for words in my head. Kimmy earnestly seconds his compliments, standing beside him in the foyer, not out on the doorstep where she belongs. The Morellis have moved away, the guests have vanished, the three of us are alone. The two of them continue to congratulate me, finding a dozen details to praise. It's over, tonight was my last chance, and now he expects me to say good-bye with grace, composure, and intelligence.

"Rot in hell, Gordon," I say, "and fuck you, Kimmy, you little bitch."

Head high, I swirl out the door.

36

THE DARKLING PLAIN

Anne

THAT'S IT. THEY'RE GONE. Thank heaven.

I take my file from the side table in the foyer and beck-on Leon to join me. Together we scan the breakdown list, a five-page, room-by-room summary of every last chore to be done before we lock up the house for the night.

"I'll need an accident report form for Fiona, too," I remind myself, but before I can move, Leon says, "I'll get it for you," and veers away toward the rear office. From the ballroom a hostess and a butler hurry toward me, bear-ing gifts. They've saved me a centerpiece, and there were extra truffles on the tables—would I like to take some home? I thank them, though I'll probably leave their offerings for the day staff instead. At various times tonight I have also been presented with a ginger ale, a cappuccino, a half dozen compliments, a discount pass to an upcoming flower show, and numerous eager inquiries on the order of, "Can I do anything for you, Anne?" Somehow, I see Leon's hand in this, and if he's told them about the divorce, I don't mind. It's easier than telling them myself.

Glen Gold and the band roll out the last of their amps and instruments. Hank comes to report the kitchen is almost clean, and Leon will sign off on it. It's one chore I'm glad to relinquish; after ten years at Rosecourt, it's still hard to see the travesty in the kitchen at the end of the night. Bread and salad, steak and swordfish and sweet potatoes, chocolate éclairs and pastry and cream puffs scraped rapid-fire from the fine china plates into industrial-sized garbage barrels by the dishwashing staff. The uneaten food glomps and clumps into the buckets, festering into a sickly sweet, carnivorous-smelling stew.

"Can't you donate it?" I'd blurted, speaking out of turn on one of my first nights as a Rosecourt hostess. "Not the dinners on the plates, but at least the leftover food here in the kitchen that none of the guests have touched? Wouldn't someone be glad to have it? A homeless shelter? A church?"

"You can take some," replied a dishwasher, tossing a huge bowl of fresh fruit salad, "but we can't send it to anyone else. If the people we gave it to didn't handle it properly and someone got sick eating it, we'd get sued."

I leave the file and breakdown list for Leon and head up the grand staircase. There's a personal ritual I like to observe at the end of every wedding that I call the Acid Test. If nothing else, it's amusing, but I contend it can predict whether the marriage we've just witnessed will last. All it requires is a quick visit to the suite after the bridal party has departed but before my staff goes in to clean up.

The Acid Test can be stated as follows: the probability that a marriage will succeed or fail is in direct proportion to the state of cleanliness or messiness in which the bride leaves the suite.

Does that make sense? It seems it should, and often, walking into the suite presents no surprises. A bride who's acted spoiled and peevish all night will leave the rooms dirty and disheveled. Granted, she doesn't do it alone. Add seven bridesmaids, a junior bridesmaid, a flower girl, and a mother primping, and the rooms are bound to get untidy. It's our job to empty the wastebaskets, wipe up the bathroom, vacuum the floor. But the bride sets the tone, and I've seen nights the suite was trashed as if on purpose, the comforter yanked off the bed, perfume splashed on the mirror, discarded pantyhose clogging the toilet. I've seen nights when the floor was literally ankle-deep in debris. It's as if the bride said, *I've paid for this place*—although she hasn't, Daddy has—*and I'll do what I want with it. Why should I care whether it's damaged? Let someone else clean up!*

What man would want to live with a woman like that?

No matter how beautiful you are, the sex is going to wear off. If you're already living together, chances are the first flush of passion is over and done. And no matter how rich you are, you're off Daddy's payroll now and onto your husband's; it's not going to be quite so cute when you pull your pouty princess act months and years after the honeymoon. This is the long haul, the lifetime voyage as the minister would have it, and soon your husband will expect you to start demonstrating those boring qualities like maturity and consideration that make it not only possible but wonderful to live with another human being till death do you part. If we offered a gentlemen's suite for the male contingent of the bridal party, the same Acid Test could probably be applied to the behavior of the groom. It would be interesting to track our wedding clients and see if there's any validity to the results. But of course, I have no proof, only my own observations and two very distinct memories.

One is of a plump young woman my staff dubbed the Hillbilly Bride. Her family must have put their life savings into booking Rosecourt because they obviously had little money left for any flourishes. The wedding gown was homemade and looked it. The bride's mother baked the cake and cookies that accompanied coffee for dessert. There was no band, only a DJ, and the groom's mother had created artificial flower arrangements in bright purple for the dinner tables. A family friend who owned a hot dog stand did the catering, and the passed hors d'oeuvres consisted of Cheez Whiz on Ritz crackers. At the evening's end, the bride and her two attendants brought down the garbage bags from the suite, and the bride beckoned me aside to ask the location of the Dumpster. When I took the bags from her with the assurance that we would dispose of them, she answered with a downright beam, "Why, that's real kind of you! You sure do think of everything here." She and her skinny husband were holding hands like high school sweethearts as they waddled out the door, and when I visited the suite, the only item she'd left behind was a plate of her mother's homemade cookies as a thank-you to the staff.

My second memory is of the Perfect Bride. She was beautiful: flawless bisque skin, her shining brunette hair close-cropped yet feminine, her features classically sculpted. Her dress was custom made of antique lace with a high neckline and dainty cap sleeves, and her carriage was so naturally elegant, every eye turned to follow as she passed through the room. Her family and fortune were blueblood, her groom was a handsome blond doctor of equal lineage. I know what you're thinking—that she destroyed the suite beyond recognition—but you're wrong. The Perfect Bride arrived at Rosecourt exactly on time, already dressed, and so confident she never felt the need to check her makeup or run to a mirror to comb her hair. The Perfect Bride was so gracious she spent the entire evening circling the ballroom, letting the old ladies admire her diamond, asking after everyone's health and well-being, introducing her new husband to her relatives, and gracefully accepting compliments as she was introduced to his. Why, the Perfect Bride never went upstairs to the suite at all. She was so perfect you could see everyone there falling in love with her, and you could see why her husband would keep falling in love with her over and over and over again. It was only my second week at Rosecourt when she appeared, and I've been longing to see her like ever since.

Wherever they are now, I know the Hillbilly Bride and the Perfect Bride are still happily married to two very lucky men.

And tonight? Can I predict what lies ahead for Allison and Mead?

It's hard to tell. On one hand, the VHM code is rarely wrong, though Mead seems such a laid-back type he may take his wife's selfish habits in stride. Yet when I enter the suite, the damage and debris are minimal. The garbage is stuffed into the wastebaskets; no food stains spot the upholstery or rugs. Only one window is open, and a few forgotten safety pins litter the bathroom sink. Did some of

my staff get in early or did Allison delegate her bridesmaids to tidy up? Maybe it was Pammy, perhaps with
Susie's help. If you're the kind of bride who can always
cajole, command, or afford someone else to clean up after
you, perhaps it won't ever matter how messy or careless
you are. You have the luxury of simply sailing through life,
while others navigate through the garbage you strew in
your wake.

Greg and I would have passed the Acid Test.

I blunt the memories before they can start up again and
head back downstairs to find Leon waiting with the accident
form. I thank him and take it to a quiet corner. Fiona's mishap
could provoke a lawsuit, so the trick is to be complete, factu-
al, and objective, emphasizing the promptness and efficiency
of our search. The issue of liability will be rigorously discussed
at an in-house meeting. Should we have foreseen this accident? Could we have prevented it? Is there anything we can
do to ensure it never happens again? Yes, ban children under
age ten from weddings, make parents sign a disclaimer that
they'll be responsible for their child, station one of our staff as
a full-time lifeguard, drain the fountain, close the rose garden.
While we're at it, let's prohibit candles in the house—they're
a fire hazard—and permanently rope off the grand staircase—
what if the bride tumbled down and broke her neck? Or let's
just ban weddings period, because they might end in divorce,
like mine.

I bring the finished report to Leon and slip it in the file.

"Would you care to walk around the verandah with me
to make sure it's swept to your satisfaction?" he asks. "And
I noticed one of the light fixtures in the kitchen flickering
on and off. Maybe you'd like to come check it?"

"No, I'll take your word on the verandah, and we'll leave a note for the custodian about the light."

I glance around at my staff. Nobody moves faster than they do at night's end. Their aching feet transform to Mercury's winged heels as they run brooms, mops, and vacuums over the floors; their sagging shoulders take on Atlas-like strength as they cart away heavy tables and stacks of gilt chairs. Room by room, the tasks complete, the lights switch off. They hurry out with a wave as I dismiss them, their faux smiles replaced by genuine ear-to-ear grins. Home looms on the horizon, home and a comfy bed.

Leon escorts me to the door, pausing to straighten a mirror that doesn't need straightening, stopping to pick a piece of lint from the vestibule rug. As I lock the front door, he glances at his watch, frowning. It's two a.m.

"Did anyone shut off the fountain?" I ask.

"I sent a butler to do it," says Leon, "but if you want to wait, I'll double-check." His face brightens at the opportunity for one last, unspoken good deed.

"No, I'll go," I say, as a pair of headlights turns in at the front gate, probably a guest who's forgotten something. "Will you take care of that, Leon? I don't feel like talking to anyone."

The night is quiet as I cross the lawn to the rose garden and step through the archway in the privet hedge. A needless trip—the fountain is off—but I sit a minute on the wide marble rim, trailing my hand in the water. It was six o'clock that Sunday evening Greg and I returned from our weekend in the Berkshires, and he dropped me at the house while he swung by the office to check for messages. It was past ten when he got home to find the self-stick farewell note I'd left on the newel post. He was shocked that I wanted our marriage to end. *Why, Anne? Can't we work on this?* But then his firm got a big new contract—a lavish resort in the White Mountains—and when he saw what it would take to sustain a relationship that made me as well as himself happy, he just didn't have the time. In his interpretation, the failure of our marriage became largely my fault. I was jealous of his career and success. I'd neglected his needs in favor of the girls. Though Miranda's deafness had imposed a strain, I'd aggravated it by becoming an activist for deaf education. Why was I off counseling others when there was barely time for us? Nor had I tried hard enough to secure another teaching position. Instead, I'd taken the Rosecourt job, which not only paid less but demanded nighttime hours on an irregular schedule—did I have any idea how that had impacted our income and family life? Is it any wonder he had to work overtime to compensate? And when, exactly, were we supposed to have sex?

I am willing to share the guilt.

"We'll make the divorce quick and amicable," we agreed.

The girls were furious. *You can't!* Miranda signed. *Why didn't you tell us there were problems? We could have helped! This isn't right!* Then Rachel joined in, both of them crying, their four hands flashing so fast we could barely keep up with them. *This is wrong and a mistake and the worst thing you've ever done! Please, please, we don't want this to happen!* They stopped speaking to us for a week, and they still stubbornly refuse to forgive us. All the more reason to conclude it swiftly, we decided, and let them get back to normal. Once, during our negotiations, both our attorneys left the conference room simultaneously to take phone calls, and Greg and I sat suddenly alone, facing each other across this cheerless table for two. Neither of us knew what to say or do, and the air was palpable with sadness, like a pale gray sky weighted with unshed water, accumulating tears. Greg started to speak, then the lawyers returned and business resumed.

The sound of running footsteps comes toward me, and I look up to see Leon in the archway. Except it's not. For a minute, my heart doesn't beat.

"I've been phoning and phoning, all the way back from the White Mountains," Greg heaves, pressing his chest, "and finally Leon picked up in the office, and I said, 'Don't let her leave!' We had the ground-breaking today, and I kept watching all these people celebrating and shaking hands, and all I could think was, I don't want this to happen . . ."

He catches his breath, and I let out mine. "Oh, Greg, I've been so miserable!"

His arms go around me, and he buries his head in my hair. "Paper can be torn up, Anne."

The ocean laps at the cliff down where Rosecourt's lawn meets the sea. The moon rides high and bright above the water, and we hold each other tight in the dark.

ABOUT THE AUTHOR

Arliss Ryan is the author of a historical novel, *The Kingsley House*, and numerous short stories published in literary magazines. *How (Not) To Have A Perfect Wedding* was inspired by her experiences as a wedding hostess in one of the famous Newport, Rhode Island, mansions. She now lives in St. Augustine, Florida, where she works as a writer, teacher, and professional storyteller. She is married with two children.